ALSO BY

CARYL FÉREY

Zulu
Utu

MAPUCHE

Caryl Férey

MAPUCHE

Translated from the French
by Steven Rendall

Europa
editions

Europa Editions
214 West 29th Street
New York, N.Y. 10001
www.europaeditions.com
info@europaeditions.com

This book is a work of fiction. Any references to historical events, real people, or real locales are used fictitiously.

First Publication 2013 by Europa Editions

Translation by Steven Rendall
Original title: *Mapuche*

Library of Congress Cataloging in Publication Data is available
ISBN 978-1-60945-120-2

Férey, Caryl
Mapuche

Book design by Emanuele Ragnisco
www.mekkanografici.com

Cover photo © Enrique Shore/Woodfin – Getty

Prepress by Grafica Punto Print – Rome

Printed in the USA

On the copyright page of *Mapuche* by Caryl Férey copyright was erroneously attributed to Mondadori.

MAPUCHE

Part One
LITTLE SISTER

0

A dark wind was roaring through the plane's cabin door. Parise, belted in, bent his bald head toward the river. He could hardly make out the muddy water of the Rio Plata where it emerged from its delta.

The pilot in the khaki bomber jacket was heading out to sea, toward the southeast. A night flight like dozens of others he'd made years earlier. He wasn't as calm as he'd been then. The clouds dissipated as they moved away from the Argentine coast and the wind grew more violent, buffeting the little two-engine aircraft. The noise from the open door was so loud that he almost had to shout to make himself heard.

"We'll be leaving the territorial waters soon!" he said, turning his head toward the man behind him.

Hector Parise looked at his watch. By that time, they should have dealt with the package . . . The crests of the waves shimmered on the ocean, pale undulations lit by the moon. He clung to the walls of the cabin—a giant lurching through the air pockets. The "package" lay on the floor, motionless despite the plane's bouncing about. Parise shoved it closer to the door. Six thousand feet: no light glimmered in the turbulent gloom, just the distant lamps of a freighter, not important. His seatbelt flapped in the cramped cabin.

"O.K.!" he bellowed to the pilot.

The man gave him a thumbs-up.

The wind whipped his face; Parise seized the unconscious body by the armpits. He couldn't help smiling.

"Go play outside, kid . . . "

He was about to tip the package out of the plane when a spark appeared in the open eyes—a spark of life, terrified.

The colossus pitched and tossed, in the grip of stupor and fear: injected with sodium pentothal, the package wasn't supposed to wake up, much less open its eyes! Was it death mocking him, the play of nighttime reflections, or a pure hallucination? Shivering like a leper, Parise grabbed the body and pushed it into the void.

1

"*La putas al poder!*
(Sus hijos ya están en él.)"[1]

The shed was covered with bright red graffiti. Jana was nineteen at the time, her anger fully intact. All the ruling classes had been involved in the theft: politicians, bankers, service industry bosses, the IMF, financial experts, labor unions. Carlos Menem's neoliberal policies had imprisoned the country in an infernal spiral, a time bomb: increasing debt, reduction of public expenditures, flexible work schedules, exclusion, recession, widespread unemployment, underemployment, to the point that bank deposits were frozen and withdrawals limited to a few hundred pesos per week. Money flowed out of the country, banks closed in fast succession. Corruption, scandals, cronyism, privatizations, "structural adjustments," externalization of profits. Menem, his successors, who marched to the tune of the markets, and then the financial crash of 2001-2002 had completed the destruction of the social fabric begun by the military junta's "National Reorganization Process."

The crash turned into bankruptcy. Argentina, whose GDP after World War II was equal to that of Great Britain, had seen the majority of its population sink into poverty and a third into indigence. A hopeless destitution. In the schools, children fainted from hunger, and the cafeterias had to be kept open dur-

[1] "Power to the whores! (Their sons hold it already.)"

ing vacations so the kids could receive their only meal of the day. In the *barrios* of Quilmas, kids compared the taste of grilled toad with that of rat, while others stole copper telephone lines, aluminum covers protecting the electrical circuits of traffic lights, and bronze plaques on monuments . . . Jana had seen old women bloody their hands clawing at the gates to the banks, old men wearing threadbare suits brought out for the occasion weeping in silence, and then the anger of ordinary people: the first riots, the looting of supermarkets (seen by the media as testifying to a lack of security rather than to desperate need), *que se vayan todos! y que no quede ninguna!* (Let them all go! and not one remain!), mounted police charging into the protesters to disperse them with riding crops, Molotov cocktails, smoke, women beaten with truncheons, their daughters dragged down the sidewalks, nervous shots fired into the crowds—thirty-nine dead—their blood in the streets and squares of the capital, a state of siege declared by President de la Rúa, growing protest, women beating on cooking pots and people shouting—"the state of siege means nothing to us!" The blockage of the roads by *piqueteros*, scarves covering youths' faces, their naked chests inviting bullets, paving stones, shattering display windows, rocks thrown at the tanks, water cannons, anti-riot squads, shields, mothers' cries, Argentine flags brandished as a kind of challenge, fear, fire, statements on state television, *que se vayan todos!*, bundles of cash leaving the country by the truckload, eight billion dollars in armored convoys while the banks were locked up tight, bigwigs taking refuge abroad in their air-conditioned villas, the stench of gas, overturned cars, food riots, the black smoke from burning rubber, chaos, President de la Rúa fleeing by helicopter from the roof of the Casa Rosada, the delight of middle fingers raised to bid farewell to those retreating in disarray, political officials throwing in the towel one after the other, four presidents in thirteen days, *que se vayan todos*, "and not one remain!"

Jana had just begun studying at the School of Fine Arts

when the country went bankrupt. She had hitchhiked out of her community a few weeks earlier, wearing the woolen poncho her mother had made for her and carrying the old bone-handled knife that had belonged to her ancestors, a few personal items, and enough money to pay her enrollment fees at the university. That was all. Even if millions of people had been ruined by the financial crisis, even if the middle class had been blown to smithereens, even if Argentina as a whole was up for sale, a deracinated Indian woman without connections or housing could still fight for her share with the dogs and poor people who roamed the streets of Buenos Aires.

Like other women students without resources, Jana had been forced to prostitute herself to survive. She refused to surrender the metal forms that moved through her brain. She had stood in front of the Fine Arts building after class, with packets of Kleenex in her bag and an icy fury between her legs.

Rich men drove by in Mercedes, the same men who had bankrupted the country, guys who could be her father and who came to shop. Sell her body to save her mind: the very idea repelled her. Jana had wept while giving her first blow jobs, and then she had swallowed everything: her Indian anger, these swines' sperm, the madness that gnawed at her heart and shook her like a pit bull to make her let go. She'd become barbed wire.

Three years of study.

She had sucked cocks in rubbers, little, big, soft, all of them disgusting, when they wanted to put it up her ass she defended her territory with her knife; they could think what they wanted, treat her like a rag doll on which they wiped off their virtue the way a mechanic wipes off grease before going home and playing the good father ruffling up the hair of his youngest child, Jana had taken refuge behind her barbed wire with the remains of her moral integrity and the body they occupied like a place paid for in parking lot, their pricks still stiff and proud . . . The swine. The war profiteers. Jana tried to calm down—Art, Art, think of nothing but Art. She slept in parks, squats, and theaters where the artists had decided to perform for free ("Buenos Aires would stay Buenos Aires"), with various people, sometimes strangers; Jana never stayed long, drew sketches in the bars or nightclubs where she ended up, exhausted, after evenings spent prostituting herself.

It was in one of these rather seedy downtown clubs that she had met Paula, right at the height of the economic crisis.

Paula, alias Miguel Michellini, a transvestite with a porcelain doll's face and robin's-egg blue eyes that seemed anchored in some distant port. "She" had immediately approached the Indian woman who was keeping a low profile and, after briefly looking into her dark, almond-shaped eyes, given her a passionate kiss as a kind of welcome: "You can do whatever you want with me!" she'd said, smiling under the spotlights as if the world were just great.

Jana had remained dubious: with her white stockings over her bowlegs, her plastic pearls around her slender neck, her false eyelashes and her cherry-red lips, Paula looked to her like a doll that has been abused. "You can do whatever you want with me": the poor creature seemed sincere . . .

The beginning of a millennium, here on Earth: a storm warning for the weakest, most vulnerable people, the ones with little armor. On the margins, it was worse. Two months afterward, Jana had picked up the tranny lying half-dead on the docks of the old commercial port after running into fans of the Boca Juniors: Buenos Aires's favorite team had just lost a game against River, and it cost Paula one of her front teeth.

That night, Jana cared for her with what she had at hand, a few caresses on her forehead damp with fear, three reassuring words she didn't much believe in, always affectionate. They became and remained friends, as much out of a sense of solidarity as out of aversion to the brutality of the world: that great stupidity. Beneath her lost-puppy appearance, Paula was funny, generous, and endowed with a drum majorette's enthusiasm that contrasted with an underlying distress no normal person could envy. Over thirty, without a degree or any obsession other than dressing as a woman, Paula still lived with her mother, a laundress in the working-class neighborhood of San Telmo, and made ends meet by turning tricks on the docks. The tranny wanted to become an artist, what a surprise, and like Jana, she dreamed of better days. Paula was also rootless—in her body. In her, Jana found a companion in poverty and hope. That would not restore the femininity that had been stolen from her. Nor her breasts . . .

Almost ten years had gone by since their shady meeting. The neighborhoods that had been inhabited by bums and by sailors had been transformed into a cluster of steel and glass towers where the multinationals had established their headquarters—the Catalinas, the few structures that had radically changed the city's landscape. Jana lived in the wasteland on the other side of the avenue, squatting in the old Retiro rail station, opposite the four-star hotel Emperator.

Sculptor: "One who brings to life," according to the ancient Egyptians.

Jana had taken over the workshop of Furlan, the artist who had taken possession of the wasteland before her; a full-time mentor, occasional lover, and chronic drinker, Furlan had taken off one day leaving everything under construction—their rickety love affair, the mildewed Ford Taunus in the yard, the shed alongside the tracks in the disused train station, which was henceforth marked as her territory. Jana spent her nights twisting iron, welding, bending sheet metal, composing the monstrous forms that would be applied to the mask of Men.

Conveniences consisted solely of water, electricity, and a stove for heating that gave off toxic fumes. The place was suffocating in summer, freezing in winter. Jana had been living there alone for four years. Furlan was said to be in France; she didn't care.

She no longer needed him or anyone else to survive. Welfare payments and the sale of her first sculptures kept her just above the threshold of indigence. The new president, Kirchner, had gotten the economy back on track without paying attention to the IMF's demands, the country was breathing again, and she felt free. At the age of twenty-eight, that was her only luxury.

Jana had no iPhone, no television, no credit cards, and her closet wasn't overflowing with clothes; Art was her only escape hatch and her ancestral lands her only target in the workshop.

Her current work—her masterpiece—was a map of the southern cone of America, set up monumentally on a base of reinforced concrete, into which she whacked the ancient native territories with a sledgehammer.

Jana was a Mapuche, the daughter of a people who had been shot on sight in the pampas.

Exterminating natives or seeking to convert impious souls, Christians had given no quarter. She didn't either: the hammer fell on the Ranquel territory, already smashed up; jets of pulverized stone hit her eyes. Her black shorts were soaked, sweat was running down her thighs, temples, neck, her dead breasts, her muscles straining toward the objective: the world, a concrete skin she was massacring with a salvific joy.

The cartography of a genocide:

Charrúa.

Ona.

Yamana.

Seik'nam.

Araucan.

The Christians had dispossessed them of their lands, but their spirit-ancestors still roamed them like red ants in the blood. Concrete dust on a tense body: the Mapuche brought her weapon down again and, her eye fixed on the impact, noted the damage done. A real bloodbath.

Eight hundred thousand dead: no, the Christians hadn't given any quarter.

That was what united the natives.

Jana was still working hard when the telephone rang. She turned to the pallet that served as a table, saw the time on the alarm clock—six in the morning—and let the phone ring: The Jesus Lizard was making the walls of the shed vibrate and a dense rain was beating on the roof, lending rhythm to the apparent chaos prevailing in the workshop. Jana was jubilant. The wind had come up, and that old dog David Yow was screaming his lungs out from the speakers and a magnetic rage was flowing like smoking nitrogen in her Indian veins.

"Haush."

"Alakaluf."

"Mapuche!"

The hammer finally fell to the floor glittering with shards. Jana was examining the contours of the craters that pocked her ethnocidal map, her arms aching, when the telephone rang again. Thc alarm clock read 6:20. The Jesus Lizard album had just ended, the rain had stopped. The sculptress picked up the receiver, her mind elsewhere—her bare feet made wolf's tracks in the concrete snow . . .

She quickly came down to Earth—it was Paula.

"Ah! Darling, finally you picked up!" she burst out. "Sorry to bother you, but I swear I'm not calling about makeup! It's about Luz," she went on breathlessly. "I'm worried: she left me a message on my cell a little while ago to tell me that she had to talk to me about something super important, but I'm still waiting, and her cell doesn't answer: something's wrong!"

Jana wiped the layer of dust off her lips—Luz was the tranny who had been sharing the docks with Paula for the past six months.

"Is that why you're calling?"

"I don't know anyone but you!" Paula pleaded. "We were

supposed to meet at five, I've been waiting a long time and she doesn't answer her phone: something's wrong!"

"What time did Luz leave her message?"

"At 1:28," her friend replied above the background noise.

"She might have been picked up by the cops."

"No, something's happened, I'm sure. She wanted to see me," Paula insisted. "I'm telling you, something's wrong!"

Jana hated to be disturbed while she was working: she didn't allow herself to be moved by her friend's melodramatic air.

"Was Luz working last night?" she asked.

"Yes!"

"Maybe she met Prince Charming. At least give her time to come back to Earth."

"That's not funny. Listen, I'm really worried. For once she's not pretending. I need you. Can't you come?"

There was deafening music in the background.

"Where are you?"

"At the Transformer."

A transvestite bar where losers like her met after working the streets. Jana glanced at her concrete sculpture and promised it a brief respite.

"O.K.," she panted into the receiver. "I'm coming."

*

The stars on the cosmic blotter were fading out one by one; Jana slid shut the worm-eaten wooden door, padlocked it, and walked across the empty ground surrounding the shed. The big Ford was getting rusty around the grille, under the blind eye of a giant hen on acid, one of her first sculptures made from scrap metal—steel bars, bolts, welding rods, beams—that still showed Furlan's influence. The other installations were also beginning to decay.

Jana slid into the cracked leatherette seat, waved to a steel aviator at the entrance to the yard and started down the Avenue Libertador—the vein, twelve lanes wide, that crossed the city's arteries. Jana was no longer thinking about her work in progress; the wind was blowing around in the car (the month before, some jerk had broken her passenger-side window), filling the trash can on wheels with a whirlwind of ashes. All through Córdoba the shops were still shuttered, the leaves on the trees were rustling before the crowds arrived, at the hour when *cartoneros* were going home. She passed a group of latecomers, their rags steaming under a load of broken bottles, pulling their carts after a night of collecting.

Palermo Viejo. Jana parked the Ford in a delivery zone and walked to the next block. She had hastily thrown on a black combat jumpsuit and her Doc Martens, her tank top was still covered with concrete fragments, and she hadn't a penny in her pockets.

The entrance to the Transformer was a simple hole cut in an iron shutter. A lesbian with body piercings, dressed for hunting big game, was letting some people in, others not: Jill, eighty kilos of violence perched on a stool on the sidewalk. Transvestites and prostitutes obeyed her finger gestures and looks, too afraid of losing their places for later, along with the possibility of picking up some extra cash if the night turned out to be slow.

"Hi."

"Hi."

Jana hadn't been in the Transformer for years, but Jill let her in, impassive beneath her bleached military crew cut. Jana bent down, made her way through the gloomy tunnel that led to the club, and pushed open the padded door. It was almost as dark inside as it was outside, the best way of hiding the dirt and the state of the furniture. A zombielike faun was wandering in the shadow of the head-high runway; watched by everyone, two trannies with made-in-China fake diamond necklaces, two addicts she didn't know, were writhing at the edge of the dance floor. Otherwise, the Transformer hadn't changed, with its cigarette burns on the benches, its lukewarm champagne, and its sex à la carte. The couples that formed incognito in the dark reached the back rooms by the runway, lit up by flashing strobe lights, but the trannies looked tired this morning. There was no mad revue under rotating disco lamps, no laughing to cover the blows and bullying: the customers took refuge behind the speakers pumping out indifferent house music, peering at new arrivals as if they were messiahs nearing the finish line.

Jana's Doc Martens adhered to the club's sticky floor. She headed for the bar and finally spotted Paula among the rudderless and anchorless shipwrecks,. She was snorting coke on the counter, in the company of Jorge, the club's manager.

"Well, well," he said when he saw the Indian woman come into his cave. "Look here, it's 'La Pampa' . . . "

Her little nickname referred to her chest, which was as flat as the Argentine plains. Jana hated that son of a bitch.

"I thought you were a great artist," he said with the complacency of a real estate agent. "What're you doing here?"

"Isn't it obvious? I'm choking on the stink of your breath."

Jorge chuckled. Stocky, wearing a bracelet and a white shirt opened to show a tuft of hair and a priceless gold chain, the manager laid out three lines of coke on the counter and handed Jana a damp straw, giving her a sly look.

"A little hit for the prodigal child?"

"No."

"Have you quit, too?"

"Fuck off," she said, looking at him under her brown locks. "O.K.?"

Paula's mouth twisted under the beauty spot that contrasted with the pallor of her nostrils: one sign from the boss and Jill would throw them out with their Adam's apples on the back of their necks if she felt like it. Jana pulled her friend down to the other end of the bar, where the music wasn't so loud.

"You should go easy on the coke, love," she said to the tranny perched on her high heels. "There's nothing but laxatives in it. And above all you should keep away from that louse."

Jorge was taunting them from the opposite end of the counter.

"I was so nervous," Paula confessed, wiping her nose.

"Coke does calm you down, it's true."

"Listen, something happened to Luz," Paula repeated, "I'm sure of it. Otherwise I wouldn't have called you."

Paula was wearing a white dress with flounces and heart-shaped earrings; her foundation was crumbling in the early morning, and by that point her curls were attractive to no one but other homosexuals.

Jana shook her head.

"It's the coke that's making you paranoid."

"No, I swear," Paula replied, her eyes big as saucers. "I asked the girls," she said, turning toward the lap-dance fans, "they haven't seen Luz all night, either. I've used up an incredible number of credits texting her; even if Luz had lost her cell, she'd be here. I don't know what's going on."

"What did her message say, exactly?"

"Just that she wanted to talk to me about something important, that she'd meet me here at 5:00, after the Niceto . . . " The Niceto was the club in the barrio of Palermo where Paula was auditioning for a part.

"By the way, how did it go?"

"Great! They told me they'd let me know!"

Paula smiled with Bambi-on-barbiturates eyes—this was her first encounter with show business.

"Who'd you see," Jana joked, "the doorman?"

"No, no, the choreographer! Gelman, a kinda younger Andy Warhol. You know, I saw part of the rehearsal, and the show looks like it's going to be good! Listen, Jana," she said, growing more serious, "Luz couldn't have been fooling around. That's not her style, and even less if she had something important to tell me. Not to mention the audition at the Niceto." Paula put her hand on Jana's. "I've got a bad feeling, Jana. Otherwise I wouldn't have called you. You know how much I care about Luz. Please help me find her."

Paula wrinkled her little trumpet-shaped nose, an expression known only to the two of them. Her smile was missing a tooth, but the rest was still intact under the makeup. Jana sighed in the club's polluted air. "O.K." Figures were slipping into the obscurity: party animals going home, habitués, gay junkies, police informers, resolute virgins, the waltz of the backrooms was getting into full swing. Jorge's voice drowned out the Latin disco blaring from the speakers.

"Hey, La Pampa!" he roared. "There are two gauchos here asking if you'll still lay them for a hundred pesos! Hey, Indian! You hear?"

"Don't listen," Paula whispered to her friend, "he's too stupid."

Jana had a metallic taste in her mouth; on the other side of the bar Jorge was snickering. She took Paula's hand and dragged her toward the exit.

It was either that or set this rat-hole on fire.

*

Buenos Aires arose out of nothing, a land of brush and mud on the edge of an estuary that opened onto the ocean where contrary winds blew. It was there that the colonists had constructed a commercial port, La Boca, its jaws closed on the Amerindian continent. La Boca, where so many cattle were slaughtered that the blood ran over the sidewalks, along with the blood of girls who thought they were emigrating from Europe to a new Eldorado or who had been kidnapped with false promises of marriage before they were sent to the slaughterhouses, where they serviced sixty customers a day seven days a week in sailors' whorehouses—another century.

The port had been abandoned, and La Boca was now known only for its corrugated metal houses painted with the remains of ship paint pots, its craftsmen, and its pretty buildings on the Caminito occupied by rainbow-colored galleries where all kinds of portraits of Maradona, Evita, and Guevara could be found. A lookalike of soccer's golden boy, or the end-of-career version, little skirts in the Argentine national colors, merchants catering to *gringas*, kids in soccer jerseys, one restaurant after another, and as many touts. During the day La Boca had loads of tourists, but the area emptied out at nightfall: prostitutes, drug dealers, addicts, riffraff, poor people, shady characters roamed it until dawn. Even the brightly-painted houses took on a macabre appearance.

Jana's Ford cruised slowly along the docks; it was a 1980 model and did not clash with the surroundings. Leaky boats served out their time in the old commercial port, half sunk or covered with algae; grayish low-income towers rose up, clothes hung to dry on the balconies like so many tongues stuck out at Buenos Aires propriety. Paula looked at the sites of perdition outside the broken window; coming down from coke made her anxious, she felt responsible for Luz and her premonitions were tying her stomach in knots.

Bosteros, bumpkins—that's what the people of La Boca are called. Also known as Orlando, Luz had begun his career as a transvestite blowing truck drivers in Junin. But he'd fled his life in the service stations on Route 7 after his only contact in town, a cousin, had thrown him out when he found women's clothing in his suitcase. Luz had felt pretty much at home when he landed in La Boca. He'd made the rounds of the bars and clubs, looking for a man who would take him as he was, and finally found Paula.

Most of the transvestites saw their peers as amateurs at best and as competitors at worst. But Paula had enough heart for two. Above all, the Samaritan was in a position to see how Luz's story would end. Overwhelmed by her need to dress as a woman, Luz had already lost everything—family ties, job, friends. After the first encounters at traffic circles, more phantasmal than profitable, prostitution had quickly become her lifesaver. She would die worn-out and toothless, in the gutter. Lost in Buenos Aires, Paula had suggested that they work as a team on the La Boca docks; they would protect one another while waiting for something better, and Paula would teach her the trade.

"Don't worry about anything," Jana said. "I'm sure Luz took some guy home with her."

"No," Paula replied. "Rule No. 1 is always to fuck at other people's places, never at your own. If the guy is a nutcase who wants to kill you, he'll have to get rid of the body, whereas at your place he can just leave and shut the door. No," she repeated as if to convince herself, "Luz would never have done anything that stupid."

Jana drove slowly under the flickering streetlights, peering into the shadows between abandoned warehouses and vacant lots. A steamboat in the last stages of decomposition was creaking against the broken-down dock, while farther on a couple of worn-out cranes and a sand barge completed the impression of neglect and decay. At dawn, the streets had emptied out: the trannies, the junkers of the prostitution game, had gone home.

"Except for sniffing dogs' hind ends, there's nothing to do here," Jana said.

Paula, sitting beside her and clutching her fake zebra-skin purse on her knees, agreed.

"Let's have a look over by the stadium," she said. "There are a couple of regular customers over there, you never know."

The La Boca stadium was a cube of yellow and grayish-blue

concrete painted with Coca-Cola signs: it was there that Maradona performed his first exploits before avenging a whole country for the Falkland Islands humiliation by beating England all by himself.

Dieguito was thinking about Maradona's sombreros, about the way he left the English team mystified, about the Goal of the Century, over and over.

"Whaaaa . . . "

Dieguito was dribbling the stars. An effect of the *paco*, the dregs of the dregs of crystal meth he'd just sniffed after making the rounds of the neighborhood.

A hundred thousand *cartoneros* came down from the suburbs every day to collect and resell recyclable garbage: paper, metals, glass, plastic, cardboard, for forty-two centavos a kilo—a few cents. Among them were many children who knew each other from their neighborhoods or soccer clubs. Dieguito and his gang wore the jersey of the Boca Juniors, the club formed after the Río de la Plata team's departure to the wealthy neighborhoods—a betrayal that had never been pardoned. Naturally, number 10 was reserved for their leader.

"Whaaaa . . . "

Dieguito was delirious. The rest of the gang was drinking a mixture of orange juice and 80-proof alcohol in plastic bottles, sprawling on the trampled flowerbeds at the north entrance: no one saw the Ford park in the shadow of the stadium.

Dieguito soon felt a presence over him, blinked his eyes to define its contours, and jumped back: a tranny was bending over him in a cream-colored coat with a stained collar and a dress below the knees . . . It took him a few seconds to come out of his trance and recognize Paula.

"What are you doing there," the *cartonero* stammered.

"We're looking for Luz," his guardian angel replied. "She was working the docks tonight: it's your sector, you must have seen her, no?"

Dieguito leaned back against the concrete pillar. There was an Indian with the tranny, whom the kid eyed with a disgusted air—she didn't even have any tits.

"Luz?" he said, his mouth feeling woolly. "Uh, no . . . "

"You didn't see her because you were high or because she wasn't here?"

"Whoa!" the boy snorted. "We worked all night while you were getting fucked: you know where you can stick your comments?"

"Hey, do you want me to smash your face in with my purse?"

The rest of the gang slowly emerged, bandy-legged; they got up without enthusiasm.

Jana rephrased the question. "We're just asking you if you've seen Luz working tonight."

"I don't know anything!" the kid yelped.

"You didn't see her all night?" Paula insisted.

"No! How many times do I have to say it?"

"Would it kill you to be friendly, Pinocchio?"

"Up yours! Yes!"

The gang started to form a circle around the trio.

"Is there a problem, Dieguito?" asked one of the *cartoneros*.

Paula shivered under her flounced dress: some of the kids bent down to pick up stones.

"Let's get out of here," Jana whispered.

Followed by scruffy kids in shorts insulting them, they made their way back to the car and took off. Dark clouds weighed on the rising sun. The tranny's spirits were plummeting.

"Maybe Luz is sick," Jana said, "and stayed home with the crud, she's probably sleeping like a stone. The thing she wanted to talk about may not be all that important . . . You're overreacting, honey."

"She would have told me," Paula said sullenly. "We had a date . . . "

At the wheel of her old crate, Jana yawned.

"We'll find out tomorrow," she said. "I'm dropping you off at your mother's house."

"Can't I sleep with you?" her friend simpered, "just for tonight?"

"No, you kick too much."

"That's because I run a lot in my dreams."

"A cheetah with fingernail polish, sure."

"I'm afraid I'll have an anxiety attack, Jana. Look," she said, putting her hand on her fake breasts, "my heart is fluttering."

"Yeah, sure."

The Ford was moving down Don Pedro de Mendoza, an avenue that took them along the harbor on the way back downtown, when they saw the rotating light of a police car at the end of the docks.

*

The old car ferry was slouched in the brackish water of the Riachuelo, exhaling an odor of mud and decomposition. A few spindly bushes had grown up against the worm-eaten dock, and there were patches of reeds where oily trash accumulated, corks and plastic bottles. A big guy weighing around 250 pounds was bending over the murky water, flanked by a puny fellow who was running a flashlight beam over the metal structure.

"It doesn't smell good, boss," the man said.

"Shine the light on it, you fool."

Sergeant Andretti grumbled as his eyes followed the beam of trembling light: a body was floating among the jugs and greasy papers, half submerged in the dense mire. The pale body of a young boy, clearly naked, that somebody had thrown next to the ferry.

The policeman turned to look at the vehicle that was

parked at the end of the docks: a strange couple soon emerged from it, a transvestite and a girl with black hair wearing an urban guerilla outfit.

"What are you doing there?"

Paula took a few steps toward the cops bending down in front of the bridge and saw the body swimming in the muck that was illuminated by the flashlight. She dug her nails into Jana's arm, her eyes popping out: it was Luz.

2

What's the matter?" Andretti asked. "Does she smell bad, your pal?"

Paula was throwing up her guts on the pavement, while two cops called in as backup were teetering at the foot of the ferry. Jana examined the policeman by the intermittent flashes of the revolving light.

"Does that amuse you?"

Fabio Andretti wore a boar-bristle mustache and carried a good fifty pounds too many. He shrugged in response. He was paid to get the parasites out of the neighborhood; he left the trannies to the social workers. His partner, Troncón, whom he'd had to kick in the ass to wake him up in a cell at the station so they could go on patrol, kept back. A pimply man in his twenties wearing a cap too big for him, Jesus Troncón was not feeling well: he'd never seen a naked body floating in shit. They were just now pulling it toward the docks.

Andretti hitched up the belt that supported his equipment and the inexorable bulge of his belly. The early morning sunlight was touching the tops of the gray low-cost housing towers—there were no witnesses other than these two clowns. He turned toward the Indian with her high cheekbones, her eyes still fixed on him.

"O.K.," he sighed. "We'll start over from zero. What's her name?"

"Luz," Jana answered.

"Luz what?"

"No idea."

"I thought you knew her?"

"I only know her tranny name," Jana explained.

"Sure. How about you, over there?" he asked the guy in a dress. "Do you know the stiff's real name?"

Paula was choked with sobs, perched on her stiletto heels, ridiculously small compared to the former butcher's boy. She didn't want to believe that this little monkey curled up below the ferry was Luz.

"Or . . . Orlando," she finally said.

"That's all?"

Paula nodded, realizing bitterly that she didn't even know Luz's last name. She pulled a Kleenex out of her zebra-striped bag and wiped her mouth while Andretti scribbled the information in a notebook, his big, sausage-like fingers covering half the pen.

"What are you doing down here at this hour?" he asked again.

"Luz didn't show up for a date with my friend," Jana said. "Since we knew she was working the docks, we went to see."

The cop's smell washed over her, a kind of aftershave for the feet.

"See what?"

"Why she hadn't come. Luz and Paula work together, you must know that because you're from around here."

Andretti looked at her shrunken breasts.

"And you, who are you?"

"Just a friend."

"How about her," he said, pointing to Paula. "Who's she, his aunt?"

Fabio Andretti had the bulk of an aging wrestler and a dark sense of humor.

"If it was a mother crying over her murdered kid, you wouldn't talk like that," Jana remarked. "But a homo crying over a whore, that's really funny, isn't it?"

"Watch what you say, kid."

"You too."

Troncón stiffened as if he'd been stung. In Argentina, people often spoke informally but the *negrita* was playing with fire. The sergeant's bovine expression became sharper.

"You want me to take you in, you and your tranny friend?"

The colossus was putting his hand on the nightstick that hung from his belt—it would be a pleasure to smash in her ribs—when one of the cops behind him cursed.

"*La concha de tu madre!* Boss! Boss! Come have a look at this!"

"What's going on?"

"Boss . . . "

Andretti looked at Luz's body, which had just been pulled up on the pavement, dripping with putrid water, and swallowed his indignation: the kid no longer had any genitals. His penis, testicles, and everything had been cut off from the pubic bone to the scrotum. All that was left was a black, festering wound, mixed with mud.

"Shit," he mumbled through his mustache.

Terrified, her face ashen, Paula retched one last time and vomited a black liquid on Troncón's shoes. Andretti also paled on seeing the young man's emasculated body. The cops on the night squad remained silent, their hands crossed, in accord with their duty.

"Cordon this off," Andretti panted, "now!"

People were starting to gather at the end of the docks. Andretti was still crouching over the body, the crack of his big buttocks showing between his shirt and his pants. It was against the rules, but he did it anyway: he put on a pair of plastic gloves and turned the body over. There was no sign that the boy had been shot in the back, but there was a deep wound under the left shoulder blade. A knife, maybe—it was difficult to tell with all the mud. Neither the head nor the abdomen seemed to have been injured. There were no clothes lying around, nor a purse. They'd search all the nearby trash bins; if they were lucky, the murderer would have thrown things away in a hurry. Then one detail attracted his attention. He shined his Maglite on the corpse's rectal area, which was in particularly bad shape: there was something shapeless there, a clump of flesh and hair. He swallowed. Was it a penis? What else could it be? What could it be but the kid's penis?

Andretti stood up rather heavily. His men had cordoned off the crime scene, the emergency services men were arriving, attracting crowds of onlookers.

"O.K.," he said to his team. "Let's pack this up."

Troncón stood nearby, his shoes covered with vomit.

"What do we do with the two whores, boss?"

The tranny was sitting on the pavement, trembling, supported by the Indian.

"We'll take 'em in," Andretti growled.

*

"*Pelotudos*," "*Cornudos*," "*Soretes*," "*Larvas*," "*Culos rotos*," "*Flor de san puta*"[2]: to judge by the graffiti that peppered the walls of the police station, opinion regarding La Boca's cops was unanimous.

Head of the night squad, Fabio Andretti had begun his career as a butcher's assistant in Colalao del Valle, a village in Tucumán, when a friend of his uncle suggested that he join the police, where he "knew some people." Fabio had taken him up on the offer and very quickly understood what could be gotten out of this line of work. Working lousy jobs in shabby police stations, he had more than once fought with officers

[2] "Balls," "cuckolds," "bastards," "worms," "pain in the ass," "whore-flower."

and their subordinates who supplemented their paychecks by robbing the local scum, thieves or drug dealers who were unlikely to file complaints. He received promotions for good and loyal service and was transferred. Fabio Andretti had joined the night squad in La Boca, Buenos Aires, where his rank of sergeant made him responsible to no one but the chief of police, who, between delivering official speeches referring to new directives that no one would follow, spent his time collecting bribes. A common and long-standing practice. At the end of the dictatorship, President Alfonsin had cut off a few too prominent heads, but since Menem closed his eyes to anything that did not involve money, most of the policemen had kept their jobs and still operated with near impunity. Murders, cases of "itchy trigger finger," sequestrations, tortures or beatings, every year there were an enormous number of complaints concerning minors tortured or strangled in the police stations.

The station at La Boca smelled of worn-out shoe leather and mothballs. Two broken chairs next to a dead plant decorated the room where Paula and Jana had been waiting for three-quarters of an hour, sitting on a bench opposite the desk. They had been refused a phone call, a glass of water, and access to the toilets, which were, it seemed, plugged up.

"It's going to be okay, precious," Jana whispered to her friend. "It'll be okay when we get out of here."

Tears were running down Paula's cheeks, completing the ruin of her makeup.

"It's horrifying," she repeated into her Kleenex. "Did you see what they did to him?"

In death, Luz had become a man again.

"Try not to think about it," Jana said, stroking her feeble hand.

But Paula wasn't listening.

"What kind of animal could do something like that? What

monster? And Luz? I don't understand how he could have let himself be taken in like that."

Luz was her protégée, her kitten by the roadside, her associate; Paula had taught her about the night, the neighborhoods, the hours to avoid, suckers to be cajoled, hotels that welcomed prostitutes, backrooms, the risks and the rules that had to be observed: it was just incomprehensible. And then why did they have to kill her? Because she was different? Because she was on the bottom rung of society, and it was eternal human nature to take revenge?

"It's disgusting."

"Yes," Jana agreed. "But it's not your fault."

"If I hadn't had that appointment in Niceto, I could have been there: things would have turned out differently."

"It's pointless, I'm telling you."

Agent Troncón was watching them out of the corner of his eye, and was less frisky than he'd been when his boss was around. Raised by a father who kicked him in the ass and who even in the morning looked like he'd just come out of a *pulpería*—a country bar in the time of the gauchos—Jesus Troncón came of age on a high, arid plain, afflicted with shortsightedness, persistent acne, and a downy mustache that caressed downturned lips. The apprentice policeman walked up and down a few times in his too-short uniform and finally beckoned to them from the hall.

"Hey! It's your turn!"

Paula cringed beneath her cheap cream-colored coat. She knew Sergeant Andretti by reputation—he was to be avoided. Jana helped her get up from the bench where they'd been marinating and shot a withering look at the greenhorn in his cap. The boss's office was situated at the end of the hall, after the empty vending machine.

"Come on, we've got lots of things to do!" Troncón bawled for form's sake.

Paula moved forward, teetering.

"You won't do anything stupid, will you?" she whispered to her friend before going in.

"No. I promise."

A smell of old sweat emanated from the walls of the office, which were covered with search bulletins, drug-abuse prevention posters, and tattered pictures of naked women. His burly body wedged into a groaning chair, Andretti sized up the couple—a transvestite with a giraffe's neck decked out in an unlikely white dress with flounces and an Indian with a torso like a female monkey's, her buttocks poured into a black combat suit: faggots disgusted him, but the little whore, with her round ass and her Amazon's legs, would be well worth visiting in a cell.

"Can you tell us what we're doing here?" Jana asked for openers.

"What do you mean, what are you doing here? We're dealing with a murder, kid," the cop snapped at her, "and I'm the one who asks the questions. Three out of four guilty parties are friends or relatives of the victims, did you know that?"

Paula shrank on the nearby chair.

"So far as I know, we're witnesses," Jana said, "not suspects."

"And the story of the killer who returns to the scene of the crime, have you heard that one?"

On the wall behind Andretti was a poster showing a girl with Teflon tits who was biting her thumb with a naughty air.

"Bull," Jana said.

"We'll see about that: where were you between midnight and six o'clock this morning?"

"At home," she replied calmly. "In my workshop."

"Workshop for what?"

"I'm a sculptor."

"Is that right. What do you make, totem poles?"

"Hilarious."

"The thing is, you don't have an alibi, sweetie, that's what I see," the head of the night squad declared. "And you, tranny," he barked, "where were you?"

Paula's tears had made her mascara run, her heels and stockings were spotted with vomit, the sight of Orlando mutilated had struck her dumb, and this jerk terrified her.

"She was at the Niceto for an audition," Jana replied for her. "A club in Palermo: two thousand people can confirm it for you."

"That means that your pal Orlando was alone on the docks when he was attacked," the policeman deduced.

"Massacred would be more exact."

"Yeah. Did he have enemies, this Orlando?"

The Mapuche shook her head.

"No . . . We know lots of sons of bitches but nobody who would do that."

"A matter of settling scores, did you think of that?"

"Orlando and my friend here were working for themselves, and they earned hardly enough to live on: that doesn't deserve that kind of ruthlessness."

The policeman pretended he hadn't heard.

"Who else was close to Luz?"

Jana turned to Paula, or rather her colorless shadow.

"Only us," she mumbled from her chair.

"You've started talking again!" the sergeant observed. "So: you don't know anyone who might give us information about Orlando?"

"No."

The giant receded like a tide of fuel oil into the chair, and crossed his meaty hands behind his head.

"If I understand correctly, you claim that the victim has no friends other than you, and that you're close to him but not to the point of knowing his last name," he laughed. "That's some friendship!"

"It's not friendship," Jana said, "it's loneliness."

"Oh ho! Do you at least know where he lives, your best friend?"

The Mapuche grimaced. "No idea."

"In a barrio," Paula threw in. "La Villa 21."

A slum in the center of town.

"Family?"

"In Junin . . . At least that's what Luz, Orlando told me. He broke with his former life and came to Buenos Aires."

"Where he ran into the wrong person at the wrong place," Andretti continued.

Paula was interlacing her fingers on the chair. The sergeant pushed back the keyboard of his computer, which resembled the shabby buildings in the neighborhood.

"Since you don't have anything else to tell me, you can go home," he announced.

"You're not going to take our deposition?" Jana said, astonished.

"To write what, that you know his first name?"

"You're going to inform his parents, at least?"

Andretti scowled at her in a special way. "You know what they say around here, Indian: mind your own business."

An old adage that had been widely repeated during the dictatorship. At that time, Jana hadn't yet been born.

"Our friend was massacred by a psychopath and there's every reason to think he's still roaming the neighborhood," she said. "Luz had a purse and clothes; if you haven't found anything, that's because the murderer must have picked up Luz in his car and taken him somewhere to kill him and then throw his body in the harbor."

"Listen, no little whore is going to tell me how to do my job!" the policeman grumbled, shaking his chops. "Now get out of here, *India de merda*, before I lock you up. Naked, how would you like that?"

Paula shivered on her chair. The station's walls oozed violence, arbitrariness, and beatings. Jana held her breath, her eyes burning with hatred. It wasn't just Jorge, the manager of the Transformer; for the cops too she would never be more than someone who sucked cocks, a subhuman or alien of the species that you fucked in cars, a bastard who grew up in the dirt and was thrown into the city like a prison, an Indian who pissed her kind's blood: nothing.

Nothing but a whore.

She took Paula's icy hand.

"*Rajemos*!"[3]

[3] "Let's get the hell out of here!"

3

"The Mexicans descend from the Aztecs, the Peruvians from the Incas, the Colombians from the Mayas, and the Argentines descend from boats," goes the old joke. In fact, Buenos Aires existed chiefly through European eyes. A play of mirrors and reflections that honed the soul of *Porteños*. After the natives were wiped out, losers from the old world gathered in this silted-up port without docks, which was reached by half-submerged wagons drawn by horses. Hardly had the dust raised by the Indians settled than the colonists began building the city of Buenos Aires that Daniel Calderón loved so much.

Was that why he left it so often, like a passionate mistress, the better to return to it? When he talked about the city, Daniel had the *duende*, that creative brilliance dear to Lorca that is sometimes found in a bullfighter's pass, a singer's voice, or the trance of a flamenco dancer. Rubén found this *duende* that "rejects muses and angels / as learned dogs in the mud" in his father's poems, the fire and light that had dazzled his childhood. Daniel and Elena Calderón had given him this name in honor of Rubén Dario, the instigator of their language's independence movement and a precursor of the manifesto of *Martín Fierro*, the avant-garde poetry magazine that had put its stamp on the beginning of the century in Argentina, and of which Daniel was one of the most innovative heirs.

Rubén had discovered Buenos Aires through the eyes of his father, a poet bound to his city the way the plain is bound to the rain: very early on, Daniel had told him about his tricks of sleight-of-hand, his bars where they smoked and talked until dawn about politics, about the tango that had returned from the whorehouses and its women bent under the other's desire, the colors and prism of the Europe that haunted them. As they sat for hours on benches or café terraces in the Florida neighborhood of Buenos Aires, his father had taught him to observe people, to recognize that a young girl was walking alone in the street for the first time, so proud in a touching way to show everyone that she was free, the elegance of lovers on the paving stones shining in the night, to divine the reflections of old men in parks, the lost thoughts that had to be recuperated for them, the insouciance of cats in cemeteries, the peaceful happiness of mature women when they had fallen in love again, the stirring vitality of some women when they gave the gift of their grace to the world, thus restoring its enchantment. Together, they imagined the lives of passersby, like the man in a hat they saw near the opera house who, by following Borges's itinerary, would end up shaking Pinochet's hand (a typical joke, the great writer having both drawn up his "ideal itinerary" through the checkerboard of Buenos Aires and shaken the hand of the Chilean dictator before retracting his act "to some extent"). As Rubén grew up, women became their favorite playground, where passionate abstraction proved most fertile. Poems and ideas piled up in the notebooks he filled, the Hispanic *duende* being the target:

Beauty, beauty . . .
I would like to die with you,
Beautifully . . .

Rubén was advancing with giant steps when Videla's coup d'état—*la Golpe*—happened on March 24, 1976.

"One death is a cause of sorrow; a million is news." Thirty

million was the number of the *desaparecidos,* those who "disappeared."

The method applied by the military junta duplicated the Nazis' practices during the war: they simply picked people up without warning. The advantages of proceeding in this way: no information about the conditions of detention, the preservation of their image on the international stage, and the possibility of liquidating individuals who would otherwise be protected by their age (minors), their sex (girls, pregnant women), or their fame. Contacts established with French officers who had fought in Indochina, and then with members of the OAS Delta groups who had returned from Algeria,[4] were soon to add to the terror by introducing electroshock torture that was henceforth used systematically on prisoners: the *picaña*. These methods and the ties established with Nazism were in no way unprecedented: the national icon, Juan Péron, had received a considerable sum in exchange for providing eight thousand passports for Axis agents fleeing Europe. In this way, many Argentine police had been trained by former Nazi officers, and pamphlets circulated in the barracks—"SS in Action," "Hitler may have been right," and the famous forgery, "The Protocols of the Elders of Zion," which was still to be found in the used bookstores on Corrientes Avenue. In addition to the instructors, the greatest war criminals had passed through the country, Mengele, Boorman—who was said to have possession of the "Nazi treasure"—and Eichmann, whose house looked out on a Jewish cemetery.

Following the example of the commander of Auschwitz, one of the high-ranking officers in the Argentine junta, General Camps, had declared that he had "never personally

[4] *Organisation de l'armée secrète,* a clandestine organization within the French army that resisted the liberation of Algeria in the late 1950s and early 1960s.

killed a child," which did not prevent him, however, from proposing, at the height of the repression, that every subversive child in primary schools be arrested in order to muzzle all future opposition. Under pressure from the persnickety Carter administration, Videla, the first head of the dictatorship, had finally given up the idea—it was a matter of image.

All the military men had been involved in these secret operations, and were regularly rotated. They were forbidden to talk about or to comment on these "purification" missions, but rumors were allowed to circulate in order to terrorize the population. Threatened with reprisals, some people turned up their radios in order to mask the cries of neighbors who were being taken away. Ford Falcons roamed the city without license plates and with an officer in the back seat. The actions took place chiefly at night or in the early morning, and on weekends, if possible: the Intervention Group cut off the neighborhood's electricity if the operation looked like it was going to be tricky, and, in the event of resistance, shot into the crowd—in his report, the officer in charge described this as an "anti-terrorist assault." Afterward, they emptied the building before taking the subversives to "processing centers."

Participating in meetings of left-wing students or labor union activities, expressing overt criticism of the military, having the same name as a suspect, having witnessed an abduction, being Jewish, teaching or studying sociology, providing advice to poor people or suspects involved in legal proceedings, taking care of suspects or poor people, writing poems, novels, or speeches, being a foreigner and "too noisy," being a refugee from a country ruled by a military regime, being sought for political reasons, practicing as a psychologist or psychoanalyst—that is, influenced by Jewish theorists—giving a piano recital before workers or peasants, being "too" interested in history, being a young soldier who knows too much or who protests, being "too" fascinated by the West or making films that are "too" focused on social subjects or that contravene "good morals," being active in a human rights association, having a brother, sister, cousin, or friend close to a *desaparecido*: the military and the police abducted people for any reason at all. Anyone who opposed the "Argentine way of life" was considered subversive.

"Subversion is what opposes the father to his son," General Videla had explained. A phallocratic paternalism that drew its ideology from Catholicism extended to the whole of society: three hundred forty concentration and extermination camps distributed over eleven of the country's twenty-three provinces, for a maximum efficiency—90 percent of those incarcerated never returned.

Rubén Calderón was one of the survivors.

One day in July 1978 he had been freed without explanation, amid the popular jubilation after the national soccer team won the World Cup.

Probably people were needed to talk about the atrocities that took place in the clandestine prisons, in a way sufficiently convincing to scare off the recalcitrant. Or rather he had been spared so that he could tell what happened during his imprisonment, so that he could tell it to Elena and her Mothers who gathered on Plaza de Mayo every Thursday: to drive her mad, precisely.

But Rubén had said nothing.

To describe what could not be described was to relive it, to make the fear, sorrow, and pain rise up again, to speak was to restore to his tormentors the power to crush him. He had said nothing to his mother about his months in captivity at the Navy Engineering School, or what had happened to his father and his sister—impossible.

Since Elena Calderón had joined the Madres de la Plaza de Mayo resistance movement, Rubén could not remain in Buenos Aires without giving the oppressors a way of exercising pressure; he had been hidden in the countryside, with friends who were not involved in politics—like many people of the time, "they didn't know," or didn't want to know. Hiding out in the converted attic of their home, barricading himself with books like a literary lab rat, Rubén met his mother with deceptive smiles.

He was the friend of owls, of stones. At night, he went out on the plain to spill his guts and didn't come back until he was out of breath, his lungs burning; he collapsed on the grass to revisit the stories they used to tell each other on the terraces of bars—the poet was dead but his voice still echoed in the prodigious memory of his son—stories in which women moved like pumas through the darkness, stories of woods where groups of people set out on horses pierced with nails, stories about encounters with women that Rubén repeated to himself under the stars to give himself the courage to write someday, if he could not speak. But the words fled. They still fled.

His mother brought news from Buenos Aires, where protest was growing. The economy was in tatters, the government's legitimacy was questioned, and there were strikes: after six years of dictatorship, hope was being reborn. He said nothing, he was flayed at the heart of the underworld, a coffin open to the great silence, a messenger of news he had never delivered.

But Rubén had a blue soul. He fooled the sisters at the neighboring *estancia*—how had such a sweet lover accumulated such scars?—developing a rangy animal musculature, invigorated in the outdoors, that would later make him a lady-killer.

"How handsome you are, my son!" Elena said, dazzled, when she visited.

It was true that Rubén resembled his father more and more—in his way of walking, the tilt of his head, the vivacity and color of his eyes, and the disarming smile that unsettled even the surliest women. Naturally, Elena was partial and his mother on top of it, but above all she was in love with her husband who had disappeared. She did not see that Rubén was hatching a monster that kept quiet as it grew stronger every day. The country girls loved his stormy eyes without knowing on whom they would one day fall, his muscular arms that tried to embrace them, taking his shivers for responses to their caresses. Rubén returned from their beds panting, divided between gratitude and fear. The people with whom he lived subscribed to *La Nación*, didn't notice anything.

Rubén was twenty years old when the defeat in the Falklands brought about the fall of the dictatorship. The Grandmothers of the Plaza de Mayo and other victims' associations soon filed a civil suit against the abuses committed during the "National Reorganization Process": it was the time of the first trials, which were to go on for years. Laws granting amnesty followed laws of exception, weariness grew over time, and the army, the police, and most of the oppressors slipped through the judicial system's net. The Grandmothers were the only ones preaching in a desert in which the country's memory was being lost.

Rubén gave up journalism, which had provided him with a living since his return to Buenos Aires, and found the apartment at the corner of Peru and San Juan that was to become his agency. He studied relentlessly the torturers' techniques of interrogation, the resistance to pain, the ways of shadowing people; he studied history, politics, economics, Nazi immigration networks, international law, legal anthropology, shooting moving targets, the martial arts of the combat teams of the *Montoneros*,[5] the ERP[6], and the Mossad: in order to fight back.

[5] *Montoneros*: A Peronist urban guerrilla group

[6] Ejército Revolucionario del Pueblo: an armed Trotskyist group in Argentina.

His detective agency's goal was not to find the *desaparecidos*—he had seen enough to know that they had been killed—but rather those responsible.

In a country where nine out of ten judges who had been on the bench during the dictatorship were still in office, Rubén Calderón was the declared enemy, the Grandmothers' enforcer, the one who received animals' heads by mail, threats by telephone, and insults. For his part, he collected reports on investigations and settled accounts.

The military men hated him, and half the cops in town would have gladly riddled him with bullets, while others would not have shed many tears over his death: Calderón was hunting on their terrain.

"Ricardo Ravelli, born 07/07/1952, corvette captain who had attended the ESMA[7], where he served as an interrogator until 1981, suspected of being involved in a false automobile accident that killed Monseigneur Angelleli, a bishop close to Vatican II and opposed to the ultraconservative Argentine Church, which supported the generals: committed suicide."

"Victor Taddei, born 01/19/1943, member of the Federal Police from 1967 to 1984, where he worked with military intelligence: left the country and his family in 2000 without providing a forwarding address."

"Ricardo Perez, born 05/02/1941 in Mendoza, judge on the military tribunal (1975-1982), then on the Supreme Court: found soaked in his own excrement a few steps from his home."

"Juan Revalde, born 11/25/1950, interrogation officer at the Campo de Mayo (1976-1980), agent of the intelligence services (SIDE) until he was forced to retire in 2003 after

[7] Escuela de Suboficiales de Mecánica de la Armada: a facility of the Argentine Navy employed as an illegal detention center during the National Reorganization Process (1976–1983).

Néstor Kirchner took office: has not spoken for two years; interned at the Rosario psychiatric hospital."

"Hector Mancini, born 06/14/1948, frigate captain in the Navy (1971-1981), twice decorated during the Falklands War; heroin addict, currently without fixed address."

"Miguel Etschecolaz, born 1929, director of investigation with the provincial police from March 1976 to December 1977, suspected of having planned the 'Night of the Pencils' during which several students were taken away, tortured, and killed: found naked at dawn, on an empty lot in Greater Buenos Aires."

"Juan Cavalo, minister to Carlos Menem and former minister of Labor in Isabel Perón's government, in 1975 signed the decree providing for the 'eradication of subversives' in the province of Santa Fe: bankrupted, went into exile in Paraguay in 2006."

The list was long, not exhaustive. Elena Calderón did not know everything—that was their fate as survivors. In fifteen years of working for the Grandmothers, Rubén had survived two attempts to gun him down on the street, a gas leak, a car without license plates that tried to run him over in front of his home, promises to rape his mother, and three physical attacks with no serious consequences. "Memory, truth, justice": since he'd gotten out of prison, the Grandmothers had in no way changed their method of harassment. It was too late. At this point, no threat, law, or decree would make them let up: now, they were the Jaws of History.

*

Summer was coming to an end, and the heat wave that had weighed on the city for a month had suddenly been swept away by a strong gale: as it grew dark, a cloudburst fell on the sidewalks of the Avenida de Mayo, driving the lottery-ticket vendors to take refuge in the newspaper kiosks.

Soaked tourists were lining up in front of the Café Tortoni, despite the late hour; Rubén made a crack to the aging doorman carrying an umbrella and wearing an impeccable uniform who accompanied him to the heavy door with brass knobs. The Tortoni was the oldest bar in Buenos Aires: Borges still had his table there, and Gardol had his statue under the polished stained-glass windows. The muted hubbub of the customers contrasted with the concert of the dishes that the smartly-dressed waiters were sending back to the kitchen. Dripping rainwater on the thick carpet, Rubén crossed the room, which was luxurious in the style of another age; he spotted Carlos's easygoing face behind the glass window of the smoking room and greeted his friend with a brotherly *abrazo*, the local embrace.

Carlos Valkin, descended from a family of Ukrainian Jews who had fled the pogroms, had been active in the Montoneros, the Péronist revolutionary party. Arrested in 1975 (when the imprisonments were still official) at the offices of the newspaper where he worked, he had been saved by the protests of Daniel Calderón and other artists and celebrities, and was able to take refuge abroad. Carlos had not been a Montonero since the Falklands War, when the leaders of the exiled party had attempted, confronted by patriotic frenzy and on the pretext of opposing English imperialism, to recruit soldiers to fight under the command of their murderers. A generational disillusionment that had not diminished his thirst for justice: Carlos had abandoned his activism but not politics, because today he was an investigative reporter for *Página 12*, a left-of-center daily. A dangerous job in Argentina.

Rubén had worked with him on *Página 12*. Together, they had solved the world's problems during late-night talks in bars, at an hour when people blow off their despair, and talked about women and love, about time past and especially time to come. At sixty, Carlos lived as if he were thirty, wore a short white beard on a smiling face, was eternally optimistic despite the turpitudes of the past, and had hungry eyes that seemed to have drained all the blue from the sky.

Old paintings decorated the walls of the little smoking room, which was deliciously empty. They ordered a bottle of Malbec and two *bife de lomo* and exchanged a few bits of news. Since their inveterate ritual forbade them to report bad news before having eaten a large meal, they waited to be served and then attacked the main course.

The McDonald's culture had hardly taken root in Argentina, where beef raised on the grass of the pampas was the basis for the traditional *asado*, the Sunday barbecue. A gourmet with a strong carnivorous atavism, Carlos complained about the fact that the best meat, the Premium, had recently been reserved for exportation.

"You'll see, someday our cattle will be offshored as well!" he prophesied, waving his fork in the direction of the rococo ceiling.

"Where? To India?" Rubén replied with amusement.

"Go ahead, laugh: our best red wines cost an arm and a leg, our whites taste like vanilla, and our women have even started eating salads!"

"I'd as soon they ate salad as knitted," Rubén said, finishing off his meat. "By the way, are you still with your girlfriend—what's her name?—Alex?"

The two friends hadn't seen each other all summer.

"No," Carlos replied with a touch of nostalgia, "the poor thing got sick of me. But I found a widow, a German woman: very nice, intelligent, rich, sexy . . . That is, as sexy as one can be at sixty," Carlos enthused; he was a chronic lover. "Ah, Ruth! 'The charm of knowing someone would be slender if, in order to achieve it, there were not so much modesty to be overcome!'" he recited, his heart and eyes full of passion.

"Who is that," Rubén asked. "Goethe?"

"Nietzsche. But translated into Argentinian, right?"

"Right!"

"And you, you rascal, do you still have nobody to introduce me to? No? Ha!" he burst out when his friend shrugged. "These ladies' men!"

"One at a time would be enough," Rubén said.

Carlos wasn't sure whether he was joking, but, ladies' man, he acted as if he were.

A couple of old Americans, both wearing checkered shorts, made a brief appearance in the smoking room. Rubén lit a cigarette to smoke while Carlos ate dessert.

"O.K.," he finally said, "you didn't want to see me to talk about women."

"Well, actually I did, in a way . . . "

Carlos wiped his mouth with a paper napkin, threw it amid the remains of his tart and pulled a photo out of his jacket; it was a digital portrait that he pushed across the table. Rubén saw the face of a brunette in her thirties, with the vague eyes of those who are thinking about something else when the shutter clicks. Curly hair, rather pretty . . .

"Do you know her?" Carlos asked.

Rubén shook his head.

"No."

"María Victoria Campallo. She left me a message yesterday at the newspaper, telling me that she would call back. She didn't call. I tried to reach her several times, without success. I went by her place a little while ago but she wasn't there. María Victoria is a photographer," he explained.

"What did the message say?"

"Nothing. Just that she wanted to see me, that it was urgent. I was away, and I didn't get her message until this morning, on the answering machine."

"What's the problem?"

"María is the daughter of Eduardo Campallo, the businessman. You know that there will soon be elections: Campallo is the chief financier for the mayor, Torres. I don't know if there's a connection, but Campallo's daughter has to know where our newspaper stands."

His steely eye shone under the curls of smoke from the cigar he had just lit. He was watching to see his friend's reaction.

"Did she leave you her cell phone number?"

"No; she was calling from a phone booth."

"Campallo rarely appears in Torres's company," Carlos went on, "but he provides the funds for his election campaigns. Campallo began in concrete, taking over his father's firm in the 1970s, and he multiplied its sales before lining his pockets by bidding on procurement contracts during the wave of privatizations. Since then he's been doing favors all around, beginning with his political friends: he's also greasing the palms of the labor unions and the *alcahuetes*[8] who hover around the Casa Rosada, the lobbies . . . An investment, so to speak," he added ironically in order to mask his bitterness. "We've been onto Campallo for a long time, but the guy is a big shot. I don't know what his daughter wanted from me or why she hasn't gotten back to me, but at the beginning of the electoral campaign, you have to admit that it's tempting to see it as more than a mere coincidence."

Rubén looked at him with an inquisitive eye.

"Why are you telling me all this?"

"Because you're a detective," Carlos said, with an ambiguous smile.

"I'm concerned with the *desaparecidos* and their children," Rubén reminded him. "Not with rich people's kids."

"María Victoria is now one of the *desaparecidos*."

Rubén didn't seem convinced.

[8] "Bootlickers."

"If she called from a phone booth," he objected, maybe her cell phone was no longer working, or she left on a reporting assignment or a honeymoon."

Carlos shook his white locks.

"No. I asked the building's concierge; he hadn't seen María Victoria for two days and her cat was meowing for her mistress's return, except that she seems to have vanished into thin air . . . I have no proof of what I'm saying, Rubén, unless you find something."

Rubén looked at his friend the journalist.

"Money, politics, power: you're asking me to put my hands in deep shit," he summed up.

"You're the only one who isn't dirtied by it."

Rubén shook his head: "That's what you say."

"María Campallo is no longer showing any sign of life," Carlos insisted, his voice becoming more serious. "Maybe she's hiding, maybe she's been told to keep quiet, to get out of town, I don't know. Help me find her."

Carlos crushed out his cigarillo in the marble ashtray. Their glasses stood empty on the well-worn wood of the table.

"I'll need information about Campallo," Rubén sighed, "about his daughter . . . I don't have anything."

Carlos pulled a manila envelope out of his jacket.

"You'll find everything in this," he said.

A superimposition of buildings, paved streets, marble, scrap metal, and garbage, the home of Latin American revolution, coup d'états second nature to it, cultural, Péronist, and haughty, Buenos Aires knew that its golden age was past and would never return.

Now kids in rags wandered in front of the buildings of the Centro, people slept on pieces of cardboard in the streets and parks, picked through refuse or lay on the sidewalks, sandwich men walked down Florida or hung out at red lights, taxis that were worn-out and not always legal drove up and down avenues smelling of gasoline, the antique stores in San Telmo were full of old chandeliers, furniture, silver, and authentic family jewels that fed an intense nostalgia. The giant movie theaters and broad boulevards had given way to franchised businesses or huge, impersonal, luxurious edifices, and if the bistro culture persisted, the prohibitive prices downtown kept the citizens of Buenos Aires away; the banks and multinationals had punched holes in the political cadaver of the country, leaving only gobs of spit on their icy glass towers.

The art of the insult was practiced naturally and without moderation; anger impregnated the capital's walls, but the odor of exile that emerged from them did not prevent couples, both young and old, from giving each other uninhibited passionate kisses in the streets, as if to ward off the fate that was hounding Argentina. The skin and the hearts of the people here were as blanched as the iron ore that had marked the century.

The San Telmo neighborhood where Rubén lived had been deserted by the middle class after an epidemic of yellow fever; now weeds were growing over the walls of decrepit houses and their cast-iron balconies. A working-class bastion on the south side of downtown, the municipality was trying to rehabilitate the neighborhood around the Plaza Dorrego, its bars and flea markets. Rubén Calderón lived on Peru Street, in an art-nouveau building whose old-fashioned charm suited him—gray marble on the floors, period woodwork, doorknobs and a bathtub from 1900. A window with blue-tinted panes looked out on the inner courtyard; the kitchen was windowless but the bedroom window gave on the corner of San Juan.

The rain had stopped when the detective pushed open the agency's reinforced door. He laid the manila envelope on the coffee table, opened the window in the living room, which served as an office, in order to get rid of the smell of cold tobacco, and made himself a drink. Pisco, lemon juice, sugar, egg white, ice: he mixed it all vigorously in a shaker before filling a stemmed glass. A pisco sour, energizing effects guaranteed. He put on the Godspeed You! Black Emperor CD he'd bought the day before, and drank his pisco sour gazing at the sky above the roofs and listening to the lascivious moans of the guitars.

Over time, the agency's office had taken over more and more of the apartment, whose private space was now limited to a bedroom at the end of the hall. Computerization had made it possible to reduce the number of volumes, to expand the field of his research, and to cross-reference sources—to produce a DNA register of the bodies of identified *desaparecidos*, a pedigree of the torturers who were still at large or of those who had been granted amnesty, testimonies—all of it connected with the files of the Mothers of the Plaza de Mayo, which Elena kept up to date, and to those of the Grandmothers, who were looking specifically for the children of the *desaparecidos*. The agency was financed by the royalty payments on his father's works, which were still published abroad, the fees that his customers could pay, and private funds or resources that had been taken away from former oppressors. In any case, he wasn't much interested in money—he would have to spend time counting up the money that was missing, and his own losses were final.

The air coming in the window was humid, borne by a capricious breeze that was blowing up to him. Rubén put his glass on the coffee table, sat down on the 1960s couch that faced his overloaded bookcase and opened the manila envelope.

Carlos was well equipped to decipher the financial setup of the Campallo empire and its ramifications: a specialist in economics, the journalist was also a member of a pressure group composed of jurists, intellectuals, and lawyers who were calling for the establishment of a CONADEP[9] to judge those who had

[9] A national commission similar to the one devoted to the *desaparecidos*.

bankrupted Argentina during the financial crisis of 2001-2002. Carlos's group concentrated on property owners who, controlling the main source of currency in the country, had sequestered the dollars derived from their activities and hidden their real revenues in order to reduce their tax bills. This oligarchy, which was connected with the world of finance, had exported its enormous amounts of surplus capital, speculating against the peso and their own country, to the point of draining it dry.

Eduardo Campallo was one of the men who had been able to take advantage of the situation. Trained as an engineer and urban planner, he had studied in the United States before taking the reins of the family business after the early death of his father, who had died in harness, so to speak. In 1975, Eduardo began running Nuevos, a construction firm based in Buenos Aires. The following year, the military hired Nuevos to tear down the slums in the center of the city and build new apartment buildings, a gigantic project that had given the young entrepreneur a leg up and at the same time expanded his networks. Martínez de Hoz, the minister of Finance under the dictatorship and subsequent governments (he was nicknamed Robin Hood, because he robbed from the poor to give to the rich), had studied at the same business school in the United States from which Campallo had graduated. A simple ideological acquaintance? Nuevos, which was later to become STG and then Vivalia, had quadrupled its turnover during the dictatorship and during the Menem years its sales exploded. Pursuing its policy of privatization, the state had then sold off land with full services in the center of Buenos Aires, hiring Campallo to build a business center there—at a profit of 200 percent. The same type of operation was repeated two years later, with the development of luxury residences in Puerto Madero and the conversion of old buildings on the docks into lofts, once again with record profits that had propelled Campallo into the upper economic spheres. Commissions, money transfers to offshore banks through dummy companies, forgeries—Carlos and his friends suspected Eduardo Campallo of having paid off the political class involved in these transactions in exchange for its generosity.

Campallo subsequently diversified his activities by moving into the media and communications; he owned several newspapers, celebrity magazines, and scandal sheets, a private radio station and shares in several cable channels. The 2001 bankruptcy slowed the expansion of Campallo's empire in the center of the capital, but not in the province of Buenos Aires, the most heavily populated in Argentina: Vivalia built, among other things, the ultra-secure community of Santa Barbara, surrounded by walls, some fifty kilometers from the city, with a special highway, reserved for residents, providing access to the international airport, armed guards, sport facilities, urban services, green spaces, etc. Campallo mixed with the country's elite, who had no lack of supplicants. Some them had naturally become his friends, beginning with the mayor of Buenos Aires, Francisco Torres.

Rubén finished his pisco sour. Although Carlos had put together a complete file on Campallo, he'd given Rubén little information about the businessman's family. In 1974, Eduardo Campallo married Isabel de Angelis, who came from the local upper middle class. Now fifty-nine years old, a Catholic, and the mother of two children—María Victoria and her brother Rodolfo, who was two years younger—Isabel Campallo was involved in various charitable activities unrelated to those of her husband and his large personal fortune. Their son Rodolfo worked as a host on his father's radio station, while María Victoria worked as a camera operator. Often away on business, according to the concierge, who was at those times assigned to feed the cat. What was he doing behind the scenes? Carlos had added a digital photo of María Victoria and the address and access code of the building where she lived.

Rubén dressed in black and prepared his equipment.

*

The bohemian youth had moved into Palermo, attracting designer clothes shops, bars, and restaurants in the cosmopolitan fashion that delighted tourists and real estate speculators. The neighborhood was now cut in two, Palermo Viejo and Hollywood, which had been renamed since artists and film people had taken up residence there.

1255 Nicaragua, three o'clock in the morning. A chrome bus in exuberant colors passed by, a fabulous vessel sailing through the night. Rubén crushed out his cigarette in the gutter of broken slabs of marble and punched in the building's access code. The lobby was empty, and there was no elevator; he passed in front of the drawn curtains of the concierge's loge and climbed the stair to the landing on the third and last floor. Music was playing in the neighboring apartment. Rubén examined the lock on the door, selected one of his lock picks, and manipulated the lock until a click indicated that it was open. Silently, he slipped into María Victoria's loft, making his way by the light coming in from outside, lowered the shades on the street side, and then turned on a lamp. The apartment was spacious, modern, and sober: an American-style kitchen, two long black sofas decorated with multicolored cushions, an architect's table near the tall bay window, and a photography studio set up behind a screen—umbrella lamps, floodlights, a white background for photo shoots. Rubén took a few steps across the brown wooden floor: a dozen photos were hanging from a string stretched across a corner of the room, held in place by clothespins. Her most recent prints, no doubt. He recognized the concerned look of the attractive brunette with curly hair—María Victoria's self-portrait, with a charming little lizard tattooed below her ear. The other photos, stage photos, showed a rock singer; his shaved head, eyes with black makeup, and convoluted poses rang a faint bell. He copied them on his BlackBerry, put on a pair of plastic gloves, and had a look at the office area.

A slogan was attached to the wall above a vintage lamp: "Don't create models of life, create model lives." There were piles of press kits, fanciful postcards thumbtacked to the wall, an enlarged portrait by Helmut Newton in which a tall, nude blonde perched on stiletto heels stared into the lens, an ashtray without butts holding a neighborhood shoemaker's card, a small box in the Peruvian style filled with coffee beans, and, in the middle of the desk, what seemed to be the place usually occupied by a portable computer. Ruben observed the loft, imbuing himself with its atmosphere.

Food in the fridge, recent purchases, clothes in the washing machine, there were multiple reasons for rejecting the hypothesis that Victoria had run away or committed suicide. An open bottle of fruit juice, leftovers, a few eggs and containers of soy yogurt—all perishable foods. Nothing that told him much. An ancient Polaroid was set on the chest of drawers, next to the landline phone. Rubén picked up the receiver: an electronically-generated voice announced a new message, recorded at noon—a certain Miss Bolivia, who was thanking María for her photos. Rubén took down her name and number. No address book or appointment calendar was visible anywhere around the telephone. He briefly flipped through administrative papers that had been put in folders, stuck the latest phone bill in his pocket, and called María's cellphone number, just to see: telephone out of order. Had she cut her line? Rubén went upstairs, doubtfully, and refrained from smoking.

The bed was made, clothes were scattered across the quilt. No sign of a cell phone. María had probably taken it with her. He went into the adjoining bathroom and opened the medicine cabinet: a bottle of sleeping pills, antianxiety medications, the rest beauty products. No prescription. He returned to the bedroom, went through the drawers in the night table—trinkets, condoms, a short, chrome dildo, heat-rub, a few photography magazines, a small bag of marijuana that smelled rather stale, a packet of powder . . . Rubén wet his finger: cocaine. Very poor quality. You could find anything in Buenos Aires, and coke in particular, but the proximity to Colombia did not prevent it from smelling of kerosene. He left the little chest of drawers and opened the closets, counted about twenty pairs of shoes. A careful search of the jackets and pants yielded nothing, as did going through the clothes lying on the bed. He bent down and saw three black hairs intersecting on the pillow: long, curly, similar to the photographer's hair. Rubén put them in a plastic bag before going back down the spiral stairway.

On his way, he picked up the shoemaker's card in the ashtray, went into the vestibule and took out the clothes that had been stuffed into the washing machine. They had not been washed. He inspected the pockets and found a crumpled cigarette paper at the bottom of a jeans pocket, with a few words scribbled on it in pencil: Ituzaingô 69 . . .

He'd already been there for half an hour. Ruben looked around the loft one last time. It was impossible to tell whether someone else had already searched it, whether María had left in a hurry, or why she was no longer giving any sign of life. He had seen no scratches on the lock, and so the front door had not been forced, but something was bothering him; he could not say what it was. He glanced into the toilet room before leaving—the cat litter was dirty—and noticed a strange series of pendants on the door, artistic compositions in plastic hanging on a string. Her specialty, it seemed. A series of humorous ready-mades, some with punning titles, others without. Then Rubén saw the pregnancy test hung on the toilet door: "*Terme au mètre.*"

The pregnancy test was positive.

4

Rubén didn't have a cat. Cats spent their time crawling all over him, curling up in his clothes if he'd been so unfortunate as to leave them lying around, rubbing them with their muzzles as they looked for the armpit, and he much preferred the company of women, even if it was episodic. The fact that he had never lived with anyone did not change his image of women, his desire for new romantic adventures: women just didn't last, that's all. He had spent years reconstructing himself after his detention. The balance was fragile, and certainly unpredictable, so what. Rubén lived in a pit of archives, faces that had disappeared, too much dust, file folders, with corpses between the pages and on the walls, a cage from which he watched women pass by. None of them had stayed long, or he had not held onto any of them, which for him amounted to the same thing: Rubén told himself that at the age of forty-seven it was too late. He was not expecting anything in particular and his solitude didn't need anyone. The time for affairs en passant was over, his father's poetry, which he knew by heart, would be of no use to him, he was reduced to silence, to nothing, words had long since betrayed him, and the stars didn't give a damn.

He was attached to the void. As for seeking a kindred spirit, it was already there, in the closet, near the bed where no woman would ever sleep again.

Rubén put on a Ufomammut CD to drown out the noise of the air lane that passed over the intersection of San Juan and

Peru, aired out the bedroom where he woke up, and had a coffee-croissant-cigarette breakfast that struggled to compensate for too little sleep. The business with the cat continued to bother him: if the building's concierge had found it meowing on the landing, María Victoria must have deliberately put it out so that it would be taken in—in which case she had fled without even taking the time to leave it with the concierge—or else it had escaped. How? The loft's windows were closed, but the animal might have been able to sneak out when the front door was opened. Had it been frightened by someone breaking in?

Sparrows were chirping excitedly outside the window, charming little monsters imported from France that had driven out the native *calandria.* Rubén gave them the remains of his breakfast, took a shower, and mentally drew up a list of his leads.

–A telephone message left the day before from a cell phone ("Miss Bolivia").

–The photos of a singer that were hung on a string.

–A crumpled piece of paper in the bottom of a pocket of a pair of jeans thrown in the dirty laundry, with what looked like an address ("Ituzaingó 69").

–A neighborhood shoemaker's card.

–Three hairs on the pillow.

–A phone bill for the preceding month.

–A small amount of dope in the night table—marijuana, cocaine.

–A pregnancy test, positive.

On his way back from the loft, Rubén dropped the pregnancy test in the mailbox at the Center for Forensic Anthropology, along with the bag containing the hairs and an explanatory message for Raúl Sanz, who led the research team. According to the SMS he received on his BlackBerry, he would have a reply by the end of the day. It was noon. Rubén began by calling the number saved on María Victoria's answering machine, let it ring. "Miss Bolivia" didn't pick up, so he left a message on her cell phone before continuing his research on the internet.

"Ituzaingó 69": dozens of hits came up, ranging from the famous battle between Argentine and Brazilian troops that was to result in Uruguay's gaining independence to a city in Corrientes province, by way of a garage rock group and several addresses in Greater Buenos Aires. Rubén wrote down the names and addresses, and then went to the photographer's site, which she seemed to update regularly. María Victoria Campallo followed artists on tours or films, which explained her frequent travels. He made a list of the musicians with whom she had worked: the most recent was a saccharine pop star who was very popular in South America and had performed in Santa Cruz a month before, but he and his staff had continued the tour in Colombia. Surfing on the site, Rubén came across the face of the man in the photos hung up in María Victoria's studio. The date of the concert indicated that the pictures had been taken toward the end of November, during the rock festival in Rosario. A black leather outfit, boots, pomaded hair like a stallion's mane, black eyeliner emphasizing his tormented eyes, a little too heavy, but an undeniable aura that would elicit the screams of the groupies that he must collect in large numbers: Jo Prat, that was the vampire's name, the former leader of the Desaparecidos, unrecognizable under his makeup and his extra weight. Rubén called Pilar, a friend of his who handled the cultural pages in the celebrity gossip magazine *Clarín*.

Pilar Dalmontes liked to fuck her husband and also other men. She answered on the third ring.

"It's been a long time, you little bastard!" she said, seeing Rubén's number come up on her phone.

"Nice to know you remember me."

"I'd have preferred to forget you," Pilar admitted, clearly in great form at lunchtime. But you know how I am."

"Marvelous."

"Flatterer! Don't tell me you don't have an hour for me?"

"How about a minute?"

"I'm not sure I can do much for you in such a short time."

"I need a contact," Rubén said. "Jo Prat. Can you get it for me?"

"Hmmm. I like it when you put on your velvet voice," Pilar said, ironically. "What do you want with him, with Nosferatu?"

"I want to bring a little sunshine into his life."

"How is yours going?"

"Great."

"I don't see you anywhere, night owl: have you got something against your contemporaries? Married women?"

"On the contrary. So?"

Pilar looked through her address book.

"Gurruchaga 3180," she reported. "Do you want his number, or would mine be enough for you?"

"Guess."

"I have only his landline."

"I'll make do with that. Do you know if Prat is around here just now?"

"I think he's on the program for the Lezama festival next week."

"O.K."

Rubén wrote down the number, thanked the gossip queen, who pretended to simper, and called the singer. Another answering machine. He left his name and number, asking Prat to contact him right away. Outside the windows, the sky was still threatening. He warmed up some leftover paella, and called thc numbers that appeared on María Campallo's telephone bill, all of them administrative or professional contacts that were of no help. Same with the shoemaker's shop, which was closed that day and the following—the shoemaker, whose name was Gonzalez, took Mondays off. All that didn't get him very far. Miss Bolivia finally called him back.

Pleasant, the young woman agreed to meet him in an hour at La Trastienda, a nearby bistro where she was appearing to promote her album. She was also a rock singer: Rubén found her profile on Facebook, and saved the information. Outside, a storm was brewing. The sparrows had left the windowsill, driven away by the wind. Rubén left the agency in a downpour.

The covered market in San Telmo did not attract an upscale crowd, with its dilapidated stores displaying antediluvian underwear, its bric-a-brac and shops with dusty ironwork. On the Plaza Dorrego, a few retirees were playing violins to supplement their pensions, which Menem had trimmed. They played on imperturbably, despite the gusts of wind that were whipping the displays of the itinerant vendors and second-hand sellers. Rubén crossed the square, where tourists who had taken refuge under plastic windbreakers were standing around, and found Miss Bolivia at the bar in La Trastienda.

A representative of an ethnic, explosive variety of rap, less than five feet tall and lost in a pair of shorts and big sneakers, Miss Bolivia was surrounded by her fans, half a dozen little lesbian dolls who followed her everywhere. They immediately hit it off. Rubén paid for a round of Coca-Cola. The rapper confirmed that she had called María the day before regarding the cover of her next album. The little Bolivian had not seen her since the photo shoot ten days earlier, it was the end of vacation, everyone was still a little here and there. In any case, María Victoria wasn't a close friend, they had just met through work: she didn't know if the photographer had a steady boyfriend, what she did with her nights, if she was interested in politics, astrophysics, or dog grooming.

"All I can tell you is that María is hetero," Miss Bolivia said.

The little dolls giggled behind her. He left the bar with the rapper's CD.

On badly photocopied flyers, girls with breasts like artillery shells pretended to be hungry for sex: Rubén brushed off a dozen hawkers soliciting on the Plaza Dorrego and went home. As he came in the door, half-soaked, Jo Prat called back on his cell phone.

*

Jo Prat had created his rock group in the early 1980s, when the junta had had to make concessions to social pressure. *Los Desaparecidos* had saluted the victory of democracy at the Obras Sanitarias stadium, supported by a vengeful crowd:

> *Milicos, hijos de puta! Qué es lo que han hecho con los desaparecidos? La guerra sucia, la corrupción son la peor mierda que ha tenido la nación! Que paso con las Malvinas? Esos chicos ya no estan, no podemos olvidarlos y por eso vamos a luchar!*[10]

The rest had been less glorious: the group had worked the concert halls and festivals for four years without taking time off, endured stress, lack of privacy, and drug addiction, and finally sank into quarrels about matters of ego and alcoholism. Colombian marijuana and the spangles of the Menem years had ended up disgusting him: quarrels, depression, treatment, Jo Prat had crossed several deserts where he'd dried out over and over. The disappointments and the wounds inflicted by people who the day before were rubbing him the right way had made him taciturn, somber, and bitter—"open-pit coal," as he said in his songs. Courageously or rashly, at the age of fifty Jo Prat was resuming a solo career with an album and a tour that had begun in November, before the summer festivals.

[10] "Military men, you sons of bitches! What have you done with the *desaparecidos*? The dirty war, corruption, that's the worst shit the country's been through! What happened in the Falklands? Those children are already gone, we can't forget them, and that's why we're continuing the struggle!"

Gurruchaga 3180, Palermo Hollywood. The paved streets were shaded by sycamores with trunks covered with romantic slogans. Jo lived two blocks from the Plaza Cortázar, famous for its beer taverns, its giant screens, and its high-priced, fashionable stores, in a white three-story building shaded by the foliage of a rubber tree.

An acrobatic painter harnessed to his pulleys was repainting the shutters of the little apartment building next door, accompanied by a mutt's shrill barking: Rubén looked at the worker's overwhelmed face, kicked the dog to make it go away, threw his cigarette in the gutter, and went into the lobby. A polished marble stairway led to the upper floor. Informed of Rubén's visit, the singer immediately opened the door.

The last Grinderman album was playing in the living room of the apartment decorated with a refined taste that clashed with the lugubrious look of its owner: pasty-faced, made-up eyes, dressed in black leather pants despite the humid heat, Jo Prat received him rather coolly.

"You don't look like a private eye," he said when Rubén came into his lair.

"Were you expecting some guy with a fedora and a flask in his pocket?"

"I no longer drink anything but green tea," declared the former rocker. "Do you want some?"

"*Vamos.*"

A Fender guitar hung on the wall, and there were engravings and a finely-worked teapot steaming on the table of the Japanese-style living room. A white angora cat straight out of an old Disney film jumped off the armchair from which he dominated the scene and, intrigued by the stranger's Italian shoes, sniffed them with the assiduity of a professional feline.

"Ledzep," Jo Prat said in lieu of an introduction.

The animal rubbed against the leather as if he wanted to make a genie come out of it, then relaxed a bit. Rubén folded his legs underneath the Japanese bench while the master of the household did the honors. An inhaler lay on the table. Ventolin.

"Well?" inquired the singer.

Rubén explained the situation, María Victoria's phone call to *Página 12*, the silence that had since surrounded her. As Rubén talked, Jo Prat's face contracted, which only made his double chin more noticeable.

The cat was doing his best to settle down on his knees, and Rubén was struggling to stay perched on the bench.

"Have you seen her or talked to her on the phone recently?" he asked, his face full of cat hair.

"No," Jo replied. "Why, do you think something happened to her?"

"That's what I'm trying to find out. Do you mind if I smoke?"

"So long as you don't blow your poison in my face."

Ledzep didn't much like the cigarette, but he remained concentrated on his objective.

"Did María talk to you about herself or about her problems?" Ruben went on.

"Not really. On tour, people say stupid things to each other. It's either that or stress," added the musician, pragmatically.

"I found antianxiety medicine in her apartment. Does María have a tendency to get depressed?"

"Huh?"

"Is she in therapy?"

"Like everyone else here, no?"

Buenos Aires has more psychoanalysts per capita than any other city in the world.

"Hm. What kind of relationship does María have with her parents?"

Jo shrugged. "Normal."

"And that means . . . ?"

"I had the impression she doesn't see them much."

"Do you know why?"

"Goodness no."

"Her father is one of the wealthiest men in the country," Rubén insinuated.

"Right. That's nothing to boast about," the rebel grumbled, pouring another round of green tea.

"Does María have a reason for being angry with him?"

"With her father? I know that María went through her grunge, or gothic, period when she was a teenager, but that's no reason to throw yourself off a bridge. And then that's the time when you resist your parents: hers may be rotten with money, but in photography María found her way and the means to be independent, with regard to her parents and the rest of the world."

"A loner?"

"Rather someone who knows how to compartmentalize her life: private on the one hand, professional on the other. That's what we have in common."

At the cost of a stubborn battle against gravity, Ledzep had found his balance between Rubén's thighs.

"Is María involved in politics?" Rubén asked.

"You mean on the left?"

"Yes."

"Do you know any right-wing artists?" Jo Prat laughed.

"Nobody's perfect," Rubén admitted, pushing aside the angora tail that prevented him from seeing his interlocutor. "And you haven't answered my question."

"No, not especially involved. Just in what she does. That's already enough," Jo remarked, calling upon Rubén to witness what he'd said. "Look, Calderón, why don't you ask her parents directly? If anybody can help you, they can, can't they?"

According to Carlos, who had ended up contacting their servant, María's parents were returning that day from Mar del

Plata. Rubén crushed out his cigarette in the bowl of sashimi without disturbing the cat.

"You live in the same neighborhood as María and you haven't seen each other for weeks," he noted.

"I've been on tour since the beginning of the summer," the singer replied. "I'm at home between two series of shows. In any case, we almost never see each other outside work. Why are you asking me all these questions?"

Ledzep played dead; Rubén had to helicopter him to the floor in order to reach his jacket pocket. He turned on his BlackBerry and showed Jo the pictures he'd found in María's loft.

"These photos were taken in late November," he said, "during your concert in Rosario. What do you think about them?"

"They're pretty flattering, don't you think?"

Annoyed, Ledzep shot the stranger a haughty glance.

"María Victoria hasn't contacted you since she developed the shots?" Ruben asked.

"I'd have told you."

"Unless you've got something to hide."

"My fat belly gives me enough to worry about," Jo replied.

"I found marijuana and cocaine in her night table. Was she taking drugs?"

"If fucking on Ecstasy is a problem for you, you're the problem. María is not a junkie," Jo assured him. "By now I can tell one a thousand miles off."

Sure.

From the other side of the table, Rubén looked at him hard with his coal-black eyes.

"Can you tell me why you're looking at me that way?"

"Because María Victoria is pregnant," the detective told him point blank.

Jo Prat paused. "Pregnant?"

"Three months gone, according to analysis," Rubén confirmed. "I don't know much about kids, but in my opinion María plans on keeping it."

The seducer frowned, covering his forehead with deep wrinkles.

"Do you sleep together often?" Rubén asked, taking for granted that they did.

"Almost every time we meet," Jo Prat replied without blinking.

"The last time in Rosario, at the end of November?"

"Possibly. If you're including me among the potential fathers, keep in mind that in thirty years of touring I must have fathered at least a dozen rug rats."

Rubén lit a cigarette, less courteously.

"Paternity moves you to the point of tears, doesn't it?"

"I've never wanted children I couldn't take care of," Jo explained. "So far as the rest goes, get used to it. Not to mention that María could have slept with other men during the same period."

"She got pregnant at the end of November, according to the analysis. You were together that week, and your portraits are hanging in the middle of her loft. Sorry to have to tell you this, but everything suggests that the baby is yours."

The bags under the singer's eyes got a little heavier under his makeup.

"I imagine she never told you about it to avoid having to get a clandestine abortion in the event that you insisted on it," Rubén added.

Abortion was still not legal in Argentina. Jo Prat emerged from his thoughts.

"Do you think the fact that she's pregnant has something to do with her disappearance?"

"I don't know."

A siren howled in the street. The news left the ex-star in the middle of a minefield. For a moment, he remained perplexed in front of his cold tea. Images were rushing through his head: María's smile when they'd had sex in the hotel room in Rosario, the champagne she'd hardly touched, his not using a condom—as usual with women he already knew—her sweet, peaceful look on the pillow when they fell asleep in each others' arms after making love . . . Did María already know, by some feminine magic, that she was carrying his child? Was she planning to tell him someday?

The silence that followed the revelation brought him back to the voice of Nick Cave coming out of the speakers. Jo ran his hand over his slicked-back hair.

"Do you know anything else, Calderón?"

"That María Campallo's father is financing Torres's campaign, that she left a message with an opposition journalist, and that nothing has been heard from her since. For the moment, that's about it."

The vampire paled in the gloom of the twilight that was filtering through the venetian blinds. Even if María had concealed the existence of this child from him, even if she was only looking for someone to father her child, she'd chosen him. He couldn't leave her like that, lost out there somewhere.

"Who are you working for?" he asked the detective.

"Nobody."

"You think María has disappeared?"

"Yes."

"Why?"

"That's what I'm trying to find out."

Jo Prat hesitated a moment. Then without a word he got up, stepped over the white cat lying on the floor, and went to the desk near the front door. He dug around in a drawer and came back to Rubén, who was still the prisoner of the Japanese bench.

"Here's thirty thousand pesos," he said, his eyes dark. "As an advance." (An envelope dropped on the tea table.) "Find her," the rocker said. "Her and my damned kid."

5

A short note in the day's newspapers referred to an unidentified body found the day before near the old ferry in La Boca: a man about thirty years old. Nothing more. The barbarous mutilation, the possibility of a sex crime, the victim's gender, and all the sordid details of the affair were not mentioned.

Jana had risen early to buy the newspapers and after reading them she called the La Boca police station to obtain explanations: according to the cop she talked to on the phone, the investigation was proceeding. It was impossible to determine the victim's full identity, to find out whether his family had been informed, whether the police had questioned any suspects or found Luz's purse in the area. Jana had persisted, but the cop on the phone got exasperated: if she had revelations to make, she could request an appointment with Sergeant Andretti; if not, there was no point in calling back.

A violent wind was blowing on the metal structures in the shed in Retiro. It was ten in the morning, and Jana was pensively finishing her breakfast when Paula slid open the door to the workshop.

The transvestite was wearing a raw-milk dress over black tights, a necklace of opalescent pearls, and a wall of old makeup after making the rounds of the city's clubs.

"Hi!"

"Hi, Jana! Up already?"

Her heels squeaked on the bits of glass and concrete that were all over the floor, and stopped in front of the monumental sculpture.

"Are you remodeling?" she asked, kidding.

Great Tortoise Island and its autochthonous territories, which she had pulverized—her masterpiece. Jana let it go.

"You want a beer?"

Paula eyed the remains of Jana's breakfast on the bar; the *alfajores*, cheap little cookies that kids loved, tempted her to risk everything.

"You don't have any coffee?"

The rain started pounding on the roof again. Jana went off to the kitchen while her friend collapsed on the seat from an old Peugeot 404 in the "living area." She had listened to the message Luz had left on her cell phone the night of the murder: a few brief words—"I've got to talk to you about something really important," without any clue except vague music in the background.

"Well?" the Mapuche said, screwing the top on an Italian expresso pot.

"I made the rounds of all the bars, clubs, after-hours hangouts, and fuckodromes in the area," Paula sighed. "Nobody had seen Luz, nowhere. Damn, I've had it."

Paula checked her eyeliner in the mirror she took from her bag, it wasn't great, either.

"Here," Jana said, handing her a cup of black coffee.

"Thanks."

Jana sat down with her on the car seat.

"It was past one o'clock when Luz left you the message, and there was music in the background: maybe she hadn't gone to work that night."

"She would have told me."

"Unless she had a reason to keep it from you: a date with a special guy, for example," Jana suggested.

"Who might have had something to do with that 'really important' thing?"

"Maybe, yes."

Paula screwed up her badly-powdered face in disgust.

"If this guy was the murderer, Luz wouldn't have taken the time to call and make a date with me; she would have asked for help, or said what he was up to."

"Hmm."

Jana worked out scenarios but none of them fit. The La Boca cops kept their information to themselves, probably to stay clear of the scandal sheets, which were just as terrible here as elsewhere, to avoid creating a climate of fear, and certainly to conceal their enormous incompetence. According to Paula, for the police to solve the crime, the perpetrators had to be stupid enough to use their victims' cell phones.

"Who are the johns, generally speaking," Jana asked, "people on drugs?"

"Them too, yes. Often people who are alone."

"Was she using drugs?"

Paula shrugged and clasped her knees on the seat.

"Maybe."

"Crack? Coke? Heroin?"

"No. A little line from time to time. But she didn't use drugs."

"Like Chet Baker, for example."

"Not even."

"Was she dealing?"

"No, I would have known that, too." Paula yawned in spite of herself. "Poor Luz," she sighed sadly. "To think that I don't even know his last name. You do know mine, at least?"

"Michellini. Miguel Michellini. Don't worry, you're not cut out for anonymity." Jana crushed out her cigarette in the saucer, where the butts from breakfast were already piled up. "In any case, it's out of the question for you to go back on the street, my love: not so long as there's a sicko out there on the docks."

Paula narrowed her eyes.

"That's lovely, Cinderella, but I don't have more than two hundred pesos left in my pocket. If I don't work a little, my mother's laundry won't make it through the month. Things are going badly, you know," she added, looking contrite. "The bills for Mama's treatment are piling up, we don't have the money to pay them, and her head's getting no better, either. Did I tell you the latest? Last night I found her chewing up receipts and bills! She'll eat anything! Shit, what if she even swallowed money?"

The Mapuche grimaced.

"The Old Witch with Horns."

"You know very well that it's more complicated than that," Paula sighed.

Jana thought it over—she'd seen the old woman once in the laundry, completely bonkers.

"We've already talked about that," she said. "Why don't you go sit down outside? Your room's all ready, all you need to do is put your stuff in there and lay down a mattress."

"That doesn't solve the problem of my mother," Paula retorted. "I can't leave her in that state, especially not just now: with debts, her state of health, and the choreographer who hasn't called me back . . . What will become of us? I have to work on the docks!"

"Not while a psychopath is on the loose around here," the sculptress repeated, categorically. "Do you want to end up like Luz?"

"No, but . . . "

"Promise me! Just until we find a solution."

Looking into Jana's dark eyes, in which a pure friendship glowed, Paula acquiesced.

"O.K. But we'll have to find one, and soon." She looked at her watch and jumped on the car seat. "Oh, shit—it's Sunday,

I'm going to be late! Damn, I have to get my makeup off or she'll swallow her rosary!"

"Good idea," Jana commented.

Paula put on her heels and crossed the workshop on an invisible thread.

"I'll call you soon, O.K.? Bye, angel, bye-bye!"

Jana wanted to tell her to send her mother to graze at the other end of the cosmos, but half of "her" had already gone out into the rain.

Few transvestites were effeminate men: their psychology was feminine, not their shoulders. Miguel Michellini had delicate features, a slender body, and refined manners. Jana never understood why he hadn't changed sexes: Miguel had never been a man.

That was exactly what people had against him.

*

Miguel had dreamed of having a woman friend who would lend him her clothes, or better yet, a women who would give him the illusion that he was being forced to dress as a girl—and that he was merely yielding to her request. As long as he could remember, the feminine universe had always attracted him: women's movements, their clothes, their games. At first, Miguel had repressed this impulse, but the attraction resurfaced depending on the circumstances and the witnesses—always feminine. And then there was that day in his early puberty when a girl cousin who had amused herself by dressing him in women's clothes noticed the growing bulge under the dress he was wearing: the contact, the feeling of being armed with silk as he slipped into the dress, the burning shiver on his skin—all that was simply delicious. His sexual orientation had been set that day, in a summer room where his cousin was laughing.

The desire to do it again had grown with his body. Miguel had always felt alone in the world. It was as if he lacked a part of himself, lacking a father, a brother, and especially a sister: his passion for the opposite universe would make up for his solitude. He had never been at ease in his body. Or if he was, it was in the body of unknown other. As if his place were not his own, as if an intense void filled it, as if he lacked himself, his own identity. Very soon he had to have women's clothes; hiding what he was doing from his mother, Miguel had started going through trash bins, and then roaming through the markets and discount clothes stores. The sight of certain garments or fabrics produced in him a sexual panic that soon led him to masturbate only when he was wearing women's clothes. He still had to go out in public. He understood that sober dress wasn't sufficiently deceptive, while sophistication was too deceptive, and he dressed accordingly. Miguel learned to walk, to show himself to others, to feel with a thrill what a passerby perceived at the moment they met, to sit down keeping his knees together; in time Miguel had learned to become Paula. In front of the mirror, "she" could repeat the same gesture countless times, as if to imbue himself with it—all that autoeroticism that made him so lonely. The transvestite's first audience was himself.

"I made an appointment with the doctor for you," Rosa called from the back room of the laundry. "This time you'd better go!"

Miguel turned to his mother: the old woman was fingering the rosary that hung from the armrest of her wheelchair, looking at him with her seagull eyes. Miguel put the iron back on its base.

"I don't need to go to the doctor, Mama," he repeated. "I'm not ill."

"That's not what the pope says!" Rosa put her sick fingers back under her checkered blanket. "Nor Brother Josef!"

"Aaah . . . He's beginning to get on my nerves, that guy."

"They say it's against nature!" she choked out. "Ah! Ah!" She was getting upset. "They know more about it than you do!"

Miguel went about piling up the shirts and stopped listening to her nonsense. The old woman mixed everything up, the pope, the Virgin, Guadalupe, God and his mother . . . Miguel couldn't bring himself to hold it against her. Rosa had had a hard life, and as she grew older, her misfortunes increased: after thirty years of widowhood and loneliness, the economic crisis and the sharp cuts in retirement expenditures had cut her military pension to almost nothing, her hip had given out, condemning her to spend the rest of her life in a wheelchair. Miguel, who kept the books and helped in the laundry, brought enough money back from the docks to keep their heads above water: half the neighborhood knew that he was working as a prostitute, but his mother? After her hip, her spirit would give out, too: the slightest thing would send the poor thing into mad fits of rage in which the angels and the Church became completely mixed up, and then there was this new mania that was gnawing her.

Rosa had started rolling into balls everything within reach: she tore up pieces of paper, chewed them with her remaining teeth, and then swallowed them. Periodicals—all right, she read nothing but stupid magazines anyway, but bills, receipts, the account books? The situation was becoming impossible: Pascual, the only cousin with whom Miguel was still in contact and who had just gotten married, had been clear about this ("one hysteric in the house is enough"), they hadn't enough money to hire home help, a retirement home, or a nursing home. An insane asylum, that was the fate reserved for his mother: the laundry in Peru Street wasn't worth anything, the few customers who brought their clothes there did it out of charity, and Rosa had no savings, nothing she could sell, and her only monument was a hero who had died in battle and this accursed son.

Rosa hadn't understood that, either. Or refused to. Or it was too much for her brain. She thought that the good Lord was ruining her life, that he was putting her to the test: she had wanted a child, preferably a son, not . . . *this*, a kid with pale skin who shut himself up in his room instead of playing soccer with the other boys in the neighborhood, an effeminate weakling mocked on the schoolyard by decent idiots dying of laughter as they swung their hips along an imaginary line, Miguel the laughingstock, the sickly kid incapable of running ten yards without getting out of breath, an out-and-out sissy, Miguel the girl sniffing hawthorn blossoms and grotesquely sensitive, his unbearable, disgusting inclinations, Rosa was outraged with shame. No, she refused to understand why her husband had gone away leaving her with this package of dirty laundry, why she found herself alone with this useless quarter of a man, his mind twisted by this damned sex: it obsessed him, the filthy thing! They'd really been duped when they bought that! Not at all what they'd ordered! The good Lord had allowed it to happen, that was her penitence, her intimate Calvary, a secret between her and God, who'd pulled all kinds of tricks to teach her. Things got mixed up in her head, memories and the present, Rosa no longer knew if it was the economic crisis or divine punishment that was driving customers away from the laundry—as if people no longer ironed their shirts!—if she had to pay for her sin, this child possessed, and then she suffered like a martyr, always that damned hip, these mysterious headaches, these children's cries in the streets that she could no longer bear, these nightmares that made her head feel like a pressure cooker. Yes, Miguel had caught the girl-sickness: that was one more dirty trick played by the Lord, something she'd have to discuss in the confessional, like the day when she'd caught him in his room, dressed as a woman from head to foot, in the company of another boy! Enough to make you throw up, for God's sake!

"Do you hear what I'm telling you?" she wheezed, brandishing her cane.

Miguel was breathing in the lavender fragrance of the shirts piled up on the ironing table: he yelped with pain.

"Ouch!"

Surprised by the prick, he spun around and grimaced: the old woman was holding a cane fitted with a spike, like the ones trash collectors use to pick up papers in the gutters, and she was shaking it before his frightened eyes—where did she get such a thing?

"You hurt me!" he complained, rubbing his buttock.

Rosa didn't listen to him, she was too proud of her anger, with her bits of chewed-up paper on her shining lips.

"What are you eating now? Mama!"

"You've always been sick!" she screamed. "Always!"

A lightning bolt of hatred trembled in her eyes. Her thin, withered arm waved the point of her cane in his face. Miguel met her demoniacal eyes and drew back against the ironing table.

"Put that down, Mama."

"Don't touch me!" She was stabbing the air. "You hear me?"

"Put down the cane, please."

"Never!" Rosa cried. "Never!"

"Mama!"

But she was already lurching out of her wheelchair. Miguel dodged the spike that was aimed at his chest and grabbed the cane as she fell back on the chair, but Rosa clung to it stubbornly: she was drooling her balls of paper all over her flowered blouse.

"Give me that damned cane!"

"Help!" She braced herself against the chair. "Help me!"

The fury refused to yield: her face crimson, curls of hair escaping from her bun, she screamed, her faded eyes popping out of their sockets.

"Brother Josef!" she howled. "He's going to come, you'll see!" she declared. "You'll see that he's going to fix your brain!"

Miguel let the harpy have the cane and retreated into the back room, frightened. This time it was clear: his mother was going insane. Completely insane.

*

Jana had put on the faded shorts hanging on the antique screen that marked off her bedroom before going to work on her sculpture, the plastic cartography of an organized ethnocide. The "Conquest of the Wilderness," according to the official expression, as if the Mapuches didn't exist.

Crushed militarily during the Great Roundup on the pampas, shot like rabbits with Remington rifles, sent to religious schools or handed over as slaves to the *estancieros* who had divided up their territories among themselves, acculturated, impoverished, reduced to silence, lying about their origins during the infrequent censuses, forgetting their culture out of shame or inertia, the Mapuches had gone through the century like shades. Ghosts. By abrogating twenty-five years of treaties signed with Spain, the Constitution of 1810 had simply denied the Mapuches' existence, the existence of the "people of the land" who had lived there as nomads for two thousand years.

The land was everything for them; the sanctuary of the ancestors, the dwelling place of the gods, the myth and point of departure for any symbolic representation, the ritual foundation and constitutive element of their identity. Without the land, the Mapuches were nothing. Some communities had clung to their farms and flocks, but many of them had had to sell their land under threat, at the risk of disappearing all the more easily because they did not appear on any civil register. Today, the Mapuches represent only three percent of the Argentine population, concentrated in poor regions in the South or scattered in the slums of distant suburban areas.

Jana worked furiously all afternoon: she cut the iron, accentuated the concrete craters, added collages of fabric and glass in the colors of the native peoples, but in spite of her efforts to concentrate, Luz's death and its consequences continued to pollute her mind.

Paula was a brainless hothead when she was acting in her own interest, but she was right about one thing: if she didn't work the La Boca docks, who would pay the bills and take care of her mother? The situation seemed impossible. A killer had attacked Luz and the barbarity of the murder suggested that he would kill again. For reasons that escaped her, the cops weren't doing anything, and the fate of an anonymous tranny was of no interest to anyone. Unless she talked to someone: who? A private detective? Jana stopped working and opened the phone book. She went down the list of names in alphabetical order. She noticed that a "Calderón" had his agency in Peru Street, a few blocks from the laundry. Was that a sign?

The sun was going down over the old Retiro rail station when Paula came rushing into the workshop, frantic: the choreographer had just called, and he wanted to see her again at 10 P.M., before the Niceto opened, about the revue she'd auditioned for, that very evening! The transvestite was in a tizzy; he'd just left his mother's, dressed as a man, obviously; a good makeup job took two hours, and, flopping about like a moth around a lamp, he didn't know what to do.

"Ten o'clock! I'll never be ready!"

"Calm down, sweetie," his friend said. "The sun has just begun to set."

"Crash, you mean!"

Jana smiled. It was odd to see Miguel with his slick short hair, his natural eyes, and the shapeless pants that concealed his figure.

"Oh, Jana!" the tranny said passionately, gripping his friend's hands. "Just imagine—Gelman is taking me for the revue! With everything that's happening right now, it's . . . so crazy!"

Confusion reigned: the docks, Luz, the Niceto, the good all mixed up with the bad. Should they laugh or weep?

"By the way," Jana asked, "do you know the detective in Peru Street?"

Paula stopped short a moment amid the sculptures and searched the tumultuous river in which her memories swam.

"Calderón? Yeah, we meet from time to time in the market. Why?" she went on, "Are you thinking about him for Luz's case?"

"Him or somebody else."

"He's better."

"Why?"

"When he walks he looks like a puma rolling his shoulders!" Paula said with enthusiasm.

Jana shook her mop of hair, which was full of dust—whatever.

"Who is he," she asked, "a former cop?"

"I don't know, I think he looks for *desaparecidos.* I've never dared to talk to him, but I've been told that he was connected with the Grandmothers."

"Aha."

"He might be the solution," Paula said. "You'll see his eyes!"

"The relationship escapes me."

"That's because you haven't seen them! I don't know how old he is," she went on, "but he doesn't look it!" She saw the time on her plastic watch. "O.K., I've got to hurry or I'm going to miss everything! But the detective is a good idea!"

The transvestite swayed toward the sliding door, then suddenly drew back.

"There's a problem, Jana," she said, turning around.

"O.K., what?"

"How are we going to pay him? We don't have any money."

Jana shrugged. "I'll figure it out. Go make yourself beautiful."

"I'm on my way!"

Paula took off toward the yard without seeing the Mapuche's somber look.

*

Vega 5510, Palermo Hollywood. The Niceto Club's sign flashed on and off behind the Ford's greasy windshield. Paula adjusted her brown wig, checked her face powder for the fifth time in her mirror with a picture of Marilyn Monroe, finally put her makeup kit back in her striped sheepskin bag and turned toward her friend at the wheel.

"Apart from the broken tooth, how do I look?" she asked with a smile.

Jana pulled an appropriate face.

"It looks a little too perfect, otherwise it's okay."

It was 10 P.M., Paula's face scintillated under the streetlights, the night owls were laughing on the rain-washed sidewalks of Palermo, cruising the neighborhood's bars and restaurants before the nightclubs opened.

"Go on, get in there or you're going to melt on the seat," Jana said.

"You're right. Full steam ahead!"

Paula got out of the car carefully, holding her knees together, gave Jana a last friendly wave through the broken window, and slalomed around the puddles, using her plush bag as an umbrella. The sculptress waited until she had disappeared into the artists' entrance before heading back to San Telmo.

1030 Peru Street. The rain was beating on the sidewalk when she pushed the intercom button.

6

The obelisk, immaculately white, rose proudly over the Avenida 9 de Julio. For a few centavos, barefoot boys were juggling in front of the cars stopped at the red light: one of them, who was not even four years old, dropped one of the two circus balls in front of the hood. His big brother, six years old, had practiced longer: three balls flew through air loaded with exhaust gas. Rubén gave the two scruffy kids a couple of coins before the light turned green and made them shoot off like sparrows.

Two million poor families, one child out of five suffering from malnutrition. Rubén saluted the statue of Don Quixote around which traffic turned at the intersection with the major artery, and headed back toward downtown and its apartment buildings with fenced terraces—looting, burglary, the memories of the economic crisis had left their mark. A shower was whipping the storefronts, driving guys in suits toward the commercial banks that were springing up again like mushrooms. Rubén opened the window to smoke, casting a venomous eye on the jerks in white collars who had bankrupted the country. Not far away, a handful of protesters carrying flags and signs with left-wing slogans were blocking Sarmiento Avenue, which was covered with flyers. They were surrounded by helmeted policemen: anti-riot water cannons, armored vehicles, Torres's elite cops were not shy about intimidation. The approach of the elections, probably. Rubén drove around the parade and continued as far as Malba, the contemporary art center.

La Recoleta was the quarter of foreign embassies, private properties, old money not subject to the hazards of the virtual, republican gilding. The avenues were broad, clean, and gave off a perfume of private homes in a very European style, with cracked Milanese facades and age-old architecture. Rubén parked the car in a side street and walked under the big mangrove trees whose roots cracked the asphalt: the Campallo family lived a little farther on, in a building barely visible behind tall foliage. It had been constructed in the early nineteenth century and was partly covered with ivy.

A peaceful place after the turbulence of the city center, in any case for people who were not much inclined to mix with others. Access to the property was controlled by a black grill with sharp points and a state-of-the-art surveillance camera. Rubén rang on the intercom, the panoptic eye targeting him.

Finally someone answered. A woman.

"Yes?"

"Hello," he said, moving closer to the intercom. "Are you Mrs. Campallo?"

"Yes," the metallic voice replied. "What do you want?"

"To talk to you about your daughter María Victoria. I'm a friend."

"She's not here. What's it about?"

"Well, that's just it," he said in an affable voice. "No one has heard from her for days, and I'm looking for her."

A brief silence.

"What do you mean, no one's heard from her?"

"Have you?"

"Well, no. Who are you?"

"Rubén, a friend."

"I don't know you."

He crushed out his cigarette on the sidewalk.

"Mrs. Campallo, if I were you I'd open the gate . . . "

The intercom went quiet for a moment, the distant echo of

a doubt that seemed to last two or three eternities, and then the click of the gate opening.

A white gravel walkway wound among the giant plants in the garden. The businessman's main residence was a large, beautiful white house, a veritable little manor in the middle of a shady park. Rubén breathed in the aroma of the flowers and followed the spiral of insects that were coming out as the weather cleared. María Victoria's mother was waiting on the front porch, her arms crossed under a deep red cashmere shawl, dark glasses with a garish frame covering half her face.

A very attractive woman, Isabel De Angelis could have had a career as a beauty queen had her aristocratic name not prevented her from working. Eduardo Campallo had plucked her to decorate his buttonhole at the age of twenty, when she had just begun to bloom, and he kept her as a talisman of a perfect success story. Isabel Campallo had dyed hair put up in a bun, a designer dress over prominent kneecaps, and a severe look for someone who had just returned from a vacation. From afar, the businessman's wife could pass for one of those old tanned beauties on tranquilizers fighting anorexia one sees at the American Express, but close up you saw two pinched lips covered with too much orange lipstick and a vertical posture intended to keep the world at a distance.

A chubby man in his thirties wearing a suit waddled alongside her.

"Who are you?" he asked the visitor.

"I imagine you're María Victoria's brother?" Ruben replied.

His belly bulging under a white shirt without a tie, Ray-Ban glasses perched on a bald head, a Porsche watch and gleaming loafers, Rodolfo Campallo flaunted the plump figure of a complacent success.

"Rubén Calderón," he said, showing his detective's badge.

"I thought you were a friend of María Victoria," his mother said, astonished.

Rodolfo sized up the private eye: brown hair that was too long, falsely calm elegance under a black suede jacket, athletic and arrogant despite the veneer of class, his provocative air, his grayish-blue dark eyes, everything about him was annoying.

"What are you doing here?"

"It's about your sister," Rubén replied from the foot of the stairs. "She isn't at home and hasn't answered her cell phone in three days. I thought that might interest you."

The younger brother, put in his place, frowned. There was a teak table in the shade of a great willow trembling in the wind, the echo of a gardener trimming the roses at the back of the garden; Rubén turned toward Isabel Campallo, bundled up in her shawl.

"Do you prefer to remain standing?" he asked thoughtfully.

"No."

Walking mechanically, the woman moved toward the nearby patio furniture and, ignoring the look her son gave her, sat herself down on a chair as carefully as if she were a faded bouquet.

"What do you know about my daughter?" she asked, peering through her tinted glasses.

"Not much," the detective replied, reassuringly. "Have you seen María Victoria recently?"

"Well, no, not very recently. My husband and I were on vacation at Mar del Plata," the ex-star of high-society balls said: "I was there all month, my husband for two weeks, and María Victoria isn't a great fan of the telephone. You say that she hasn't been in contact with anyone?" she said, sounding worried.

A gold crucifix hung in the cleavage between her old breasts.

"Let's say that she can't be reached. When did you talk to her for the last time?"

"Let's see . . . I left her a message about ten days ago, but you know how kids are, they call back when they have time. All I know is that she was hoping to use the vacation to work on her photography. That was what she usually does at this time of year."

A sigh half emptied her. Rodolfo had joined them under the willow.

"Who are you working for?" he asked.

"That doesn't matter," Rubén answered, concentrating on the mother of the family. "Do you have any explanation for your daughter's silence?"

Isabel shook her lacquered hair and drew her shawl around her against the gusts that were singing in the trees.

"No," she said, disconcerted. "No . . . "

"No trip, rendezvous, or particular event?"

"No." Her memory was skating on a river with horses caught in the ice. "Why? What's going on?"

"María Victoria is expecting a child," Rubén announced.

For the first time, the mother and her son wore the same expression on their faces.

"She's in her third month," he went on. "Obviously you didn't know."

Isabel pulled herself together on the garden chair.

"No."

"Where did you get this information?" Rodolfo interjected.

"Why do you think your daughter didn't say anything to you about it?" Rubén continued.

"I don't know," Isabel stammered. She was shaken. "We're a very Catholic family, María Victoria knows that having a child outside the bonds of marriage would make us terribly sad, but . . . I just don't understand."

"Any idea who the father might be?"

"Heavens no!"

"María Victoria hadn't introduced you to anyone? Never?"

"No . . . Unfortunately, getting married isn't one of her priorities."

"The prospect of having a baby could have turned her life

upside down," Rubén suggested. "It might explain her silence or her flight."

Rodolfo was pacing up and down underneath the willow, exasperated.

"You don't answer the questions you're asked," he said, changing the subject. "Who are you working for?"

Rubén ignored him. "It appears that María Victoria went through some difficult times during her adolescence and afterward," he said. "Did she rebel against her social milieu?"

"What are you implying, Mr. Calderón?" Isabel replied coldly.

He lit a cigarette—something about these people annoyed him, something that didn't have to do with the money, luxury, or the ostentation.

"Did María Victoria ever take a political position?" he asked.

"What do you mean?"

"Against your husband and his powerful friends, for instance."

"That's outrageous!" Roldolfo said angrily. "My sister's not a communist!"

Rubén smiled wryly—funny how some people can go to extremes to justify their point of view. Porky was beginning to irritate him.

"Your husband amassed his fortune during the National Reorganization Process, and then profited from the economic crisis," he said, looking at Isabel. "María Victoria might have wondered about how that wealth was acquired."

"Why are you here, Mr. Calderón," Rodolfo burst out. "To dig up filth?"

"Is that how you see your sister's life?"

"No," Rodolfo replied furiously. "Your trade."

"I get the impression that yours isn't too bad either, fatso," he said to bug him. "Radio host, right? Stupidities and laughs galore. I hope you thanked your papa."

Rodolfo grew pink, cramped in his white shirt. He was the comedian on the morning show of a radio station that in fact belonged to his father, and his job consisted of pissing people off on the telephone by pretending to be someone else, making "trick" calls that were usually rigged; it would have been hard to say who, if anyone, they amused.

All that could be heard was the sound of the pruning shears among the rosebushes and the rustling of the wind in the willow over their heads.

"I won't spend another second in the presence of this individual," Rodolfo hissed to his mother.

"Good idea," Rubén said.

"Throw him out, Mama, or I'm calling the security men."

"Yes."

Petrified behind the screen of her dark glasses, Isabel Campallo did not move. Rodolfo hesitated a second: his mother was upset, this troublemaker provoked them, but a vague fear kept him from making the call himself, and anyway he'd left his cell phone at home.

"I'll call Papa," he said curtly, turning on his heel.

Isabel drew the shawl around her skinny shoulders, pale in spite of the carotene and the vacation at the beach.

"You know something, don't you . . . " Rubén said.

"No. But my son's right," Isabel resumed. "I don't know where you're getting your information, but I beg you to leave my home. Now, immediately," she ordered, recovering her dominant status.

Rubén crushed out his cigarette.

"I'm trying to find out if your daughter is still alive. Is that a problem for you?"

"You're making me crazy with worry, if you want to know the truth."

"You know something, something I don't know."

The blue arrows of his irises pierced her.

"No," she said, feeling threatened. "I don't know anything and you are not welcome in our home. Leave," she panted. "Right now!"

Isabel turned toward the porch and started to get up, but he grabbed her wrist.

"You're lying," Rubén insisted. "Why?"

"Stop bothering me. I have nothing to say to you. Let me go."

The air in the garden was charged with electricity. Rubén tightened his grip on her wrist, almost without noticing.

"You're hurting me!"

"You're lying."

"No!"

"Then tell me what you're scared of."

Isabel Campallo trembled when she met the eyes of the detective, who was staring at her maliciously. He'd have liked to break her wrist. To grind her bones.

"You," she replied in a tremulous voice. "You . . . "

*

A truck slit the twilight, howling. Rubén crushed out his cigarette against the railing of the balcony, deaf to the clatter of the wheels on the metal plates. His bedroom looked out on the bridge leading to the airport, part of the superhighway that cut a deep scar through the neighborhood, at the corner of Peru and San Juan. Trucks hurtled past day and night, spewing diesel fumes, but Rubén heard nothing but the wailing of the baby under the concrete pillars, which had been going on for two weeks.

A family lived under the bridge, a couple of *cartoneros* and two scruffy children who had never slept in a bed or gone to school. Only this bridge. They'd made it their shelter for two years now, with kitchen utensils, bottles of water, canned goods, the wretched mess that constituted their possessions. A baby had recently been born, a catastrophe, their third, clothed with what was at hand. Where had the mother given birth? In the street? Those people not only picked up cardboard boxes, they lived among them. A whole family, anonymous and recycled as well. They had constructed a barricade, an empty shell that they closed behind them when night fell to protect themselves from the cold, stray dogs, down-and-outs; they came out in the morning, stiff after a sleep without memory, all rags and dirt, incapable of saying thank you to the rare passersby who gave them a coin.

They had become cardboard themselves.

Rubén rocked in the humid breeze, the baby's tears like obsessive reminiscences. Time went on, its back to the future. All these sobs, these cries of the children who ran over his ceiling, the little footsteps of careless orphans above his cell . . . A silent hatred gripped his heart. The first stars appeared in the mauve sky. Rubén swallowed hard, his knuckles white. Soon there was only a ghost hung on the balcony, and this baby wailing in the night . . .

Will Papa come back?

Of course, why do you say that?

Foreign countries are far away. And then he always tells stories . . .

Oh, yes. That's even his specialty.

Holding his little sister's hand, Rubén smiled—he found her amusing. And a smart cookie: when she was only two, Elsa already spoke almost fluently, without adopting the intonation of a soppy princess that some people found charming. His little sister had a ready tongue, like Lucky, the big black dog that escorted them on their way to school.

Foreign countries are someplace you come back from, Ruben decreed to reassure her. Otherwise they become home.

Elsa had lifted her face toward the long-haired teenager hold-

ing her hand—how old he looked for someone not even fifteen!—without really understanding what he had just said, but she pretended she did, anyway.

Do you think we'll have to leave, she asked. Leave the house? Would that bother you?

Elsa had shaken her little brown curls.

No. Maybe a little.

Rubén smiled on seeing the freckles around her nose, the marks of her feline mustache. She was starting middle school, and didn't yet know many people.

Leaden silence in the streets of Buenos Aires, a diffuse threat, teachers stuffed into blouses that looked like they belonged to someone else, as if the chalk on the blackboard might betray them: except for the dog Lucky (but they could take him), Elsa wouldn't be sad if they had to leave Argentina. Go into exile. Many people had done that.

What is France like? she asked.

Rubén had shrugged.

Full of cheeses, it seems.

She laughed. That was his goal.

The Argentine World Cup victory was still a few months off, but the junta would take advantage of the event to strengthen the feeling of national identity, to con the foreign media by mobilizing a whole people behind its soccer team: on the pretext of giving lectures, Daniel had left for France to organize the resistance, to denounce the trick of the World Cup unofficially before journalists that he would have an opportunity to rub shoulders with or media figures who had committed themselves to their democratic aspirations. They had to rain on the parade, turn the situation to their advantage. Rubén knew nothing about all that. His parents hadn't told him anything, but Daniel had asked him to take care of his sister while he was away; he would be the man of the household.

It was late summer, the sun ran over the puddles left behind by the thunderstorm that brought them home from school. Elsa and Rubén were walking hand in hand, Lucky was sniffing his way down the sidewalk as if an army of bones were running away under his snout, they arrived in front of the florist's shop at the corner of Peru and San Juan: the dog had stopped dead and then lowered his ears. A car suddenly came out of nowhere, almost hit the bouquets that had been set out on the sidewalk, a Ford Falcon without plates that blocked the street. Three men in civilian clothes immediately jumped out of the doors, guns in their hands. Rubén pulled his sister back but a hand grabbed her by the nape of the neck. Rubén protected himself without letting go of Elsa, whom he heard screaming next to him.

Rubén!

The men tried to separate them. Lucky bit one of their assailants, who swore until a man unholstered the gun he was wearing under his leather jacket and emptied his magazine, shooting first into the belly of the good old dog, and then finishing him off by putting a bullet in his eye. Clinging to her brother, Elsa was shrieking with terror. Rubén tried to pull away, hitting out haphazardly, and his sister was also kicking desperately, but in vain; the men flung them to the ground, calling them names, grabbed them and put a gun to their temples, roughly hustled them off to the Ford and flung them into the backseat. Rubén was no longer resisting. He couldn't see clearly. Everything had happened in a few seconds and blood was running over his eyelids.

The florist's frightened look, Lucky's body on the sidewalk, the passersby turned into stone statues, the back of the Ford Falcon, the burlap sacks put over their heads, the oppressive dark, the muffled sobs of his sister at his side, her trembling body pressed up against his on the seat, more insults, threats, the ride in the car: time had contracted.

Rubén . . .

Shut up, you stupid kid!

Miles of fear and anxiety. Finally the vehicle stopped. They were taken out of the backseat. The dark under the hood grew even more opaque when they were pushed with rifle butts toward a cooler place. Forbidden to speak or move. They were not alone, Rubén felt it in the air: other people were being held prisoner there, and they were scared too. An odor of tires and grease. Not until the hoods were removed did Rubén regain his footing in the real world. A lightbulb that dazzled them for a moment hung in the basement of a garage: there were a dozen of them under the harsh light, men and women alike, trembling like sheep before the bitter laughs of the wolves that surrounded them. Young men full of haughtiness and military certainties, others with unbuttoned shirts and holsters under their armpits, masticating their chewing gum with their mouths open.

Take your clothes off! the man who seemed to be the leader ordered.

Any hesitation was corrected with the blow of a truncheon. They obeyed, cold fear in their bellies. Their naked bodies were soon shivering on the frigid concrete of the Orletti garage. Elsa was crying silently, her bare feet curled up: anyone who opened his mouth would be beaten within an inch of his life, they had been told, and so she pressed her pink lips together, emitting little squeaks like a mouse. The men laughed to see them naked—it was funny. Rubén hardly dared raise his eyes. His sister was the youngest, and also the most terrified: he sensed her silhouette alongside him, terribly embarrassed to be naked in front of all these people, with her little pointy breasts and her young adolescent's public hair, which led to indecent remarks. But they didn't laugh long: the officer with a mustache barked insults, "red dogs," "hippies," "communists." Rubén didn't know what they were going to do to them, even if one evening he had caught his parents talking in the kitchen about kidnappings. He didn't lose heart. Not yet. They were separated, the men on one side, the women on the other, in the greatest tumult: blows rained down under the garage's obscene lightbulb.

Rubén! Rubén!!!

That was the last image he had of his sister; a little woman writhing in tears who implored him with her big green eyes, trying desperately to cross her thighs over her pubescent vagina. She was calling to him for help as they suddenly dragged her back to take her away, amid cries of fear:

RUBÉN!!!

The rumbling of the trucks penetrated from the balcony of the bedroom. Rubén sniffed the dress that he was holding in his hands, his favorite, the orangey-red one with the little black collar, deeply. The fragrance had evaporated long ago, but he smelled it whenever he wanted.

"A *desaparecido* is someone who is not there, and to whom you speak."

Returning from his exile in the countryside, Rubén had found Elsa's clothes in their place, carefully folded in the closet in her room. Their mother wasn't going to touch anything, not even a pen or a pair of shoes, until her husband and her daughter "reappeared alive," the slogan of the Mothers of the Plaza del Mayo. But neither Daniel nor Elsa had come back. They would never come back. Like thousands of others, they would remain phantoms forever. Finally, years having gone by, Rubén had urged his mother to give the clothes to the needy—there were plenty of those in the city, and even if by some miracle Elsa were to come back someday, her clothes would no longer fit her, would they? Elena had accepted, weary of waiting. Maybe it was better that way . . . But Rubén had lied to his mother. He hadn't given his sister's clothes to the poor: he had taken them to the apartment in Peru Street that he had just bought, across from the accursed intersection with San Juan where they had been abducted one summer day in 1978. He had put Elsa's things in his bedroom closet, the forbidden closet, which he still watched over.

All her dresses were there, folded on the top shelf, the orangey-red one that reminded him of her freckles, and the others, her T-shirts, her shorts. Rubén slept with the remains of his sister, her sad little bones and the school notebook in which he had closed up their nightmare.

Prey.

Or carrion.

Rubén put down the dress and closed his eyes, wishing he'd never have to open them again.

"My little poppy . . . "

Rain was falling when she rang on the intercom.

7

Jana was tall for an Indian, a svelte woman with medium-length hair as black as her eyes, whose ancestral sorrow seemed to drip with the raindrops on the doormat.

"Are you Rubén Calderón?" she asked in a hoarse voice.

"Yes . . . "

A Mapuche, to judge by her almond-shaped eyes. She was holding a half-soaked cloth jacket in her hand and wearing a dark, close-fitting jumpsuit, an old pair of Doc Martens with worn toes, and a tank top that emphasized her round shoulders. No bra—no need.

"I've been told that you're looking for *desaparecidos*," she said. "The daughter of the laundress downstairs . . . "

"Yes, yes, come in . . . " Rubén emerged from his fog, and gestured toward the club chair that his visitors usually sat in. "Sit down."

"My name is Jana," she said. "I prefer to stand."

The sculptress briefly surveyed the agency—American-style kitchen, bookcase, a messy desk with a turn-of-the-century lamp and missing person posters tacked to the wall, witnesses in trials who had been kidnapped, dozens of faces that seemed to be looking at her from their tombs without burial. She turned back to the detective, who had just closed the reinforced door, and recognized the painting over the 1960s sofa: Velásquez's *Las Meninas*.

"Is that an original?" she asked playfully.

He smiled.

"Coffee?"

"No."

"Something else?"

"No, nothing, thanks."

Paula had been right about Calderón—pure elegance compared to her scruffy clothes, and two coal-black eyes speckled with little blue forget-me-nots whose translucent, brilliant blue left her speechless. You'd think he'd just been crying.

"Am I disturbing you?"

"No," he lied. "I wouldn't have invited you to come up."

Jana relaxed a little.

"Calderón—is that your real name, like the poet?"

The detective raised his eyebrows.

"You know him?"

Jana shrugged. Daniel Calderón's dark poetry had rocked her in the shadows—and vanquished them. The writer had disappeared during the Process, like Haroldo Conti, Rodolfo Walsh . . . Tortured, beaten, liquidated.

Rubén didn't want to talk about his father.

"May I ask what brings you here?"

Jana forgot the dead people's faces on the wall and the little blue flowers that were sending distress signals.

"A crime was committed the other night at the port in La Boca," she replied. "The body of a man was found near the old ferry. Have you heard about it?"

"Yes, I saw it in the newspaper."

"You've got sharp eyes, it went almost unnoticed."

Rubén lit a cigarette he took from the package that was lying on the coffee table, and let Jana continue.

"The victim is a friend of ours, Luz, a transvestite who turns tricks on the docks. The police haven't revealed the info, but Luz was tortured before he was thrown into the harbor. He was emasculated," she added, her voice more serious. "I think he'd also been raped."

"How do you know that?"

"We were looking for Luz when we ran into the La Boca cops, who were fishing his body out of the water down at the docks. They took us to the station to interrogate us, but they refused to take our deposition and threw us out. I called them this morning to find out how the investigation was going, but they blew me off. Somebody has to look into this. The guy who massacred Luz won't stop there. No one could possibly have anything against him, I mean personally. The killer's a sicko, a pervert of the worst kind."

Rubén looked at her, her and her dark eyes washed with rainwater.

"My work consists in tracking down *desaparecidos* and their torturers," he sighed. "I'm sorry, miss, but private matters are not my line."

"The laundress's son is a transvestite too: he's my only friend and I care about him. A killer attacks the trannies of La Boca, the cops don't give a damn, and I don't want Paula to be the next one on the list."

"Is your friend also a prostitute?"

"Not everyone is lucky enough to be a variety show performer."

"Or to grow old."

"That's why I've come to see you. No one saw Luz before the murder, neither on the docks nor elsewhere. We don't know what happened, whether the killer was a customer or a sadist: all we know is that Luz left a message on Paula's cell phone during the night to tell her she wanted to talk to her about something important, and then she was found in the harbor the next morning. Paula had taken her under her wing," Jana added as an explanation. She drew a sheet of paper out of her jumpsuit, a page torn out of a notebook. "I don't have any photos of Luz to give you, but I drew her. From memory," she added, handing him the piece of paper. "Maybe this will help you."

A bus thundered past, making the agency's windows vibrate. Rubén unfolded the paper she gave him and saw the face of a young man with melancholy eyes. A charcoal drawing.

"You're an artist?" he asked, looking up.

"Sculptress. On the back I wrote a list of the places that Luz and Paula usually work at night. My friend looked around there yesterday. She didn't find anything, but you might be luckier. There was music in the background of Luz's message. Obviously a public place."

Jana held her drenched jacket in her hands, trying to decipher the thoughts of the man behind his veil of smoke. He was standing in front of the coffee table in the living area, a little taller than she was.

"So, is it a deal?"

Rubén handed the drawing back to her.

"Sorry, I don't know anything about the transvestite scene. And above all I don't have time."

"But you're going to accept the job," Jana retorted.

"I am? What makes you think that?"

"It's the only way to find out what happened."

She was speaking in syllogisms. She refused to take the drawing back, and Rubén put it down on the table.

"You're wrong about me," he said. "I'm not the man you need, not for this kind of investigation."

"You don't know that before you've tried," Jana insisted. "Help me stop this bastard before he attacks someone else. Before he attacks my friend."

Rubén took another puff. He should never have let her come up.

"I am concerned with the people who disappeared under the dictatorship," he repeated. "Only *desaparecidos*."

"Paula has to turn tricks to earn a living. I'm scared for her, scared of what might be done to her. Do you understand, or are you made of stone, too?"

Tears had dried in the depths of her dark eyes, a long time ago. Rubén was contemplating the disaster when Jana took a step toward him.

"I don't have any money, but I can pay you in a different way," she said boldly.

Rubén froze when she put her jacket on the back of the armchair.

"I don't need money," he said.

"But you must want to fuck me."

He sized her up briefly.

"No."

Her pupils shone. He was lying.

"Don't play thc classy gentleman," Jana taunted him. "Everyone wants to fuck. And I don't give a damn."

Rubén stubbed out the butt that was burning his hands.

"I'm sorry for you."

"You're the only one."

Her Indian eyes were fixed on him like a wolf in the line of sight.

"You've knocked on the wrong door, miss. I can't help you. And still less in that way. I don't take advantage of war, or of despair, call it what you will."

Jana's throat was dry. She drew herself up to her full height and looked at him.

"You don't like me?"

"Go home," Rubén said, suddenly tired.

Jana didn't open her mouth. That would teach her to ask for help from a *winka*. She blushed when she thought about her ratty chest underneath her T-shirt. Sure that he must be disgusted, the Porteño with fine, delicate hands, sure that he must be used to another kind of merchandise. She would petrify with shame, right there in the middle of the agency.

"I'm sorry," Rubén repeated, seeing tears welling up in her eyes. "I don't have time right now, but I have a woman cop friend who knows what she's doing: I can speak to her about it . . ."

"Forget it," she interrupted.

Jana grabbed her jacket and left the room without looking at the detective. A draft helped her slam the reinforced door, animating for a moment the faces of the dead on the wall.

The thunderstorm was raging outside the open window. Rubén remained motionless, sifting through his contradictory feelings. A mantle of depression fell on his shoulders, inexorable. He saw the notepaper left on the table, the face in charcoal that the Indian had made for him, no doubt convinced that he would accept her proposal. His throat tightened with pity—the drawing was magnificent.

*

On her deathbed, Jana's great-grandmother had given her a knife. Angela was the last woman of the Selk'nam, a people related to the Mapuches that had lived for centuries in Tierra del Fuego. One day fishing boats had come to their cold and icy islands, bringing diseases and weapons, and the Selk'nam all died. Angela was the only one left, and she was so old that her hands were all wrinkles. Jana was seven years old but she was the eldest daughter, and a little Selk'nam blood flowed in her veins. Angela had given the little girl her old knife with the whalebone handle so that at least her memory would be preserved. And especially, she had told her the secret of the Hain, that fantastic drama. Jana had kept both of them warm in her memory full of stories that the old woman had been telling her since she was an infant: Shoort, Xalpen, Shénu, and Kulan, who came down from the sky to torment humans, fabulous stories.

Jana had grown up on the pampas of Chubut province, in the middle of the world's most fertile plains. At that time, there were two cows, a heifer so timid that they'd had to pull her out of her mother's body, Eyew ("down there," in Mapudungun), and her sister Ti kude ("the old one"; it wasn't clear why she was given this name). An affectionate, lively, and curious child, Jana knew the sound of tall grass and the wind that blew over it, deciphered its many voices, the strings with gloomy sounds and the brief whistles in stems as rigid as wires, the moaning of the wind that grew and died away among the smooth reeds of the marshes, bearing light rain or a thunderstorm. The flatness of the place made her see what we can only guess, and guess what we do not see. She was eleven years old and, like all little Mapuche girls in the countryside, knew little about the world around her. She knew her father's resolute voice, her mother's strong hands and rare smile, races and fights with her brothers, but she did not yet know the *winka*—the outsiders. Traditionally, the Mapuches saw the state and Western society as at best a foreign body, at worst an implacable enemy. For her, they were still only abstract silhouettes, names.

Some of them occasionally came along with their big cars, their skimpy clothes, and their neckties. They discussed matters with her father, who was the community's envoy, its *werken*. His name was Cacho, and his eloquence authorized him to speak in the name of the others. The fate of all of them depended on his know-how. They counted on him, because problems were multiplying. Cacho became gloomier day by day. He had not told his children about the expulsions to which the community was being subjected, about their claims to retain their ancestral lands—and let them continue to go to school, study, and become lawyers in order to defend the rights of their people.

No one suspected what was about to happen. Jana was asleep in bed with her sister when the *carabineros* broke down the door of their house. Giants with steel heads stormed into their home, howling like devils, guns in their hands. The girls woke up, terrified. The men pulled them out of bed and then threw them into the arms of their mother, who was trembling with fear in the kitchen with the rest of the family. They insulted them in Castilian Spanish, breaking everything of the little they had with a ferocious frenzy. Their spiked boots slammed the furniture into the wall, their soldier's physiques, their voices like roof beams falling on you, the military insignias on their uniforms, their caps: Jana was petrified, hypnotized by the fury of their violence.

When there was nothing still standing, when everything had been reduced to ruins, they started beating her father, the messenger, kicking him with their boots and hitting him on the head and spine with their truncheons: the *carabineros* went at it full tilt, several of them at once, shouting to egg each other on, while the *werken* writhed on the floor. His wife was moaning the way pumas do when facing the hunter's rifle, crushed by fear, pressing her daughters to her nightshirt. Jana couldn't see anything but them: the *winka* were ugly, frightening, as tall as cranes, destroying everything in their way, bellowing insults that she could not understand at the age of eleven. Beaten, lying amid the debris of the devastated kitchen, he father no longer protested. A thread of bloody saliva was flowing over his split lips. His eyes closed, Cacho did not see the men in helmets push the children away to seize his wife. Jana did see it.

She had looked Evil in the eye. She had seen its pale, grimacing face, pupil to pupil, and her mother groaning with terror when, laughing, they tore off her nightshirt to humiliate her.

Jana was then eleven years old, and her breasts had not grown since. Not the slightest stirring. Days, months, years had passed, but her chest had remained hopelessly dry, an arid land, without life, like her ancestors who had been driven off their lands. Her chest had become her taboo, her pain and her shame. A supreme and cruel insult to femininity that all men would mock, breasts of bone, scorched earth, two dead fish floating on the surface, butterflies on pins, breasts that had nothing to give, or milk of curdled blood, breasts that would never nurse children: at the age of eleven, Jana had amputated herself.

She had never talked about them, never showed them to anyone, not even Paula. The first boy with whom she had made love had not asked any questions, and the later ones thought only about sex, Furlan about his sculptures, no other man had counted for more than the time necessary to satisfy her needs. Jana banged her jaw on the steering wheel of the Ford—what was she thinking, that she was going to seduce Calderón with her dirty little monsters?

The windshield wipers struggled against the storm. Vega 5510, Palermo Hollywood. Paula was waiting in front of the Niceto, sheltered from the rain, when she saw the old jalopy's headlights: her heels clattering on the sidewalk, her striped purse held over her head to protect herself from the rain, she ran over the paving stones without falling, opened the door, and broke into tears in Jana's arms.

"What's wrong? Did it go badly?"

She tried to calm Paula down, but her frail shoulders were heaving under her coat glistening with raindrops. Impossible to stop her. Jana gently pushed back her friend, whose mascara was running down her cheeks that were burning after the interview she'd just had.

"Well?"

"I . . . I got the job in the revue," the transvestite stammered. "Someone backed out . . . I saw the choreographer, Gelman. He's hiring me for the three dates in Buenos Aires . . . It's . . . more than I hoped for, Jana, so much more!"

The Mapuche grinned with pugnacious joy at the transvestite's tears: three shows in a fashionable club weren't going to get Paula out of her rut, away from blowjobs in cars and teeth knocked out when she met the wrong person, but the first steps are always the hardest, aren't they?

"That's great, old girl, I'm sure you're going to make a great hit! Come on, stop crying, you're getting mascara all over!"

Rain was still falling on the Ford's cracked windshield. Paula was gripped by a vague happiness so intense that it took her a good two minutes to pull herself together. Jana handed her the packet of Kleenex that was gathering dust in the glove compartment and helped her dry her tears.

"Thanks," Paula sniffed. "Thanks . . . and how about you?" she asked, hardly over her emotions. "What happened with the detective?"

"He sent me packing," the sculptress replied, growing somber.

"Ooh . . . "

"Yeah."

"I'm disappointed," Paula said sadly. "He looked like such a nice guy."

"You see, that's not enough."

Before getting back in the car, Jana had walked a quarter of an hour in the storm to calm herself down—yes, she had really acted like the stupidest of idiots.

"But that's all right," she declared. "We'll manage without him."

"Ah?"

"Next week the troupe will have left the Niceto and you'll be on the street. You definitely can't be out there when there's a killer on the loose. Luz might have left papers in his squat that would allow us to identify him; then the cops will be forced to notify his family and undertake an investigation worthy of the name. You know where Luz lives, right? Let's go to her place and see if we can find anything."

There was a cosmic silence in the car.

"In the *barrio*?" Paula gulped. "In the middle of the night?"

"Don't worry. No one's around at this hour."

"Precisely. What if we're attacked?"

Her grimace circled her mouth three times. Jana chortled and that did them a world of good—she too was near the breaking point.

*

Poverty had been spread out over the Buenos Aires checkerboard. Unlike the shantytowns of Greater Buenos Aires built on public dumps or flood zones, the *barrios* formed pockets of poverty in the heart of the city. The people crammed into them experienced unbearable living conditions unimaginable for the middle classes and without equivalent on the South American continent. Driven out of the center of the city during the dictatorship, there were now a hundred and fifty thousand of them living scattered in the *barrios*, lacking everything—potable water, education, medicine. Illiteracy and delinquency completed the picture of the impoverished group that was here, as elsewhere, in a very bad situation.

Squeezed between the Retiro bus station, through which employees came in from the suburbs and tourists left for Iguazú Falls, Villa 31 was the gaudiest shantytown in Buenos Aires. Luz lived in the nearby wasteland, a dozen acres left vacant alongside the San Martin rail station that hundreds of families, many of them foreigners, had taken over a few months earlier during the excitement—and with a few gunshots to settle disputes. Francisco Torres, the mayor of Buenos Aires, had sent in the police, but the squatters had driven them back, laying claim to the land and access to water and electricity.

With the expanding holes in the floorboards and the bath towel stuffed in the door to protect against the rain, Jana's Ford was not much out of place in Villa 31: they were coming into a disaster area, a succession of hovels made of bits and pieces of junk that were hard to identify in the dark. According to Paula, who had helped her protégée move in, Luz lived in a shack next to a stable.

The dirt path that crossed the *barrio* was strewn with rubbish; the Ford dodged potholes and sleeping dogs, braving the shadows that danced just beyond the headlights' range. They passed several unlighted shacks with crisscrossing illegal electrical hookups before finding the stable in question. Luz was squatting in the structure next door, a pile of red bricks and concrete blocks roofed with corrugated iron.

Jana turned off her headlights, immediately plunging them into darkness. The place was sinister, deserted.

"Let's go," she said, grabbing the flashlight in the glove compartment.

They shut the car doors carefully, as if the shadows might betray them. Paula walked with great caution, but her heels still slipped in the mud.

"You O.K., Lady Di?" Jana whispered.

"Fuck," she grumbled, catching herself by gripping Jana's arm.

Two luminous points appeared in the flashlight's beam: the eyes of a scruffy dog that was lurking behind the shack. A padlock lay on the ground. The chain was gone. Jana pushed open the rickety door and, guided by the flashlight, swept the interior of the squat with her eyes. Kitchen utensils, cobbled-together furniture, a wardrobe, a screen of fabric with an oriental design, hangings on the brick walls: everything had disappeared. All that was left was the windows covered with plastic bags that flapped in the night wind. The neighbors had probably taken what they could. Jana looked at the floor, found food packaging, bits of plastic, clothespins, photos from magazines that had been trampled.

"If Luz had any papers, they must have disappeared along with the stuff they stole," she said.

"Hm."

Paula thought about the wigs. Luz had begun with cheap ones, the hair as long as possible that accentuated the masculinity of her features as much as possible, but Paula had chosen a shorter wig for her that had transformed her face.

"The wigs," she whispered in the darkness.

"What about the wigs?"

"Luz had a hatbox that I gave her when she came here. She must have hidden it somewhere. Those beautiful wigs cost an arm and a leg: Luz would never have left them lying around where they could be seen. Without a wig, you're nothing," the transvestite added. "If she had to put valuable or important things somewhere, that's where she'd put them."

The wind was rushing in through the shredded plastic. Jana ran the flashlight over the floor of the squat.

"In any case, I'd be surprised to find a hidden trapdoor under this pile of shit."

Paula pulled her cream-colored coat more tightly over her breast while the Mapuche tapped on the brick walls. The thickness was the same everywhere, except between the kitchen area and the bedroom, where the wall was thicker. Jana bent down and noticed a dozen bricks that were not mortared to the others. She handed the flashlight to her friend, who was shivering behind her.

"Take this, hold the light for me instead of jerking off."

"Hey!" Paula cried, taking offense for the sake of appearances.

Jana stuck the blade of her knife into the crack and quickly pulled out a first brick. The others came out more easily. Finally, she extracted a round object from the wall.

"That's it," Paula said over her shoulder.

The hatbox she'd given Luz. Jana dusted it off before opening it. There was in fact a wig inside it, a short square-cut blond Venetian one that Luz often wore, a boa, a pair of black velvet gloves, a pink fountain pen, and envelopes. Dozens of sealed letters without stamps, all bearing the same address: Mr. and Mrs. Lavalle, Junin. Her parents? The Mapuche dug around in the bottom of the box and found two aspirin bottles whose contents she emptied into the palm of her hand: little bags holding crystals appeared under the flashlight. She put a little on the tip of her tongue and grimaced: clearly it was *paco*, chemical residues that demolished even the hardest users. Paula was coming apart underneath her makeup.

"Didn't take drugs, huh?" Jana grumbled.

*

They returned to Jana's place before reading the contents of the envelopes, with a glass of iced vodka to restore their strength.

There were about thirty letters written in the form of a diary, strange to say the least. Orlando "Luz" Lavalle seemed to maintain a correspondence with his parents in the purest South American style. The first missives dated from his arrival in the federal capital. In them, Orlando wrote about the beauty of Buenos Aires, the abundance of its museums, its enchanting parks where cats slept between neo-Romantic sculptures, the architecture of public buildings, the opera, so Parisian. An aesthete's soul animated the feverish lines composed by the young man, the archetype of the provincial coming to the metropolis. In the following letters, Orlando told how he had found a first job as a dishwasher, then as a waiter in a cafe, and finally got a position as a server in a restaurant on Florida, the downtown artery. According to what he told them, the pay was good, and he hoped to be able to leave the attic room he was renting for a fortune from a cantankerous old rascal who answered to the name of Angelo Barbastro. The subsequent letters talked about his meetings with Alicia, a young woman he often met at the restaurant. One evening, Alicia had asked him when he got off work so that he might join her in a fashionable cafe in Palermo, where the bohemian youth hung out. Alicia was a painter and very beautiful. She had noticed the portraits of customers that Orlando amused himself by sketching during his breaks. Alicia thought the one he'd drawn of her was particularly successful; she had many artist friends, people who were a lot of fun and would help him if he wished. Someone who worked hard could hope for anything: the price of passion, the galleys—Orlando was prepared for anything. And then one night Alicia walked back to his attic room with him, they had kissed at the doorstep to the building, and since then they had been inseparable, her artist friends ended up adopting him, his marvelous drawings, blah, blah, blah. Orlando was fantasizing from start to finish.

The reality was dirt, hunger, fear, getting up in the cold or the suffocating heat of a squat without water or electricity, going to shit in a field full of garbage, rinsing yourself in the basin, helping the flour collector make bread, feeding kids whose eyes were covered with flies, finally getting ready to go out, dreaming for a moment in front of the mirror before going back to the blows, the threats, the cops, the violent, homophobic fans who had to be avoided on pain of ending up without all your teeth like Paula, Jil the lesbian with fists of iron at the entrance to the Transformer, Jorge the cocaine addict and all the others, the reality was Luz, the little tranny who worked the end of the docks, who'd do you for a few pesos, unless instead you gave him a good beating to teach him to be a homo, the *paco* that he unloaded on other losers, all the pathetic lies that Luz/Orlando invented to hold up without upsetting his parents, who knew nothing about what was going on.

Paula felt deceived, betrayed. Not only had her protégé failed to tell her everything, but he had lied to everyone. Jana, sitting on the car seat in the workshop, also looked downhearted. The young transvestite had not been the victim of a barbarous random crime on the docks: he had been killed for a precise reason that escaped them.

8

A smell of incense floated up from the marble walkways. Rosa Michellini drew the curtain in the confessional a little further, as if someone might see her there. However, the church was empty at this hour.

"Have you spoken to your son?" Brother Josef asked.

"Oh, no! Good Lord, no!"

"But the matter you told me about the other day," the priest insinuated.

Rosa looked out of the corner of her eye at the man in a chasuble she could make out behind the grille: what was he talking about?

"Your son, Miguel," he went on in a soft voice. "Do you remember?"

"Oh, yes!" Miguel's mother burst out, as if saved by the bell. "Yes, I told him to get treatment! That he had women's disease! Yes, that's it," she recalled, "I told him to go to the doctor!"

She fingered her rosary the way she thought the Chinese counted.

"Is that all?"

"Isn't that enough, Father?" the old woman replied boldly. "After all I've had to put up with for him! Last night again he didn't come home until almost dawn!"

Rosa didn't remember any more. Too many frogs croaking in her pond.

"You didn't say anything else to him?" the priest asked again. "You don't remember everything, you know. The ways of the Lord are mysterious, but the repose of your soul comes through confession. Speak, and God will help you."

"Yes."

But Rosa Michellini once again seemed to be absent: she tore the program of the mass on her knees into little bits that she rolled into balls with maniacal intensity. A sign of great nervousness, thought the priest, who had already see her do the same with her hair—a rather frightening sight, moreover.

"Rosa," he said in a soothing tone, "Rosa, I can help you."

The laundress smiled like a baby, sensitive to the caress of his voice. A brief moment of calm in a head where a storm was raging: she was praying, praying especially for Miguel, however, she prayed night and day for the salvation of his unnatural body and soul, Rosa was tired of praying for nothing, as if her joined hands were not the right ones, as if they too were paying for sins they hadn't committed—not all alone. It was true after all, she thought, that her husband was also involved, even if she was the one who had insisted on having a child, you could certainly say that the unfortunate man did a damn poor job of it!

She nervously rolled her balls of paper, her mind elsewhere.

"You haven't said anything to your son about the visit you received last week?" Brother Josef persisted, all velvety.

"I never receive any visits!" Rosa certified, bouncing on her handicapped person's wheelchair. "Miguel even less: I wouldn't allow him to!"

She swallowed a ball of paper without even noticing.

"Rosa, I'm talking about the visit you mentioned the day you came with the paper. Do you remember? Do you still have it? Did you show it to your son?"

"Nothing at all!"

"What do you mean?"

"Did you know he takes pills? I saw him do it in the backroom the other day: they're hormones, I'm sure of it! To make him grow breasts!" the unhappy woman cried, enraged. "You'll see, someday he'll have his member reduced! Aah! My God!" she moaned in the confessional box. "My God, what have I done to deserve all that? Life is such a burden! I beg you, Brother Josef, save me, save me from Evil!"

The young priest cleared his throat and persisted.

"The document you showed me, Rosa, do you still have it?"

"It's a secret!"

"Yes, yes," he reassured her. "Did you tell anyone else?"

"What?"

"Miguel, your son, perhaps?"

"You have to come talk to him! Right away! You have to come before it's too late!"

"What . . . what are you talking about, Rosa?"

"About his member!" she said, swallowing a ball of paper. The demon is capable of anything! Even having it cut off! It's awful. You have to . . . you have to help me!" she said, barely able to get the words out.

The laundress was seized by a fit of coughing so violent that it brought her to tears. In the darkness on the other side of the grille, Brother Josef sighed, perplexed: this old woman was becoming demented.

"All right," he finally said. "I'll come speak with your son."

Bits of chewed-up paper adhered to Rosa's lips.

"Ah! Ah!" she choked. "Watch out for him! This time, watch out for him! Oh, sparks are going to fly!"

Yes, thought the priest, more and more demented.

9

Rubén and Anita Barragan had grown up in the same neighborhood, San Telmo. At first, they were not close—the little girl was really too blonde to interest him—but then Anita grew six inches the year she turned twelve.

The metamorphosis did not go unnoticed in the neighborhood, but Anita's problem remained the same: her ugly face, which she hid behind her light colored hair, her locks like a curtain drawn over her unfortunate stage. Her measurements didn't matter, this brand new big body which begged to be put to use, Anita still woke up every morning with the same homely mug. "Rendezvous at the OK Corral," as she used to say. The aquiline nose that she saw as crooked, too-small eyes, too-white skin, lips that looked like cigarette papers—Anita found it hard to endure this neutral, static, even dissymmetrical face that refused to conform to the canons of any period. Hiding behind a smiling mask, she avoided mirrors and reflections in shop windows as if her "ugly mug" was all that could be seen. In any case, boys were not taken in: although they followed her in the streets and sometimes whistled at her, none of them turned around when she passed.

Anita lived backwards.

Flipside.

She'd lost face.

Anita was delirious.

She had been in love ever since her early puberty: thinking herself ugly, she had chosen the handsomest, most impressive, most inaccessible of the neighborhood boys, Rubén Calderón of course, a big brown-haired boy with an incredibly sexy walk who had lost his father and his sister during the Process: in short, a hero, with eyes that would break your heart, an imperial bearing, and a small nose the exact opposite of her own. Anita had first confronted him in the street, while he was talking to a pretty brunette in a miniskirt; she had planted herself in front of him, holding out a carefully wrapped package that the young man had ended up opening with amused curiosity. Inside was a falsely naive drawing, a ship sailing over a sea of tears, with Anita as the captain waving from the bridge. "To accompany you in the life that we will never live together," read the legend that she had added in her best handwriting. Rubén had left the pretty brunette standing there and bought Anita a strawberry gelato, the best she'd ever had.

Years later, they'd seen each other again in front of the residence of Juan Martin Yedro, an amnestied policeman. Anita and her student friends, intoxicated by the songs of vengeance sung by young people hopped-up on the illusion that followed the fall of the dictatorship, were throwing red paint bombs at the torturer's walls, locking arms and jumping up and down, shouting slogans denouncing the federal police. Rubén, who was at that time a journalist, had remained alone on the sidelines, as if scouting out his future hunting grounds, and then asked her to have lunch with him. The beginning of their adult friendship. The fact that seven years later Anita Barragan joined the federal police was not the least of her paradoxes. With her law degree in her pocket, she'd passed the examination to become a police inspector and was then transferred from one position to another by a macho administration. Finally, she had ended up in the police station in the neighborhood where she'd grown up, San Telmo, in the "911" brigade that patrolled downtown Buenos Aires. The police chief, Ledesma, an old, paternalistic cop relatively immune to corruption, led the team of about forty officers, which had ended up seeming old-fashioned after the mayor set up a new elite police unit.

An attorney, businessman, and former president of the Boca Juniors soccer team, Torres was aiming for the top, the Casa Rosada, the presidential palace. His father, Ignacio, had made his fortune in the wine trade during the boom in the 1990s and had financed his son's first campaign: Francisco Torres openly supported the Peronist right wing that constituted the main opposition coalition, and it was well known that the mayor would become its head. Equipment, weapons, techniques of investigation, scientific policing, training—the mayor had modernized Buenos Aires's system of repression by greatly increasing communication. Torres had assigned Fernando Luque to manage this elite unit that was supposed to become the "Argentine police of tomorrow." There was no skimping on resources or methods: the preceding year, Luque had been indicted in an case involving illegal wiretaps before being cleared—by a judge close to Torres.

In the meantime, the 911 brigade's two-tone patrol cars picked up drunks, wifebeaters, troublemakers, and a few thieves and pickpockets. An inspector not assigned to any investigation, Anita found herself training pimply interns who spent more time ogling her breasts than keeping an eye on the streets, a kind of work she found not very motivating and far from her initial areas of competence. About to turn forty, Anita, who had aspired to radiant passions, was living alone in a studio apartment in Parque Patricios with Mist, the gray cat that had taken up residence on one corner of her bed and vegetated there like a police officer on patrol.

Anita and Rubén met at El Cuartito, an ancient pizzeria in the city center that was jammed at lunchtime. Enormous numbers of yellowing posters covered the walls, showing Maradona and other soccer players in the tight shorts of the 1970s and

1980s that made people forget the smell of melted cheese constantly emerging from the kitchen. Amid office employees, Anita and Rubén ate an extra-large pizza, incognito in the racket of commentaries on the next match. He was wearing a shirt and a suede jacket that absorbed the greasy smell of the chair; she wore her navy blue uniform with three buttons open to allow her prodigious lungs to breathe. The detective told her about María Campallo's phone call to the newspaper, his visit to her parents, her mother's reaction on hearing about the baby, and the singer father who had hired him to find the photographer.

The waiters were weaving among the chairs in the cantina, their hands loaded with steaming platters. Anita leaned toward her childhood love so she wouldn't have to shout.

"What do you want me to do? Send out a missing person bulletin concerning the daughter of one of the most powerful men in the country, just like that?" she said, cracking her knuckles.

"Nobody has reported her disappearance," Rubén replied.

"Have you thought about suicide?"

"Have you ever seen a pregnant woman commit suicide?"

"That depends on what she has in her belly," the old maid added. "Suppose the child isn't Jo Prat's, that she's carrying a monster, the result of a rape or God knows what else?"

"You read too many women's magazines, *querida*."

"Darling," the nickname he called her to help her like herself. Rubén wiped his lips with a paper napkin, crumpled it up and tossed it on his plate, which he had hardly started on.

"O.K.," Anita continued. "Let's assume that María Victoria has vanished, that she found out something about her father's activities, or about one of his friends connected with the Torres campaign, and let's suppose that she's in hiding or scared. Have you seen many children reproach their parents for lining their pockets?"

"María didn't call Carlos at the newspaper to talk about baby clothes," Rubén objected.

"Was she politically engaged? I mean against her father?"

"Not to my knowledge."

"That's not much of a basis for putting out a missing person bulletin, you have to admit."

"Her computer has also disappeared, either that or María took it with her when she fled. It might provide the key to the problem. Carlos is working on that, but it's going to take time. I need you to find her, Anita. If Campallo's daughter felt threatened, she might have left the country. Ask Immigration if they have any trace of her somewhere. I also need detailed bills for her cell phone," Rubén added, writing numbers on a corner of the paper tablecloth. "I've been able to get my hands on only last month's bill." He tore off the paper and slipped it under her glass. "Here's her number."

Anita blew away her blonde hair—she was sweating under her shirt, among all these males braying as the pizzas came spilling out of the ovens, and Rubén was giving her one of his disarming smiles the secret of which the divine SOB knew only too well.

"You don't have to worry about losing your job with the cops," she reminded him. "If I tell them that the information comes from you, I'm going to get my knuckles rapped."

"You're too smart for that."

"You're not the one who's under the hammer."

"Nor holding the handle. You have a friend in Immigration, don't you?"

"We haven't slept together for a long time."

"I'm sure that it hasn't caused him to lose the faculty of speech."

Anita didn't answer. She was ruminating over the pizza crusts. Her years as a cop had dulled her complexion, her uniform had destroyed her sex appeal, but Rubén saw her again as a girl, with her strawberry ice cream in front of the stand and her teenager's eyes that were eating him up.

"O.K.," she sighed, putting the number in her pocket. "I'll see what I can do."

"Thanks, *querida*."

"That's it, right."

Anita got up amid the brouhaha, threw her napkin in Rubén's face, and with a century-old wink disappeared toward the restroom, swinging her hips. He ordered two coffees and took advantage of her absence to pay the bill.

The blonde soon returned, re-powdered, almost spruce despite her outfit.

"Thanks," she said, seeing the money on the table.

"It was disgusting," he said, to reassure her.

Anita's soft smile reminded him of the pizzas. They slugged down the coffee.

Dark clouds were sliding through the sky as they left the cantina. Rubén lit a cigarette and felt better in the open air. He was thinking about the sculptress from yesterday, about her request regarding the murder in La Boca. A little earlier, he had shown Anita the charcoal portrait of the transvestite; she'd heard about the body found near the ferry, but not about what had been done to it.

"Shit!" she exclaimed when she saw the time. "I'm late!"

She embraced him—she smelled like vanilla, the world's most popular flavor.

"By the way," Rubén said before letting her go. "Does *Ituzaingó 69* mean anything to you?"

Anita frowned.

"No," she said. "What is it, a swingers' club?"

*

Ituzaingó 69, a few scribbled words found in the pocket of María Campallo's jeans. Rubén had visited an apartment building on San Martin and questioned a couple of unionized workers who had lost everything, their jobs and their dignity, during the wave of privatizations, surviving one way or another by participating in trading clubs, people who had never heard of María Victoria Campallo or her father. The preceding night, the detective had followed another lead, a rock group, Ituzaingó, from the neighborhood of the same name in the Castelar Norte area: the musicians had played two weeks earlier at the Teatro de la Piedad, on the corner of Bartolome, a rather homey co-op bar where the group's bass player was performing solo that evening. A simple voice, sounds produced by a computer, a CocoRosie-on-the-moon atmosphere: asked after the set, the young brunette had stated that she had never met the photographer—they were only a self-produced group from the northern suburbs.

The trail was cold. Rubén gave up and drove to Palermo, where María Victoria's shoemaker had reopened his shop after his weekly two days off. Rubén showed him the card he'd found in the ashtray in the loft, trying not to dwell on the odor of leather and feet that permeated the shop. The shoemaker, who was very affable, confirmed that Miss Campallo had in fact left a pair of shoes with him the preceding week, to be resoled.

"María didn't come pick them up?"

"No," the gray-haired man replied. "It was urgent, it seems, but I'm still waiting . . . These young people!" he sighed with empathy.

"Do you know why it was urgent?"

"To go dancing!"

"Dancing?"

"The tango, obviously."

Obviously.

"Can you show them to me?"

The man soon put a pair of heels on the counter, tango shoes that must have polished many a floor.

"If you're planning to take up the tango, I would advise you to choose another model," the shop owner joked.

"It looks like María dances often. Do you know where?"

"I know that she takes lessons at La Catedral," he answered. "She's been taking them for some time now."

A tango club not far from downtown. Rubén tried to pay for the repairs, for the trouble, but the shoemaker refused.

"She'll come pick them up herself!"

Maybe not.

Rubén went home, his heart a little heavier. He was still thinking about the Indian woman who had rung the bell at his office the preceding evening, her black eyes awash with rain, about her proposal. The poor girl, was she really so desperate? Night was falling on the facades of Peru Street when Anita called him back on her cell. According to Immigration, María Victoria Campallo had not left the country the preceding weekend, but she had gone to Uruguay, round trip to Colonia and back, on Wednesday—that is, two days before she disappeared.

"Colonia?"

"Yes, by boat."

Rubén searched the name on the internet. Bingo. "Ituzaingó 69": it wasn't an address in Argentina, but rather in Colonia del Sacramento, Uruguay.

*

Scrap metal sculptures were piling up along the disused warehouses—bits of iron, motors, bicycle frames, tricycle wheels, pipes, rusty plates, bolts off locomotives, crankshafts attacked by brambles. Paula's "dressing room" was at the back of the yard, beyond the ridiculous bent sheet metal giant representing the Federal Police. It was a moss-covered trailer sitting on concrete blocks, where the transvestite had collected her feminine treasures, far from her mother's sight.

Paula needed spangles, perfumes, people like her, with echoes of loneliness in their wild laughter: Miguel needed men who would see him as a woman. His mother had never understood or accepted him as he was. Would things have been different had there been a male presence in the house? Miguel remembered little about his childhood, and almost nothing about his father, Marcelo, who had died during the Falkland War, when the flagship of the Argentine fleet sank with its three hundred sailors. A black page in history: their history ended there. Miguel was five years old, and his mother Rosa was his only guardian, a pious woman attached to cleanliness and order who very quickly revealed her manic-depressive tendencies. When he was still very little, she tucked him in so tightly that the bed looked like a sarcophagus: his chest restricted by the covers, Miguel slept feeling that he was suffocating—a psychosomatic explanation for his heart problems? Objects and furniture were arranged with a positively military rigor, his toys limited to a set of little cars or soldiers in which the boy took no interest. Life had come to a stop after the death of his father, the hero whose cult Rosa maintained. In the household, laughter was considered an affront to the deceased, who, by his absence, occupied all the space.

Miguel hardly went out, except to go to school or to accompany his mother to church, where the atmosphere was not very different from that at home. Conversely, he told himself that the arrival of his cousins was just a matter of acting out his feelings. Miguel had to fill the void in his heart, a terrible void he couldn't explain. Without a diploma, forced to help Rosa in the laundry, the transvestite had never had or seized the means to become independent. A shared love would no doubt have helped him leave his mother, but his need to transform himself intervened between desire and *the other*: at twenty, Miguel understood that he could never love anyone. Never really—never the way one imagines. And that he would die of it. He was himself *the other*.

Narcissus. A matter of reflection, of a cruel lack of self he tried in vain to fill by cross-dressing. Miguel was not the only one who was "sick": alerted by the sudden aggravation of her case, he had informed himself about his mother's maniacal lunacy.

People afflicted by geophagy ate earth, coprophagics ate excrement; people suffering from the Rapunzel syndrome ate their hair, chewed-up paper, or various kinds of food wastes. Rosa was risking intestinal occlusion and other serious complications connected with what medical science considered bulimic behaviors: in any case, psychiatric treatment was indispensable. One more worry for Miguel. How long had his mother been suffering from this syndrome? Was she swallowing all sorts of stuff when his back was turned? How much? Should he have her hospitalized, as soon as possible? And the choreographer, the revue at the Niceto: what would happen if he was given an opportunity to go on tour with the troupe, as Gelman had just suggested? Should he once again give up any idea of having a happy life to take care of his crazy mother?

It was the evening of the premiere: Paula had hardly had time to rehearse her choreography, and the telescoping of reality put her in a state of confused excitement—would she be up to her dreams? A blond Venetian wig, her favorite, was on the dressing table stand; she was putting on the last of her makeup when Jana found her in front of the mirror, a headband over her pulled back, pinned up hair, amid ribbons and bows and cotton balls.

"Are you ready?" she asked on coming into the transvestite's "dressing room."

Her long eyelashes fluttered briefly.

"Almost!"

There was a smell of spangled powder and patchouli in the trailer: Paula put down her beauty tools and examined her face.

"What time does your revue begin?"

"I go on stage at 2 A.M.," Paula replied. "But I have to be there at eleven for makeup and costumes. Oh, Jana! I'm scared to death but it's great!" she cried impatiently, her eyes popping in front of the mirror. "A tour, just imagine! I could get my tooth fixed, and maybe even buy myself, buy myself . . . "

"Some chewing gum," her friend suggested.

"I got through the audition, but I've never done a show like this!" Paula continued, in her made-up bubble. "If that happens, I'll be completely petrified! You know what they say about stage fright? You can shit your pants!"

"Your show is going to be great," Jana said.

"You're coming, right?"

"Of course."

Paula had gotten an invitation for her friend, who hardly ever left her metal sculptures. It would do her good, too.

"Paula?"

"Yes, my love?"

"Why don't you come live here permanently? Don't wait for your mother to be institutionalized. That's unavoidable anyway, and this tour may be the chance of a lifetime: don't spoil it."

In her mind's eye, Jana saw the madwoman, her stringy old dirty graying red hair and her malicious face, incapable of loving: let her die and go to Hell.

"What do you say?" she persisted.

"I don't know, I don't know anymore . . . "

"This kind of opportunity doesn't come along every day, Paula. It's a sign you've been given. Life is full of them. Follow it."

"Maybe you're right. Maybe it's Luz sending me a sign from wherever he is . . . poor dear."

"Well?"

Her wig adjusted, the transvestite turned around on her seat of pink plush.

"I'm ready!"

Paula smiled, made-up as if for a wedding to be held on Venus. Jana sighed—Paula was so pigheaded . . .

*

Sarmiento 4006, at the corner of Medrano: far from the clubs in San Telmo, where the city's great singers performed for a select audience, La Catedral didn't look like much, with its old-fashioned lobby lit by neon lights, its stairway in 1950s tiles, and its ten-peso entrance fee.

But on the second floor everything changed.

Testosterone, toxins, dance steps, and pheromones collided like blind passions in the half-light. Rubén made his way into the cavern of the tango, the theater of dance born more than a century earlier in the *conventillos*, old buildings rented to immigrant families or converted into brothels. The place owed its name to the ancient wooden cathedral that now housed a different kind of temple. The light was warm and brilliant on the immense red curtains that marked off the space, which was of an impressive beauty. A giant portrait of Gardel dominated the dance floor where the couples competed: there they danced transverse tangos that were always astounding. In the shadows, the dancers waiting their turn watched each other from the tables with a subtle play of glances: soon they would have to take each other in their arms. Often without being acquainted or saying a word, they would have to sense and divine their partner's intention before taking the first step, which was henceforth ineluctable.

Two young Scandinavian blondes were waiting near the dance floor for a stallion to come break them in; Rubén thought of his father (Daniel Calderón had written several poems about the "bicephalous monster" of the tango), then moved toward the heavy red curtains. Behind them was the bar, a long counter of polished wood where aficionados came to have a drink between dances. Old posters climbed up the walls under long Chinese lanterns; an artist's sculpture hung from the main beam of the ancient cathedral, a large scarlet gagged heart that seemed to float under the roof.

"Does that remind you of anything?" asked a voice while he was gazing upward.

Rubén turned around and saw a large-breasted woman in her forties, a brunette who was very attractive despite her sinuous nose.

"Love, no?" he said.

She examined the work that hung over them.

"Uh-huh," she acquiesced. "Do you dance?"

He saw that she was wearing suitable shoes.

"Like a foot," Rubén replied.

"Ah? That's not the impression you give!" she burst out with an open laugh.

"Don't be misled by the poor light, I'm a terrible dancer. Do you come here often?"

"No."

"Too bad."

"Yes," she said. "Too bad."

An elegant young man with an unkempt beard was collecting the empty beer glasses on the bar. Rubén left the solitary dancer, asked the bartender to make him a pisco sour, and showed him the photo of María Victoria.

"Do you know this girl? Or have you ever seen her here?"

"No," the young man promptly replied. "We see a lot of people."

"María Victoria Campallo," Rubén announced, while the man was crushing the ice. "She comes here to dance, I've been told."

The bartender finished mixing the drink, glanced again at the photo on the bar, and pulled an evasive face as he agitated the shaker.

"I don't know." He filled a glass with white foam. "Ask Lola and Nico, they know everybody."

"And where would I find them, these turtledoves?"

"Over there," the barman said, with a jerk of his head.

Lola and Nico were taking a break at a nearby table, away from the dancers. Rubén left the barman a generous tip and picked up his glass.

Outrageous makeup, a black hat, fishnet stockings, a red dress tight over the hips—except for the sneakers she had just put on to give her feet a rest, Lola was still wearing her full tango regalia. Forced, like many Argentines, to work several little jobs, during the day the couple performed on the terraces of bars in La Boca, where, fascinated by the tango's mimed coitus, oafish tourists had themselves photographed for a few pesos, hanging on each other's necks in sensual poses. In the evening, they gave dance lessons at La Catedral. Nico spoke *lunfardo*, the slang of the *conventillos*. His girlfriend Lola looked sour; she would have preferred to work in a nursery rather than as a street dancer taking in the bumpkins. Rubén found them sitting at a table in a corner, massaging their weary feet after the evening's dance lessons. He introduced himself, briefly explained his request, and showed them the photo of María Victoria. Nico, who was very angular, bent over the face printed on matte paper.

"Yes," he promptly replied. "I've given her a couple of lessons this summer . . . A nice girl, rather talented."

Next to him, Lola retained her haughty pout.

"Have you seen her recently?" Rubén asked.

"We ran into each other last weekend. She was sitting there," Nico said, pointing to a table shaded from the spotlights. "But she was taking lessons."

The detective felt his skin prickle.

"When was that?"

"Friday."

The day María had called Carlos at the newspaper. New, shadowy couples were entwining on the dance floor, but Rubén was no longer paying attention to them.

"Was there anyone with her?"

"Yes. A little redhead, all tarted up," Nico laughed to avoid his panther's wrath. "The girls must have stayed an hour. Why?"

"The girls?"

"No need to be a physiognomist to see that the redhead was a tranny!" the dancer with the slicked-down hair chortled over the sound of the concertina.

Rubén still had in his pocket Jana's charcoal drawing, which he had shown to Anita at lunch. He unfolded the sheet of notepaper, trying not to show how nervous he was.

"This kind of transvestite?"

Nico smoothed his mustache and glanced at his companion, who assented with a detached look.

"Yes," he said. "That looks pretty much like her."

Rubén shivered in the warm light of the spots: Luz.

10

A Yankee, young, drunk out of his mind, got out of a taxi holding in his hand a beer and a few pesos that he threw to the driver to pay his fare. Determined to impress the four cheerleader types who were accompanying him, he tried to cut into the long line at the entrance to the Niceto Club, emphasized his status as a natural leader of the Free World, protested when Rubén passed in front of his court, and got himself tossed by the bouncer, who sent the starlets to the end of the line, accompanied by the night owls' sarcastic remarks.

The most hyped club in Buenos Aires was jammed full for that night's show, which was in full swing: the sound machine blared, and under strobe lights, an ecstatic crowd was gathering in front of an immense stage. The show that was being presented left Rubén stunned for a moment.

A tall blonde straight out of an erotic comic book, wearing a miniskirt and a sailor's jacket, was dancing voluptuously under the lights, occasionally giving a French kiss to her feminine alter ego, a willowy brunette with slicked-back hair and a man's suit, who wrapped the super bimbo in her voracious legs. Blind to the petting of the two beauties, a bald tranny weighing at least 350 pounds and draped in silk was sodomizing a young gladiator, masked, muscular, and armed with a trident; his colleagues in the Roman legions were sinking their swords into the asses of terribly consenting ephebes, licking the plastic blades and making gluttonous gestures toward the audience, which was exulting along with them, caught up in the trance. A sexual execution, an act of unbridled lust, multiple partner-swapping, lesbian, homo, tranny, men or women dishonored, all kinds of combinations followed one after the other on the stage of the Niceto, a sort of orgiastic brothel orchestrated by one of de Sade's henchmen, one in high form. Club 69 was the troupe's name: an extravagant porno-comic choreography.

It was four in the morning, it was the third club that Rubén had scoured, and Paula was stage right, wiggling her behind in a red dress with glinting fake rubies; radiant, a ten-carat smile making up for her missing tooth, the laundress's son was giving a blow job to the beak of a pink swan who decorated the backdrop. They had been running into each other in Peru Street for years. Sated, Paula tapped the bird's spangled hind side to emphasize its good taste, turned toward an audience that would applaud anything, and recognized the man in front of the stage—the detective, who signaled to her that he'd be waiting for her in the bar after the show.

Rubén passed through the wasted crowd and ordered a drink at the nearest bar. He recognized the young Americans with pasteurized sex appeal who were swaying their hips to techno house music, had his drink passed to him over a hedge of drinkers whose average age couldn't have been more than thirty. He was watching, pensively, the drunken parade of peacocks around blondes when he saw Jana at the other end of the bar. Auburn hair that evanesced, a black tank top, and fairy-like arms: she had seen him, too.

Rubén made his way through the fauna.

"What are you doing here?" the sculptress asked him, still surprised by what could only be a coincidence.

"I was looking for you," Rubén replied in the din.

Jana wanted to make room for him but they were being pressed against the bar.

"I thought we weren't worth your trouble? How did you know that we'd be here?"

Ruben leaned toward her ear.

"You left me a list of places where your tranny friends hang out," he said into her hair. "I made the rounds of three dance halls before the guy at the door told me about the show this evening. Naturally, that put a bug in my ear!"

"Bravo, Rin Tin Tin!" she laughed over the bass.

Rubén put a bill on the bar sticky with beer.

"Can I buy you a drink without you throwing it my face?"

"I wouldn't want to ruin your *hidalgo* outfit," she said considerately.

Calderón was wearing a shirt under a 1960s-style leather jacket that must have been worth two or three of her sculptures.

"I wasn't born with a silver spoon in my mouth," he informed her.

"Was it too big?"

Rubén broke out laughing amid the drunks, and suddenly looked ten years younger.

"So, what'll you have?"

"Same as you," she said.

He caught the bartender's eye and ordered two pisco sours. Jana was almost as tall as he was, and so close he could smell her musky odor.

"What do you want from Paula?" she asked.

"I'll explain it to you when we've gotten our drinks: it's too noisy here."

They almost had to shout at each other to make themselves understood.

"In any case I lied to you the other night," Jana confessed, jostled by the sticky crowd. "I no longer have any desire whatever to have sex with you!"

"You'd have tired yourself out anyway."

"Not my type."

"What?"

"You're not my type!" she shouted.

Rubén handed her the glass that had just landed on the bar and led her off in search of a less deafening place. People were dancing even in the club's corridors and hallway, where the boozers were walking back and forth. They found a table covered with empty glasses far enough from the dance floor so that they could talk; a man with an eye-patch was snoring on the neighboring bench, his shirt unbuttoned, probably abandoned by his pals. They sat down on the vacant stools without disturbing the drunkard. Rubén took off his jacket and rolled up his shirtsleeves.

"So," Jana asked, her cloth jacket tossed on the bench, "why did you want to see us?"

"Your pal Luz was seen in a tango club last Friday. A woman was with him, María Victoria, the daughter of Eduardo Campallo, a rich industrialist who is financing the mayor's campaign. Do you know her?"

Jana was looking at the skin on the inside of her forearms: she slugged down half the pisco, the little straw stuck between her lips, and answered with a pout.

"Never heard of her."

"María Campallo disappeared the night that Luz was killed," the detective went on. "I don't know what happened to her, but I've been looking for her for days. It happens that two witnesses saw them together at La Catedral a few hours before the murder of your transvestite friend." Jana frowned. "María Campallo is a photographer. I was hoping you or your friend Paula could help me put the pieces together."

"Your story's pretty strange," Jana commented.

"Yes."

"Do you think Campallo's daughter was murdered too?"

"We'll find out when the cops drag the harbor. But as you said, they seem not to be doing anything."

Over her drink, the Mapuche was thinking hard, and forgot the shame that had overcome her at Calderón's office the night before—a strange reunion.

"Odd how things turn around, isn't it?" she remarked.

"That's because they go together," Rubén replied.

Their eyes met, familiarly. The ice was broken.

"I don't know whether this might help you in any way, but I searched Luz's squat last night, with Paula. We found letters addressed to her family; apparently they live in Junin. I tried to contact them but I couldn't find their name in the phone book. Maybe they have an unlisted number, or maybe they're dead. Luz made up things about everybody," she explained, "starting with her parents: we'd have to go there, but I'm not sure my old junker would make it."

Junin was about three hundred miles away, in the middle of the pampas.

"What's their name?"

"Lavalle. Luz's real name was Orlando, Orlando Lavalle. We also found dope in the squat," Jana added. "Bags of *paco*, which Luz must have been dealing in the neighborhood. She never mentioned that to Paula."

Rubén nodded. The photographer had coke and weed in her night table, nothing very serious compared to *paco*.

"Do you know who was getting her the stuff?" he asked.

"No, but Luz could have been dealing on some mob boss's turf, and he killed her as a warning."

A battle for territory, with Eduardo Campallo's daughter caught in the crossfire . . . The neighborhood of La Boca was adjacent to San Telmo: Rubén knew the dopers in the neighborhood, who would put a knife to your throat to pay for their fix and who would be found dead one morning in the courtyard of a *conventillo*. María might have been at the wrong place at the wrong time, in Luz's company, but something didn't fit in that scenario.

"María was pregnant when she disappeared," Rubén said, "and *paco* is the worst shit on the market. I can't imagine her poisoning her baby with stuff like that."

"Unless she wanted to kill it."

"You have strange ideas."

"Something must have brought Luz and Maria together."

Jana finished her drink, the bass throbbing in the background. Over the detective's shoulder, she spotted Paula perched on a Greek column that two gladiators in G-strings were pushing into the mosh pit: she was wiggling in her dress with rubies lit by the spotlight, blowing powdered kisses to the hysterical crowd, smiling with happiness, as if happiness existed.

Rubén was looking at her, his mind obviously elsewhere. She took the opportunity to study the fine brown locks that covered his forehead.

"Do you know the name of the cop who pulled Luz out of the harbor?" he said, waking from his trance.

"Andretti," Jana replied. "The head of the night squad. The kind of cop that would eat bats."

Rubén knew him by reputation: a zealot. He glanced at his watch: almost five in the morning.

"O.K.," he agreed.

"O.K. what?"

"I'm going to have a couple of words with him," Rubén said, his eyes somber.

He put his glass down on the wet table. Jana's glass was already empty. In her Indian veins ran alcohol and electricity.

"I'm coming with you."

*

Crooks and gang members considered the Argentine police a rival force, one that was armed and whose job was to protect big-time criminals from small-time ones. A tenuous porosity: weapons moved in illicit circuits linked to the police and the army; when young thieves were arrested, they were severely beaten before they negotiated their freedom in exchange for part or all of what they had stolen, the meagerness of their take explaining the cops' inclination to liquidate them; going over to the enemy was a way for delinquents to earn money "legally" and save their skins at the same time.

Scapegoat, teammate, jack of all trades—the role of Officer Troncón varied with the moods of his superior, Andretti. At first, Jesus Troncón had cleaned the police station's toilets and winos' cells before it occurred to the sergeant to use him for specific operations. The greenhorn was officially employed as an "apprentice electrician": he could always rig alarm systems and start fires in squats for the benefit of real estate developers.

Troncón was on the reception desk that night. He recognized the Indian woman who burst into the station, but not the big, brown-haired guy with 220-volt eyes who swooped down on his counter.

"Is Sergeant Andretti there?" Rubén asked, without introducing himself.

Jesus put his skin mag under a pile of badly photocopied papers. The guy's elegance didn't go with the shabbiness of the place, and he couldn't understand what he was doing with the *negrita*.

"He's not available," Troncón declared, adopting a suitable tone. "What is it about?"

"The murder of the transvestite you fished out of the harbor," Rubén replied

"Oh, yes."

"Go find Andretti, I'm telling you."

Jana was fidgeting near the plastic plants. The station was deserted, without even a drunk or a doper howling for a fix in the cells.

"I have orders," Troncón said angrily, his forehead low and stubborn. "I'm the one who makes decisions."

The dolt was getting flustered.

"Fine," Rubén said impatiently. "Where's the chief's office?"

"End of the hall on the right," Jana replied.

"He's not there!" Troncón cried.

"You squint when you lie."

"Nobody's going down there!" Troncón stationed himself in the middle of the hall, his hands on his hips, on his belt. "You have to make an appointment."

Rubén pushed the idiot against the wall.

"Boss!" Troncón shouted, picking up his cap. "Boss! Boss!"

"What's going on?" a voice thundered from the end of the hall.

Alerted by the noise, the colossus came out of his office: Sergeant Andretti, 250 pounds, a little pudgy but still capable of knocking a mare's eye out with one punch.

"What the fuck is going on?"

He knew Calderón. He'd seen him around and knew his reputation: he was a violent, nosy troublemaker who was high on human rights and was building up files on the former oppressors. Andretti scowled when he saw the Indian woman behind the detective; she was the one he'd questioned the other night. Rubén went up to the big cop.

"I'm investigating a disappearance and the murder of Orlando Lavalle," he said without showing his badge, "the tranny you pulled out of the harbor. I know he was tortured before being thrown in the water. What did the autopsy show?"

"I don't have to answer your questions," Andretti replied, his shirtsleeves folded up on his hairy forearms. "And I don't like private eyes. Get the hell out of here with your whore!"

The former wrestler was running on testosterone.

"This lady is a witness to a murder. Would you prefer that I speak with the journalists? A tranny from La Boca emasculated and thrown into the harbor like a piece of shit, that would make the headlines of more than one newspaper. What do you say to that, big guy?"

The sergeant scowled. He saw Troncón's head sticking up at the end of the hall and snorted.

"Well?" Rubén persisted. "What did the autopsy show?"

"Nothing at all," Andretti replied. "It didn't show anything because there was no autopsy. We didn't find the tranny's purse and there was nothing in his squat, either, no documents, nothing to identify him, zip."

"That doesn't mean you don't have to do your job."

"Our job is to save money: do you know how much an autopsy costs?" the sergeant said, turning to Jana.

"Convenient, isn't it?"

"I'm not the one giving the orders."

"Where's the body?

"In the potter's field."

"That's the place for people like him, right?" Rubén focused on the policeman's vague gaze. "You get rid of the body, and that allows you to avoid conducting an investigation."

"We conducted an investigation! We're still conducting it, what do you think? At this moment there are two cars patrolling the docks: you can see for yourself that the station is empty, that we're doing all we can!"

"All you can to prevent a second murder from revealing the way you operate," Rubén added. "What does your report conclude, Andretti? That an unidentified tranny cut off his cock while shaving his crotch before falling naked into the harbor?"

"Ha ha!"

"What then?" he insisted icily.

The sergeant sized up Calderón, who was clearly ready to fight about it, and weighed the pros and cons.

"No one saw the tranny hooking that night," he said. "That doesn't help us much."

"Luz, Orlando, was keeping dope at his place," the detective shot back, "dozens of doses of *paco* that he was dealing in the neighborhood. Do you know who his supplier was?"

"No," growled Andretti, leaning his massive body against the office door.

"You, Andretti, you and your little pals on the night squad, who must be getting their share."

The giant flexed his pecs.

"Listen, you little shit . . . "

"I don't give a damn about your trafficking: you've buried the investigation so that no one will go nosing around in your affairs, right? Now answer me one question, the only one that interests me. I know that María Campallo saw the transvestite a few hours before his death: why?"

Troncón's cap could still be seen at the corner of the hall. His boss was getting visibly annoyed.

"I don't know your María," he replied promptly. He shook his jowls. "Who is she?"

His innocent air made Calderón grind his teeth.

"The daughter of Eduardo Campallo," he said, "a rich man who's financing the mayor's campaign."

He showed Andretti a picture of the photographer, which the policeman examined prudently.

"I don't know . . . Never saw her in this neighborhood or elsewhere."

"But she was with Orlando shortly before his murder."

"Maybe," Andretti replied, shrugging his enormous shoulders. "But not around here."

Rubén glanced at Jana in the harsh light of the corridor—for once, the fat jerk seemed sincere.

"Did Luz have regular customers?" he asked. "High-class customers?"

"I don't know," the policeman grumbled. "That's not my business."

"No, your business is just to provide dope to a loser tranny so that he can ruin the lives of other losers. Are you trying to win a gold medal for humanitarian acts?"

Their eyes met, two crocodiles in a pond during the dry season. The cop said nothing, fulminating in an eloquent silence.

"If you're involved in this, Andretti," the detective hissed, "I swear I'll make you eat your own lard."

"Go fuck yourself, Calderón."

But the head of the night squad was uncomfortable. Rubén signaled to Jana that it was time to get out of there. They left the La Boca police station without even looking at the dolt behind the counter.

Outside, the air was warm, the sky the color of amethyst. Jana, who had observed the joust, let Rubén come back down to a more hospitable terrain. They took a few steps along the sidewalk, between a damp mist and a dusty wind. Rubén had almost been scared when he'd looked at Andretti. He was ruminating, the alkaline core smoking under the electric wires connected to the *conventillos*.

"We were on the wrong track, huh?" Jana said, reading his thoughts.

"Looks like it, yes."

The car was parked a block away.

"What do we do now?" the sculptress asked.

Rubén met her eyes sparkling under the setting moon.

"I'll take you back."

*

The headlights awakened the aviator with springs for eyes who was on guard in courtyard, at the entrance to the wasteland. Jana had left the keys to the Ford in the dressing room at the Niceto, but Paula hadn't yet returned. Rubén parked the car in the courtyard.

"I'm going to look for the parents' address," the Mapuche said as she pushed open the gate.

He let her take off toward her workshop, and took advantage of her absence to have a look around her turf. Huge red ants were feeding in the nettles, their antennas rising over their heads, under the mocking gaze of a crocodile with teeth made of screws; farther on, a rusty Varan made of bolts off a locomotive wandered through the brush, and was being left to disintegrate there. The sun was coming up behind the shed, and a few birds were chirping on the stripped poles. Jana came back to the courtyard.

"Here," she said.

Rubén crushed out his cigarette butt on the aviator and pocketed the envelope with Orlando's parents' address.

"Thanks."

"Are you planning to take a trip to Junin?"

"Uh-huh. To get a little info, in any case," he replied evasively.

He'd asked Anita to follow up the lead in Colonia. How could Orlando be connected with María Campallo's round-trip excursion to Uruguay? Somewhere nearby a bell was ringing six o'clock, and he was beginning to feel very tired.

"Shall we have a drink while we wait for Paula?" Jana asked. "If I know her, she won't be back before ten in the morning."

He raised his arched eyebrows.

"I lied to you a little while ago in the club," she said confidentially. "When I said that I didn't want to have sex with you."

Rubén looked at her under the fading stars: for the first time, there was something merry in her almond-shaped eyes.

"You've got energy to spare, it seems," he said softly, smiling at her.

"It's free. Everything about me is free. Haven't you noticed?"

Rubén tried to escape her deep black eyes, but failed. She locked onto her target and wouldn't let it go. Their hands had been waiting to touch for a long time.

"Jana . . . "

"Quiet," she murmured, coming closer to him.

Jana pressed her lips to his mouth and felt herself melt like chocolate when he entwined his tongue with hers. Soon all she could hear was the birds cooing. With one hand, Rubén clasped her bottom and pressed it to him, so tenderly that she let herself be carried by his open eyes: black, gray, blue, stormy bouquets exploded in the courtyard. Jana no longer wanted to think or breathe, she caressed his unkempt hair, the little curls on his forehead, and felt his penis against her crotch and groaned with pleasure. Desire, light and wild, electrified her. His hand under her ass seemed to lift her off the earth, their tongues were two little sweet-water serpents that ran down between her thighs. They were kissing passionately when the sound of a car horn interrupted them.

The birds flew away from their perches, hearts beating like theirs at a hundred miles an hour.

Jana remained speechless for a moment, her lips still wet, while the garbagemen moved on. She wanted to say simple things, things she'd never said because she'd never experienced them, but a shadow fell across Rubén's face.

"I've got to go home," he said, removing his hand.

Jana stepped back, disconcerted.

"Now?"

"Yes." Rubén moved toward the car. "I'll see you later."

And he left her there, under the skewed gaze of the aviator in an iron suit.

11

The sudden low pressure system that had been dominating Buenos Aires weather for three days had given way to a blue late-summer sky. Rubén put out his cigarette in the flowerpot; the glassed-in enclosure of the harbor station sheltered souvenir shops, a tobacconist, and a row of female employees stuffed into tight-fitting uniforms in their companies' colors.

A bleached blonde smiled under her toucan makeup: he bought a Buquebus ticket for Colonia, on the other side of the estuary, and showed his passport to the immigration officer. The ferry for Uruguay was bobbing in the brown water of the harbor: Rubén joined the passengers who were marveling at the imitation luxury of the main lounge, his face somber despite the sunshine. He had slept a few hours after returning from the wasteland, but he still felt just as feverish and shadowy images kept clouding his mind. A voice coming from the loudspeaker announced the ferry's imminent departure. Rubén ordered an espresso at the varnished wood bar, and opened the newspaper to forget the mood music: there were articles about the coming elections, about Francisco Torres, the city's mayor, who would receive almost a third of the votes, according to recent polls, about soccer and Maradona's latest escapades, but there was still not a word about the disappearance of María Victoria Campallo.

The boat had hardly left the dock when a crooner in a ruffled shirt sat down at his piano on the stage of the main lounge to do a song recital. Before an audience of old ladies with saggy arms overloaded with gold jewelry, the seducer began singing "My Way," exchanging coy winks with his listeners.

This was a long way from the Pistols.

Rubén climbed upstairs—there was an open-air bar and the gilt was getting on his nerves—but it was no better: two walls of loudspeakers were spitting out a deafening techno house, driving the tourists toward the benches on the top deck. Were they that afraid that people would get bored? Thinking they were filling dead time, they ended up creating voids. Far from the bass tones that were emptying the deck, Rubén found a place that was more or less quiet at the rear of the ship and stood at the rail, smoking and looking out over the muddy water stirred up by the propellers. The cranes in the commercial harbor loomed over the container ships as they were going out to sea. A shiny new three-master was coming back toward the marina. He was still thinking about Jana, about her fragrance in his arms, and what had led him to kiss her in the courtyard. The Mapuche had come out of nowhere. And for what reason, if not to return to it? Age, social and ethnic background, everything separated them. The ardor of their kiss at dawn betrayed a deep and common despair that he didn't feel up to confronting. In any case, it was too late, too late for everything. The wind freshened under the maritime sun. Pollution formed a gray band in the distance over Buenos Aires, adrift under the pall of smoke from the outlying factories. Rubén forgot the young Indian woman and the undulation of waves beneath the swell.

Anita had collected precise information about the address in Colonia and María's trip there three days before she disappeared. Jose Ossario, the man who lived at No. 69 Ituzaingó Street, was not in the phonebook, but Anita had found a record of his car in the highway police's files—a white Honda registered in Colonia del Sacramento. The rest was on the Internet.

An Argentine citizen, Jose Ossario had first worked for various science fiction magazines before publishing in 1992 his first book, *The Hidden Face of the World*, a hodgepodge of scientism on a bed of conspiracy theories that combined espionage, astrology, and acute paranoia. In the book, Ossario elaborated his own crazy, earnestly believed truth, gaining notoriety among initiates. Later on, he had worked as a paparazzo before starting up several press agencies that all ended up the same way: unpaid bills, outlandish accounting practices, bankruptcies, and various con games. An expert in blackmailing and extorting scoops, Ossario had come through without a scratch until 2004, with the publication of a series of photos showing the former head of Menem's cabinet, Rodrigo Campês, with the daughter of the country's leading labor leader, scantily clad, on the beach at Punta del Este, where the lovers were staying in a palatial suite—for which, naturally, no one was paying the bill. After the scandal hit the headlines, Ossario had thought his day of triumph had come, but he was rapidly disabused. This not being his first scrape with the judicial system, buried in fees for documents and lawyers, blacklisted, he had ended up throwing in the towel. There had been no news of him since he went into exile in Uruguay three years earlier, except a book, *Counter-Truths*, a sensational story brought out in a thousand copies by a small publisher in Montevideo, but the only response had been a wall of silence. Now fifty-one years old, the former paparazzo lived at No. 69 Ituzaingó Street, but clearly . . .

Rubén stamped out his cigarette on the metal deck.

They were arriving in Colonia.

*

As in Brazil, the amnesty for the dictatorship's henchmen had been the cornerstone of the transition to democracy in

Uruguay. Recent developments suggested there was light at the end of the tunnel, but the country seemed to be living in slow motion, as if hiding the past had encased the present in wax.

Colonia de Sacramento, the country's former colonial capital, was no exception to the countrywide somnolence. Old, abandoned buildings, streetlights from 1900, ruins with balconies eaten away by rust, beat-up Fords from the 1950s, Rambler Americans and ancient Fiat 500s keeping cool under the orange trees. Although outwardly reminiscent of the old-fashioned charm of the Gay Nineties, inside the souvenir shops were full of manufactured horrors—porcelains, clothes, craftworks, everything was in turgid bad taste. Rubén walked down paved streets shaded by palm trees and came out on the Plaza Mayor.

Sparrows were chirping under rotating sprinklers on impeccable lawns, brightly colored parrots perched on an ancient tree took flight into the sky to flirt briefly with the wind; a few old men dozed on a bench as the sun suffocated everything. Jose Ossario lived a little farther on, at the end of a cement lane that led to the sea.

Ituzaingó 69. The sun was beating on the perimeter wall, hiding a flat-roofed house that was almost invisible from the street. Rubén rang the intercom, located the surveillance camera above the reinforced grille, rang again. No response. He stepped back to widen his angle of view, but over the wall he could see only a bit of whitewashed facade and two closed shutters. He glanced through the interstices of the grille, saw a garden with tired flowers and more closed shutters on the ground floor. The lane was empty, the heat pounded on the sidewalk as if it were an anvil. Just then, Rubén felt a presence.

Somebody was watching him from behind the neighboring hedge: a puny, balding little man about sixty-five, with small, pale, deep-set blue eyes with bags under them. He looked worried.

"Are you looking for something?" he asked.

Rubén pointed to the former paparazzo's house.

"Jose Ossario," he said. "This is where he lives, isn't it?"

"Yes."

The neighbor wore discreet glasses, a polo shirt, and shorts that allowed his white, hairless legs to be seen. Rubén approached the hedge.

"Do you know how long he's been gone?"

The little man shrugged.

"Several days, I think." He examined Rubén with curiosity. "You're Argentine, aren't you?"

Rubén's accent left no doubt about that.

"Martin Sanchez," Rubén said. "Yes, I come from Buenos Aires."

"Franco Díaz," the neighbor replied, smiling behind the wire fencing. "Retired botanist. Are you looking for Mr. Ossario?" he asked in a friendly way.

"Yes, I work for a collection agency," Ruben lied. "It's a rather complicated matter and it's . . . well, urgent."

"Ah?" Díaz hesitated. He was holding his pruning shears in his hand, and a glimmer of interest appeared in his close-set eyes. "But you must be hot in this sun," he said as if just remembering his manners. "Come have an orangeade," he added considerately, "we can discuss this more comfortably. Do you like flowers?"

Poppies.

The old man opened the gate, going on about the return of the sun after the strong winds of the preceding days. Franco Díaz lived alone in a house by the sea where he seemed to be enjoying the most peaceful of retirements: an eminent botanist—his garden was splendid, unlike that of his neighbor—he had put in a water lily pond on the roof terrace of the former *posada*, from which one could contemplate Río de la Plata. A little creek ran below the house, in the shade of a weeping willow, its muddy banks littered with plastic bottles.

Rubén sipped a cold drink as he listened to the retiree talk about the rarity of his flowers before turning the conversation to the subject that interested him.

Sensing that Díaz had reservations about his neighbor, Rubén wholeheartedly confirmed them—Jose Ossario owed money, an old debt concerning an insurance policy that he had just cashed in. Díaz listened to him, his face pale, almost melancholic. He acknowledged that his relationship with his neighbor was not so good, and as the conversation went on, he became voluble: litigious in the extreme, the preceding year Ossario had filed a suit against him over a complicated matter involving the water table, which Franco was supposedly polluting with his herbicides. Was it his fault if his neighbor didn't have a green thumb, that everything died on his land while his own paradise was in full flower?

"The kind of people who attack manufacturers of microwave ovens because their cat got fried inside!" the old man summed up with a dose of youthful humor.

"The shutters are closed," Rubén noted. "Have you seen him recently?"

"Not since Friday or Saturday. In any case, his car's no longer there."

"Do you know if someone visited him?"

"No, I don't think so. To tell the truth, no one ever visits my neighbor." Díaz's bald head was sweating despite the coolness of the pond. "Another orangeade?"

"Yes, thanks."

Rubén took advantage of the friendly retiree's absence to have a look at Ossario's house. It was a rather common building whose balcony looked down on the river; a little farther on, the dike at the marina could be seen, with its motorboats and sailboats bobbing in the current. The shutters on the upper story were closed as well. Franco Díaz returned to the terrace, carrying cool drinks.

"Do you think my neighbor has left?" he asked, without hiding his curiosity. "I mean, for good?"

"I hope not," laughed the temporary insurance man. "Why? Do you have reasons to think that he might take off?"

"No, why would he do that? Because of his debts?"

"You know how people are with money," Rubén insinuated.

Díaz agreed and took a sip of his orangeade. He also had a slight Argentine accent. Then his affable face froze. Rubén turned toward Ossario's house: a car had just stopped in the street. A single car door slammed, then a gate creaked. The detective said good-bye.

A white Honda was parked at the curb. A recent model, like that of the former paparazzo. Rubén put his hand on the hood: the motor was hot. He rang at No. 69 and stood under the surveillance camera waiting for a response. Finally a voice crackled over the intercom.

"Who are you?"

"Calderón. I'm a detective and I've come from Buenos Aires. You're Jose Ossario, I assume."

Rubén showed his badge to the video camera trained on him.

"How did you know I'd come back today?"

"I didn't know. I was talking with your neighbor when I heard the car," Rubén explained. "I have to talk with you, it's important."

"Talk about what?"

"María Victoria Campallo. I'm looking for her. Let me in, Mr. Ossario."

The crackling went on for several seconds. Rubén put out his cigarette on the sidewalk softened by the afternoon heat. A click finally opened the gate. A garden full of weeds led to the half-open door. He went up to the porch.

"Are you armed?" Ossario asked from behind the security door.

He had left the chain on. One kick and it was gone.

"No," Rubén replied.

"I am."

"Don't hurt yourself."

The man took off the chain and let the detective come into his cave. The contrast with the light outside left Rubén completely blind for two or three seconds, long enough for Ossario to size up the intruder. Rubén raised his hands as a sign of passivity, and realized that the man was behind him.

"Who are you working for?" the man said, closing the door.

"Myself."

"Don't move," the man said, walking around him.

Rubén saw the glint of a gun barrel in the semidarkness. The ground floor contained a photo lab and an editing unit.

"Open your jacket," Ossario ordered.

Rubén obeyed.

"O.K., you go first."

The stairway led to the living room, whose half-open shutters filtered the daylight. Rubén saw Ossario's pale face: he was looking at him stubbornly, a revolver in his hand. Thirty-two caliber. He was wearing a khaki jumpsuit, a shirt, a safari vest, and leather ranger boots. Muscular, with a shaved head, a goatee, and the jowls of a beer-guzzling metalhead, Jose Ossario seemed better prepared for self-attack than self-defense.

"Can I smoke or will the detectors make us pay a fine?"

Ossario didn't much care for the detective's humor.

"How did you find me?"

"Your address was scribbled on a piece of paper in the pocket of a pair of jeans that María Victoria didn't have time to wash. Put your artillery away, please."

Ossario thought it over, stroking his goatee. There was a sofa bed and photo gear near French door. Rubén took a quick look at the bookshelf while Ossario was ruminating—

Meyssan, Roswell, Faurisson, UFO stories, the Bermuda Triangle . . .

"What do you know about María Campallo?" Ossario asked without putting down his gun.

"That she came to see you two days before she disappeared," Rubén answered.

The man paled a little more.

"Go on."

"María was trying to contact a newspaper hostile to her father, Eduardo, and nothing has been heard from her since. I've been looking for her for almost a week now. You'd be better off putting up your little popgun if you don't want me to take it away from you."

Rubén lit a cigarette while observing his reaction, but Ossario remained silent for a long time. A tripod with a digital video camera stood in front of a window that gave on the neighbor's garden.

"The idiot," the former paparazzo finally whispered.

Rubén gave him an interrogative glance.

"I told her to keep quiet," Ossario mumbled, clearly torn between the shock of the revelation and anger. "I told her to let me handle it . . . the idiot!"

He put the gun in its holster, his eyes distracted, shaken.

"To keep quiet about what?" Rubén asked. "Her father Eduardo's activities?"

"Her father Eduardo? Ha!" he laughed with malicious pleasure. "He's not her father! Oh, no!"

"What do you mean?"

Ossario clamped his protruding eyes on Rubén, delighted by the effect he'd produced.

"You didn't know?"

"What?"

"María Victoria was adopted. She and her brother! Ha!" he said triumphantly. "You didn't know that?"

Rubén paled in turn.

"Are you saying that María was adopted during the dictatorship?"

"Obviously!"

The sound of the surf below the terrace rose to their ears. The news changed everything—that's why María had tried to contact Carlos at the newspaper, why she'd been kidnapped: she was one of the babies stolen by the soldiers.

"Do you have proof of that?"

"Proof!" the former paparazzo exulted.

Rubén felt like he was talking to a madman, but the madman wasn't lying.

"You're the one who told María the truth about her adoption, right?"

"Yes. I wanted her to testify for me in the Grand Trial."

"You were planning to sue Eduardo Campallo?"

"Oh! Not only Campallo! The rest of them, too! All those monopolists, those so-called elites and professional neoliberals who sealed my lips to keep me from talking! The Grand Trial: that's my response! Of course, Campallo's press killed me," he laughed, "I'm a thorn in their sides! A critic of their ideology! I've chosen that as my standard!"

He was jubilant, a prisoner of his resentments.

"Do you know what has happened to María Victoria?" Rubén asked.

"No," he said with a frown. "No, but I can guess! The idiot wanted to find her brother! You see where that got her!"

Rubén felt the atmosphere change around him. Suddenly he was sweating.

"María Victoria has another brother? A brother other than Rodolfo?"

"Rodolfo was born at the ESMA, but he's not her brother," Ossario blurted out, almost frighteningly. "Her real brother was exchanged with him at birth! The poor kid was sick, or they'd cut up his mother too much in the clandestine maternity ward: Campallo exchanged him for another baby born in detention, the infamous Rodolfo, the one in perfect health! But he isn't her brother! Not at all!"

The ESMA, the Navy Engineering School. For Rubén as well, history stammered.

"A man was murdered the night María disappeared," he said, trying to retain a neutral tone, "a transvestite witnesses saw with her that evening. Do you think he's her brother?"

Ossario was becoming more and more agitated.

"The little idiot!" he grumbled in his delirium. "I told her not to move, that I'd take care of everything. She disobeyed me! And this is what happened!"

Rubén heard a noise outside, on the terrace, a slight creaking. He moved away from the bookcase in front of which he'd been standing and pushed aside the blind on the window that gave on the street: a white van with tinted windows was parked in front of the Honda.

"The idiot," Ossario mumbled.

Rubén leaned over and saw the broken garden gate, then shadows on the balcony dancing behind the blinds.

"Look out!"

The frame of the French door yielded in a brief explosion of wood: two hooded men broke in before Ossario's eyes; for a second, he remained petrified. A red laser beam was fixed on his chest. Surging forward from the wall against which he had flattened himself, Rubén struck the shooter in the throat, a violent direct hit that made him drop his Taser. The man groaned, and stumbled over the debris. Seeing his partner in difficulty, the other man pulled the trigger on his Taser. But Rubén was using the partner as a shield, and the man took the full force of the shock. The detective didn't leave the shooter time to reload: he cast aside the shocked puppet in front of him, leapt on the other man, and gave him a wicked kick in the testicles.

"Get out of here!" he shouted to Ossario.

The assailant remained immobile in the half-light of the room, a dull pain radiating through his crotch. Ossario finally reacted: he grabbed the pistol in his holster, ran toward the stairway and found himself face to face with the second team, who had just come through the ground-floor window. He fired on them. The Taser beams hit him point-blank in the chest, a shock of fifty thousand volts that threw off his aim: the first bullet hit the stairway ceiling, and the second blew off his forehead as he collapsed, shaken by spasms.

Rubén had no weapon: he was making his way toward the balcony over bits of window blind and glass when he gave a cry of pain. A fifth man was on the terrace. Rubén retched when the piano wire dug into his throat, and immediately understood that he would die as soon as the man tightened his grip and destroyed his windpipe. With his head, he struck three furious backward blows and hit his target, while he crushed the man's instep with his heel. The killer was shaken, but held on. Rubén was suffocating. Ossario was lying at the top of the stairs, the upper part of his skull pulverized, and the two other guys were running up. Rubén reached back and grabbed the killer's testicles and twisted them with all his strength. The man fell back against the guardrail. Rubén felt the man's body; blood was running onto his shirt, more and more as the lethal wire cut into the skin; he was crushing the man's testicles but the brute refused to let go. Rubén put an arm over his shoulder and, pulling him along with all his weight, fell over backward.

Two laser beams grazed him as they went over the guardrail.

There was a twenty-foot drop to the river: the two men fell head over heels into the muddy water that was flowing under the terrace. The current immediately carried them away. Rubén couldn't see anything in this dark water, the waves and the killer clinging to him were dragging him down. He struggled furiously, his lungs burning. He threw his elbows around wildly but it was no use. They were drifting along in the dark, pulled down by the current. Rubén twisted around in the molasses, out of breath. He saw his aggressor's head among the bubbles and stuck his thumbs in his eyes. He was swallowing a first gulp of water when the man let go. Rubén gave a final kick to get back to the surface, saw the light, and sucked in the air like it was a piece of eternity. He was no longer thinking about the killer, his bleeding throat, or Ossario, he was just thinking about breathing. About surviving, escaping the trap they'd set for him in the house. He swam blindly, pulled along by the waves; the marina was two or three hundred yards away. He came up in the eddies and algae, a taste of mud in his mouth, and looked behind him. The former paparazzo's house was no longer visible, hidden by the trees on the corniche, and there was no trace of the killer who had fallen from the balcony with him. There was nothing but the white dock of the little harbor in front of him, and the rays of the sun that was sinking into the water.

Rubén made it to the shore, exhausted, and dragged himself as far as the part of the beach in front of the dock. Lukewarm blood was running from his throat as he panted. He lacked oxygen, and points of reference; his head was spinning. Water and mud were dripping off him onto the wet sand, his body still trembling after the attack. He sat down among the bits of plastic and seashells, his lungs aching after being under water so long.

"Are you all right?" a fisherman asked from his boat.

Rubén didn't answer. The stench of mud was in his mouth and fear was running down his legs. He retched and vomited a black liquid onto the pearly fragments of seashells.

The bastards had almost killed him.

12

Among the five hundred babies stolen during the dictatorship, many were not listed at the BNDG, the genetics bank. Most of their parents had never reappeared, having been pulverized by dynamite, burned in clandestine centers, incinerated in cemeteries, cast in concrete, thrown out of airplanes: without exhumed bodies or searches by their families, these children would remain ghosts forever.

The babies were given to sterile couples close to those in power—officers, policemen, sometimes even torturers, adducing false documents. *Apropriadores*: that was the term used to describe the adoptive parents. The waiting lists were long, special privileges acceptable. The *apropriadores* waited until a prisoner had a baby, and then recuperated the fruit of her womb. If the mother was liquidated after giving birth, that was not their problem: these babies were part of the "spoils of war."

Except that, since they were illegally appropriated, these children did not have access to their family history: it had been stolen from them. The men and women who had doubts about their origins thirty-five years later could call upon CONADEP, an organization whose job was to determine the identity of the *desaparecidos*. When they learned the truth about their origins, affection often won out over affliction, and many of them erased the past and reestablished contacts, when they could, with their original families—grandparents, uncles, cousins. In every case, these children underwent a veritable psychic earthquake: diverted filiations, interrupted transmissions, the bonds that bound these stolen babies were based on lies and crimes. They could not love, hope, build, or progress in their adult lives, mendacity insinuated itself everywhere, made minds and acts opaque, contaminated feelings.

The Grandmothers had understood this, and opened a psychological unit to help these children overcome the trauma. They had found more than a hundred of them: María Victoria Campallo was one of the four hundred children who were still lost. She and Orlando, the brother she was looking for.

In extremis, Rubén had found a seat on the last ferry for Buenos Aires. His cell phone had not survived its time underwater, and the remarks made by Uruguayan immigration officials and the foul humor he'd been in since his forced dip into the river had not sated his desire to kill.

On the boat taking him back to Argentina, he finally reached Anita by phone: and it got worse.

*

The Buenos Aires ecological preserve bordered on the Río de la Plata, whose muddy waters emptied into the ocean. Inextricable thickets, marshes infested with mosquitoes, pink flamingos, and puffins fishing provided some idea of what the first conquistadors found when they landed here five centuries earlier. Adjacent to Puerto Madero, the preserve was separated from the business quarter by a simple avenue that was more or less unused; the sunset was flaming on the reflective sides of the buildings when Anita Barragan's patrol arrived at the site. They were the first on the scene.

Novo, the current trainee, was driving the emergency squad's two-tone Fiat. Wearing a cap and a green uniform, Jarvis, the frumpy guardian of the preserve, made his rounds every night to chase out the little wise guys that liked to picnic in the fresh air and smoke joints while playing music: he was the one who had found the body and immediately called 911.

The Fiat bounced over the rocky track that wound through the bit of jungle and stopped within sight of the ocean.

"It's there," Jarvis said.

The shore was twenty yards below, beyond a clump of acacias. They left the police car at the side of the road and went the rest of the way on foot. Tall reeds anticipated the skyscrapers that could be seen in the distance. By the light of the setting sun, they traversed a cloud of particularly persistent mosquitoes and made their way through the stunted trees to get to the beach, a bit of earth covered with branches and various kinds of rubbish.

Dirty brown water was lapping in small, oily thrusts, exhaling a sickly sweet odor of decay. The low-pressure system that had struck the Argentine coast had changed the currents; hundreds of plastic bottles had washed up on the beaches and riverbanks, carrying mussels and empty seashells into the estuary. Full of apprehension, Anita walked up to the edge of the water and held her breath in order to confront Death. The body was floating among plastic bags and algae, the top of the head torn off. Blue cloth pants, a T-shirt, no shoes. A woman, to judge by the tufts of brown hair full of sand and parasites that were jumping around. A swollen, unrecognizable body. Anita shuddered as she bent over the face: attached around the eye sockets, dozens of whelks were eating away the rest of the eyes. The smell got more intense; Anita didn't know what to look at first, if she could go on looking at this poor woman with the top of her head gone, half devoured by the sea.

Novo stood at a distance, preoccupied by the churning of his bowels; the guardian had turned his eyes away and was looking toward the thicket. Anita was trying not to vomit. She believed she'd seen the worst when she picked up burned bodies; but there were no limits to the worst. She thought about her cat to keep her mind off the body, swallowed even though her mouth was dry, ignored the putrid emanations and the mosquitoes harassing her, and crouched down in the mud. To be in this condition, the corpse must have been in the water for several days. The top of the skull had been scalped, a clean cut, probably made by a boat's propeller. It was hard to look at the face, with its orifices teeming with whelks, but the neck was intact. A tattoo was visible under one ear: a little lizard crawling toward the lobe.

Anita stood up, cold sweat running down her spine. She had seen the tattoo somewhere else. The digital photo Rubén had shown her. María Victoria Campallo: she had the same little lizard below her ear.

*

A greasy sandwich was dripping on Alfredo Grunga's shirt. El Toro knew the city like the back of his hand. He had roamed it in a Ford Falcon—in the good old days, as they said, or at least the times they constantly referred to as the good old days. Sitting at his side, El Picador was scanning radio stations, trying to find a love song to relax. Quite a lot of traffic on Buenos Aires's main artery: office workers going home, confident in their positions as officials, their families, their cobbled-together everyday lives.

O divina . . .
Toda, toda mia . . .

El Picador had found a suitable station. He gave his partner an angular smile. El Toro, who was driving the converted van, was finishing his cheese empanada; sweat was running down his flabby jowls, like the grease running onto his shirt, which was still more or less white—what a pig, this Toro—ho, ho, ho!

"Turn down that stupid fucking music!" the big bald man in the backseat growled.

Parise knew these wild-eyed fanatics, and this time there could be no slipups.

A charter member of the Triple A (Argentine Anticommunist Alliance), Hector Parise belonged to the group that had awaited Perón's return at the Ezeiza airport in 1973, when two million people stormed the airport to give the old hero a welcome he wouldn't forget. Parise and his team had taken up a position near the speaker's platform and fired into the crowd, concentrating their fire on the Montoneros, the most virulent activists. Thirteen dead, four hundred wounded, Perón's plane diverted to a military base, and a terrible panic that prefigured the general's split with the left wing of his party: on May 1, from the balcony of the Casa Rosada, where the Montoneros had assembled en masse to show their support for him, Perón called them "immature imbeciles," "traitors," and "mercenaries." A perfectly orchestrated coup, because Perón died two months later, leaving power to his wife, a dancer under the influence of López Rega and his death squads, of which Parise was a member—the beginning of the scramble for power that led to Videla's coup d'état.

Ancient history.

Avenida Independencia. El Toro was wiping his fingers on his shirt when Parise barked from in the back of the van, "Take the first right."

*

Miguel had opted for a white sheath dress under a belted, flared coat that showed off his ankles—the transvestite had a fetishistic taste for high-heeled pumps, which he wore smaller than his feet in order to "shrink" them. His debutante's outfit. People were going to laugh or cry, it didn't matter. The show at the Niceto had changed everything. The magic of the stage that you felt in the pit of your stomach and that liberated you. After her mad night spent dancing, laughing, and drinking with other artists, Paula had understood that her life was changing. One stroke of good luck following another, Gelman and Club 69's performers hired her for the tour to Rosario, and other gigs were coming her way, from Mendoza to Santiago. The shock had been staggering, the response urgent (they were leaving two days later), and from then on the decision was final: Miguel would give up prostitution on the docks for an artist's life. He would replace his broken tooth and maybe even one day,—why not?—change his sex, his name, his life, far from the mother who was blocking his way. Miguel was going to become Paula, like a butterfly leaving its chrysalis: forever.

The transvestite looked at her watch, a little candy-red dial that emphasized the edging on her dress: it was closing time, and the laundry's metal shutter was already down. Miguel clicked his heels in the alley that led to the back room ("the artists' entrance," he called it), his heart pounding—"Steady, old girl, be a man for the first and last time in your life!"

He had hardly opened the door before he was met with a cry.

"There he is!" Rosa jumped on her chair. "Aah! Aaahh!"

The old woman almost suffocated on seeing her son dressed in that way, gripped the armrests as if the Devil had given her wings, and clutched her checkered quilt in her scrawny hands.

"How dare you?" she said furiously, shooting him a murderous glance. "How dare you, you demon?"

Rosa was not alone in the laundry's back room. A man in a cassock was there with her, a man about forty with a soft smile and a white clerical collar. Brother Josef, no doubt, the priest the old bigot was always going on about.

"Did you bring in reinforcements?" Miguel asked his mother.

"Look at him, Brother Josef! Do you see the sickness in him? You have to exorcise it! Oh, Lord!"

"Now then, now then . . . " The priest patted his parishioner's withered arm. "Take it easy, Rosa."

Miguel shook his head under his wig, offended but almost amused by the situation.

"What a horror! Just look at his homosexual clown getup! To do that to his mother! In front of you, Brother Josef! And it makes him laugh on top of it! Brother Jo . . . "

"Please, Rosa." The man was trying to cool her outrage. "Calm down and let me talk to your son."

His paternalistic manner reeked of conspiracy: Miguel was tired of all this.

"I don't have anything to say to you, old friend," he said, to cut the conversation short. "It's my mother I want to talk to, not you."

"Lout!"

"Let him say his piece, Rosa. Your son has important things to tell you. Speak, my son. I'm here to help you, you and your poor mother."

The priest from the Immaculata Concepción was wearing discreet little glasses on a pale and mousy face that oozed Christian benevolence. Miguel ran his hands over the folds of his dress and shrugged.

"All right." He took a deep breath. "Mama, I've come to tell you that I'm packing my bags and leaving the house. I've found a job in a transvestite revue; in two days we're leaving for Rosario, on a worldwide tour, and I won't come back. Not here anyway. I don't care what you think, since you've never thought about me, but always about yourself. I don't even hold it against you. If Papa had lived, we wouldn't be in this situation. In any case, it's too late. From now on, Miguel will dress as Paula, whether you like it or not. You've never loved me," he continued, pulling the rug from under her feet: "even when

I was a child, I could never do anything right. You scolded me all the time, as if you wanted to suffocate me, as if I weren't the person I was supposed to be, and well, that's too bad. Now I'm leaving. I'm out of here. I'm disappearing!"

"What?"

"Yes, Mama, I've had enough of living in mothballs, of listening to you tell me I'm sick and doing your ostrich act. I didn't come here to ask your permission or your opinion, I came to get my things. I'll come back to help you now and then, if you want me to."

"Selfish brute!" Rosa yelped.

"Yes. In the meantime, I'm going to live with people who love me as I am."

"Impostor!"

"Right."

"Impostor!" the old woman shrilled. "I'm ashamed of you, you libertine! You want me dead, admit it! How ashamed I am, my Lord, what shame!"

"Miguel," the priest interrupted, "why leave your mother so suddenly? Something must have happened recently that forced you to make your decision."

"It's funny," Miguel remarked. "It's when you become free that people start thinking that you're talking rubbish. You know what, Brother Josef? Since you and your God are so clever, why don't you take care of my mother."

"Miguel," retorted the priest in a solemn tone, "if I were you I'd talk . . . Your mother told me about a visit last week: were you present?"

"Impostor," Rosa grumbled, gulping down a cough drop she took from the box she held under her quilt. "You've never been anything but an imposter."

"What visit?" Miguel asked.

"A woman. She gave your mother a document, an important document. Rosa says she no longer remembers where she put it, but you must know: you're the one who takes care of papers, aren't you?"

His conciliatory voice rang as false as a rescheduling of debts. Miguel turned towards his mother, but her faded gaze was lost in the abyss of her madness.

"Listen," Miguel said, "I don't know what my mother has told you but she's not right in the head."

Rosa was digging around in her box, wild locks of her hair sticking out of her bun, repeating in a dull voice: "Impostor . . . Impostor . . . "

The priest shifted from foot to foot in front of the ironing table.

"Miguel," he persisted, "I have to know whether you saw the document that woman left here."

"Good God, what are you talking about?"

There was a moment of hesitation in the back room. Brother Josef was now sweating heavily under his cassock. He came closer to Miguel and whispered confidentially.

"Didn't your mother tell you?"

"Tell me what?"

"Well . . . that she isn't your mother."

Miguel frowned with his carefully plucked eyebrows.

"What do you mean, she's not my mother?"

"You should tell me the truth, Miguel," the priest urged him in a low voice.

"What truth? Mama!" he cried, turning toward the laundress. "What have you gone and said now?"

"You're the one who's sick!" she shouted. "Impostor!"

Everything was jumbled in Miguel's head, the past and the present, up to that point carefully kept separate.

"What is this all about?" he cried. "What do you mean, you're not my mother? Is it true, Mama? You're not my mother? Damn it, answer me!"

But the old woman sat on her invalid's chair, chewing something and fixing her predatory gaze on an imaginary prey. Disconcerted, Miguel shook his head.

"All right, that's enough," a voice behind them growled.

A giant with a heavily-veined skull burst into the room, followed by two fairly unpalatable men, a stocky, dark-skinned man with a thick neck, pot-bellied but solid as a rock underneath a shabby suit, and a kind of old lady-killer with slicked-back hair and the haughty look of someone who ultimately has nothing to say. Miguel backed up to the ironing table: the three men had hidden in the shop, the metal shutter was down, and their scruffy appearance was almost scary.

"Who are you?" he asked. "What are you doing here?"

Parise positioned himself in front of the door to the storeroom, cutting off any route of escape.

"Didn't your mother tell you anything?" he asked, a threatening gleam in his eyes.

"Tell me what?" he quavered.

No one was paying attention to Rosa Michellini. In the background, Brother Josef was dripping with sweat.

"Do you have the document?" the bald giant asked.

"What document? I don't understand anything you're saying!" Miguel replied. Parise's inquisitive gaze made him shiver, in spite of himself. "Who . . . who are you?"

Parise turned to El Toro, a cube of muscles with protruding eyes and a skullcap.

"Let's hurry this up."

Miguel gulped when he saw the strange weapon aimed at him. The electric impulse bit him in the shoulder, two harpoons connected to a thread that petrified him. The transvestite hardly had time to cry out: a puppet charged with volts, Miguel looked one last time at his mother's crumpled face before the floor came at him at high speed.

"What . . . "

Parise put the blade of his switchblade to Rosa's flabby neck.

"Shut up, you old bat," he warned her, "or I'll nail you to the wall. Understand?"

The poor old woman was paralyzed with fear, her hands clutching her precious box of cough drops. Her son was lying near the ironing table, writhing with convulsions. El Toro bent down to grab the weakling while El Picador unrolled the tape. Miguel felt the floor tiles against his cheek, the hoarse breathing of the men who were tying him up. He was incapable of moving at all.

"I'll bring the van around," El Picador announced.

"O.K."

Parise knelt in front of the tranny, now bound hand and foot.

"Are you the one who told Ossario?"

"N . . . N . . . "

"It wasn't your mother, so who was it?"

Miguel shook his head helplessly. The giant turned toward the laundress who, from her chair, was looking at him venomously: terror seemed to have shut her up in her world of dead angels and divine furies, unmasked by her lies or unable to hear them. Parise muttered—they had searched the apartment without finding anything.

"I think he doesn't know anything," Brother Josef broke in, indicating the tranny lying on the floor. "He . . . he would have told me."

The walkie-talkie in the team leader's pocket crackled: the coast was clear. He gestured to El Toro, who threw the tied-up "package" over his shoulder—light as a feather, like the Campallo girl and the other tranny they'd taken for him . . . Dropping her box of cough drops, which rolled against the baseboards, Rosa jumped up and down on her chair, as if she'd been struck by lightning.

"What are you doing to my son! Let him go!" She brandished her spiked cane in the direction of the two men. "Let him go, you demons!"

El Toro chortled at her flailing about.

"That's my son!" Rosa spluttered, her chin shiny with saliva. "My son!"

The laundress slashed the air with her cane, almost fell forward off her chair, and returned to the attack with all the energy of despair.

"Almighty God! Almighty God!"

Parise picked up the tranny's scarf that was lying on the floor and went around the wheelchair: in a single movement, he took away the cane that was trying to put his eye out and sent it flying to the other end of the room.

"Almighty God! Almighty . . . "

He grabbed the old woman's scrawny neck and wound the scarf around her throat. Rosa struggled on her chair, quickly suffocating in the killer's grasp. It takes five minutes to strangle someone, much less to break a neck. Parise flexed his muscles and gripped her throat with all his strength: Rosa let out a long death rattle, her eyes popping out of their sockets. The vertebrae broke, sounding like jacks. Her head fell forward, forever inert, on her flowered blouse.

Parise relaxed his grip, his shirt soaked with sweat. It reeked of laundry powder and death in the shop, the others were waiting in the van: it was time to get out of there. The bald man scowled one last time at the tousled mummy on her chair, her tongue hanging out like a pink snake, lumpy saliva running down her chin . . .

The old witch.

*

Jana hadn't slept a wink. She wasn't up to doing anything, not even sculpting: that never happened to her. She had begun polishing the edges of the craters on the cement base, sharpening the steel rods to insert the fabrics in the colors of the native nations into the devastated territories, but the memory of that night shook up her slender certainties. Sculptor: someone who brings to life . . . Rubén had placed his warm hand on the small of her back and almost lifted her off the ground to press her against his sex, and in a dream in which his eyes gave off comets, he had given her the most sensual kiss she'd ever had before leaving her standing there like a dope, in front of the aviator with the unhinged smile. What was he up to? Did he reserve a special electroshock treatment for her or did he do that with every woman? Jana no longer knew what to think. The world had shifted its axis, changed color—anthracite gray, powdered with forget-me-not blue. She'd fallen into the trap. How could she get out? Paula had retired to her "dressing room" shortly before noon, her head whirling after her mad night at the Niceto, and she had immediately noticed that there was something odd about the Mapuche's eyes.

"Hey, girl, you're in love!"

Jana had shrugged.

"Humph."

"Nonsense! Your eyes are shining, my beauty! So, what did he do to you? Did you kiss?"

"Hardly."

"Did you sleep together?" she asked excitedly. "Come on, tell me about it!"

"You know about Fukushima? It was like that, all rotten."

"I don't believe you, you little kamikaze! Ha, ha!" she laughed, waving her arms around in the shed. "You're in love, Jana, that's great!"

And how. She hadn't been able to sleep, and hardly to work, now the floor was covered with tools that cast a menacing eye on her convoluted monsters. Paula had left in the Ford to see her mother, and Jana no longer knew what to do with her feelings. She was making herself a cup of coffee to get rid of the taste of sleepless nights when the sound of an engine resounded in the yard, soon followed by the slamming of a door. Jana looked up, suspiciously—no one ever came there. Someone was walking through the grass to the sliding door, which had been left half-open. Rubén Calderón came into the workshop, but he was far from being the imposing presence he'd been the preceding evening: his beautiful black jacket, his shirt, his short Italian boots, all his clothes were covered with mud.

"Are you competing with me?" Jana asked.

Rubén forgot to smile. His hair was sticky and a long welt ran around his throat—a narrow, red, straight wound where blood was beginning to coagulate.

"What's going on?" Jana said more soberly. "What happened to your neck?"

"Some guys attacked me in Colonia. The ones who killed Luz and María Campallo."

"Who?"

"They just found her body in the wildlife preserve. She'd also been dead for several days, apparently."

Jana was looking at him as if he'd just emerged from the earth.

"I talked to a guy in Colonia," he went on, "Ossario, a former paparazzo who had compromising documents. María Campallo is supposed to be the daughter of *desaparecidos*. Your pal Orlando too. He was exchanged for another infant born in detention, Rodolfo, María's official brother, biologically speaking. In any case, the Campallo family is involved in the theft of babies. Ossario didn't have time to tell me more; he was killed. The killers were waiting for him, at his house. I was barely able to escape."

Jana was still staring at him, overcome—too much information all at once.

"You've got to clean that up," she said, pointing to the terrible wound on his neck.

"I cleaned it on the boat."

"With what, seawater?"

"It'll be okay."

"Doesn't look like it to me."

Rubén pensively lit a cigarette from the packet he'd bought on the ferry.

"What are you planning to do now?" Jana asked.

"Persuade Orlando's parents to testify. They also stole a baby: they can tell what happened at the ESMA, illegal adoption, exchange of babies, and bring down Campallo and the people who are protecting him."

Jana remained doubtful.

"There's something wrong with your story," she said after a moment.

"What?"

"Orlando: he was twenty-five years old when he was killed on the docks."

When he heard that, Rubén stared.

"Right," she sent on. "He was too young to have been adopted during the dictatorship. The guy in Colonia was lying to you."

Rubén recalled Ossario's words regarding the missing brother, his sister's search when she learned of his existence, which led to the docks in La Boca where the transvestite was hanging out. He suddenly paled.

"The laundress's son—how old is he?"

"Thirty-four," Jana replied.

The current age of the children of the *desaparecidos*.

"Shit."

Jana gulped. She was also beginning to understand.

"Orlando Lavalle is not the brother that María was looking for," he breathed. "The killers kidnapped him along with María as they left the tango club, but they took the wrong transvestite."

They'd mixed things up, gotten everything backward:

Miguel was the photographer's brother, not Luz. That's why she had called him the other night, that was what was so important, what she wanted to tell him, before she was murdered. Miguel had been adopted during the dictatorship.

*

Jana was trembling with rage on the seat of the car: Miguel's mother was pure poison. She was the *apropriadora*, and not Orlando's parents, she, with her soldier-husband, had accepted the sordid deal offered by the rich Campallo family. Whether or not Rosa Michellini had a choice left her cold: her husband having died in combat, the perverse woman had taken her revenge on their adopted son, as if she held him responsible for her misfortunes—the disappearance of the hero-accomplice, Miguel's sexual orientation, the state of her health. The other way around, everything became comprehensible. That was why the disoriented boy felt so alone, misunderstood, and scorned: he'd lost his sister, his parents, his identity, the very origin of his life.

Jana had called Paula's cell phone but there was no answer. Avenida 9 de Julio. Rubén was driving; he was worried. On the way they'd said what mattered, and now a heavy silence prevailed in the car. They got there at twilight and drove down Peru Street, which was deserted. The laundry's metal shutter was down.

"There's a rear entrance," Jana said.

Rubén parked the car in a side street, took a Colt .45 out of the glove box, and put it under his jacket.

"Let's go."

The orange cat lounging on the pavement arched his back before suddenly running off. They slipped into the alley and into the little weedy backyard through which the storeroom was reached. Jana was wearing a pair of simple cloth shorts and a black tank top—she hadn't had time to change her clothes. She knocked on the door but received no response. Their eyes met. Rubén grabbed the revolver and pushed open the door to the storeroom. It was completely dark. He gripped his gun in one hand, and with the other held back Jana, who was following him: Rosa Michellini was sitting in her wheelchair, her blue tongue hanging out of her mouth, a scarf still wound around her throat. Rubén crossed the room in an instant and disappeared into the shop, leaving Jana alone for a moment. She turned on the lights and shivered when she saw the old woman with her eyes protruding from their sockets, her crimson face resting on her torso: Miguel's mother was dead. Rubén reappeared.

"Lock the door," he said.

Jana obeyed while he had a look at the other rooms. He soon came back, having found nothing. The apartment was empty. The Mapuche hadn't budged, hypnotized by the body slumped on the wheelchair. An odor of old age hung in the air despite the stale smell of laundry powder.

"The scarf," she said. "It's Paula's, I mean Miguel's." Not long before, it had been around his neck.

Rubén thought for a moment. Was it a clue meant to accuse Miguel of murder, or to throw them off the track?

"Do you think they kidnapped him?"

"If they'd wanted to kill him, we would have found his body," Rubén replied.

He put on latex gloves. Miguel's mother seemed to have shrunk to half her size with her quilt wrapped around her sick hips, her blouse covered with saliva, and her box of cough drops scattered all over the floor. The angle of the neck suggested that it had been broken; the body was lukewarm, indicating that she had died no more than an hour or two before. There were no other traces of wounds, just this face disfigured by strangulation, with little balls of chewed-up paper stuck to the lips and this satiny scarf that belonged to her son. It was growing more humid in the back room. Rubén lifted up the laundress's head, opened her mouth and saw something stuck in her esophagus. A little ball of paper, half chewed-up. He pulled it out with the tips of his fingers.

"What's this?"

"The old woman was crazy," Jana said. "The Rapunzel syndrome."

He grimaced.

"Rosa chewed up her bills, her papers, her hair, anything she got her hands on," she explained. "Miguel was planning to ask a psychiatrist for help, and then . . . "

The sculptress, wavering between anger and nausea, didn't finish her sentence. Rubén wiped the saliva on his jacket and unfolded the little ball of paper he'd taken out of Rosa's throat. The writing was minuscule, typed: he could distinguish numbers that resembled a table, a series of letters . . . Rubén bent down and saw the box of cough drops and its contents, which had rolled against the wall. They weren't candies to suck on but more little balls of paper that Miguel's mother had torn up with maniacal care. The detective picked them up; there were about half a dozen of them. He flattened them out on the ironing table: they contained more numbers, but also names.

"What is it?" murmured Jana, leaning over his shoulder.

"They're not bills, in any case. They look instead like . . . file cards."

The numbers seemed to correspond to schedules. Then Rubén saw a date, September 9, 1976, with a cryptic code alongside it. September 1976. The dictatorship.

"It's an internment form," he said.

Rubén turned toward the body. There were only seven intact pieces of paper. How long would the autopsy on Rosa take, ten, twelve, twenty hours? Too long, in any event. Between now and then her gastric juices would have eaten everything up. He straightened up the corpse on the chair, then took off his jacket and rolled up his shirtsleeves.

"What are you doing?"

"She swallowed the rest of the document," he said, indicating the *apropriadora*. "With a little luck, the acid won't have erased everything yet."

Jana didn't immediately understand what he had in mind. Rubén's eyes had changed, as if he had fallen into himself. Jana stepped back, speechless: he breathed out to relieve the stress, took out the blade of his knife, and cut open the old woman's blouse. Her empty eyes were fixed on the ceiling and her withered flesh appeared in the harsh light of the storeroom.

"If I were you, I'd look the other way," he said.

The Indian woman kept her eyes fixed on him.

Her choice.

Ruben stuck the blade into Rosa Michellini's abdomen and disemboweled her.

13

The moon was climbing over the roofs when they opened the reinforced door of Rubén's office. No one had seen them leave the laundry and go down Peru Street. The detective lived two blocks farther on. Jana had followed him on the unreal sidewalk, her head full of images of dead people, hardly listening to the phone conversation he had with his cop girlfriend on the way: she was thinking about Miguel, about the horrible fate that seemed to have hounded him ever since his birth. It was hot in the apartment, one of those muggy nights typical of a Buenos Aires summer. Rubén threw his stinking jacket on the sofa, drew the drapes, and spread his precious masticated papers on the desk. Most of them were damp, in poor condition. He let them dry in the open air. The soles of his boots squeaked on the marble floor. They were shot, too.

"Do you want a drink?" he asked.

Jana shook her head. She felt like throwing up. Rubén still had that dreadful mark along his neck and the old madwoman's blood on his shirt.

"I'm going to take a shower," he said.

The Mapuche didn't react; she stood there with her arms crossed, her big, dark eyes in freefall. Keep cool, don't think about what they might be doing to Paula at this very moment . . . The pipes moaned behind the tiles in the bathroom. Jana listened to the long moan of the water in the pipes, far, very far, from the sobbing of the wind in the grass.

A mixture of blood, water, and organic materials had spilled out on the quilt when Rubén pulled out the *apropriadora*'s stomach; he had put it down on the ironing table, lukewarm and bloody, as in the courses in forensic medicine, opened the membrane with a disconcerting skill, and using the point of the knife, slit it open lengthwise. The gastric juices had begun to eat away the food, but the balls of paper were still visible among the stale-smelling contents of the stomach. He found seven of them, which he cleaned briefly before taking off with Jana.

The shower finally stopped. A bad dream.

Rubén soon reappeared, barefoot, clad in black pants without a belt and a plum-colored shirt that hugged his shoulder muscles. She felt pathetic in her worn-out shorts, tank top, and old Doc Martens, as if the difference in their ages was to her disadvantage. He filled a glass with cold water from the tap and handed her a pill.

"Take this," he said. "It'll help you hold up."

"What is it?"

"A tranquilizer."

"I don't want to be tranquilized."

"And I don't want to see you in this state . . . Please."

He was looking at her in a friendly way again. Jana swallowed the pill with the glass of water without seeing that he was looking at her lovingly. She was still thinking about Paula, about her spangled dreams that were collapsing, about their sleepless night that turned into a nightmare.

"Do you do this sort of thing often?" she asked, getting a grip on herself.

"What?"

"Disembowel old women."

"No . . . they're not all so crazy."

Some kind of balm glistened on Rubén's neck. He went to the bar to make a pisco sour.

"It would be better for you not to go home," he said while mixing the ingredients. "Stay here tonight . . . afterward we'll see."

A night bus rattled the windows of the office. Rubén filled a glass to the brim, lit a cigarette, and glanced at the bits of paper spread out on the desk. They were almost dry. His hair was dripping on his bruised neck. Poc, poc, a rain of tears over what happened to them.

She came closer.

"What are you doing?"

"A puzzle . . . Anyway, what remains of it."

Parts of the writing had disappeared as a result of the gastric acid, but the density of the balls of paper had preserved a good half of the content.

"How did the old woman get her hands on these papers?" Jana asked.

"Through the intermediary of María Victoria, I suppose. Or Ossario. Unless she had had them ever since the time of the adoption, and tried to destroy them. That's what we're going to find out."

Rubén started reconstituting the document under the art deco lamp, while Jana watched from outside the circle of light. He didn't know when the crazy old woman had begun swallowing these precious papers, or how many pieces were missing: he was weaving his fabric, laboriously, fitting together the bits of paper on the table one by one. The minutes passed. Jana yawned in spite of herself.

"You can sleep in my bedroom if you want," Rubén said. "This is going to take me a while, I think."

The sculptress was dead on her feet. Probably an effect of the pill, accumulated fatigue, or nerves that were relaxing.

"What about Miguel?" she said quietly. "Do you think they're going to make him disappear, too?"

"Like all the witnesses to this business," he replied in a voice that he tried to keep neutral. "You're one of them."

"You too."

"Yes. But I'm not going to let you go like that."

Jana wasn't certain that was reassuring. They hadn't touched each other since their kiss at the base of the aviator, three centuries ago. Absorbed in the puzzle's game of musical chairs, Rubén was no longer paying attention to her. Names soon appeared, places, then the ESMA's coat of arms. An identification form, as he'd expected. The one Ossario had shown María Campallo as a proof of her adoption? How had the former paparazzo obtained such a document? He pursued his task, no longer feeling any fatigue: sleep had fled, the world had disappeared into an abyss that took him back thirty-five years. He rotated the debris, established connections. The apartment was silent, hardly disturbed by the rumble of traffic on the airport superhighway beyond the accursed intersection. Jana had curled up on the couch without even taking off her Doc Martens. Another hour went by before he obtained a coherent result.

It was clear that what he had before him was not one but three pages of a single document: three badly printed photocopies of an identification form created at the ESMA and dating from the summer of 1976.

Rubén worked out an initial scenario on the basis of the evidence at his disposal. Ossario had contacted María Victoria to show her the internment form that condemned her adoptive parents, with the goal of getting her to testify in his "Grand Trial," but the photographer had not followed the paranoiac's instructions: she had tracked down the laundress to whom her biological brother had been given, with a copy of the document as proof. Miguel being away, his mother had kept the copy, probably promising to show it to her son, to confess to him, one on one. María must have doubted what the old madwoman said; pursuing her search by questioning people in the neighborhood, she had been sent to the La Boca docks, where the transvestite son of the laundress had been turning tricks for years. María then happened on Luz, and had taken her away or made a date to meet at the tango club, without knowing that the killers were tailing her. They had been abducted as they came out of the club.

Rubén mulled over the reassembled fragments of the puzzle. There were gaps, names, dates, or places censored by the time it had spent in Rosa's stomach, but it still constituted an organizational chart of the military men involved in the kidnapping and sequestration of María Victoria's parents. The latter's names were legible: Samuel and Gabriella Verón. Eduardo Campallo's name was also on the document: the children had been handed over to him on September 21, 1976. The detective remained for a moment hunched over the lamp on the desk, troubled. Despite its condition, he'd never seen such a precise internment form: names, dates, movements, everything was carefully recorded. It would take him hours to inventory it, index the names of all the guilty parties and their accomplices, and compare them with his files. No, this time he wouldn't be able to handle things by himself. He needed help. Carlos, Anita, the Grandmothers . . .

Old ghosts were roaming around the office when he looked up. Jana had fallen asleep on the red couch in the living room. She was there, hardly six feet away, knocked out by the pill. The curve of her brown legs gleamed in the light of the art deco lamp, a bit of her face, her hair falling over the armrest. Barefoot, he slipped silently to the sofa where she was sleeping off her misery. The Mapuche, curled up like a hunting dog, was holding her arms hugged to her chest, but her sleeping face was that of a child. Muddy tears that had risen from the underworld beaded on her eyelashes. Rubén knelt down beside the little angel and caressed her forehead with the tips of his fingers.

My sweet . . . my sweet little sister . . .

Part Two
THE SAD NOTEBOOK

1

Franco Díaz had tears in his eyes when he saw the majestic ombus rising against the Argentine sky—trees that botany classifies as giant grasses and that are typical of the pampas. The retiree from Colonia hadn't seen them for how long—fifteen years?

A fervent Catholic and a patriot, Franco Díaz was a man with principles—never regret, never betray. For more than thirty years the Argentine army had been his sole mistress—demanding, faithful. A family was fine for civilians. But as he got older, his early retirement guaranteeing him a comfortable pension, Franco had become attached to the idea of growing old with a woman—a sweet and submissive woman, like his mother; to make him happy, she would have only to respect the order of things. Nothing complicated, he thought. He had retired to Colonia del Sacramento, the Uruguayan port opposite Buenos Aires, hoping to find what he was looking for. He'd had to lower his sights. The ancient colonial city receiving primarily tourists or families in shorts with digital cameras, available women in his age bracket were few, under surveillance, or even atheists, so that after a number of episodic or unhappy experiences, Franco Díaz had ended up forgetting the idea of growing old with a woman.

Perhaps he should have thought of it earlier. Perhaps, too, he had see too many ugly things—women must sense that. Franco had no regrets: what had been done had to be done, and above all he had found in flowers the otherness that was lacking in his life in the barracks.

At first, he thought botany would help him fight loneliness and idleness: better than a hobby, in flowers he had found another time. The time of growing . . . Wild irises from the marshes, gleaming gladiolis, haughty roses or azaleas, flowers would be his redemption.

Franco Díaz wanted to die in peace.

The liver cancer that was gnawing at him was spreading. The doctors he'd consulted in Montevideo gave him hardly six months to live. No one knew. Not even his former superiors. The illness developed in successive crises, more and more violent, and soon nothing would be able to hold it back. Franco was alone with Death, his metastases and his Secret, which was killing him perhaps even more than the cancer.

"Speak, and God will help you," his friend and confessor at the time told him.

As the last months of his life fizzled out, Franco Díaz had become a mystic. Sometimes he heard It as a result of prayers and ecstatic appeals, when his reason gave way or when the pain in his guts became too much to bear. The Voice counseled him, omniscient and yet so near, more comforting than the morphine tablets: it was the Voice that had given him the idea of hiding his Secret, of letting time do its work. He had planted a *ceibo*, the Argentine national tree, like a stele, a mausoleum. The world was not yet ready: first, his generation had to pass away. An irony of fate: it was at the moment that Franco Díaz was getting ready to bow out that his past caught up with him.

It had all begun the preceding week, when the retiree had seen unusual things on his street: a gray car and figures prowling around his neighbor's house. The following day, a man had come to ask him questions, a big, husky man with a strong Argentine accent who claimed to be a friend of Ossario's passing through the area. Ossario hadn't opened his shutters for three days, and his car was not there: everything suggested that he had left. The big guy tried to seem friendly, but Franco guessed that he was lying. Ossario never received visits from friends, and his house seemed clearly to be under surveillance. The insurance agent who'd come from Buenos Aires had also lied about his identity. What did all these people have against Ossario? Franco Díaz had sensed danger. Something had filtered through, inevitably, something that concerned him. Blackmail, the extortion of money, putting "revelations" up for bids, the former paparazzo had been capable of anything. Diaz could have looked into it, found out through a traitor or a convert who he was. Familiar with interrogations, Díaz knew that the men who had visited him were professionals, cops or secret agents connected with some office. If the men prowling around his house were sent by his own people, *they would have told him*. Ossario's impromptu return and the attack on the house had accelerated everything.

Unlike the former military men who'd been driven out and put their houses in the Florida neighborhood up for quick sale, Díaz fled, leaving everything behind him: his property, his *posada* on the banks of the river, the precious plants that he'd spent so many years raising and that would fade without him in his secret garden. He crossed the border in his Audi that very evening and slept in Argentina, his beloved country, in a small hotel where he registered under an assumed name. Now he was driving along a tree-shaded road, ill at ease, on the run. "Speak, and God will help you," his confidant repeated. Yes, but speak to whom? Viola, Camps, Galtieri, Bignone—most of the generals involved in the Process were dead. Who else knew? Who had betrayed them? In this treacherous game, whom could he trust?

Of the men from that time, the only one left was his confessor. And the Voice told him to look for him, so long as he had the strength to do so, and to find him before it was too late.

2

It was Thursday: the sun had returned, the sparrows on the Plaza de Mayo were taking a bath in the fountain at the base of the obelisk while waiting for the Grandmothers to arrive.

They were converging toward the assembly point, two by two or in small groups, shuffling along, the eldest holding the arms of their daughters. They greeted Elena Calderón, who was laying out the association's flyers, DVDs, and books under the impassive eyes of a police squad—the infamous elite police. Rubén's mother arranged her *pañuelo*, which the wind was blowing around, and returned the greeting of her companions in misfortune.

Elena Calderón would never have thought she would share the fate of these women.

Elena was a daughter of the old upper middle class of Buenos Aires, a descendent of the oligarchies that had gotten rich at the end of the nineteenth century, when Argentina, having liquidated its native peoples, had opened itself up to international trade. Her grandfather, an officer who had served under General Roca, had received immense lands as his reward and consolidated his fortune by allying himself with other great families that had divided up the country among themselves. His son Felipe had inherited thousands of acres on which the world's best beef cattle grazed, fed Europe as it was rebuilding itself, made substantial profits, and woven networks of influence in the various Argentine political groups, whose waltz of coups d'état was orchestrated by the army, which was still closely connected with the government.

The fall of Juan Perón, who after the death of his wife Evita went about in public with a thirteen-year-old girl, changed nothing. Coddled by her family, Elena had grown up in a middle-class household in La Recoleta where, once her beauty was recognized, she very soon found herself courted by the most eligible suitors in the capital. But unlike her brothers and sisters who sacrificed themselves to the rites of passage of their social class—for girls, parties to celebrate their fifteenth birthdays, balls to the sound of boleros and an exacerbated romanticism—the youngest daughter dreamed of emancipation. While reading in the Querandi, a smoke-filled cafe where the counterculture youth met, Elena had met a young poet and polemicist, Daniel Calderón, whose verbal skill competed with his fiery eyes: the lightning bolt made a direct hit on both of them and they were inseparable from then on.

Two years later, Rubén was born, and then Elsa.

A progressive, like every good Argentine petit-bourgeois or intellectual, Daniel had managed to slip through the nets of the ever-present military censorship. His poems began to be translated abroad and his wife encouraged him to write, sure that the best was still to come. Daniel Calderón had the *duende*, the gift of enchantment. Someday everyone would be like her, dazzled by his personality and his power of expression, this smile that by its luminous peace disarmed everyone—Elena was a woman in love.

And then came the Golpe, on March 24, 1976.

Videla, Massera, Agosti. Because of her social origins, Elena thought she was protected from the generals who, each representing his respective corps, erected themselves as guardians of morality and Christian order: the famous National Reorganization Process. Despite the life she had chosen, Elena represented the old right wing of the country, which sometimes supported Peronism. She was very quickly disillusioned. Foreign creative works were outlawed, publications were put under surveillance, there was an auto-da-fe of books on history and culture in general that were deemed to be too influenced by "Marxism," and the literary landscape dissolved in the widespread terror and self-censorship.

Books on sociology, philosophy, psychology, politics, and even mathematics soon became impossible to find. The review and then Daniel Calderón's books met with the same fate. According to the government, subversives would disguise themselves "as ordinary men-in-the-street," which justified no-holds-barred repression.

Each case of disappearance constituted a universe of its own, an inexpressible totality of pain and an irreversible upheaval for those who remained.

Fear: every Argentine became a potential target, and was concerned first of all to ensure his own security and that of those close to him.

Ignorance: the media did not mention the kidnappings, ratified the official communiqués issued by the police and the military, according to which the ghastly daily discoveries were the result of conflicts with subversives, or even between subversives.

Confusion: hadn't this violence begun before the coup d'état, amid the disorder and corruption of the Peronist regime? Hadn't the guerrillas fought against the preceding military dictatorship, hadn't they refused to play according to the rules of democracy and carried violence to inadmissible extremes?

In Buenos Aires, the repression was terrible, the atmosphere sordid. People avoided greeting each other in the street, speaking to strangers on pain of being accused of conspiring or arrested for having given a light to a passerby. Elena and Daniel temporized. Something had to be done, but what? Who could resist the military? The Church? It was in bed with the military. The political parties? They'd been muzzled. The intellectuals, the journalists? They were in the line of fire.

But they did finally decide to act.

Since the junta controlled the kind of works that could be sent through the mail, Elena had had to move heaven and earth to get her father's friends to help her obtain a visa for Daniel, who had been invited to participate in a lecture series at the Sorbonne on nineteenth-century Argentine poetry. After months of negotiations, the exit visa was finally granted. Daniel Calderón had left for France in early 1978 with his manuscripts hidden in the lining of his suitcase—a publisher in Paris had agreed to bring out his most recent collections of poems under a pseudonym, whereas Daniel would establish contacts with the groups opposing the dictatorship, most of them composed of political refugees who were trying to alert defenders of human rights to the reality of the country as the Mundial approached. France, the country that took in the Argentine exiles: Daniel had convinced Simone Signoret to become their spokesperson in the media—the actress had shown great generosity and paid for the banners and flyers out of her own pocket—and Danielle Mitterand to use her influence in political circles, whose secrets she knew, as a former member of the French Resistance.

Daniel Calderón was giving his lectures in Paris when he learned of the abduction of his children on their way to school.

Had someone betrayed him? Where, in Argentina or in France? In any case, he had to find them before they disappeared forever, sucked into the machinery of the state. He immediately returned to Buenos Aires, despite his wife's fears, and was picked up by the agents of the SIDE before he even got out of the airport.

"Operation Return," as the military called it, was a tactic consisting of setting a trap for exiles by infiltrating their associations abroad. Had the visa for France been granted with this end in mind? Elena Calderón had gone to great lengths to track down her family, had called upon people she thought were close to her, without result: "Your husband ran away," they had dared to tell her. She had turned to Daniel's supporters in France. The affair had been brought before the highest authorities, but if the country of the Rights of Man condemned Videla's coup d'état, behind the scenes things were more complicated: the French intelligence service had been informed of the issuing of false papers for agents of the junta assigned to track down dissidents on French soil, but Poniatowski, the Minister of the Interior, had taken no steps to arrest them. Former members of the French Secret Army Organization were still found in the secret services, in France and in Argentina, where some secret agents returning from Algeria had become instructors in no-holds-barred interrogation. And it was not just the Secret Army Organization: from 1957 to 1983, regular army staff members and officers gave classes in Paris, via the "French mission," training future torturers for war against insurrections and for the use of psychological terror in bringing the people into line. Were they playing a double game? Elena Calderón had met with the French ambassador in Buenos Aires, an affable and cultivated man who had proven more interested in improving his passing shot than in demanding information regarding the disappearance of a poet on his return from Paris.

Like other women and mothers of the *desaparecidos*, Elena had had to resign herself to the arbitrariness: the military men struck when and where they wanted, sarcastically throwing *habeas corpus* requests back in the faces of the humiliated plaintiffs.

Every day, there were dozens of these women in front of every police station in the neighborhood, asking for news of their loved ones; Elena Calderón joined these women eaten away by anxiety, most of them workers' wives whose children had been kidnapped by police forces operating without badges or identities. Through her contact with them, Elena discovered with alarm the condition of her compatriots, some of whom were going out alone for the first time in their lives. Reduced to housekeeping and childcare, these women knew nothing. Politics did not concern them—at least they had ended up believing that—and any notion of rights was foreign to them. Few read, or if they did, they picked up by chance *La Nación*, which spoke for the Process. Women who above all did not understand what was happening: "they" must have made a mistake . . .

For hours, these mothers remained prostrate, powerless, sleepless in a pit of despair. The authorities laughed in their faces: "You son must have run away with a chick!" "Another case of terrorists settling accounts among themselves." The most fortunate of them received a coffin containing the body of their son or husband, with armed soldiers present to forbid them to open it—then they would have seen the marks of torture, or that there was no body in the coffin.

The women decided to join the resistance.

There were only fourteen of them when they first gathered around the obelisk on the Plaza de Mayo, on April 30, 1977. There was no square in Argentina that was kept under closer surveillance: the Plaza de Mayo was the center of military power, the symbolic site of the country's political memory, situated between the Cabildo, the seat of the former Spanish colonial government, and the Casa Rosada, through which had passed all the heads of state since the eviction of the last viceroy of Spain in 1810 and the proclamation of the Republic.

The women had assembled in front of the obelisk, wearing a cloth diaper—the *pañuelo*—on their heads like a scarf, as a symbol of their stolen children. Openly defying the government, the Mothers insisted that their loved ones must "reappear alive," rejecting mourning on that principle: the children had been alive when they were taken away, and as long as the torturers had not admitted their crimes, these *desaparecidos* would remain alive. The police had quickly threatened them, and then ordered them to disperse, but the Mothers, locking arms, had started circling the square, clockwise and counter-clockwise, in an ultimate act of defiance. "Madwomen" had mocked the government's power.

But they came back. Every Thursday.

Dogs had been unleashed on them, mounted police had charged them, mass arrests were made: after they were dispersed, the Mothers of the Plaza de Mayo returned every time, re-formed their ranks, which were soon increased by their sisters, daughters, and friends. They began making files on their aggressors, questioning the rare detainees who had been freed, and gathering a quantity of information for which they paid a high price: abandoned by the high clergy of the Church, infiltrated and then betrayed by Astiz (a military man so ferocious that his colleagues had given him the ironic nickname of "the blond angel"), overwhelmed by the abduction and disappearance of three founding Mothers and the two French nuns who supported them, the women continued to demand justice as they circled, every Thursday, in front of the Casa Rosada.

The fall of the dictatorship did not long calm their ardor. To the laws of "national pacification" issued by the military, Alfonsin, the new president elected by universal suffrage, had at first responded by abrogating the amnesty, with the result that the leading generals were indicted and half the officers were forced into early retirement, while at the same time he condemned the violent acts committed by the revolutionary army of the people and the Montoneros, whose leader was arrested. A theory of "the two demons" that proved fatal: the army threatening to call out the soldiers in the barracks, Alfonsin retreated and announced that trials for human rights violations would be held in military courts, abrogating the "duty to obey" clause and thus de facto disinculpating the perpetrators, except in the case of "proven atrocities."

A commission on the *desaparecidos*, the CONADEP, was set up, but its role was more to provide a death certificate for the persons abducted than to prosecute the guilty. The "Full Stop" law [11] soon gave plaintiffs no more than sixty days to indict accused members of the armed forces before Menem drove the point home by decreeing the *indulto*, a pardon. After fifteen years of legal proceedings, Videla, Galtieri, Viola, and Massera, the leading generals, got off with a few years in detention in comfortable prisons, while the pillagers, the torturers and their accomplices, everyone who had not attained the rank of colonel, was acquitted.

An insult to the Mothers and Grandmothers of the Plaza de Mayo, who became more than ever unbending. No exhumations of bones without investigating or judging the guilty, no posthumous homage or indemnities to clear the slate, no reconciliation with the Church.

Iglesia! Bassura!
Vos sos la dictatura![12]

The Grandmothers would fight on to their last breath, not in a spirit of vengeance, but without pardoning, without forgetting. "They may have succeeded in killing our husbands and children, but they have not killed our love," they repeated.

More than thirty years had gone by, and Elena Calderón was no longer the haughty, distinguished woman who handed out daiquiris to the Chilean refugees passing through her home, but her determination was as young as ever.

A furious wind was blowing over the Plaza de Mayo. Elena was preparing the display table where she would distribute the

[11] Law No. 23492: dictates the end of investigation and prosecution against people accused of political violence during the dictatorship.

[12] "Church! Garbage! You're the dictatorship!"

association's latest information bulletins when her son appeared among the tourists in shorts suffering from the humidity. Rubén was wearing a pseudo-casual plum-colored shirt and impeccably cut black trousers, his walk was supple, alert, as if something in him wasn't aging, either. Elena smiled at her partiality: she now had only her son, who reminded her so much of Daniel.

"Hi, Mama."

"Hello, honey!"

Rubén hugged his mother, smelled her light perfume and felt her heart beating against his with a special emotion.

"You look tired," she said, smiling as she looked at him.

"It could have been worse."

Then Elena saw the terrible red welt around his neck, the bloody scab covered with a healing cream, and her beautiful blue eyes dimmed.

"What's going on?"

"A body was found last night, washed up on a bank at the ecological preserve. The body of María Victoria Campallo, the daughter of Eduardo Campallo, a friend of the mayor. María had discovered that she was a child of *desaparecidos*. At least that seems plausible. And she was murdered before she talked."

Elena forgot her son's wounded neck, her information bulletins, her *pañuelo*.

"My God!"

"Yes. I also found a document, an ESMA internment form that traces the sequestration of María's biological parents and the birth in detention of her brother. Eduardo Campallo is named as the *apropriador*."

Rubén cast a hostile glance at the rows of overequipped cops keeping the square under surveillance. His mother was digesting the information, surprised and dismayed.

"The poor little thing," the old lady said.

"Uh-huh. Especially since María was pregnant when she was kidnapped."

"Ooh . . . But why didn't she come see us? We would have helped her! Why contact *Página*?"

"She wasn't going to call *Clarín*."

The editor of the center-right newspaper was herself suspected of being an *apropriadora*. Elena conceded the point, still under the shock of the revelation. The affair reeked of sulfur and her son's general tendency to stir up hornets' nests. All this didn't tell her anything worthwhile.

"I don't know how far Campallo is involved," Rubén continued, "and even if the papers I found accuse him, María remains his daughter. The whole thing is getting complicated. I need you to decipher the document and track down the murdered parents. I have their name, but they don't appear in our files."

The wrinkles on his mother's face deepened. Elena no longer had the energy she'd had at the time of the first demonstrations, the first trials (when she thought about it—thirty years!—the bitterness of the fighting made her dizzy), her legs had grown heavier, her dresses hung loosely on a body that had become virgin again, but her thirst for truth and justice was still intact. She squinted in the direction of the square and the Grandmothers, who were closing ranks behind their banners: the vice president of the Grandmothers was beckoning to her from the obelisk, where the female warriors were about to begin their Thursday rounds, wearing a baby diaper instead of a helmet. Elena put a stone on the tracts being ruffled by the wind.

"I'll tell Susana and be right back," she said to her son.

*

At the age of seventy-six, Susana Arguan wore springlike polka-dot dresses on a body that was still lively (she was the only one who wore her *pañuelo* like Marilyn Monroe) and wielded irony with the false levity of a bitter despair. The daughter of a communist worker, Susana had lost everything when her daughter was kidnapped at dawn, along with her little boy, one day in April 1977. A portrait of her looking like a damned angel hung in a place of honor near her desk, a darling in black and white as intact as her faith in their quest.

Elena Calderón, known as "the Duchess," wondered whether this little old woman was a force of nature or a congenital worker like a red ant: a friend, that was sure.

Specializing in searching for children who had disappeared during the dictatorship, the *Abuelas* learned of their existence through letters, anonymous appeals, or when victims tormented by doubts presented themselves at the association's office in Virrey Cevallos Street. This office, more a town house than a bureau of investigation, was where the *Abuelas* had established their headquarters, a veritable war machine directed against the state's lies. A secretariat, accounting office, press bureau, a reception desk for people who showed up spontaneously, with a psychological team, an investigative bureau and another for attorneys who came on Fridays to offer their advice, a kitchen, and the head office near the entrance, shared by the president and the vice president: the headquarters accommodated forty persons working permanently or episodically for the *Abuelas*. Here they received witnesses, supporters, journalists, and schoolchildren, wrote to judges, and harassed politicians, military men, and retired policemen. Like the Mothers of the Plaza de Mayo with whom they worked hand in hand, the *Abuelas* had experienced everything: intimidation, sacking, and disappearances of important files or computers. Their time was limited, and that made each victory all the more precious.

They were getting ready for the celebration of the one hundred and sixtieth baby reunited with its true family when the association's vice president arrived at the headquarters with Elena Calderón and her detective son in tow.

On the way, Rubén had told them what he knew: Ossario's revelations before he died, the killers in Colonia waiting in front of the house, Miguel's abduction, and the copy of the document held by Miguel's mother, her death by strangulation, the call he made to Anita to ask her to pick up the corpse, the transvestite's hair that he had taken that morning from a wig in her "dressing room," and deposited at the Center for Forensic Medicine, and then his visit to the Duran hospital, where the *desaparecidos*' DNA was stored. If María Victoria had doubts regarding her origins, the only way to track down her biological parents consisted of asking for DNA tests, which would amount to launching legal proceedings against Eduardo and Isabel Campallo. And that she had not done.

"She probably didn't have time," he said.

"Yes, but if Miguel's DNA matches that of María Victoria, that would prove that the Campallos stole the children!"

"They'll never agree to have the tests unless an official complaint forces them to."

"What about her so-called brother, Rodolfo?"

"His big ass is sitting on a pile of gold; he won't budge."

"Great attitude," Susana commented. "All right, let's get started."

The office was minuscule. They sat down without even taking time to drink a cup of tea. The Grandmothers adjusted their glasses while Rubén spread out his fragments: three sheets like jigsaw puzzles, made of torn up paper that was sometimes illegible, and that the detective had Scotch-taped together. Several pieces were missing in the triptych, but the whole left the Grandmothers speechless.

Identified by numbers, each detainee imprisoned in the clandestine centers had a "strictly confidential and secret" file. Indicating identity, background, activity, level of dangerousness, this file was known only to the interrogating officers. That was the kind of document the Grandmothers had before their eyes. The writing was small, typed, and the photocopy was poor in quality, but it was possible to decipher the different places where the *desaparecidos* had been transferred, the names of some of the interrogators, the date and time of the torture sessions, the prisoners' condition afterward—"normal" or dead . . . A document of a very administrative precision that elicited vengeful growls from the old women: Samuel and Gabriella Verón had been kidnapped on August 13, 1976, and taken to the Navy Engineering School along with their little girl, aged one and a half. At that time, Gabriella Verón was eight months pregnant. They had not tortured her, but they had tortured her husband, every day. The girl who was to be renamed María Victoria had been taken away and put with other children of the *desaparecidos* while waiting to be adopted by people close to the government. On September 19, Gabriella had given birth to a boy in the clandestine maternity ward at the ESMA (the name of the military doctor involved had been eaten away). Since the infant suffered from a cardiac insufficiency, his appointed *apropriadores*, the Campallo family, had exchanged him for another baby born to *desaparecidos* ten days earlier, "Rodolfo," who was then in the possession of Javier Michellini, a noncommissioned naval officer, and his wife Rosa.

The Grandmothers' hearts beat faster. The identity of the child-stealers was not the only information on these forms: they also contained the names of the torturers, their accomplices, the places, the dates . . . An exceptional document, of which they had only a partial copy.

Susana was the first to react.

"The paparazzo," she said. "He's the one who had the original?"

"*Had.* Yes, probably."

"You think the killers took it back?"

"Maybe." Rubén rummaged in the pockets of his coat while the Grandmothers were considering. "Can I smoke if I open the window, Miss Marple?"

"Sure," the old communist replied. "When I'm canonized a saint."

"What a stubborn person you are."

"I still don't have cancer. Great, huh?"

"What are you planning to do with this document, Rubén," his mother said, returning to the subject at hand. "Attack the Campallo family?"

"We have only a half-legible copy of a thirty-five-year-old internment form," he said, frowning. "In its current state, Campallo's lawyers would dispute the authenticity of the document, three pieced-together sheets of paper that could just as well have been falsified. No, you'll have to track down the parents, Samuel and Gabriella Verón, members of their family, and find out why they've kept silent. Witnesses may still be alive, people who are in hiding, who are afraid or who no longer want to remember . . . "

The Grandmothers discussed the matter as they looked at the puzzle. About one fourth of the words had disappeared, but they could reconstitute an organizational chart of the military men and their accomplices who were involved in the couple's sequestration and the theft of the children, establish correspondences, and work their way back to the *desaparecidos'* families.

"Yes," Susana said, her mind elsewhere. "Yes, we'll take care of that."

"I've given a copy of the document to Carlos," Rubén told them. "He will look into the connections between Campallo and high-ranking officials at the time who could have gotten him the babies. He will contact you."

"Fine."

The air was heavy in the *Abuelas'* office. Rubén looked at the black and white portrait on the wall, a young woman hardly twenty years old whom he had not known: why did she have such a sweet smile? Why, on seeing her, did he want to *love* her? Because of what they had done to her? Elena plumbed her son's feverish look, which was not due simply to his lack of nicotine.

"What will you do?" she asked him.

"I'll look for the bodies of the biological parents," he said, coming out of his meditations. "If I find them, their DNA will prove their connection with María and Miguel, with or without the Campallo family's agreement. I also have to find a safe place for a witness, a friend of Miguel's at whose place he kept his tranny gear. She was with me at the laundress's when we discovered her body."

"A witness? Where is she?"

"Locked up at my office."

"That's not very prudent," Susana observed. "By this time, the killers in Colonia might have found out who you are."

"Precisely," he warned them, "be on your guard: the name of the person who ordered the abductions and murders must be on the form."

Rubén wasn't telling them everything, Elena felt, just as he had never talked about his months of incarceration at the ESMA, not even to Carlos (she had asked him about it one night when she was feeling bold), who was certainly his closest friend. What was keeping her son going could kill him—did he know that? When they released him, Elena had asked if he had heard anything about the fate of Elsa and Daniel: Rubén had replied in the negative. They had probably been sent to different clandestine camps. The problem was that he had repressed the subject rather than worry about it as she did. Everything that had to do with his detention was taboo. Torture had made him very resistant. She couldn't talk to him about women, children, and grandchildren, all the things a mother hopes for from her son. That didn't prevent her from knowing him right down to his fingertips.

"Don't worry about us, if that's what's bothering you," she said, looking him in the face. "You're the one who's in danger, Rubén. You and your witness."

3

Rubén knew the risks he was taking. When he came to office in 2003, Néstor Kirchner had abolished the amnesty laws, not hesitating to dismiss fifty-four generals and admirals, take down the portraits of the oppressors in the barracks, and transform the ESMA into a Memorial Center. But during the very first trials, a carpenter who had been tortured and was an essential witness for the prosecution had disappeared without a trace. Subsequently, other persons who were implicated in these crimes or who were prepared to testify died under suspicious circumstances—bullets in the head, cyanide poisoning—or simply vanished.

Thirty officers convicted of crimes committed under the dictatorship were thus freed because the period set by the statute of limitations had run out. In 2008, of eight hundred cases brought since the cancellation of the amnesty, only twelve had gone all the way to sentencing, with thirty-six convictions pending.

"They're eliminating everyone," the president of the *Abuelas* had complained.

Christina Kirchner had been following her dead husband's policies, and the rate of indictments had increased since 2010 and the ESMA trial. Eight hundred new indictments and almost three hundred sentencings, and even if that represented hardly two accused per clandestine detention center, the former oppressors were being prosecuted and the number of suspicious deaths among the witnesses were legion, scandalous crimes whose perpetrators were never found. Although some judges and ministers seemed to be acting in good faith, the law of silence usually reigned among the investigators: there were suspicions about the networks of interests and protection that were said to have survived the collapse of the dictatorship, but nobody dared to utter the names of those who were trying to cover their tracks. The Grandmothers had demanded the dismissal of passive judges and the extension of preventive detentions, but the pressures were still enormous. Was the abduction of María Campallo connected with one of the cases currently being investigated?

Rubén had spent part of the night entering into his files the names and places that appeared on the internment form. He deposited one copy in a locker and another with Carlos, and left the puzzle with the Grandmothers. He did not understand how a paranoiac like Ossario could have procured such a document, but if he had had the original, it had disappeared along with him. Someone had involuntarily betrayed him: María Victoria. The kidnappers must have made her talk, and followed the trail back to Ossario, whom they were waiting for when he returned to Colonia. But María—who had betrayed her? The laundress, with whom María had been imprudent enough to leave a copy of the document? Was Rosa Michellini demented to the point of handing her own child over to the oppressors? In any case, the killers had had some lead time. A double kidnapping in the middle of Buenos Aires, the transvestite thrown into the harbor to make the murder look like a sex crime, Ossario's house put under surveillance, the attack, the almost simultaneous murder of Rosa and the abduction of her son—operations on that scale couldn't be improvised: logistics were involved, vehicles and weapons that couldn't be traced, a hideout where interrogations could be carried out, trained men, complicities, all advantages Rubén didn't have.

He spent an hour in a shop in Florida, long enough to pick

up two cell phones with prepaid cards, and another hour organizing his retreat before he took off for San Telmo.

Anita Barragan was waiting for him in a store in Peru Street that specialized in art books, not far from the police station: no cop ever went in there.

At the back of the store, Oscar, the bookseller, had set up two wicker and leather chairs with worn armrests where people could read while drinking *maté*. Anita wasn't a great reader but she liked the peace and quiet of the place, looking at the customers and drinking the bitter beverage that was served there, as much as you wanted. More nervous than usual, she glanced at her watch—something she'd got in some promotional deal; she didn't care about watches or jewelry in general. Thanks to Rubén, she had found two corpses in less than twenty-four hours; the guys in charge of the crime unit limited her to a token role, but she was determined to show them that they were wrong, all down the line.

Rubén arrived on time for their rendezvous, which had been set a little earlier, greeted the shop owner, who had a salt-and-pepper mustache, and spotted the blonde sitting in the reading area. Anita was wearing her policewoman's uniform, her hair let down from her regulation bun, hiding as much of the down covering her cheeks as possible—an *eau de* bearded woman according to her complex no. 12.

"You don't look so good, you heartbreaker," she observed.

Her black cotton jacket with seams overstitched in blue was in harmony with her eyes; the rest seemed very tense.

"I must be getting old," he conceded, collapsing in the chair put there for that purpose.

"Impossible," his childhood friend said. "You're immortal, like David Bowie."

Rubén shook his head: he was brown-haired, a dyed-in-the-wool Porteño, trained for combat, and he spoke English with a Mexican coyote accent. Then she saw the red line that ran across his neck, repressed a shiver—those guys in Colonia, no doubt.

"Nice collar," she commented. "Is it decorative?"

"Yeah, I brought it back from Uruguay. There were also things made of seashells, but you would have found those a little too gay." Rubén glanced over the rows of books and saw the last customers chatting with Oscar at the cash register. "Do you have any news?"

"Yes. Ossario's house burned down after you were there yesterday. A body was found in the ruins, that of a man who seemed to correspond to the description of the renter. I don't have any further information for the moment, neither suspects nor possible witnesses."

"There was one, however," Rubén objected. "Díaz, the neighbor I questioned before the attack. I tried to fool him but he knew that I'm an Argentine: Immigration would have no trouble finding me on the passenger list."

"I can call a couple of colleagues to get some tips. But if I were you, I'd try to disappear for a while. I'd tell you to come to my place," the blonde added, "but I have only one bed."

"I'll figure something out, *querida*," he said, replying to her oblique smile.

Rubén had called her the preceding evening as he left the laundry. Anita had had to make up a story about clothes she had to drop off at the dry cleaners on her way to work, and a metal shutter that was pulled down earlier than usual that led her to worry about the old invalid's state of health and to find the scene of the crime—which was moreover not very palatable.

"The murder in Peru Street—what happened with that?" Rubén asked.

"It's not the discovery of the corpse that's the problem," Anita replied, "but who will conduct the investigation."

"Did Ledesma take you off the case?"

"I fiddled my report, but the Old Man needs to restore his

image: he's the one heading up the investigation. I'm still involved, as an auxiliary, as usual. For the moment, we're trying to contact her son Miguel: that's to say that they are not about to find the murderer," she added with acid irony.

Anita inhaled her *maté* while he mulled things over. The "Old Man" Ledesma wasn't the worst of cops, but Rubén couldn't have them on his back.

"Has María Victoria's body been identified?"

"Yes," Anita replied. "Her father came last night to identify the corpse. It's not yet officially a murder, but an investigation has been started. The forensic team is handling it, of course."

"Luque?"

"Roncero," she said. "Same difference."

The head of the police force's elite homicide squad.

"You saw María's body on the beach," Rubén said. "Was there anything indicating that she been physically abused?"

"The top of her skull had been taken off, what would you call that?"

"Any clear signs of torture?"

"I didn't see anything like that. Hard to tell, given her condition." Anita shuddered as she recalled the sight of the corpse washed up among the shellfish and whelks. "We'll know more after the autopsy. Muñoz is doing it."

The head physician at the Institute of Forensic Medicine, a bootlicker who followed Luque's orders. They were going in circles.

"You're well-informed for a patrol officer," Rubén complimented her. "Who's your source?"

"Guillermo, the intern at the morgue. He's a pal of mine."

Anita smiled, pleased with herself.

"Well done, Barbarella."

"I couldn't say the same about your visit to Colonia," she said, slightly annoyed. "The Uruguayan police will soon be on your case, and the Buenos Aires police will love grilling you about it. Luque will kill the first person who trespasses on his territory and Ledesma has politely asked me to do my nails while he carries out the Peru Street investigation. How do you plan to get out of this? Feet first?"

"That's not a very nice thing to say to me."

"I'm kidding. The only solution is to go tell the Old Man everything."

"And put myself under police protection?" he said, cynically. "No, we need proof. When is María's funeral?"

"Tomorrow evening."

"Already?"

"You haven't seen the body," Anita said, looking distressed. "And then Campallo must be eager to bury his daughter before the press gets hold of the tragedy."

There was a muffled silence at the back of the bookstore. The last customers having left, Oscar was counting out his cashbox. Sunk in the old chair, Rubén was thinking hard.

"I have to see María Victoria's body," he finally said.

"Impossible," Anita replied. "The forensic team comes in right after the autopsy to prepare the remains."

"I also need a copy of Muñoz's autopsy: X-rays, requests for analyses, photos of the body, anything you can find."

"Huh?"

"Work it out with your intern friend, *querida*."

Anita would have liked to hear a touch of jealousy in his voice, but Rubén was smiling just as he had on the day he'd bought her a strawberry ice cream.

*

For hours, Jana had been waiting impatiently in her ivory tower, ruminating on the same fears. She had surfed the net, but the press was not talking about corpses, Miguel's abduction, or the murder of the laundress. Was it too early? The

Mapuche paced like a wild animal in its cage. Impossible to read, to find a television set, to concentrate on anything at all. She had listened to music, thinking that would calm her down: Godspeed You, Barn Owl, Marc Sens—Rubén's CD collection was full of instrumental music ranging from the tragic to the sinister, by way of light and electronic destructured. Did it reflect his soul? They had hardly seen each other this morning: she had awakened just as he was leaving, obviously not having slept that night, and asking her to stay there, securely locked in, until he came back. The sun was going down over the rooftops of Peru Street when Jana heard the clicking of keys in the lock.

Rubén, finally, his face not exactly fresh.

"Sorry to be late," he said.

"My hair has grown longer, would you like to see it?"

The detective gave a hint of a smile and put down the canvas bag he'd brought that morning from Jana's workshop.

"I took what happened to be in your closet," he said. "I hope it'll do."

"It'll do. Do you have any news?"

"Not yet, but I informed the Grandmothers and my friend Anita the cop. We'll know more soon. In the meantime I found a place where we can hide out," he said without taking off his jacket. "It'll take a few days. Afterward you can go home."

"I don't give a damn about that," Jana replied, eager to do something. "What I care about is finding Miguel."

"So do I, you know. Listen, the killers saw me in Colonia, and they may have already identified me. For the moment, the most urgent thing is to get out of here."

"O.K. Where?"

"To a guy's place. I'll explain on the way there."

She pulled a face but agreed. Rubén took along the portable computer in his office while Jana dug around in her things. He let the young woman change clothes and went down the hall.

The air was humid behind the bedroom curtains; Rubén pulled out the old, tattered leather bag underneath the chest of drawers and stuffed the computer, a pair of shoes, and a few clothes hanging in the closet into it. The Sad Notebook was there, on the shelf, alongside the dresses that Elsa would never wear again, the poppy-red one and the others. He hesitated a moment. Was it the fear that the killers would break in here, that they would come across this relic, an intuition that was a priori irrational? Rubén was burying the school notebook in the bag when a creak in the floor made him jump. Jana was standing in the doorway. She was no longer wearing shorts but instead the black jumpsuit she'd had on the other night and a military jacket that was chic in a radically Joe Strummer kind of way. On the floor, she saw a brown leather traveling bag that had to date from the time of Simon Bolívar, and the consternation on Rubén's face, as if he'd been caught doing something he shouldn't.

"What's wrong?"

"Nothing . . . Nothing."

There was a tremble in his voice.

"You're all pale," she said.

"I'm just tired, that's all."

A thin layer of sweat was forming on his forehead. Rubén slipped the rug out from under the chest of drawers.

"Have you ever shot a gun?" he asked, looking up.

"My brothers had rifles," Jana said in answer.

"This won't be a matter of shooting toy balloons."

"We went hunting in the forest. I was the best shot, for your information. Why, are you planning on shooting people?"

"I hope not."

The hiding place was underneath the old chest of drawers, a false plank that followed the lines of the wooden floor. That was where Rubén kept unregistered weapons of several calibers, cash extorted from former oppressors, a rifle and its sights, a defensive grenade, and handcuffs. Intrigued, Jana bent over the hiding place. He took out the Colt .45, two boxes of bullets, a telescoping billy club, a fighting knife, and half the bundle of cash. For her, he selected a .38 caliber revolver that would not jam. Afterward, he put the chest back in place.

"Are you ready?"

"I've been waiting for you all day."

Rubén made the rounds of the room three times without seeing anything suspect. He picked up the bag, which had belonged to his father.

"Let's go while the coast is clear."

*

A Colombian dance standard was playing on the corner, being pumped out the open windows of an overloaded VW Polo: kids who were going to a party. Rubén beeped open the door of his car and followed the sculptress down the sidewalk.

It hadn't been hard to convince Jo Prat to provide them with a hideout. María Victoria was carrying his child, she had been murdered—a daughter of *desaparecidos*—and his own aunt Noemi had been kidnapped during the Process, and so had cousins he'd never seen except in photos and that the old people were still weeping for, people who hadn't mourned, without bodies, devastated by this absence that was more cruel than death itself. Gurruchaga 3180: the stairway on the left led to the upper floor, there was no other. Rubén waited a moment before ringing the bell at the apartment—they could hear music behind the reinforced door—Hint-Ez3kiel, post-rock with devastating riffs. The singer promptly opened the door. He too seemed to have emerged from a tomb.

"Well, well," he said, seeing the couple on the landing.

Calderón was accompanied by a young, slender brunette in an urban guerrilla outfit, as flat as a flounder under her black tank top—a Mapuche, to judge by her facial features, completely ravishing.

"Jo," he said, introducing himself with a jowly smile.

"Jana."

He shook the Indian's hand, invited her to leave her bag in the vestibule, and turned down the sound. Rubén closed the door behind them while she looked around the musician's loft—a living area with a high ceiling and a brick bar in the middle, a stairway of glass and steel with a fishing line as a guardrail, art photos on the walls, musical instruments, a couch and Japanese furniture, farther on a collage by Dao Anh Viet.

"Nice place," Jana said.

The rocker seemed a little cheesy with his made-up eyes and leather pants, but all in all still attractive despite his rolls of fat.

"Would you like something?" he asked with a thoughtfulness Rubén had never seen him display before.

Jo preferred women to men.

"I don't know," she said pointedly, "to see the Piazza Navona in Rome, especially Borromini's fountain, with his muse wringing a swan's neck. Do you know baroque art?"

"I'd love to learn about it. Nothing more, shall we say, accessible?"

"Do you have the means to blow up the banks and oil companies?"

"Not at hand," he conceded. "But I can make a song about it for peace in the world, if you want."

She raised her eyebrows.

"Do you believe in that sort of thing?"

"You'll see, when you get older it's consoling."

A big white cat was observing the intruders from the glass stairway, its eyes two golden balls on full alert.

"You don't have anything against old tomcats, I hope?"

"Not so long as they shit in their litter boxes," she replied, peering at the animal. "What's his name?"

"Ledzep. Of course, he's no longer young, but after the first twenty-four hours he'll be eating out of your hand."

"You don't have bowls?"

The musician smiled before turning to Calderón.

"There's a couch upstairs, you can just sleep there," he informed him, before pointing to the hall that led to the right. I've set you up in my bedroom," he told Jana. "There's an adjacent shower and a Jacuzzi upstairs, if you want to take a bath: the view is very nice if you like blue sky."

"We're putting you out," Jana interjected, not used to being hit on.

"I'm used to living in a hotel," Jo assured her.

"A stroke of luck."

"To see you again?"

"You mean see me alive?"

Rubén let them fence, and shooing Ledzep, who had taken refuge on the steps, went up the stairway with his baggage. The upstairs room had a sloping roof, with a low wooden table on casters, a sofa bed covered in white fabric, a bathroom with mosaics, and a large bay window that gave on the terrace: a sail was spread over a teak table surrounded by flourishing plants. He put his bag down on the sofa bed and reevaluated the places he'd inspected that afternoon. A barbecue for making *asado*, an outside shower and a bamboo screen that separated it from the neighbors, whose terrace could be seen down below. The front door to the loft was reinforced and, except for Carlos and Anita, no one knew that Prat had hired him to find María Campallo. The evening breeze reminded him that he hadn't slept three hours in the past two days. He sorted his things on the couch without seeing the cat hiding underneath them, put the computer on the table and plugged it in, heard the front door slam, and repressed a series of yawns before the digital icons appeared in their places.

Bare feet soon came up the stairs: Rubén paid hardly any

attention to her, absorbed as he was by the blue reflection of liquid crystals. Jana looked over his shoulder, an immaculate towel in her hand.

"I'm going to take a bath."

"O.K."

But he wasn't listening. Jana disappeared toward the Jacuzzi, while data flowed over the computer screen. Eaten away by gastric acid, illegible or missing, several of the oppressors' names had been irretrievably lost—the chaplain on duty if there was one, the obstetrician, some of the interrogators. Among the usable names, Rubén had listed Victor Heintze, Pedro Menez, and Manuel Camponi, the successive guards in charge of the parents who disappeared. The first two appeared in his files (rubric "deceased"), while the third had gone into exile in Italy in the mid-1980s. The principal actors in the fate of the Veróns remained.

According to the copy of the document, Samuel, the biological father of Miguel and María Victoria, was tortured every day until his wife Gabriella gave birth on September 19, 1976. The couple had been extracted three days earlier, but strangely, Samuel and Gabriella Verón had been shot only two days later, on September 21. The notation of the place where the execution took place had unfortunately been destroyed, as had the name of the officer assigned to the task: all that could be deciphered was part of the name of the petty officer involved (" . . . do Montañez") who accompanied him. The latter did not appear in any of his files. Rubén pursued his research in the Internet phone book: Leonardo, Fernando, Orlando, Eduardo, Ricardo, Bernardo, Alfredo, he ran through dozens of Montañezes scattered all over the country. After a while, Jana emerged from the Jacuzzi, a large white towel wound around her torso and hips.

Wet, her hair looked longer, falling over her naked shoulders. She saw the traveling bag and the detective gear, sat down without a word, and curled up on the sofa bed.

"You O.K.?" Rubén said mechanically.

Since she did not answer, he looked up from the screen. Her almond-shaped eyes were distressed, dark. Sad. No dream in them.

"Why did you kiss me the other night?" she asked him point-blank.

He sighed a little.

"I wanted to, probably."

Jana looked at him from under her wet locks.

"What does 'probably' mean?"

Rubén did not reply. He'd been practicing for almost thirty-five years. Jana pulled her towel a little tighter, a slender defense against the fire that was consuming her.

"Well?" she persisted.

"I'm forty-seven years old, baby doll," he finally said. "I'm afraid that all my responses are bad."

"I'm a sculptress, I can give you different ones."

Rubén could smell her soaped skin. He lit a cigarette to hide his embarrassment, but it didn't work.

"I've fucked rattlesnakes to survive," Jana said, showing her pretty teeth. "That doesn't mean that I'll kiss just anybody. My friend has disappeared, you're my only hope of finding her, and you don't say anything to me, you don't show me anything except a mysterious Great Silence that reeks of the cosmic void for miles around. What's your problem, Calderón? You kiss me at dawn as if I were all you had in the world, and then you leave me standing here like a crane in front of my bits of scrap iron, come back and whisk me away to the home of an old madwoman whom you cut up before my eyes before locking me up amid your dear *desaparecidos*, forbidding me to go out: what do you take me for, a good-for-nothing princess? Don't I deserve at least an explanation, a couple of tender words to let me know where I stand in this mess? Do you think I'm a throwaway girl, a simple Kleenex you can use to wipe away your moments of abandon?"

"That's not the point."

"With you, it never seems to be the point," she said, stifling her rage. "What's in your heart, apart from dead people? You're living in the past, Rubén, to the point that you are incapable of imagining the future. You're the one who has lost your senses along the way, *winka*, not me. You've lost your ability to smell shit, which is what makes us different from all those sons of bitches. I have faith in what I'm doing, in what keeps me going. Now it's you. Because we still have a chance of finding Miguel and because no one has ever kissed me so sweetly."

Jana kept her eyes on him, wrapped in the towel, her copper-colored legs folded under her.

"I'm sorry," he said.

"For what, for having kissed me? I don't believe you, old man."

"We're on the run."

"What does that change, the color of my eyes?"

Jana wanted him to take her in his arms as he had the other night in the yard and to run her heart through with his damned forget-me-not eyes so she might die of him once and for all, since fate had reduced them to one another: then the BlackBerry on the coffee table rang. The detective saw Anita's name on the screen and answered. The discussion was short—they had a one-hour window.

Jana was still looking at him from the sofa bed, her jade-colored hair dripping on her thighs.

"I have to go," he said.

It was 11:30 P.M.

"Where?"

"To the morgue."

*

Anita Barragan was not really a sex maniac; was it her fault if men, who were usually so proud of their reasonableness, lost their heads over a pair of tits? What did that remind them of, she laughed, their mothers? Her tendency to relieve the little darlings being equaled only by the obstinate resistance to her charms on the part of the only bachelor she found really attractive, Anita preferred to have affairs with married men that normally went nowhere. One would never have expected Guillermo Piezza, a hirsute forensic scientist fifteen years her junior who was completing his training at the Morgue Judicial, to have been her lover. He didn't plan on getting married, and at the age of forty, Anita thought herself too common to inspire youthful ardor, but the intern must have liked old maids who handled sex and humor with all the contradictory guile of a depraved neurotic (that was how she defined herself to sugar-coat the pill). Guillermo sometimes sodomized her in the upstairs toilet, an exciting little game without consequences that would go on as long as no one felt injured by it. Anita didn't expect anything from him: Guillermo couldn't refuse her anything.

The old Buenos Aires Institute of Forensic Science, which used to be adjacent to the medical school, had been transferred to the Avenida Comodoro Py, not far from the Retiro and the new port. Opened with great ceremony in Antepuerto, a new zone filled with public buildings, the Morgue Judicial, a resolutely modern structure, contrasted with the Mussolini-style austerity of the past century; a large marble hall sheltered the reception area, the cafeteria, the educational sector, and a private space reserved for victims' families. The upper floors—containing laboratories, forensic clinics—were reached by a two elevators, one reserved for the public and employees, and the other exclusively for the medical staff, corpses, and authorized persons.

Anita was waiting in front of the ambulance entrance, worrying about being caught there, when Rubén arrived.

"Did anyone see you?" she whispered.

"Apart from a few spy satellites, no."

"Ho, ho, ho." Anita pinned the badge Guillermo had given her on her lapel. "Come on, let's not waste any time."

With its long marble corridor, soft lighting, balustrades and glass staircases, the smooth architecture of the Forensic Institute was more reminiscent of the international airport than of a morgue. A little Bolivian woman was distractedly mopping the floor, a white mask over her tanned face, which she hardly raised as they passed by. Anita walked fast under the filtered neon lights: Rubén had no business being in the lair of the forensic police, and her job was absolutely on the line here.

"The body was prepared for burial," she whispered as she guided the detective through the labyrinth of the high tech bunker. "Damn, the funeral service is going to start any minute now, and it's crazy to be here!"

Rubén avoided the surveillance camera at the corner of the corridor and followed the blonde to the cold storage area.

"We have five minutes, no more," Anita said as she opened the door.

The room exhaled a combination of ammonia and deodorant for public toilets. The aseptic white walls, a harsh light, and a row of compartments on the right, dead bodies classified by their order of arrival. Number 23: Anita pulled out the aluminum drawer and immediately looked away.

Rubén cleared his mind as he approached the monster. Muñoz, who had just finished the autopsy, had tried to make the corpse a little more presentable, but with half her head torn off, the state of her skin and her empty eye sockets, poor María was unrecognizable. Rubén swallowed as he thought about the self-portraits hanging in her loft, and better understood why the family was rushing the funeral.

"Four minutes," Anita whispered, looking at the wall.

The skin was withered and faded, the skull had been cut

behind the frontal lobes, rather cleanly despite the gauze bandages. Probably a boat's propeller. The rest of the face was a horror. Not only the eyes but also the mouth had been eaten away by whelks. María Victoria Campallo. A diaphanous, almost milky body, round breasts, a slightly rounded belly, sewn back up in haste.

"The windstorm that hit the coast caused some damage in the ports and marinas," Anita said, keeping her distance. "But according to Maritime Affairs no shipwreck was reported in the Río de la Plata area."

Rubén nodded. The cadaver's paleness indicated that it had been in the water for a long time, several days to judge by the state of the skin, which was beginning to rot in contact with the air. No sign of a bullet wound, a knife blow, or a cigarette burn.

"What does Muñoz's report say?"

"If I knew that I wouldn't be cooling my butt here," his friend replied.

Above all, it was the odor that was boring into his head. Rubén put on a pair of surgical gloves and handed a pair to Anita.

"Here, help me turn her over."

Anita blew aside her blond locks, a nervous tic she had. They grabbed María's corpse and flipped it over on its stomach. No visible lesions, despite multiple apparent fractures. The body must have floated to the surface and then been ground up by a freighter, ferry, or trawler, whose propeller had cut off the top of her skull. Rubén forgot the ugliness of death and put his gloved hands on the drowned woman's back. His senses very quickly became more acute, as if the lessons in forensics taught by Raúl were coming back to him through his fingertips: carefully, he felt the bones, followed the uneven shapes of the fractures. The jawbones were broken, the clavicle, the ribs.

"The results of the toxicological tests won't be in for several days, but Guillermo has some stuff for you," Anita said to hurry things up. "Let's get out of here, please."

The young intern on duty that night knew Calderón's reputation as a troublemaker, like himself, but to hell with his superiors, for whom he had only moderate respect. The future forensic scientist had stoned the police's armored cars during the crisis, and when those responsible for the bankruptcy fled from the rooftops by helicopter, he'd flipped them the bird, along with thousands of other bare-chested longhairs. Guillermo had not assisted Muñoz during the autopsy, but he had cleaned up after the heavyweight had done his work. In particular, he had found two X-rays in the waste bins, rejects that he had made off with before they could be destroyed.

Rubén put the pictures on the lighted screen that lit the small room where the intern had been waiting for them. Certain fractured areas were not clear. He spent a long time examining them. It was not only the jawbones, the clavicle, and the ribs that had been caved in, but also the femoral heads and the heel. María's body seemed to have imploded.

The characteristics of the fractures left no doubt. María Campallo had not been beaten with iron bars or crushed by the hull of a ferry while she was floating on the surface: she had been thrown out of an airplane.

"What is it?" Anita asked.

Rubén paled. The Death Flights.

*

Drugged with sodium pentothal, loaded into trucks or cars, gagged, bound, and hooded, subversives extracted from the prisons were taken to military airports and thrown alive into the Río de la Plata. Night flights, in helicopters or more often in airplanes. Sometimes the cadavers were found trussed up on the coast of Uruguay, dismembered or mutilated bodies that the waves brought in depending on the variations in the currents. The unexpected storm the preceding week had driven the photographer's body back toward Buenos Aires, as often happened during the worst days of the Dirty War.

Lost in these reminiscences, Rubén saw the scene once again in violent flashes, the kidnapping of María Victoria and the person she thought was her brother as they came out of La Catedral, the transvestite whom they tortured in front of her to make her talk, the screams, the confessions, their separation, Orlando sent to the deserted quays of La Boca, María drugged to transfer her to an airport in the countryside, the rich industrialist's daughter reduced to a package thrown into the trunk of a car, a simple number to be erased, to be made to disappear, María inert on the floor of the fuselage, flying over the drop zone, the black skin of the ocean crinkling under the moon, she still deep in her chemical dreams, feeling neither wind nor fear, the voracious and muddy waters at the mouth of the river far below, and then María Victoria cast into the void, her fall, her interminable fall toward the ocean. Hitting the sea after falling 6,000 feet is like hitting a concrete wall: María's bones had exploded in her flesh.

Rubén was driving down Corrientes, shaken after his visit to the Morgue Judicial. His hand snatched at the night air through the open car window. His shirt was drenched with sweat, his loaded Colt was in the glove compartment. Big cars were rolling down the swarming Centro Avenue; the signs on the luxury shops were still illuminated and sparkled under the eyes of old ladies in furs whom aging *hidalgos* were taking to dinner after the show. The people downtown seemed rich, happy, healthy, guardians of the *porteño* soul. His father would be their age if he'd lived.

Rubén arrived at the apartment in Palermo, his eyes burning with fatigue. The lamp in the Japanese living room was lit and the curtains were drawn, but the room was empty.

"Jana?"

The smell of weed floated down the glass staircase. He found her upstairs, sitting cross-legged in front of the low table that served as a desk, her eyes glued to the computer screen.

"Dracula left me some *flores*," she said, handing him the joint.

Jana wore a threadbare gray shirt over her shoulders and black jean shorts just as threadbare as the shirt. A butt had already dried out in the ashtray—local marijuana—under the wise eye of the big white cat who had finally emerged from his hiding place and positioned himself on the chest of drawers. Rubén chased away the images of death that had been haunting him since he left the Forensics Institute, took the joint between his lips, and leaned down to look at the screen.

"The Montañez you're looking for must now be at least fifty-five years old," she said, "if he's still alive." She showed him the notes she'd scribbled on her loose sheets. "I've found a dozen of them on the Internet: the former petty officer might be one of them."

Rubén ran through her notes: truck driver, restaurant owner, delicatessen, public scribe, none of people named "Montañez" that Jana had listed worked in a private security or caretaking firm.

"What did you find out at the morgue?" she asked.

"María Campallo was thrown out of an airplane," he drawled. "The currents washed the body up on the coast. That implies a pilot, a suitable plane, an airport close enough to Buenos Aires to be able to organize the transfer, accomplices . . . "

He passed the joint back to her.

"I can take care of that," the sculptress said.

"You don't know my files, the classification system."

"Do you think I'm retarded? Just tell me what to look for."

Her coldness perked him up.

"Pilots' names," he replied. "Compare them with the ones

appearing in the files. Also look into their backgrounds, the kind of airplanes used on the weekend of the double murder, the nature of the airports around the city, with or without control towers . . . Anything you can find."

"O.K. And Montañez?"

"We'll have to look in the Navy archives. File a request with the appropriate authorities. That can take weeks."

He yawned, weighed down by the musician's *flores* and his lack of sleep the night before.

"O.K.," Jana said. "Go to bed, I'll deal with the airports. You can sleep in the downstairs bedroom."

He nodded. The Mapuche's face was very close, her full lips delicately drawn. Rubén abruptly stood up straight and rocked back and forth over Jana, who had already turned her attention back to the internet.

"Good night," he said.

"Try to get some sleep, you stubborn ox."

Ledzep, who had been following the conversation from the chest of drawers, jumped down and followed Rubén.

The hope of finding Miguel alive was growing slimmer by the hour. One chance in a hundred, according to the detective: without him, Jana would have no chance at all. She relighted the joint and began to surf the websites. There were half a dozen airfields scattered around the city, private flying clubs perennially short of funds and therefore not very picky about the people or merchandise that passed through their facilities. The smallest did not have a control tower, and seemed to limit themselves to giving flying lessons. Two of them bordered on Route 9, the main highway nearest the Río de la Plata. Jana took down the pilots' names listed on the first one, three men with smiling faces out of *Top Gun*, and entered the data into Rubén's files. More research. Cross-checking. Available photos. Comparisons with the organizational charts of the oppressors and their accomplices—wasted time: none of the three pilots appeared on Rubén's blacklists. She made notes on what she found anyway, who knew.

The second airfield didn't have a real Internet site, just a vague advertisement with photos that looked like they dated from the 1970s. No proper names: just the fees charged and the options available. Ledzep, who must have been thrown out of the bedroom, nuzzled her bare feet with the assiduity of a wild animal reconquering territory. Jana looked at the clock; it was very late. Too agitated to sleep, she left the computer on standby and went down the glass staircase. Thoughts flashed into her head, each more sinister than the last—had the killers already thrown Miguel into the estuary? She smoked a joint of pure *flores* while looking out at the street behind the curtains. The city's lights flickered like fireflies in the violet sky. She suddenly felt lost, foreign to the place, as if time was passing without her. Without him? Rubén was keeping his distance, as if something ineluctable were going to happen and crush them both. Jana didn't give a damn about their differences, about the violence that lay just under his skin, even about his age. The body had feelings that didn't lie. His burning hands, his cock, the passionate embrace the other night, in the yard . . .

Ledzep's mewing brought her out of her night owl's thoughts—he wanted to go to bed, too. Weary, she put out the joint, drank a glass of water, and brushed her teeth in the bathroom adjacent to the bedroom. A designer mirror, king-size bed, minimalist furniture, oriental lamps that shed a subdued light to produce a voluptuous atmosphere. Jo Prat had put a bouquet of flowers on the night table, red roses, obviously; they were magnificent. Rubén was sleeping fitfully on the white sheets, having taken off just his shoes, his arms hugging the pillow as if it might escape. Hope, despair. She wavered a moment under the effect of the THC, closed her eyes to the disaster, and sank down without regret in the shadow of his arms.

Two black holes cast into the void.

4

The population of Buenos Aires, which had no land use policy, had settled along the rail lines, with the result that the city was shaped like an open hand. The industries had then slipped into the interstices, continually extending the suburbs and their three ring roads. Rubén was driving on Route 9, which was jammed, listening without flinching to the nonstop news on the radio. He'd slept eight hours straight, and the fatigue that had dogged him for two days had been diluted in black coffee. The newscaster had just announced the death of María Victoria Campallo, whose body had been found on the shores of thc ccological preserve. No other details at the moment, except that an investigation had been opened. Not a word regarding the burial, which would take place that evening, nor about her murder, even though it was fact by now. Had her father, who had contacts in the media, ordered that the matter be handled that way?

Jana had listed three airfields where María might have been taken for a night flight, one south of the city, two north. Rubén was returning from the San Miguel flying club, where all the pilots had provided information about their flights on the night of the kidnapping. It was now past noon, a stormy heat was making the air in the car sticky, and the mufflers of the stacked-up cars were rumbling. He passed depressing areas saturated with billboards, tediously flashy shopping areas that had been inflicted on them since the triumph of Wal-Mart and financial capitalism, a tacky hedonism smoking over the void that would soon submerge the planet. Bar-coded despair; Rubén was thinking about lethal waves when he turned off toward the residential suburb of El Tigre.

An area where the well-born used to have vacation homes at the turn of the twentieth century, the little city of El Tigre was located at the entrance to the eponymous delta that extended north of the capital. Rowing clubs, swimming clubs, and cricket clubs: on weekends, people from Buenos Aires crowded around the open-air cafes in the marina, from which they travelled the canals in wooden boats of an old-fashioned luxury. The houses here were surrounded by flowers and had large gardens and carefully tended lawns. The storm had given way to wicked sunbreaks during which the puddles on the asphalt glistened: according to the map, the airfield was located not far from the city.

A field of lush grass was followed by a marsh. A few cattle ready for export were grazing there, half-asleep; beyond the barbed wire, Rubén spotted the red and white windsock at the airfield, inflated by the breeze. He stopped the car at the end of the dry land that served as a parking lot and stretched his shoulder muscles.

A dilapidated shed with closed shutters stood next to the gas station at the edge of the runway. Too small to have a control tower, the El Tigre airfield consisted of a corrugated iron hangar, a prefab office, and a training plane, which was sitting on the tarmac—a little two-seater with faded white paint. A country airfield, deserted, where time seemed suspended. Rubén made his way past the office, glanced briefly at the plane on the runway, and walked to the hangar. Another plane was parked at the back of the hangar, a Cessna 185. Neither pilot nor mechanic anywhere around. He retraced his steps, moving along in the shadow of the buildings.

A fan perched on a stained counter was blowing around the damp air in the main office. An obese man was halfheartedly wiping his brow in front of a computer screen; bits of greasy paper rolled into balls were lying near the keyboard. Valdés, the manager of the flying club and head pilot, hardly raised his head when he saw Rubén come in. He had played forward on a high-level rugby team, and had even thought for a while of going pro before being taken down a peg by the steroid-charged players from Tucumán. Valdés had completed his pilot's certification and because afterward he got no exercise, he'd gained fifty kilos in pizza, which he seemed in no hurry to lose.

Rubén showed him his detective's badge.

"I'd like to talk to one of your pilots," he said, peering into the adjoining room. "It looks like there isn't anyone . . . "

Disturbed just as he was having an electronic success, Valdés raised his walrus-like chin.

"What do you want with my pilots?"

"How many of you work here?"

"My secretary is far along in her pregnancy and I have to deal with the paperwork all by myself," he replied gruffly. "There's only Del Piro. When he's here."

"Is he one of your pilots?"

"The only one. Except for me. But I no longer fly very much," the big man added.

"I can see that. Where is he, this Del Piro?"

"He took a week off to do a training course in acrobatics. Why?"

"You have no other instructors?"

"Haven't for the past two years," the head pilot said. "There's an economic crisis, have you heard?"

Rubén looked at the dusty shelves and the file drawers behind the guy.

"Was the acrobatic ace on duty at the end of last week?" he asked.

"Don't know," Valdés replied. "Here we give lessons, not information."

The old rugby man went back to his computer screen, moved a few electronic cards in the cooling breeze of the fan. Rubén leaned over the counter and pulled the plug. Valdés's face looked like that of a forward before the scrum.

"What's your problem?"

"A night flight," Rubén said. "Do you keep a record of what happens here or are your planes there for show?"

Valdés stared at him with sullen eyes. The detective didn't blink.

"Open that damned register."

The swiveling fan blew in his direction.

"There's no law that says I have to do that, fellow," he replied.

"It will take you two minutes. Maybe two years in the joint if you refuse to cooperate. I'm conducting an investigation into a murder that also interests the cops, and I'm sure that they would be delighted to nose around in your accounts. You don't seem to be doing a lot of business," Rubén insinuated, looking around.

Valdés bared his teeth, which sparkled with disdain, despite the tobacco stains.

"I just want to verify one or two things on the registers," Rubén went on in a voice he tried to make conciliatory. "Then I'll leave you to your little affairs. Unless you have some reason for refusing?"

Valdés shrugged, blew out enough air to fill two dirigibles as a sign of consent, made his way around the desk, and opened the register in which the flight plans were recorded.

"The weekend of the eighth, right?" he grumbled. "Nope, there's nothing mentioned."

Rubén turned the document over to check. Nothing.

"Maybe the pilot didn't file his flight plan," he suggested.

"Why would he do that?"

"To go take a piss at two thousand feet."

"Not Del Piro's style," the manager retorted, with a jeering look.

"Is that right? And what is his style?"

"Skirt-chasing. Like all pilots."

"I see. What about you, where were you last weekend?"

"With my wife. It was her birthday, and we've been married for twenty years. If you have a problem with that, comfort yourself with the knowledge that I do too: O.K.?"

"Can I see Del Piro's file?"

Valdés complained but pulled the file out of a metal drawer and threw it on the counter, fairly exasperated.

Gianni Del Piro, born April 15, 1954, residing in El Tigre. Tanned, emaciated face, graying sideburns, a rather good-looking man despite the look of an eagle on the hunt that he tried to give himself in the photo.

"Did Del Piro get his pilot's license in the army?"

"Like nine-tenths of the guys I've met," the manager answered.

Rubén took out his BlackBerry and took a digital photo of Del Piro's name and address. Valdés ruminated.

"Are you the one who lives in the shed outside?" he asked.

The obese man shook his jowls.

"No. It's had a leaky roof for years. I live in town."

"So the flying club is empty at night."

"Yep."

"Does Del Piro have a set of keys to the hangar?"

"Of course," Valdés grumbled. "This is a small flying club: the pilots don't wait for me to be there to give their lessons. Are you going to go on bugging me like this for a long time?"

Rubén picked up the flight plan registers.

"Give me the key to the Cessna in the hangar."

"Why, are you planning to cross the Andes in that little thing?" the chief pilot joked.

Rubén didn't laugh.

"Hurry up, let's get this over with."

Valdés threw a set of keys on the counter and pointed to the registers.

"You're going to bring those back to me, right?"

It smelled like motor oil and grease in the hangar. Rubén briefly inspected the equipment stored there before going to the Cessna at the back of the hangar. The little touring plane could carry two persons in front and the same load in the back: by taking off the door, you could very easily push out a body in flight and return to the airfield. He climbed into the cockpit.

The pilots recorded the number of hours on the motor after each flight. Rubén compared the log with the plane's timer. The numbers corresponded. Del Piro could also have disconnected the timer. Rubén pulled out the stick in the gas tank, put on latex gloves, dug around in the cockpit, ran his torch over the rear of the plane: the floor, the seats, the back of the cabin, everything was immaculate, or recently cleaned. In any case, there was nothing to indicate a phantom flight.

The sun dazzled him for a moment as he came out of the hangar. He walked alongside the tarmac and headed for the gas pump, fifty yards before Valdés's office. It was a very elementary service station with a simple pump and a register in which the pilots recorded their fill-ups. Rubén consulted the document: no fill-up was mentioned during the weekend in question.

He calculated the average fuel consumption based on how often the tank was filled, compared it with the flights made by the Cessna and the raised fuel stick on the plane, and frowned. There was something wrong. Del Piro had filled up too early following the weekend of the 8th.

Rubén checked his calculations several times. His adrenaline was surging: a two-to-three-hour flight's worth of fuel was missing.

*

Jana managed to contact three-fourths of the forty-two people named Montañez who were listed in the phone book, giving them a story about a lottery game that was based on birth dates. After a series of tedious calls, she found eleven persons who were as old as the former corporal involved in the murder of the Verón couple.

The DDHH (The Ministry of Justice and Human Rights), the ANM (National Memorial Archives, based at the former ESMA), and the CONADEP: Jana searched the lists of the members of the armed forces who were connected with the repression, the lists of the Center for Legal and Social Studies made available to the Grandmothers, and the files stored on Rubén's hard drive, without finding the slightest trace of a corresponding Montañez. She had only these eleven names lined up on the paper, eleven suspects scattered all over the country. It would take too long. Paula would have been dead for a thousand years before they found anything. There remained the archives of the armed forces.

The top secret documents connected with the sequestration and murder of thirty thousand *desaparecidos* had been burned when democracy arrived (and any possible copies probably destroyed as well), but the Navy, like all the branches of the armed forces, had kept its archives. The public did not have access to them, for the simple reason that the Navy refused to grant it: in exceptional cases only, "legitimate users" justifying the "necessity of consulting" the documents could have access to them—in other words, very few people, and at the cost of efforts that had very little chance of succeeding. That's what

Rubén had said that morning before leaving, as she was emerging from the *flores* fog.

Waking from the sleep of the dead, Ledzep made a conspicuous appearance as soon as she opened the fridge. He had feasted on the remains of breakfast left on the table in the living room, but his sly air belied a plea for meat. Jana drank a cold beer to give herself courage, and left the hideout at noon.

In a macabre ironic twist peculiar to Argentina, the building housing the Navy archives was located near the Morgue Judicial, on the Avenida Comodoro Py. The building, called Libertad, had the form of a hexagonal prism a dozen stories high, newly repainted in white, and meant to erase the memory of the sadly famous Navy Engineering School.

Jana had come on the *colectivo*, the local bus, her black canvas bag on her shoulder and her identity card in the pocket of her jumpsuit. The sky was blue after the rainstorm, and the wind was rustling through the few trees bordering the parking lot. She climbed the stairs, full of apprehension, showed her bag to the two burly guards at the entrance, walked through the metal detectors, and presented herself at the reception desk.

A woman in her forties with a parrotlike voice was talking on the telephone with what seemed to be a girlfriend: the visitor's arrival seemed not to interest her, since she continued her discussion for a while before turning to the Mapuche, who was fidgeting on the other side of the counter.

"Hang on a second," she said to her friend before pressing the receiver to her breast. "Yes, what do you want?"

Jana made a superhuman effort to smile.

"I'm looking for my cousin," she said, moving up to the Formica-topped counter. "García Márquez. He was a petty officer in the Navy. I've lost touch with him and am trying to get back in contact with him, for family and also legal reasons."

Since the woman was scowling beneath her makeup, Jana persisted.

"It's about an inheritance, papers that have to be filled out. The notary handling it told me that I would find information about my cousin in your archives. Do you know where they are?"

A few aging men in uniform passed through the great lobby, carrying files under their arms. The woman at the reception desk gestured nervously in the direction of the elevators.

"Tenth floor. You have to make an official request at the office concerned, fill out the forms, provide justifying documents, and return when you receive a response, usually not before two weeks have passed," she added as a kind of litany. "Do you have identification?"

Jana handed over her ID card, which the employee photocopied without getting out of her swivel chair. Then she mechanically threw a badge on the counter.

"You will return this to me on your way out!"

"Thank you, madam."

The woman put the telephone back to her ear.

"Hello, Gina, are you still there?"

Jana attached the badge to the collar of her black jean jacket and walked toward the elevators, her bladder suddenly tight. An armed guard was standing near the emergency exits, wearing a beret in Navy colors. The tenth floor: a vast hall with a polished floor that reflected the sunshine passing through the bay windows that looked out on the new harbor. Little signs directed the visitors to the various administrative offices; Jana called a fictitious number on the cell phone Rubén had left her and began an imaginary conversation as she had a look at the room. "Yes . . . No . . . " She roamed around without anyone paying attention to her: the archives room was at the far end, on the right.

A soldier sitting at a table in front of a crude desk was guarding the entrance, a pale Sean Penn lookalike with the air of a juvenile delinquent. A walkie-talkie, revolver, and nightstick hung on his belt. It was lunchtime, and he was eating a sandwich wrapped in paper, keeping an eye on the orderly area that, like him, was dying of boredom among the potted plants. Jana sat down some distance away on one of the vacant seats in the middle of the hall. She did not know how the place was organized or where the archives were kept, but the guard was alone. Jana found an old eyeliner pencil at the bottom of her purse and started making herself up to lessen the guard's suspicions. He took another long drink of water from a little bottle and put it back on the desk; it would soon be empty. A few minutes later he headed for the nearby toilets.

Jana didn't wait until he disappeared to take off behind him. She sped up and was a few yards from the entrance when a man came out of the restroom. He walked toward her, his uniform impeccable, frowned imperceptibly, and, showing the badge on his jacket, walked past her without saying a word. The coast was clear for the moment. Jana moved past the deserted desk and slipped through the varnished door. A shiver ran down her back.

The air-conditioning was on high in the archives room. Jana quietly closed the door behind her and positioned herself against the perpendicular wall in front of her: footsteps resounded in the semidarkness, soon followed by the sound of a door slamming. The Mapuche kept close to the wall of the coatroom, but her legs seemed to be giving way underneath her: what the hell was she doing there? She waited until the poison descended from her suddenly shaky legs and spread out and sank into the floor before finally daring to look around. The room was empty. Two computers with flat screens were humming on desks, next to impressive rows of shelves: there were about twenty of them, a cathedral of paperwork dimly lit in this windowless bunker. Jana dashed into the corridor between the closest rows and hurried, hunched over, to the far end, as if that would make her invisible. Her need to urinate was becoming more pressing. Two men soon entered, their hoarse voices echoing in the confined universe of the archives room. They were talking about soccer; she didn't listen. Sweat was running down her temples. Jana moved away, light-footed, hid at the end of the row of shelves, and looked up. D3, that was the number on the shelf.

The employees' voices were indistinct, at the very end of the corridor. She made her way through the labyrinth. M1, M2, M3. Jana found a shelf corresponding to the name Montañez in M4. Hundreds of files were piled up in the corridor that led to the open space. She hesitated a moment before starting into it: was it instinct, a sign of the times? An employee walked by twenty yards farther on, upright as the letter I, without noticing her presence.

Jana's T-shirt was soaked with sweat; she walked stealthily between the walls of documents that protected her, holding her breath. Monterubio, Monteramos . . . Montalban, Montamas, Montañez: fifth shelf, just above her head. Jana grabbed a stack of files, heard footsteps, and held her breath: someone was two or three rows from her.

A minute passed with an awful taste of eternity. The footsteps finally moved away. The Mapuche went through the military records, her heart racing. Montañez, Oswaldo, born October 2, 1971: too young. Montañez, Alfredo, born August 24, 1967: also too young. A drop of sweat fell on the yellowed paper of the file she was holding in trembling hands. Montañez, Ricardo, born June 12, 1955, in Rufino. The birth date was right, and also that of his entry into the ESMA, which he had left in late 1976 with the rank of petty officer. He was the one. It had to be him. Crouching at the foot of the storage shelves, Jana found her throat grow drier. A voice made her jump.

"What's that smell?"

Fear.

Her fear, dripping from her body.

The guy was in the next row, smelling her presence.

"Hey, is anyone there?" he called blindly

Jana had already stuck the document in the pocket of her

jumpsuit; she put the file at random on the shelf and slipped off in the direction of the emergency exit, at the end of the row. Nobody on the left, nobody on the right. She opened the fire door and disappeared.

"Hey, is somebody there?"

Ten floors. They would notify security, which would have only to pick her up at the bottom of the stairs. Jana followed the little green light, rushed down the stairs, hanging onto the rail to muffle the sound of her steps, and came out on the ninth floor, her heart beating wildly. The group of military men talking in front of the bay windows hardly deigned to look at her. Jana pushed the button on the elevator, struggling to keep calm. Still no alarm. However, the employee in the archives room must have heard the emergency door click shut. The elevator came quickly: she pushed on the button, made the doors close behind her, and began her descent. She was wiping away the beads of sweat on her forehead, imploring the gods of her ancestors to spare her this time when the elevator car suddenly stopped. Fifth floor. A tall man in a uniform with stripes came in without a word: the officer she had met a little earlier, coming out of the restroom.

"You going down?" he asked.

"Yes."

His affable demeanor didn't last. The elevator had hardly begun its descent before the man drew back: a disagreeable odor permeated the car. He scowled starchily at the Indian woman, who was staring at her Doc Martens. Finally the elevator doors opened on the main lobby: Jana gulped down the saliva she no longer had and set out for the reception area, a haven of peace in the storm. No one stopped her. Still not. She left the badge with the uninterested woman in a wig behind the counter, and forced herself not to run to the exit.

The security men's walkie-talkies began to crackle. Jana walked by them at the moment they were answering and took the broad stairway that led to the parking lot. Two men rushed out of the building, too late: the wind was cooling her face and the *colectivo* was arriving at the end of the esplanade.

*

The seaside resort of El Tigre had emptied out at the end of the summer. The rowing clubs were still busy, and a few morons were still making their jet skis howl among the rotting lemons that were floating on the surface of the water. Rubén was driving down the main artery, holding a sandwich he'd bought on the fly in one of the shops on the embarcadero. Gianni Del Piro lived at the end of the avenue, in a detached house that clashed with the sumptuous residences around it, which had been built a century earlier.

A compact car was parked in the carport. Rubén threw the rest of the sandwich to the dog that was going through the neighbor's garbage cans and rang at the front door. The pilot's wife promptly opened the door. Her name was Anabel, a plump bleached blonde with a crude red smile who, to judge by her vast heart-shaped décolleté, still refused to accept the fact that she had turned fifty.

"Hello!' she chirped to the dandy standing on her porch.

Rubén, all smiles, passed himself off as an old army pal who had been assigned to round up the squadron to celebrate the retirement of a mutual friend. Charmed by the attention, Anabel explained that Gianni had left the preceding week for Neuquén to participate in training course in "advanced acrobatics" and that he would be back on Sunday, but that she could still call him to let him know about the reunion.

"If you want me to, of course!" the coquette added.

"I'd like to surprise him," Rubén replied cagily.

"As you wish!"

Rubén briefly sounded out the woman who was fanning herself on the threshold. She'd had a facelift, and even though she was flirting with him, her innocent air was convincing. He left Anabel to her Botox and returned to his car, which was parked a little farther down the street. Leaning on the hood, he called the flying clubs in Neuquén.

One of them offered training courses given by experienced pilots, but according to the fellow he talked to on the phone, the next course in acrobatics didn't begin until the following month.

Then he called Anita.

She hadn't read Muñoz's autopsy report regarding the death of María Victoria Campallo, but according to the information she'd gleaned, the theory that it was a homicide remained in doubt: an accident, a suicide, a murder—Captain Roncero's team, to which Luque had assigned the case, was not excluding any line of investigation.

"The autopsy report is wrong," Rubén replied, "you know that as well as I do."

"Right. That makes two of us against the rest of the world. María was buried not long ago and no one will allow us to exhume the body to get a second opinion. Unless we can prove that the Campallo family is not genetically related to its stolen children. Where are you with that?"

"I've got the name of a guy, Gianni Del Piro, a former military pilot who works in a little flying club in El Tigre. I suspect him of having transported María's body and falsified his flight record to make himself invisible. He gave his wife and his employer a bogus story about a training course in Neuquén and left the conjugal household the day before the double murder last week. Could you use his cell phone number to find this guy?"

"I remind you that my functions are limited to driving the patrol car in the presence of a male colleague and typing up reports, because these *pajeros*[13] have only two thumbs," Anita retorted.

[13] Jerk-offs.

"How about your pal at the telephone company?"

"It's still possible to keep an eye on calls," she grumbled, "but Del Piro can't be located without Ledesma's permission."

The police chief in the neighborhood where she worked.

"Luque and his elite cops see this as a pile of old shit at best."

"Ledesma might want to complicate his life," Rubén suggested.

"At two years from retirement, the Old Man isn't going to take the risk of getting himself dismissed without having solid proof," his subordinate replied.

"Tell him that it's about the murder in Peru Street, the murder of the laundress's transvestite son who is supposed to have been seen in a tango club with the Campallo daughter shortly before she disappeared."

"Damn it, Rubén, if I tell him that I'm conducting a parallel investigation regarding Campallo, he'll have me picking up bums in the boonies!"

"A wonderful opportunity to change assignments, no?"

"Very nice. Do you have a job for me?"

"Del Piro is involved in this," Rubén said, "I'm sure of that. He can lead us to Miguel and the killers. Figure out a way to make that palatable for Ledesma and find this guy for me. I'll make him tell us what we want to know."

He could be counted on to do that.

"You're making me do stupid things," his childhood friend complained. "The Old Man is going to want to know who my source is."

"Tell him that the Grandmothers have serious doubts about the real identity of María Campallo, and that Del Piro is suspected of having been involved in the kidnapping of Miguel, the main witness, who has disappeared."

Anita briefly evaluated the situation—yes, the thing was doable.

"All right," she agreed, "I'll see what I can do. In the meantime, this will cost you dinner in a restaurant. With candles, O.K.?"

Leaning on the hood of his car, Rubén smiled—a girl passed by on a bicycle, her bare legs flying.

"By the way," Anita said, "I have news from Colonia. The body found in the ruins of the house was identified as that of Jose Ossario. He died from a bullet in the head, a .22 caliber that belonged to him. Obtained legally. An investigation is underway but the fire has made things difficult, especially since the call for witnesses hasn't produced anything."

"How about Ossario's neighbor, Díaz? Didn't the local police question him?"

"I'm repeating what I was told: no witnesses. Your botanist must have cleared out," Anita suggested. "Or he's scared and is keeping quiet. It's also possible that he's been liquidated. That he's been thrown out of an airplane to see if he could fly."

"Right."

But he didn't seem convinced.

"People have a tendency to die after they've been around you, have you notice that?"

Rubén received another call on his BlackBerry: it was Jana.

"Excuse me, I've got to go," he said hurriedly. "Try to convince Ledesma. We'll talk again!"

He took Jana's call, his pulse accelerating.

"Jana?"

"Everything O.K.?"

"What's going on?"

"I found the petty officer, Montañez, there, in the Navy archives."

Rubén frowned under the beating sun.

"What?" he said.

"I went there at noon today," she explained. "His name is Ricardo Montañez, that's his full name. The birth date on the military record corresponds to one of the guys I talked to yesterday on the phone."

Rubén looked for a little shade along the residential street.

"You went digging around in the Navy's archives?"

"That's where the military records are stored," Jana retorted. "You're the one who told me that."

"But I never told you to go there!"

"Who else was going to do it? You, maybe? It's true that no one in the army knows you, and I'm sure they all adore you. Am I wrong?"

Rubén shook his head, disconcerted.

"You're crazy, just think what would have happened if you'd been caught! Damn, you should have warned me."

"About what? That I was going out without your authorization? You're not my father, and I didn't leave the reservation to obey the next person who came along, if you see what I mean."

"No."

"Well, in any case it's too late," Jana said to drop the subject.

"Where are you?"

"At the house. I just got here."

"Stay there. Please."

"O.K.," she said at the other end of the line. "When are you coming back?"

"Not before 8 P.M. I've got two or three things to deal with. I'll explain."

"All right."

"Anyway, bravo," he said before hanging up. "The archives. I don't know how you did it, but you're managing like a real pro."

"You haven't seen me in bed," Jana added. "A real little lynx!"

Rubén smiled in spite of himself. Yes, she was completely nuts.

5

Gusts of wind were blowing the veils of the women assembled around the family tomb; the men were hanging onto their hats, their sorrow, the women hung on their arms. There were no children present except a newborn infant who was not yet afraid of the cemetery.

The cemetery of Recoleta received the country's elite—presidents, governors, ministers, celebrities. To find Evita's grave, all you had to do was follow the funeral sprays. The Campallo family belonged to these privileged groups. That did not console them. In the late afternoon, heavy gray clouds had descended on the city, darkening the mourners' faces a little more. There were about twenty of them, dressed in black, crowding around María Victoria's coffin. Eduardo, a large man, freshly shaven and wearing a designer suit, his wife Isabel, an invisible skeleton under her veil, clinging to him for support, their son Rodolfo, in pleated pants, his jaw pulled into his double chin. Behind this trio, a few stooped women had congregated, their handkerchiefs hanging from their withered hands, and two not very agreeable-looking teenagers in suits, who had been forcibly combed and who were constantly smoothing their hair blown about by the wind. At a distance from the familial cocoon, a heavyset man with a shaved head and a hard face behind fine black glasses was prepared to get rid of any reporters who might appear.

Eduardo Campallo had taken care to bury his daughter in the strictest privacy, after the official closure of the cemetery.

He was meditating in front of the coffin, his hands joined. He had refused to let his wife see María's body, a sight that was traumatizing in every way. A priest with an emaciated countenance was officiating in Latin; he was so skinny under his cassock that he seemed to be swaying in the breeze as he sprinkled a few drops of holy water on the oak coffin. Isabel could hardly stand up. A final prayer, the last tears; Eduardo signaled to the employees that they should lower the casket into the family tomb. The sobs grew louder.

The statue of General Richieri stood guard, uselessly, over the little star-shaped plaza. Rubén, who had played hide-and-seek with the cemetery guardian before the closure, had found an observation post not far away—a white marble monument depicting the "Conquest of the Wilderness," illustrated with rather mediocre carvings of Mapuches on horseback. The detective came down from his perch as the tomb was being closed up over the body of the unfortunate María.

The striped cat that was prowling among the tombs came to be petted, his eyes dirty and indifferent. Rubén tapped the scarred head of the tomcat and took the service road.

The funeral cortege, driven away by sorrow, had begun to disperse among the gray crosses covered with moss. Eduardo Campallo was leaving with his wife on his arm when he saw the man near the little plaza. Isabel, who was walking with her head down, also saw him. Her fingers clutched her husband's sleeve.

"I have to speak with you, Mr. Campallo," Rubén said as he approached him.

The businessman's face, his black Prada suit, and freshly shined shoes bespoke nothing but dignity, sorrow, and distress. Isabel whispered something in her husband's ear, after which Eduardo's face grew even more somber.

"I have nothing to say to you, Calderón. Your presence here is as indecent as it is inappropriate. I know about your intrusion into our home," he added, without concealing his anger.

"The police do too. I warn you right now that you're going to hear more from me."

"The newspapers will too when they learn that you adopted two babies during the dictatorship," he said.

Campallo's bodyguard came up immediately. He was wearing a coat with epaulets and had a jutting jaw.

"Is there a problem, Mr. Campallo?"

Rubén brandished a plastic bag before Campallo's eyes.

"This hair belongs to your daughter," he said with a straightforward look. "Or rather to your adopted daughter, María Victoria. I've compared your DNA: you have no biological connection. Would you prefer to speak with me now or do you want to explain to the press?"

The patriarch's waxen mask grew paler. His son was approaching the plaza.

"What's going on?" Rodolfo asked when he saw how agitated his parents were.

Rubén ignored the gorilla with a shaved head who was waiting for his boss's orders.

"María Victoria was kidnapped before she was murdered along with those close to her. She was looking for her brother—her real brother, Miguel Michellini. Does that name mean anything to you, or did you never meet the family that agreed to the exchange of infants?"

There was a moment of hesitation at the gates to the cemetery. Eduardo grew crimson with rage.

"You have no manners or compassion for . . . "

"Have you read the autopsy report?" Rubén interrupted him.

"María drowned," Campallo grumbled. "Isn't that enough for you?"

"Ask Muñoz if there was water in her lungs, ask him if she was still alive when they threw her in the ocean!" he roared, feeling a desire to bite.

"What are you talking about?"

"The fractures show it very clearly. Your daughter was thrown out of a plane, Mr. Campallo, like in the good old days of the dictatorship. Either you knew about it and you're the worst pile of shit on earth, or you didn't, and I suggest you speak to your friends about it."

"Don't listen to this bastard, Papa," Rodolfo whispered.

Isabel seemed to disappear behind her husband's back. Half a dozen people had now gathered around the patriarch.

"María discovered that you aren't her biological parents," Rubén went on, "and that her real parents were abducted and killed during the Process. She also learned of the existence of her brother, who was born in detention," he added, turning to Rodolfo. "But that is not you, Rodolfo: her real brother was exchanged at birth because he had a cardiac insufficiency. He was the person María was looking for when she was kidnapped: Miguel Michellini. What was his problem," he demanded of the *apropriadores*: "did he have a limp? Is that why you traded him in for a new one? How much did the new one cost you?"

Rodolfo was incredulous. His father didn't blink, standing there on the little plaza as if he'd been turned to stone. A tear rolled down Isabel's cheek under her veil.

"You son of a bitch!" Rodolfo barked.

"Let him speak," Eduardo breathed.

Rodolfo looked with alarm at his father.

"Your daughter was planning to file suit against you, Mr. Campallo," Rubén went on. "You and your wife. She was murdered before she could talk. That's one thing I'm sure of."

A flight of crows passed through the construction magnate's eyes.

"I didn't kill my daughter, Calderón," he said hoarsely.

"Someone else could have done it for you. María Victoria had her hands on a document that compromised you," he said, driving the point home, "you and the people implicated in the sequestration of her parents. Seven years in prison, that's the sentence you could get for stealing children."

Eduardo swayed back and forth in the breeze, livid.

"What? Is this true? Papa?"

"Don't listen to this demon," Isabel finally said.

Eduardo Campallo was stunned. The world was crashing around his ears. He remained motionless, his eyes empty, completely dumbfounded. Next to him, his son's forehead was wrinkled. Rodolfo put his hand on his overwhelmed father's shoulder.

"Papa? Papa?"

*

Rubén returned from the La Recoleta cemetery supercharged with adrenaline. He left his things in the apartment's entry hall and found Ledzep lying on his back, his front paws pedaling the air. The Japanese lamps in the living room were turned on, the curtains drawn.

"Jana?"

No response, except for the sounds coming from the street, nor any evanescent smell of marijuana. Rubén stepped over the cat and climbed the glass staircase—maybe she was in the Jacuzzi. The computer was on standby on the coffee table, his traveling bag and things were scattered on the sofa bed, the bathroom was empty. He opened the bay window, his attention attracted by the little lights on the terrace.

"Jana?"

The table was set, with a white tablecloth, plates, and an elaborate array of silverware, little islands of candle jars flickering in the warm wind, a few red rose petals scattered at random, but there was no trace of the sculptress. The cat mewed behind him, its hair ruffled, and nuzzled his pants leg. Where had she gone now? Ledzep took off in front of him as he went back down the stairs, worried. The cat rubbed against the fridge, extending its fluffy tail like a reed trembling in a gale. Rubén went toward the hall and saw the door to the bedroom open.

"Jana?"

The heat grew more intense when he went in. A heady smell of roses floated in the half-light, and a dozen candle jars surrounded the bed. He froze. Jana was lying on the sheets, her eyes closed. She wore nothing but a black tank top and seemed to be asleep, her hands lying along her body. Rubén saw the brown tuft of public hair, her mouth, the shifting reflections of her body in the golden light of the candles, and didn't dare move. Had she heard him? For a moment he would have liked to go back thirty years in the past, to the time of fleeting romances and pledges made to women and their charms, but his hands, his poor hands, no longer obeyed him: they touched the Mapuche's cheeks, which hardly stirred at the contact.

Rubén kissed her as he had the first evening, tenderly, wholly.

"Your spit tastes like grass," he said very quietly.

Jana finally opened her eyes and smiled, seeing him leaning over her, and spread her legs. Three red rose petals decorated her labia.

"Fuck me instead of saying stupid stuff . . . "

*

Jana hadn't known many men away from the docks—that wasn't a competition, either. Once the clumsy encounters of adolescence were over, she had glimpsed the gates of a paradise to be conquered with Arturo, a young man who had given her a ride when she was hitchhiking to Buenos Aires and taken her home for a night of love all the more beautiful because it would be the only one, before she arrived in the capital and collided with the wall of reality: a country in a time of crisis, in which everyone was surviving with whatever means were at hand. Furlan had picked her up like an apple that had fallen from the tree too soon in a ruined landscape and eaten her green. The two guys with whom she had slept afterward—a student she met at a vernissage and a museum curator in his fifties who had invited her to a big meal at the Taberna Basca in San Telmo before very nicely proposing that they spend the night together at a hotel—were like little seashells found at the bottom of a pocket, souvenirs that you throw away almost without noticing.

Beneath her feral cat manner, Jana was sentimental. No, her meeting with Rubén had in no way been a matter of chance. Chance was like happiness, a *winka* notion. The spinelessness of the elites and the ukases of finance had thrown her alive into the world's garbage dump, where rats lined up to teach her how to be nineteen years old, but she had put up barbed-wire barriers to keep inviolate the house where Love would grow up. For this imaginary flame she would have sacrificed anything, even her sculptures.

That flame was still crackling in the light of the candle jars. Their languid bodies were recovering after their exertions. Jana saw strange forms in the crumpled sheets—animals' ears, old men, glaciers turned upside down, as she was. They had just made love, and their secretions were everywhere; fluid was running down between her thighs, heavy stars hung from the ceiling, rose petals were scattered among their earthly humors. Jana dreaded their first contact, a sensation that was often irrevocable, but Rubén had already put his smooth hands around her legs, petted her hair like the fur of a silky animal, and lapped her up in little gulps: her ankles, the back of her knees, the hollow of her groin, her lips, the *winka* had licked her in little concentric circles without ever touching her breasts—a delicate attention—his soft tongue had gone up the length of her arms, her armpits, her neck, the electric lobe of her ear, and then he had stood up into the sky to let her taste his cock, which was so full of her that Jana, greedy and no longer caring about anything but pleasure, had drawn it all the way to the bottom of her belly.

His blue soul was fading, piece by piece. His cock slipping over and over her clitoris, hypnotically, her murmurs urging him to take her, her eyes when he penetrated her, the incandescent arrow sinking into the silk, the patient quest for her abandonment, the abandonment: Jana had loved it all. Now night was falling behind the blinds on the windows, and on the messy sheets she was dreaming of strange sculptures; the world had expanded by a third, and even more, in all directions. She lay next to him, enjoying the silence that still bound them together in the cheesy half-light of a room that was not theirs. An unknown emotion that she put down to her background—love or not, no one had ever fucked her like that.

"Tell me, do I have an effect on you," she said, to break the chains.

Rubén smiled, the sheets pulled up around his torso. Was it modesty? She'd seen the marks on his body, but it wasn't the moment to talk about them.

"Are you hungry?" she asked.

"Not very."

"I'm going to make something while you lie there and think.

"O.K."

Jana leapt up, put on her shorts and shirt over the tight-fitting tank top, which she hadn't taken off.

"It'll be ready in ten minutes!"

Jana headed for the kitchen, leaving him alone in the bedroom. Ledzep immediately climbed up on the bed, put his nose to Rubén's face, and purred like a steamboat going up the Mississippi.

"Damn," he mumbled, brushing himself off, "you're getting hair all over me."

But to judge by his reaction, the cat didn't care a bit.

A rough, pugnacious Iggy Pop was playing in the living room when he got out of the shower, "Beat 'em up." He found Jana on the terrace, where she had set up the table while waiting for him to return. The Mapuche had lightly made herself up; it was the first time. Rubén sat down in front of the steaming dish.

"What is it?"

"I haven't the faintest idea," she replied.

The macrobiotic products that were in the rocker's fridge were, in fact, not very appetizing. At the end of the table, Ledzep didn't look very convinced, either. Rubén started in on the soy steak and told Jana about his day. The petals on the tablecloth reminded him of the time they had just spent together, the night was warm, the neighbors invisible behind the bamboo hedge that protected them from the outside world. Jana listened to him, regained hope when she heard about the pilot, and told Rubén in turn about sneaking into the Navy's archives. The lax security around the archives room, her close escape, and her return by bus from Antepuerto with Montañez's record: Ruben's round eyes looked like those of the cat at the end of the table.

"What if you'd been caught?" he scolded her.

"Like an old dog?"

"Phhh."

Jana changed the subject but she had had the scare of her life that day. He opened the document she had stolen for him. A photo at the top of the page showed a young man with a jowly, pimply face: Ricardo Montañez had been trained at Campo de Mayo before joining the ESMA (May 1, 1976), which he had left at the end of his tour of duty in November of the same year, with the rank of petty officer. Everything fit, the date of birth, that of the transfer. Jana had his address and phone number on her phone company list: today, Ricardo Montañez was the owner of a hotel in Rufino, La Rosada (no Internet site), which served as his address.

"It would be worthwhile to question this guy, no?" Jana concluded.

Rubén agreed, lost in his thoughts. The Forensic Medicine Center in Rivadavia had just confirmed the genetic links between María Campallo and Miguel Michellini, but the comparison of their DNA with the anonymous bones stored in their collections had for the moment yielded no results. If the parents who had disappeared had been executed at the time of the "transfer," only Montañez and the officer commanding him knew where they had been held. Finding the DNA of the murdered couple would prove their connection with María and Miguel: Eduardo Campallo and his wife would then be forced to admit having stolen the children, thus confirming the authenticity of Samuel and Gabriella Verón's internment form, even if it was fragmentary.

Rufino, a little place somewhere out on the pampas. Jana had taken reckless risks but she had done good work.

"Pisco sour?" she asked.

Rubén emerged from his lethargy. Juicer, lemon, sugar, shaker, alcohol, egg; Jana had arranged all the fixings at the end of the table.

"I'm going to get the ice cubes," he said, getting up.

"They're already there."

A bowl, hidden under the plants: a very precise approach. The two of them set about making the cocktail, filled the glasses with alcohol-laced foam, and drank to this special day. The bamboo swayed in the evening breeze that was blowing between the buildings. The tension relaxed; they drank and forgot the investigation, the threats that hung over them, gave the rest of the soy steaks to Ledzep, and smoked to prolong the intoxication. The stars came out one by one over the terrace. Rubén realized that he knew nothing about her.

"Where did you grow up?" he asked from the bench across from her.

"In Chubut Province," Jana replied.

"In the Mapuche territories?"

"Yes." She picked up one of the rose petals on the tablecloth and began to tear it up with great care. "But we were expelled from out lands," she added. "An Italian multinational . . . "

"United Colors?"

"Yes. We must not have been the right one."

The irony didn't fully conceal her bitterness.

"Is that why you came to Buenos Aires?"

"No, I came to do sculpture," she said. "It was the *machi*, the shaman of the community where we took refuge, who encouraged me to sculpt my dreams when I was little. I began like that, sculpting my nocturnal visions in araucaria wood. Art school came later."

Jana kept her distance—slippery terrain.

"Did the *machi* want to transmit his powers to you?" Rubén asked.

"No, it was my sister who stuck to that. But that's another story. Defending the Mapuche identity doesn't mean the same thing for them as it does for me. The force that binds me to the Land is less organic: I use symbols, materials. Does this interest you?"

"Do you take me for a dolt?"

She smiled slyly.

Few Argentines were aware of the situation of the people who were still called "Indians." Jana talked to him about a world of poverty and defiance, of villages lost in the foothills of the Andes where development was limited to a few tractors, and tribal councils were sometimes corrupt and sold off parcels of the ancestral lands that had been reconquered at considerable cost, a world in which activists disappeared or got killed without an investigation being made, a world of people who didn't interest anyone. Rubén listened, attentive to the variations in her voice, which betrayed her growing emotion. Jana hadn't had to wait for Furlan or courses on the history of art to know that Mapuche culture had its place alongside the others: for her, asserting the Mapuches' identity and knowledge was not so much a matter of asserting the possibility of another world—with finance as a weapon of mass destruction, it was essentially already dead—as a pact of resistance signed with the Earth. The *winkas* had stolen the Mapuche territories, but they understood nothing about the ongoing dialogue that bound them to the world. Their ignorance would be her main focus.

Rubén was thinking again about the monumental sculpture in the middle of her workshop, and began to fit together little pieces of it.

"And you have never wanted to return to your community?"

"No." She shook her head. "No."

"Why?"

Jana crushed the last rose petal with her fingertips.

"Because it's too hard to leave it. And then I've already told you: that's another story."

Her eyes had become sad, as they were when he'd found her standing at his door. She was hiding something. Maybe the main thing.

"Can I put my head on your lap?" Jana asked.

Rubén suggested that she lie down next to him on the bench. The glasses were empty, the wind cooler after midnight. She smoked, looking at the stars, the nape of her neck resting on his thighs. With the trip to Rufino, tomorrow would be a long day, but neither of them wanted to sleep.

"How about you, haven't you ever thought of getting married, Sherlock Holmes?" Jana asked offhandedly. "Having kids?"

Rubén shrugged.

"You must have had a woman in your life?"

His sister.

"No. No woman, at least not the way you mean it."

"A guy?"

Rubén caressed her cheek.

"The missing person posters in your office, the photo off to the side, a young man with a beard and his pals in front of the Eiffel Tower. Who is that, your father?"

The sepia face of Daniel Calderón, surrounded by his comrades in arms—another Argentine poet and the exiled publisher who also translated him.

"Yes. It's the last photo I have of him. A Parisian publisher gave it to me. My father was kidnapped when he returned from France."

"I read that. Is that why you became a detective, to avenge him?"

"Avenging the dead doesn't bring them back," Rubén replied evasively.

"The living are not always better off."

"That's true."

The candles in the jars were going out one after the other. Jana raised her head—it was difficult to see if he was talking about himself, with the obscurity of the roofs. They were both pursuing the same thing, whether ancestors or *desaparecidos*: ghosts. And with a poet of that caliber for a father, she thought, Rubén must like stories. Jana told him the story of the Selk'nam, the cousins of the Patagonian giants, from whom she descended through her great-grandmother, Angela, the last representative of that vanished people in Tierra del Fuego. She told about Angela's old, wrinkled hands that she caressed when she was little, like crevices, the knife she'd inherited from her ancestors, and the secret of the Hain, which the matriarch had revealed to her on her deathbed. The Hain ceremony was a veritable cosmic drama, staged by men to frighten women and keep their power over them. For this ceremony the Selk'nam impersonated fantastic characters, putting on terrifying, extraordinary costumes, those of the spirits that composed their myths, costumes that made them literally unrecognizable; some characters proved to be violent, others ludicrous or obscene. The women, who knew nothing about the men's disguise, reacted accordingly, hooting and trembling with fear as they collected the children under animal hides. The oldest children were taken away from their mothers and subjected to three days of hell, humiliated, beaten, and chased through the snow and the forest by the most evil spirits. In this cosmogonic drama, Jana was particularly fascinated by Kulan, "the terrifying woman." A spirit of flesh and blood, Kulan descended at night from the sky to torment her masculine victims. The men announced her arrival by singing, the women and children hid. The spirit of Kulan, young and slender, was played by a *kloketen*, a child or adolescent girl whose breasts had not grown, her head camouflaged under a strange conical mask, with a white band around her body as far as the crotch, which was covered by a G-string. Kulan kidnapped men at night to make them her sexual slaves, kept them a week or more, and no one heard anything about them. The women begged the heavens, but the ogress's appetite was insatiable: the men returned to the camp stumbling, exhausted, emptied out by Kulan's excesses, fed only on birds' eggs, their hair covered with celestial excrement.

Rubén smiled as he caressed Jana's head, which she had lain on his lap, enjoying the magic of this moment that they both knew was utterly ephemeral.

"What is the secret, then?" he asked.

"The secret of the Hain? I'll tell you that the next time!"

Her dark eyes outshone the stars.

"We'll never leave each other again, if I understand correctly," Rubén said.

"No." Jana was no longer smiling. "We will never leave each other again."

Never.

6

"Montañez—does that name mean anything to you? Ricardo Montañez?"

"No. Who is he?"

"A former petty officer attached to the ESMA," Luque replied. "Montañez served over there in 1976 and I've just been informed that his military record has disappeared. Someone entered illegally into the Navy archives, an Indian woman, to judge by the surveillance video cameras. Jana Wenchwn. She left her papers at the reception desk. No police record. Wenchwn—that name means nothing to you, either?"

"No."

"She's suspected of having fled with Calderón. I don't know why she wanted that military record, but since Montañez served at the ESMA, I thought it might interest you."

"Uh-huh. You did the right thing."

Still holding the receiver to his ear, Torres thought it over. Calderón worked for the Grandmothers of the Plaza de Mayo, and those nosy old bitches would move heaven and earth. Their style.

"This Montañez," he asked, "do you know what happened to him?"

"Manager of a hotel in Rufino, according to what we know now. A remote village along Route 7. Remains to be seen what he has to say."

A knowing silence. The line was secure, the threat vague. The chief of police took the chance.

"Should I tell . . . "

"No, no," Torres interrupted. "He doesn't know anything about it. I'm going to inform the general. If anyone knows Montañez, he's the one. I'll get back to you afterward."

"All right, Mr. Torres."

"Goodbye, sir."

"Goodbye."

Fernando Luque hung up, pensively. Torres had put him in deep shit, up to his neck, and he could no longer back out. The head of the elite police rang his secretary.

"Sylvia, get me Customs."

*

Beyond the outer suburbs of Greater Buenos Aires, the wind was blowing over the plains, the wind the gauchos called the *pampero*. The herds used to be so large there that when enemy ships approached the city, its residents released the cattle whose horns would serve as ramparts. The pampas where they grazed still extended as far as the Andes, over five hundred miles, an "amorphous and harmless country, uniform and boring, like the representation of nothingness" that nourished, according to the writer Ernesto Sabato, Argentine literature's metaphysical imagination. The conquistadors had already sought in vain the fabled silver mines mentioned in legends that had given this depressive El Dorado its name: Argentina, a deserted land of grass and lakes that is now traversed by a paved highway that seems to run straight as an arrow.

Rubén was thinking about his father on Route 7, deciphering the flashing headlights of oncoming trucks that were signaling to each other in the distance. Jana was dozing in the passenger seat. As the miles rolled by he regularly checked the rearview mirror. They had passed a police roadblock not long before, as they left the province. The motorcycle cop had demanded the car's registration and written down their names before letting them drive on. Their weapons were hidden under the seat, and their bags were in the trunk, along with the items they'd bought that morning in a suburban shopping center. They still had over two hundred miles to cover before arriving in Rufino. He'd opened the window to smoke as he drove, lulled by the hum of the engine. Jana finally awoke; she wedged the soles of her Doc Martens on the glove compartment, her mind still hazy.

"You O.K.?"

The sun shone brilliantly beyond the dusty windshield, fields rolled away as far as the eye could see, green oceans dotted with brown cattle.

"Uh-huh," she replied faintly.

Her head bouncing against the side window, she had dreamed about Miguel. The memory left a bad taste in her mouth.

"I'd like a cup of coffee," she said.

A gas station came into view alongside the road. They filled up at the pump while trucks lined up for diesel, and stretched their legs as they watched the semis roar by. A dusty wind was sweeping across the station's pavement, crushed by the midday heat.

"I'm going to take a turn driving," Jana said to emerge from the mist of her dream.

"Later on, if you want."

"I drive better than you do."

Rubén also couldn't care less about cars. His, a Hyundai, ran fine. He ran his index finger over the Mapuche's lips, counting up the kisses he'd left there for her.

"What would you like to eat?" he asked.

"Guess."

A smell of soggy fries permeated the service station's snack area. They drank a cup of coffee from the machine as they observed the hovel where the truck drivers were grumbling, furtively kissed as they were going toward the toilets, and met again in the shop. They paid for the gas at the counter covered with chocolate-covered junk and bought some more or less fresh vacuum-wrapped empanadas to take with them. They were sitting down outside in the shade of a yellowing advertising umbrella when Rubén received an SMS from Anita. A laconic message: "The Old Man is O.K."

"What does that mean?"

"That we'll soon be able to track down the cell phone of the pilot, Del Piro."

Ten minutes later Jana, reinvigorated, took the wheel: she put on the Jesus Lizard CD she'd borrowed from the apartment, turned onto the highway, and followed the exhaust of the trucks polluting the blue skies. "Goat." Chacobuco, Junín, Vedia, the towns flashed past like explosions as they drove along Route 7.

*

Just a stopping point on the road to Mendoza, the little town of Rufino lived in slow motion, its cruising speed. A soybean processing plant with smoking chimneys provided most of the town's activity, the rest being limited to: a couple of service stations where heavily-loaded semis gathered; a few shops with Far West display windows; and two hotels on the main street, which was almost deserted even though it was a Saturday evening. Neither of the hotels was called La Rosada. Worn-out after hours on the road, Jana and Rubén ate in the restaurant of the less depressing of the hotels. The young waitress seemed bored to death, her breasts almost popping out of her low-cut blouse in the hope that someone would get her out of this dead end: according to her, La Rosada was on the outskirts of town, beyond the traffic circle that took the truck drivers back to the main highway. The girl's eyes, at first pleasant, had turned bittersweet.

A narrow paved road full of potholes led off to the north; following the waitress's directions, they drove past the BP station with faded paint and went on half a mile farther. Soon they saw La Rosada's sign among the bushes; it was shabby and seemed centuries old. Jana parked the Hyundai in the graveled lot. Empty parking sheds were lined up behind the building, one of them closed with a blue plastic tarp. They got out and glanced briefly around, looking in vain for the entrance to the hotel.

"Strange place," Jana said.

Rubén bent down in front of the shed covered with the blue tarp and saw the wheels of a car poking out.

"Good evening!" someone sang out behind them.

A man with a craggy face was approaching them. He was wearing a moth-eaten wool sweater flared out over his short legs, a pair of baggy sweatpants, and worn-out sandals with holey socks of different colors. He sized up the Indian woman and the white man accompanying her, and smiled, showing his remaining teeth.

"Are there two of you? It's a hundred and fifty pesos a room," he announced valiantly. "Half an hour, huh?" he added with a complicitous wink.

A toenail black with dirt was poking out of his green sock. The couple looked at him cautiously, but the man didn't get flustered.

"If you want to stay an hour, or longer, I can give you a special price! Come on," he said with jovial impatience, "a hundred pesos."

Jana turned to the open shed and saw a little sign in the form of a red heart crudely taped to the door at the back, which must lead to a dinky room. La Rosada was a hotel used by prostitutes and unfaithful husbands who came there to relieve the boredom of the great plains.

"Are you Ricardo Montañez?" Rubén asked with a grimace.

"Hell, no!" the dirty dwarf retorted. "He's the boss, I'm just the manager of the sheds, Paco! As for the rooms in the hotel, we can make a deal: how about two hundred pesos for the whole night?"

Paco was wearing a wig so tacky that it looked more like a cap. The dark lines around his eyes made him resemble a sad panda, and his brain also seemed to be masticating bamboo.

"Where is he, the big boss?" Rubén growled.

"At his place," Paco replied, pointing to the house behind the trees.

Lights were coming on at dusk, partly hidden by a high, thick hedge. The manager of the highway brothel stared at the Indian woman, met the oblique glance of the big, brown-haired man who was inspecting the place in an inconvenient way, and went all out.

"Fifty! Fifty pesos for an hour!"

The dolt. Rubén took the lout by the mop that served him as a tunic, and breathed into his drunken face:

"You're coming with us, Don Juan."

"Hey! You can't just go to Mr. Montañez's place like that!" Paco gurgled as he was dragged over the gravel. "It's private! Hey! It's private!"

"Shut up, I told you."

A small home appeared, a single-story house covered with ivy, invisible from the road. A string of lights and a wisteria decorated the front door, but the windows were closed.

"Does Montañez have a wife or children?"

"Divorced her, I think."

"What business is he in?"

"The hotel!"

"What else?"

"I don't know," the manager of the sheds stammered. "The rooms . . . I just take care of the rooms!"

A nocturnal bird chirped in the branches. Rubén pushed the guy toward the porch and handed the .45 to Jana.

"If this pile of lice tries to run away, shoot him in the foot."

"O.K."

Paco looked around him like a seagull in front of prey washed up on the beach.

"What? Are you nuts or what? Whattya going to do with . . . "

"You'll get another bullet in your ass if you do anything stupid," Rubén whispered to him. "Now ring."

Paco's short legs were trembling under his rags. He rang, several times. The sporadic noise of trucks could be heard in the distance, insects were circling under the wisteria, but no one came to the door. It was open: Rubén pushed the wigged dwarf in front of them, ordering him to keep his mouth closed. A dark hall lit by candles led to a white double door with gilt reliefs. There was an odor of jasmine in the hall, where the candles flickered. Paco walked cautiously on the pink marble floor, giving off a foul odor amid the incense. The voices became more audible behind the gilding of the double door: a woman's moans, languorous and punctuated by unmistakable cries. Their eyes met, stunned. The double door was locked: Rubén broke the lock with a powerful kick and shoved Paco into the middle of the room with the same violence.

It wasn't a swingers' party for the leading figures in Rufino, and still less an orgy with deluxe whores getting paid per moan: Ricardo Montañez was alone in the middle of the room, naked as a jaybird, a glass of ice-cold champagne nearby. A giant screen connected to a computer faced the bubbling Jacuzzi under the speakers, from which wailing orgasms were roaring. A girl in garters was exhibiting herself on the king-size screen, clitoris wet and pubes shaved, in a clichéd brothel setting. A devotee of cybersex, Montañez was communicating with the performers on a site that offered, at the rate of fifty pesos for ten minutes, erotic stimulation of all kinds: the girls responded to their customers' orders by typing short texts, moaning on cue. Montañez saw his employee on all fours on the acrylic animal hides, the couple accompanying him, and, after a moment of shared stupefaction, reacted.

"What are you doing here? It's . . . it's private here!"

In his sixties and fattened up by business meals, Ricardo Montañez had a soft, milky body lathered with fragrant oils, short-sighted brown eyes, and a elephantine belly that almost concealed his child's penis: an immature penis, not ten years old.

Rubén approached him while Jana turned off the sound. Ashamed, furious, Montañez stood up in his birthday suit and rushed toward the silk dressing gown lying on the bed.

"It's . . . it's a violation of my home!" he protested.

Ricardo Montañez had gained over a hundred pounds since his youth in the military, but it was indeed the former petty officer.

"Listen, big guy," Rubén began, confronting him. "I'm looking into a double murder that took place under the dictatorship: Samuel and Gabriella Verón. I know that you were serving at the ESMA at that time, and I also know that you took part in the couple's transfer and killing. September 1976. A couple whose children had been kidnapped."

"Who . . . who are you?" the brothel's owner asked angrily.

He looked around him, saw only a video that suddenly seemed obscene, and his sheepish employee.

"Don't expect anyone to help you," Rubén warned him.

"But . . . "

"I don't give a shit about your sexual problems, Montañez. I just want to know who the officer was that accompanied you that night, and where you buried the bodies."

The fat man pulled his dressing gown tighter around him, not knowing what to do.

"Either you talk or we'll have to cut off your little worm," the Indian woman said.

"It wasn't me . . . I . . . I was just the driver . . . It's ancient history."

"Not for us. Who was the officer assigned to extract the couple?"

Ricardo was sweating heavily under his makeup. Rubén grabbed him by the collar.

"You hear what I'm saying to you?"

"I don't know anything!" Montañez yelped. "I was never told. He . . . he wasn't at the ESMA. Or I'd never heard of him. I don't know anything, I swear!"

"Where are the bodies buried?"

"I . . . I don't remember anymore."

"Where?"

Montañez began to choke.

"In the Andes . . . near the Chilean border."

"Where in the Andes?"

"A pass!" the obese man breathed. "I don't know any more!"

Paco backed toward the door, staring with fear at the scarlet face of his boss, whom the big brown-haired guy was manhandling.

"Stay where you are," Jana whispered to him, giving him a kick.

"A pass!" the boss said hoarsely. "Near Puente del Inca! In . . . in that area!"

The former petty officer was beginning to suffocate. Rubén relaxed his grip.

"You're going to take us there," he announced in a cavernous voice.

"Wh . . . what?"

"To the pass where you buried them."

Montañez's entire body was trembling; it seemed to be deflating.

"Huh? But . . . it's over five hundred miles from here!" he

said, readjusting the collar of his kimono, which had been wrinkled by Rubén's grip.

Rubén sized up the man with a boy's penis, who was shaking beneath the silk.

"Get dressed, old man."

*

Jana drove while Rubén grilled the guy in the backseat. Looking like a Buddha curled up in a corner of the car, receptive to the detective's threats or relieved to talk after so many years of silence, Montañez told them his story.

Having grown up in the region, without plans or any qualifications other than a license to drive large rigs (his father had been a truck driver), Ricardo had enlisted in the army at the age of nineteen, on a sudden impulse that had boomerang effects. The *verdes*, the young recruits, had no choice: those who didn't obey orders, even if they were iniquitous, found themselves on the other side of the fence. Ricardo had first been detailed to the Campo de Mayo, which had been made into a vast concentration camp in connection with hunting down "subversives," and then to the ESMA, as a driver. He had been chosen for the extraction of a detained couple, but not informed of the special mission to which he had been assigned. The identity of the prisoners, who were drugged for the trip, was unknown to him, but he remembered the transfer, an endless road they'd covered partly at night and that took them up into the mountains. An officer accompanied them, a colonel in the army who had never said his name. Montañez had driven the van without asking any questions. When they arrived at the foot of the Andes, the officer had ordered him to put on one of the hoods they used to cover the eyes of subversives, and to keep quiet while he took over at the wheel. They had driven for an hour or two, without a word, as far as an isolated *estancia* somewhere in the bottom of a valley. Montañez had helped the colonel take the couple out of the van. At that point they were awakened and their hands tied behind their backs: a bearded man and a woman who was wearing a dress that was in pitiful condition and who could hardly walk. Someone was waiting for them inside the *estancia*: the colonel had gone in with the two detainees, while he remained freezing in the van. An hour later, the trio came out again. Ricardo had put the hood back on, still without saying a word, and they set off again in the night, as they had come. After what seemed to him another hour of driving, the colonel had taken winding roads before stopping the vehicle in the middle of the desert.

The prisoners were trembling with fear when they were made to get out of the van. The officer, his revolver in his hand, had ordered them to dig their own graves, but the couple had refused. In the end, it was Ricardo who'd gotten stuck with the job. The colonel had shot the two subversives himself, putting a bullet in the napes of their necks, first the woman, then the bearded man . . . Afterward, the officer assigned to the mission had commanded him to take the wheel again and to keep his mouth shut if he didn't want to get in trouble, and that is what he'd done. Montañez had left the army two months later, at the end of his enlistment, and returned to his region of origin, hoping never to hear anything about that period again.

The former driver was sweating on the backseat, his cheeks trembling with the bumps in the road. Rubén was harassing him.

"Did they give you money to keep quiet?"

"No."

"How did you manage to buy your shitty hotel?"

"My parents died . . . They left me a little money."

"This colonel—you must have run into him again after this episode?"

"No, never. He wasn't at the ESMA, I tell you!"

"Describe him."

"Fairly tall . . . thick brown hair . . . pretty young at the time, maybe around forty. It was a long time ago, I don't remember anymore."

"We'll see about that. Any identifying characteristic?"

"No. I'd never seen him before, and I never saw him afterward. It's a period that I want to forget, and . . . "

"Describe the place where the couple was executed."

"Toward Puente del Inca . . . I remember black rocks alongside a rough track, a huge landslide . . . It was a long time ago!"

Rubén grumbled in the backseat. There were gaps in the petty officer's story—the location of the *estancia*, what might have taken place there, the identity of the owner and that of the officer assigned to carry out the transfer and the murder. The interrogation had gone on for more than an hour. Montañez grew tired, his nerves breaking down after his confession. Rubén thought for a long time on the backseat. Jana was watching the road, looking out for stray cattle that could pulverize the car. Soon Rubén leaned forward toward her.

"Do you want me to drive?"

"No, that's O.K. Hey," Jana whispered. "I'm thinking about something."

"What?"

"What are we going to do about the cat? He must be hungry, poor old thing."

Rubén caressed the nape of the Mapuche's neck and smiled in the dark of the car.

"Don't worry about him, he'll be all right."

*

The valley of the Uspallata cuts deep into the Andes. The heart of the rock was yellow, red, gray, black, green—a miracle of nature escorting the defile. They had passed Mendoza before dawn and followed the road that climbed into the mountains. A few quarries with trucks standing about and improbable derricks miming the conquest of the West seemed petrified by the first rays of the sun. Farther on, a little chapel made out of a drainpipe contained a row of ex-votos. Rubén and Jana traveled through spectacular gorges, past a lake of turquoise water dominated by mesas, winding canyons in which rafting clubs often camped and which were closed to the public at the end of the summer. They drove for nine hours, almost without stopping; the lack of sleep was beginning to make itself felt, and they stopped for a cup of coffee at a mountain inn that was just opening its doors.

Awakened from his virtual ecstasy, Ricardo Montañez snorted. He was wearing linen pants, a beige tunic thrown on in haste, and moccasins without socks.

"I've got to go," he said.

The inn was empty at that hour. While Montañez was in the toilet, Rubén ordered breakfast and returned to the sunny terrace. Huge rocks lay on the other side of the road; they had probably been there for centuries. Jana mewed as she stretched her arms; her muscles were stiff. The sun was coming up over the crest of the mountains, and a bird of prey flew high above in the pink sky. The air was cooler at 6,500 feet; the landscape had a cinematographic clarity.

"I've never come this way," the Mapuche said. "It's beautiful."

They soon arrived at the Aconcagua, "the stone sentinel," the roof of the Americas, whose snowy peaks were lost in the clouds. Rubén stayed close to her, the scent of her hair as a guide.

"Do you think Montañez is putting us on?" she asked. "He's been moaning in the backseat for hours."

"We'll soon find out."

A truck passed by, whining in second gear.

"In any case, we should be wary of him," Jana said with a frown. "This guy really looks like a sneak, with his little prick."

Her slight smile grew larger. Rubén suddenly felt like kissing her, telling her that last night had been marvelous, but the old petty officer was coming back from the toilets, as white as a sheet.

Puente del Inca: the last pass before the descent into Chile. An orange dust was flying over the asphalt road. As they approached the border post they met only a few trucks. Montañez continued to sweat heavily in the backseat of the Hyundai, barely reinvigorated by his breakfast. They saw a couple of llamas lost in the stony waste as they drove out of Las Cuevas, but not a single human being. The slopes of the mountains varied in color from mauve to red; it was growing hotter. Jana slowed as she crossed an abandoned train track: an old iron bridge signaled that they had arrived at Puente del Inca, the southernmost limit of the ancient kingdom of the Incas.

"Do you recognize it?" Rubén said as he drove.

Montañez was dripping under his tunic. He was afraid of his memories, afraid of spending years in prison for a crime he hadn't committed. Since the statute of limitations on crimes against the state had been abolished, the detective had made a deal with the former military man: no criminal charges in exchange for his collaboration. They drove along the bed of a dry river, then passed dramatic scree slopes in a narrow canyon: Montañez observed the landscape attentively.

"Turn right here," he said after a while.

A sheet of ice gleamed in the lunar shadow of a rocky peak. They followed a dirt road that went to the right. The air coming through the windows was warmer. The Hyundai was traveling at the feet of titans eroded by the wind when the fat man signaled that they should stop. A lava flow had stopped near a pinnacle of black rock with steely glints.

"Is it here?"

"Yes, I think so."

The petty officer had never returned to the scene of the crime, but it was impossible to forget these contrasts. They parked the car at the side of the road. Montañez said nothing, hypnotized by the metallic reflections of the rock that ate into the sky. Rubén poked into the soil apprehensively, as if the dead might rise up. Finally, Montañez pointed to a spot at the foot of the rockslide.

"Here, I think."

The soil was dry and scattered with small stones. Rubén threw a brand-new shovel and pickaxe in front of Ricardo's tasseled moccasins.

"Dig."

The sun rose steeply in the heart of the Andes. Montañez labored, hunched over his tool: he'd been digging at the foot of the precipice. He complained about blisters and backache. The earth was hard and the heat dreadful, despite the bit of cloth that protected his large, shaved head; Jana and Rubén, who had taken refuge in the car with the door open to let the desert air blow through, watched him struggle.

Jana had never been north of the mountain range, but she knew that there was a Huarpe site in this region, a center of energy as powerful as that at Machu Picchu, where the shamans talked with the cosmic spirit. The Huarpes, those peaceful giants, had not been destroyed by the little Incas but by the Jesuits, who had recruited them in order to save them. Rubén listened to her as he smoked, keeping one eye on the progress of the work. He thought again about their discussion on the roof terrace. The Mapuches also talked with the earth. Her sister and the *machi* . . .

"By the way, you never told me," he said. "What is the secret of the Hain?"

The Selk'nam's great-granddaughter gave him a charming look.

"Maybe someday you'll find out. Or maybe never."

He spat the smoke from his cigarette out the open door. Not very precise, her story. Twenty yards away, at the foot of the rocky mass, Montañez continually swore at the barbarous soil; his tunic was dirty, his moccasins dusty, his hands covered with blisters. He was killing himself under the blazing sun, a trembling mass half swallowed up by the hole, he dug on and on until he hit a bone.

"Here's something!" he cried.

He put down his pickaxe, his eyes baleful under his head-cloth. Jana and Rubén left the car that protected them from the sun and returned to the pit, from which the heavy man was extricating himself with difficulty. Bits of bone were visible at the bottom of the hole. Rubén set down the little case that Raúl Sanz had given him and jumped down into the cavity. Jana kept an eye on Montañez, whose face was red from the effort he'd made; he was almost apoplectic. The detective swept away the looser earth using small archeological tools: brushes, rakes, a pick; his actions were precise and cautious. Jana leaned over the grave. Other bones appeared, vertebrae the color of fabric, then a human skull. That of a woman, so far as one could tell by the remains of the dress. Montañez was still wiping his face, sitting in the shade of the black pinnacle that loomed over them.

"Was that what she was wearing?" Rubén asked him.

The former petty officer approached the grave very slowly, then made an affirmative gesture. Rubén went on with the exhumation. There was another body, intertwined with the first, a man, his neck broken by the impact of a bullet. Samuel and Gabriella Verón. It couldn't be anyone else.

The detective did not separate the two skeletons of the couple intertwined in death: he detached the skulls and put them in a military sack brought for the purpose. Jana didn't say anything either. The noonday sun was beating down unmercifully. Rubén thought sadly about these two young people who had spent six nightmarish weeks in detention at the ESMA, and then found themselves in the Andes in the middle of the night, hugging each other and trembling in front of the grave that was being dug for them. The girl first, Montañez had said, then the bearded man. Two young people twenty-five years old, whose children had been stolen from them. Lovers.

*

A gray, angry thunderstorm was sweeping across the valley. They went around the cloud, following the ray of sun that passed through it. Jana was driving silently. They had just left the dirt road and gotten back on the asphalt that wound down to Uspallata. The bones were in the trunk of the car, along with the tools and their baggage. Rubén had buried the remains of Samuel and Gabriella, hoping to give them a decent grave later on. In the backseat, Montañez was slowly recovering, counting the burst blisters on his pudgy fingers. He too was shaken. They drove past abrupt cliffs of astonishing beauty without meeting any other vehicles. The detective was sending messages on his BlackBerry when Jana slowed down as she came out of a curve.

People were blocking the road.

"Rubén . . . "

He looked up. *Piqueteros*. There weren't many of them, about a hundred yards away. People who hadn't shared in the economic growth and who had assembled in haste under a billowing banner. It was hard to determine what they wanted—probably just work. Bizarre. Standing in the middle of the road, the unemployed men signaled to them: Jana braked as they approached the roadblock and rolled down her window. A man wearing an old sweatsuit came to meet them, a colored sun hat on his head. The *piquetero* smiled broadly at her; he had a nasty scar on his nose and held leaflets in his hand.

"*Hola, señorita!*" he said as he leaned on the car's windowsill.

There were six of them under the banner, their heads protected by straw hats; there was a fellow at the wheel of a pickup who was observing them from the side of the road.

"Go!" Rubén shouted, plunging his hand under his jacket. "Go!"

These guys were not *piqueteros*. The man at the door of the car dropped the leaflets that had been hiding his gun and pointed it at the Mapuche at the wheel. A shot resounded in the car as she floored the accelerator. Rubén had fired first, at point-blank range: hit in the solar plexus, the scarred man fell to the asphalt.

"Go! Go!"

Jana no longer heard Rubén's cries nor the roaring of the motor: the gun had gone off a few inches from her ears; a high-pitched whistle was piercing her eardrums, and the world seemed to be turning. She crossed the line of fake *piqueteros*, who immediately moved aside. They pulled their hidden weapons out of their shirts and emptied their cartridge clips as if they had been at a shooting range. The rear window of the Hyundai was blown to pieces.

"Keep your head down, Jana!" Rubén bellowed. "Damn it, keep your head down!"

The Mapuche was focusing on the road, clutching the steering wheel: a volley of bullets passed over them, spraying bits of glass everywhere inside the car. Jana had her foot on the floor but they still weren't going fast enough: the car was hit, the trunk riddled with bullets. Montañez was howling in the backseat. Jana was gripping the wheel when one of the tires exploded. She immediately lost control of the car, which swerved suddenly toward the side of the road. There was no guardrail, but the dry land prevented serious damage when they went off the road: bullets were still flying around them as they bumped over the desert.

"Keep going, keep going!"

Jana drove a hundred yards before she heard the first sounds: Rubén was pointing to the ruins of a building a little higher up the hill. The Hyundai climbed another thirty yards and then stopped against a talus of stone and sand. Rubén grabbed the .38 under the driver's seat and opened the door.

"Let's get out of here, fast!"

Jana climbed out as he went around the car to get the bag out of the trunk. Ricardo Montañez crawled out in turn, moaning, his tunic spattered with blood: a bullet had broken his upper arm. Bullets were whistling through the cloud of dust that still protected them. Montañez grimaced, holding his wounded arm, disoriented. Rubén dragged him toward the Mapuche, who was running in the direction of the ruins, the revolver in her hand. The pickup came up behind them, five men clinging to the bed. They stopped next to the Hyundai and fired their weapons into the swirling dust that was now dissipating. Rubén, Jana, and Montañez had a hundred yards' head start. The *piqueteros* jumped down, divided into two groups and set out in pursuit of the fugitives.

Rubén let go of Montañez, whose arm was bleeding fast, and hurried to catch up with Jana, who had already reached the first butte. The ruins were a little higher up, after the dip. He ran after her, the military bag on his shoulder, without turning around: more bullets were ricocheting off the rocks. There was a steep slope in front of them. Jana and Rubén got to the low wall first. Montañez lagged behind, his eyes rolling at his open fracture and the bullets whistling around his ears. He lost a moccasin as he ran, tried to pick it up and let out a strident scream. His shoulder blade and lung perforated, he collapsed halfway up the slope. Panic! He clung to the stones that shifted under his hands, refusing to believe that his last moments were at hand and, spitting blood, slipped down onto the pebbles. The killers ran up behind him, six men divided into two groups who were making an assault on the butte. Rubén caught his breath, counted the bullets that were jingling in his pocket. Five. Plus the seven in the Colt's cylinder. The .38 was loaded. That made twenty-two.

"Take cover," he said, nodding toward the ruins.

Firing at moving targets: his weekly meeting, with Anita. Rubén aimed at one of the two guys who were trying to circle around on the right and fired. The man slumped down, hit in the stomach. There was no cover for twenty meters around: he fired two more shots at the most heavyset of the men, a guy in dirty jeans, who stumbled back under the impact. Rubén bent over and ran under a storm of inaccurate fire. Jana was trying to open her ears, crouched behind the collapsing wall.

"You O.K.?"

"I can't hear anything!"

The ruins weren't the remains of an *estancia* lost in the mountains but a former hot springs building that had been destroyed by an avalanche a century earlier. The deluxe hotel had overlooked the Río de las Cuevas, twenty yards below it. Rubén pressed up against a window that had served as an arrow slit, and put down the canvas bag containing the skulls.

"Jana, can you hear me?"

"Yeah, it's getting better."

Rubén put the .38 in her hands.

"Who do I shoot at?" she asked.

"The group on the left," he said, pointing to the three men who were approaching.

The Mapuche had never used a revolver, only rifles: she lifted the hammer. Her cheek was bleeding; she'd been hit by a fragment of stone or windshield.

"Ready?"

She nodded.

"O.K.!"

They spun out of the opening and fired in the same movement. Jana missed her targets, who flattened themselves on the ground. Rubén took advantage of this to shoot the man who was reaching the building on the right side. Adrenaline was coursing through his veins; he grabbed the bag on the ground and fled with Jana through the passageways.

A waterfall was spewing into the canyon, pouring out water rich in iron and sulfur that gave a yellowish-orange color to the age-old rock: they ran under the cool vaults of the old spa and came to what must have been the baths. A wooden bridge crossed the green river flowing down below; they flattened themselves against the rock of the platform alongside the bridge, their hearts pounding. A cloud of spray from the summits plunged into the river, but cooled them hardly at all.

"Are you all right?" Rubén whispered as he reloaded his gun.

"Yes. Worry about these bastards instead."

There were three killers, better armed. He could hear them getting closer under the vaults. A strong odor of sulfur rose from the river, but they no longer smelled it. The *piqueteros* were only a few yards away, shadows moving along the walls, making the terrain secure as they advanced. Rubén gripped the handle of the Colt .45. Jana was crouching next to him, jammed into a crevice, her revolver pointed toward their assailants—she still had a few bullets. The killers were hiding in the darkness of the baths. Rubén kept his finger on the trigger, anxious. The *piqueteros* knew where they were: if they attacked the bridge, firing at such short distance would cause real carnage, and Rubén had only five bullets left. The water flowed toward the abyss, filling the air that had suddenly become unbreatheable. Jana held her breath, her hands sweating. Rubén thought about firing two shots blindly to disperse the killers long enough to jump off the bridge: a drop of twenty yards before hitting the water of the river. It was the end of summer, and with the water low they might very well break their necks.

A cell phone rang, incongruously, out of the grotto. Jana

looked at Rubén, who signaled to her to get ready to jump into the void. They waited, a few seconds that lasted an eternity, but nothing happened. The killers seemed uncertain what to do. One of them had retreated to the damp room to take the call; there was a moment of hesitation as the waterfall rumbled, the echo of a muted voice from the vaults of the old spa, an obscure silence, and then the sound of a pebble grating under a shoe. Footsteps. Footsteps that were moving away.

Their eyes met again, waiting to see what would happen. Rubén waited a few more seconds, then signaled to Jana to stay put and slipped off like a cat. He climbed along the wall like a tightrope walker, looked down on the river and the bridge far below: three figures were hurrying down the hill, dragging the bodies of their companions. They were retreating.

Montañez, the witness to the double murder, was dead. That was enough for them, obviously. But not for Rubén. He evaluated the topography of the site, saw Jana hiding near the bridge, her hand gripping her gun and giving him questioning looks.

"Take the bag!" he called to her from his perch.

Then he went around the rocky outcrop.

Jana saw him flirting with the drop-off as he made his way along the ridge, climbed down, and ran toward the slope that led to the road. He charged down the talus in a trail of yellow dust, slipped on the pebbles, and almost fell headfirst but caught himself on the clouds.

On the other side of the outcropping, the killers were climbing into the pickup, carrying their wounded. One of them was no longer moving, and two others, who could barely walk, were hurriedly hoisted onto the bed of the truck. The 4x4 bounced over the terrain until it reached the asphalt road. Rubén ran to cut them off, but understood that he would be too late and suddenly changed course and climbed back toward the little slope on his left. A dead tree stood at the summit of the butte; the killers were passing by it, ten meters below. He took aim. They were driving at top speed toward the curve in the road. Rubén emptied his clip onto the bed of the pickup, his hand cold in order to contain his rage.

Hit in the chest, a *piquetero* slumped against the cab; the one holding a red banner put his hand to his jaw, which had just been broken. One of the wounded seemed to jump under the impact, while his neighbor, already dead, took a bullet in the face. Rubén exhaled, his eyes fixed on his moving target, and swore: he hadn't hit the driver and his clip was empty. They were getting away.

A small cloud of powder blew away in the desert breeze. He had one last glimpse of the pickup disappearing around the curve, blood sprayed over the cab and dead men in the back. Rubén gritted his teeth, dirty and panting.

The rotten bastards.

7

Jana had observed the counterattack from the ruined bridge of the former spa. An icy breeze accompanied her as far as the rocky outcropping where Rubén was grumbling, the hot revolver still in his hand. His clothes were covered with dust, his face pale despite his run and the sweat running down his temples.

"Did you get them?"

"Not all of them."

They had scratched their hands going down the scree slope. Jana put the bag on the ground, saw the cartridge casings scattered in the brush, and met the detective's feverish eyes.

"I like being in bed more."

Rubén didn't flinch. Their bodies stank of sweat, fear, and death. They took each other in their arms to be sure that they were together, alive. The tension moved back down their legs. The killers had fled, as suddenly as they had appeared. Rubén caressed the Mapuche's wounded cheek, just a scrape. She felt the muscles in his arm that were protecting her, the tenderness of his hands on her, and breathed more easily. In the meantime, the situation wasn't great: a dead body halfway up the slope, Montañez, whose bloody tunic was sending olfactory signals to the vultures, the cartridge casings from their weapons all over the area, and the Hyundai off the road, planted like a biplane in the desert. He let go of Jana's hand, which was still squeezing his.

"Let's not stay here."

They hurried down the slope, keeping an eye on the ridges

and the road that wound through the rock. Although the radiator had survived the crash, the hood had been crushed. The inside of the car was full of broken glass, and the rear seat was still sticky with blood. Bits of rubber clung to one wheel; it seemed possible to drive on the other three, and the keys were still in the ignition. Rubén climbed in and hit the starter. The motor ran normally.

"What shall we do with Montañez?" Jana asked.

"No time to bury him. We've got to get out of here before the cops show up. Come on, help me."

Shade was in short supply in the middle of the afternoon. Rubén put on the spare tire while Jana flattened out the crumpled metal of the hood with her Doc Martens. The road started winding a hundred yards farther on, past the wasteland where they had crashed. Rubén was still trembling. He didn't know how the false *piqueteros* had been able to set a trap for them so quickly, in the middle of the mountains; he knew only that he'd almost lost her.

"Any idea where those guys came from?" Jana asked while he was struggling with the wheel.

"No. Montañez might have been under surveillance. The theft of his military record must have been reported, and the info was forwarded to the boss, who sent his henchmen after us. Unless we were tracked."

"Tracked by who?"

"The provincial border posts."

"You mean the cops are in on this?"

"I don't see how the medical examiner could have falsified the autopsy report on María without Luque's permission. He's the one who's handling all this, and he has clearly lied to the Campallo family."

She frowned, leaning against the hood.

"I thought Campallo was a friend of the mayor; it was Torres who set up the elite police force, wasn't it?"

"Yes," he conceded, his scratched hands now black with dirt. "Something's wrong in this business."

He changed tires.

"Shit, somebody's coming."

Coming down from the pass, a truck slowed and pulled over, an old blue Ford. Two farmworkers in straw hats were in the front seat.

"Need a hand?" the driver asked from the dented door.

"We're fine, thanks!"

Jana made reassuring signs to them to get them to leave. The workers set off again in their jalopy, making a friendly gesture in lieu of a goodbye, without noticing the body that was drying in the sun in the distance. Rubén finally stood up, his forehead dripping with sweat. The spare would hold until they reached the next town, but the axle seemed to have been bent. They dug out the car and got back on the section of paved road that led to the main highway.

"Uspallata 22 km" the sign read. Rubén lit two cigarettes, put the first between Jana's lips as she drove, and reloaded the two revolvers, which were still warm. Fortunately, it would take the local police some time to find the hotel owner's body: with a little luck, they would be far away. The vague testimony given by the farmworkers they'd met while he was changing the tire would be useless; on the other hand, despite the threats he'd made, the testimony of the guy at the brothel in Rufino worried him. They followed in silence the road, which wound through steep canyons as it threaded its way through the passes of the Aconcagua. An eagle was turning in lazy circles high above. Rubén was replaying in his mind, for the tenth time, the gun battle fought shortly before.

"Was it your brothers who taught you to shoot?" he asked as they came out of a long curve.

"Yes."

"What were you hunting with your rifles?"

Jana shrugged.

"Carabineros."

He gave her a questioning glance, to which she did not respond.

Route 7 meandered through the slopes of the Andes: a line of trucks going in the opposite direction had piled up, blocked by a convoy. Jana drove prudently, afraid that she would come upon a police patrol. A warm wind was blowing through the pulverized windows, and Rubén was keeping an eye on the sides of the road and the entrances to canyons, the revolvers within reach, but the killers had actually vanished.

Uspallata, "the teeth of the earth," a village sound asleep on this hot Sunday afternoon: the stands in front of the shops were empty, the terraces deserted at siesta time. The Hyundai crossed the main street and slowed in front of the closed casino that marked the intersection of the three roads. A little farther on they saw the pennants of a garage, a service station half-covered with brush.

The mechanic who came out of the workshop frowned when he saw the car that had pulled up in front.

"What happened to you?" he asked, inspecting the car's body. "An accident?"

"No, it was stolen from us," Rubén said with cool self-assurance. "It was like this when we found it."

"Hard luck!"

The mechanic was not deceived, but he pretended he was.

"We have to drive it back to Mendoza. Can you repair it?"

The man's brother came out to the little parking lot flooded with sun, wiped his hands on his coveralls, and nodded to the couple. Jana went toward the toilets while they hemmed and hawed. Rear window, headlights, axle, not to mention the holes in the body: in view of the damage, they would need at least until the following noon, and then only if they could get the right parts.

"What if I paid you double?" Rubén suggested.

"That won't bring the parts in by plane," the brother noted. "Even if we work all night, it won't be ready before noon tomorrow. At the earliest! It's full of electronic shit, your car."

"Sure . . . " A sticky silence in front of the garage.

"O.K.," Rubén said. "Noon tomorrow."

He advanced the money to buy the parts, which the brother would go to pick up in Mendoza, and the same sum in exchange for them forgetting the rest. Once the car was on the ramp in the garage, Rubén took the bags out of the back of the trunk and rejoined Jana, who was splashing water on her face in the lavatory. She had only a superficial cut on her cheek that was no longer bleeding.

"Well?" she asked.

"We're stuck here until tomorrow."

Jana sighed.

"Poor Ledzep."

Rubén washed his flayed hands in the dirty sink.

"What about the local police? Aren't they going to give us trouble?"

"The next police station is a dozen miles away," he said. "And the garage guys seem O.K. Let's go eat something, then we'll see."

A blazing sun for a soporific Sunday in the little town in the Andes. It was six o'clock in the afternoon, the wind was warm, their eyes were burning from lack of sleep, and they hadn't eaten anything since morning. A bleached blonde in a Hello Kitty T-shirt ran the only shop open in the village, a snack bar with gaudy signs that sold mainly ice cream. They swallowed homemade *bocadillos* under the breath of a capricious fan. The room was empty, the *cumbia* at full volume: Rubén could hardly hear his cell phone ring.

He went outside to take Anita's call.

Married men taking a day off for the traditional *asado*, the intern sleeping off a binge with his partying friends, Anita was spending Sunday having a nap with her cat Mist. The recent events had upset their little habits. Del Piro still hadn't shown up, but she was on the botanist's trail thanks to her "pal" at Immigration: Díaz had in fact crossed the Argentine border the preceding Wednesday, that is, on the day of the raid in Colonia. The paparazzo's neighbor had fled. Whom was he running from? The killers or the cops? Was his hostility to Ossario a façade? To hide what? At the other end of the line, Anita remained in doubt.

"Who says that your botanist is not involved in all this? He might be a military man, a former Nazi, an old piece of garbage who has taken refuge in Uruguay under a false name, or an accomplice of your famous silent partner."

"Uh-huh."

The stray dog that was sniffing the municipal garbage cans in the shade of the cracked walls went around Rubén, his tail between his legs.

"Do you have a photo of Díaz you can send me?"

"I can scan the one in his passport."

"O.K. Send copies to Carlos and the Grandmothers too. Díaz might be in our files under another name."

"When are you coming back?"

"Not for two days."

"And the *piqueteros*?"

"I hardly saw them," he said, "apart from the guy who stopped the car: a heavyset, brown-haired fellow with a scar, average size, about forty. I can ask Jana to make a sketch, if we can find some paper in this hole."

"Jana?"

"What do you want me to call her, Picasso?"

"She also draws killers on the road?" Anita pretended to be astonished. "What talent!"

"Are you jealous?"

"Terribly."

"Tsk."

"I've been in love with you since I was a girl, you jerk."

"You're not a girl anymore, *querida*. So, is it over?"

"Yes. I'll let you know if Del Piro calls from his cell phone," Anita said before hanging up. "*Ciao, bello*! Kisses to you know who!"

The enchanting friend.

Jana was waiting with the sacks in front of the snack bar. According to Hello Kitty, the only hotel in Uspallata had closed the year before; there remained only the prefab cottages visible behind the hedges of the campground, and they had all the charm of a suppository.

"Not exactly pretty," Rubén commented.

"It's either that or sleeping under the stars."

Her dark eyes were already shining.

*

Something like a desert extended for miles beyond the village, the Andean plateau surrounded by blue and mauve mountains over which falcons soared. Rubén and Jana were walking north, their weighted-down sacks over their shoulders. Animal bones were bleaching along the brown earth track; the sun's heat was getting less intense as they made their way over the bare land. The walk had reduced them to the silence of these immense spaces, as if nothing had existed before them. Soon the landscape devoured everything, shrubs and brittle grasses; they walked a couple of miles, the breath of the wind like a wave singing over the sand. Nature was so impressive that they forgot the fright of the day.

"You all right, old man?" Jana said to Rubén, who was lugging the heaviest sacks.

"I can still walk a yard or two," he assured her. "How about you?"

"I'll have to put my shoes back on."

A stony path led to the Rock of Seven Colors. Jana, who had been walking barefoot since they'd left the village, stopped to put on her Doc Martens. Strange little thing. They passed the skeleton of a cow that was lying in the shade of a stunted tree and found a sandy place where they could set up camp for the night. The site, enclosed at the end of a canyon, was blazing with the light of the setting sun. They put down the blankets and the food they'd bought—ready-made salad, industrial bread, two bottles of beer that were still more or less cool, and a piece of beef that they would grill if they could find some firewood. Jana used the lighter to pry off the caps while Rubén collected stones for the fire, waited until he sat down next to her, opposite a rainbow-colored rock, and handed him a bottle. All that remained of the Quilmes, the mountain people who had died off in the reservations on the plains where they had been parked, was the name of a beer: Quilmes.

"Odd how Christians are able to honor the people they've massacred," the Mapuche observed.

"What do you do with your victims, pull out their nose hairs?"

"Yes, with our teeth, to make the kids laugh."

Their mouths met.

"For the rest of our lives," she said.

"Yes, for the rest of our lives."

They clinked glasses, Rubén more worried than he wanted to show. He was still afraid of losing her. He wanted to hold her to him, on any pretext, to hug her tight until he could feel her Indian pulse beating in his veins, but part of him was still down there . . . He looked out blankly over the stony ground. Jana moved a little closer to him, as if she had heard an echo of the silence of his abyss, and put her head on his shoulder. The sky was turning pink as it withdrew from the Andes. For a while, they continued to contemplate the desert and the passes in the fading light. The beauty of the world: it was there, before their greedy eyes, and Rubén could no longer see anything but ghosts. The sky was melting on the rock when she murmured:

"Rubén, there's something I haven't told you. The other night, in the bedroom, I saw the marks on your skin when we made love, the scars . . . "

Dark scars in the light of the candles, on his breast, his armpits, terrible wounds that time had not erased. Rubén did not reply, but the little flowers trembled in his eyes.

"They tortured you, didn't they? Those scars—did they do that to you? Electrical burns?" He remained silent. "You were also in the ESMA's jails, weren't you? But you got out," she added to help him. "They didn't kill you."

"Yes they did." He was looking down at the sand.

"No, Rubén. You're alive, more alive than anyone on Earth."

"No."

The crack in his façade was now gaping. He had said nothing to others, shown nothing. He had seen Death, and no one must see that, on any pretext, on pain of going mad.

"Your mother survived the tragedy," Jana said in as gentle a voice as she could manage.

"She doesn't know what happened."

"She can guess."

"No."

Rubén was mumbling. She glanced at him, suddenly concerned. Spirits were floating around him, stone spirits. Jana knew this feeling of eternal solitude, all those years when her breasts had not grown—solitude, anger, and helplessness.

"We almost got ourselves killed today," she said bravely. "It might happen tomorrow, as we come out of a cafe or an apartment building, and then it will be too late. I want to share everything with you, Rubén, not just anonymous lovemaking in some bed or other. Your hands have known other women, but I don't want to be like them. Not today and not tomorrow, either. Moral niceties have nothing to do with it. What are you afraid of, me? Do you think I'm going to steal something from you? Your most precious possession, maybe? What do you take me for, a *winka*?"

He smiled wanly.

"I can handle anything," she said, challenging him. "After what I've been through with you, I can handle anything."

"No one can handle anything."

"You have to want it. And I do."

"Want what?"

"You. In my mouth, in my arms, all of you. As you are."

He looked down at the sand.

"Do you think that's too much?" she asked.

Jana was stroking his hand as it lay on the ground; she was filled with an unfamiliar, virgin tenderness. The sky was falling on the Rock of Seven Colors; Rubén glanced at his father's bag—everything was there, close at hand. Of course . . . it wasn't the fear that the killers would search his apartment that had led him to empty his closet, it was she . . . his little sister. He rose to get the leather bag, dug around inside it, and handed her a school notebook. Jana recognized the handwriting: *The Sad Notebook*. It was Rubén's. His eyes were also filled with tears.

"I'm going to find some firewood," he said.

The desert was peaceful at twilight. Intrigued, Jana opened the notebook to its first page. Rubén was already walking away, a hunched-over silhouette against the fading sky. She read the notebook, almost without breathing, all the way to the end.

And the horror electrified her.

THE SAD NOTEBOOK

The "tumba": a greasy stew smelling of tripe with bits of boiled meat floating in it, the bread we dipped in it apprehensively, closing our eyes in order to be able to swallow it . . . The indigestion of the world, the poetry of the starving. Let's talk about poetry—or rather let's no longer talk about it. When you're hungry, time stops, life is immobilized in wax, a derelict vessel crushed by ice, eyeless faces that waddle about just as bears get used to their cage, blindfolded eyes that no longer deceive, or so little, the bars they put around you and then the rumbling, the belly that twists in its emptiness, and so many other things to tell you, little sister . . . Urine oozed from the walls. There was a pail, however, with bits of dry shit on the plastic—all I had to do was to lift my hood to see that mine was red—a cellmate, provided that you had anything to shit out. Even dreams turned gray, dreams without women and without love that hardly escaped reality, the blows, the fever, the cries, the dirt. How long were we separated? I left you staggering among the lambs in the Orletti garage, with that expression of pure fear in your eyes and your efforts to hide your young adolescent nakedness. How long have we been separated, little sister? Two months? Three? First they laid me in a box upstairs, a coffin three feet wide, they left the tops off the better to keep an eye on us, the "sardines" as they called us with the infamous wit of obedient ordinary people. A first variant, to get us in condition. P-45 was my name. It was forbidden to move or speak to each other. We could stay for days in these "lion cages," captives all in a row. At first, I didn't even know that I was at the Navy Engineering School: I hadn't had my hood off during the transfer, and I'd been put in isolation in a cage-coffin. I didn't know why they were holding me that way, for how long, or whether they were going to kill me or drive me mad. And then one day they transferred me to a cell, a container five feet by seven that was, as I later learned, in the basement of the ESMA. And it was worse. Chained up, naked, my legs hobbled and bent, a hood over my head, I was reduced to waiting, lifeless, for the next session of picana. *Did they do that to you, too? At the age of twelve, did they consider you a child or an adult? I saw dead people, little sister, people who died of panic when the men came to take them away, telling them they were going to be cut up with a chain saw—they revved the motor in the hall so that they would scream louder—or when, through the slamming doors I heard the cries of another person, another person who was already me. Then the terror was so great that we forgot our own stench, the juice of fear that ran down our thighs: I could no longer see anything but the torturers' screwed-up eyes over me and the diodes that they were applying to me before skinning me alive. Skin stinks when it's burned, little sister. Some interrogating officers played the good father: "Why don't you talk, my child? Just look at the state you're in now!" I saw the blackened bodies that they were taking out of the cells, so covered with burns that you could hardly see their eyes, black as coal, some succumbed or had given up and were covered with excrement, their sparse beards repeating the same phrases, shades or what remained of them, incredulous at the idea of witnessing their own burial—people who probably resembled me . . . Where were you? Woman or child? It was on you that they avenged themselves the most: for them, women's bodies were battlefields, especially those of the most beautiful, whom the jailers relentlessly raped to teach them to stay at home, or not to wear miniskirts. Whores, or considered as such. I heard them laugh about their sexual exploits, discuss the best women, like the thirty-year-old brunette I'd met in the corridor and with whom I had spontaneously fallen in love. I didn't know her name but I'd called her Hermione, a poet's name. At that time I knew nothing about women except the kisses of girls seen in the darkness of movie theaters, Steve McQueen and Faye Dunaway as a background, but that slender brunette with such a dignified, intelligent look was for me a fantastic apparition at the heart of nothingness. I held tight to it in the evening, I clung to her, to her big blue eyes that had pierced my heart in the corridor. She brought me back to the women we followed around on the terraces of bistros, to happy life, to life before Hermione. I saw her again later, haggard, scarcely able to stand up after a "work session." She could no longer see me because her blue eyes expressed nothing at all: she had gone mad. The jailers gave scores: She was 322: they had raped her three hundred and twenty-two times. Where were you, little sister?*

Before the Human Rights Commission visited, they had walled off the stair leading to the jail cells: the naked, wet bodies lying on iron plates, the rapes, the electricity—the emissaries of the international community saw none of that. The soccer World Cup could take place. They left again with their attaché cases full of recommendations, leaving us alone, at their mercy. And everything began all over again. The prohibitions—talking, seeing, sitting down—the odor of hoods drenched in the blood of former detainees who had bitten their tongues while they were being tortured, my cries when I was taken to the workroom for the tenth time, the picana *that empties your intestines, the torturers' jokes, the unquenchable thirst, the beating of your heart that drums in your temples, a hundred and thirty, a hundred and forty, a hundred and fifty, still more blows, the nakedness, the isolation, the loss of bearings, the smell of shit become almost familiar, the fear, still more blows that I didn't see coming from behind my hood, the insults, the threats, and the despair when I thought about you. The terrible thoughts. Where were you, little sister? I heard the cries of the new arrivals who were being tortured, the television cartoons and comedies the guards turned on in the break room to drown out the screams, trembling at the idea that it was you who were being torn apart on the tables. They questioned me about Papa, asked me where he was—in France—what he was doing there—writing poems—kept telling me that I was lying, that I was the son of a Red, that they were there to clean up the mess, and I was already part of it. Papa hadn't said anything to me about communists, Montoneros, or terrorists who had taken refuge abroad. The answers I didn't have threw them into mad, or simulated, rages. The crying fits, supplications, their stubbornness, insanity loomed everywhere. Time was erased, a life in pencil. I was afraid I'd become like those zombies, the people who had never been political activists and who were not prepared to die for a cause that they were not fighting for, people incapable of getting back on their feet and who lost their minds, who played the slave thinking the torturers would spare them or collaborated so that it would all finally end.*

Die or go mad.

Die or go mad.

Die or go mad.

The elastic of the hood pressed on my skull, was slowly cutting it in half, a shooting, unbearable pain; tears flowed by themselves all night, or during the daytime, I no longer knew, time had dissolved, hanged itself, a dead life—madness that soon no longer looms but creeps closer, lies in wait, watching for the slightest weakness, to carry me off like a sheep in its claws. Through the walls I felt the presence of other detainees dispossessed, as I had been, of their names and their rights, reduced to simple matriculation numbers that could be tormented at will, the abstract universe of questions in which submission meant survival, the disgusting stew they served us, the night terrors when we were awakened on a whim so that we could be beaten, riding crops, clubs, whips, karate holds, water-boarding, hung by the feet with a cloth over the head and lowered into a bathtub full of icy water: the shock, the asphyxiation, the pain of water in the lungs, a death by suffocation. Doctors were assigned to bring the drowned person back to life, so it could begin all over again, once, ten times, repeated deaths, and then the attack dogs trained to kill that were let loose on the poor devils who had nothing left but their bones, my neighbors whom I saw when they took us out of the cells for collective beatings, burning us with cigarettes, boiling water, red-hot pokers, cut, gashed, slashed us, skinned us alive, the new arrivals who were given a choice between electroshock torture and gang rape, sadistic, systematic vexations, sitting on the floor without being permitted to lean against the wall of the cell, from six in the morning to eight in the evening, fourteen hours to stay in that position, those who fell were beaten, those who turned their heads were beaten, those who talked were beaten, and then the detainees who were forced to fight each other without taking off their hoods, the worker, number 412, who had been literally forgotten in his cell, the victim of some administrative problem, and who died of thirst and exhaustion, the sophisticated humiliations, still more blows, gratuitous, the same routine that was inflicted to punish us for being born, for having long hair, for wearing glasses, for going out to nightclubs. Where were you? In time, I succeeded in communicating with the people in the neighboring cells, whispering a few words when we were jostled together or when one of them brought our meager ration. Of you, no trace. I sometimes heard children's screams from the upper floor, but they didn't last. I still didn't know that they were being given to sterile couples close to the military. Twelve years old, little sister: you were too big to be given to just anyone. And then one evening, while I was picking up my bowl of "tumba" I heard a comrade's voice whispering to me: "Your father's here."

My heart started beating so hard that I almost dropped my food bowl: had Papa let himself be captured in order to find us, his kidnapped children? What madness!

The World Cup was in full swing, the pressure put on us by the guards had let up a little, or rather it had shifted to the Argentine team. July 17, 1978, the day I turned fifteen. A new detainee was handing the soup in through the hole in the door, closely supervised by El Turco, the jailer. I was about to go for the bits of meat that were floating on the surface when I saw the little aluminum ball mixed with the sticky mess. I licked it off in my mouth before carefully unfolding it: it was a piece of aluminum foil off a package of cigarettes and contained, on its opposite side, a treasure. A poem, little sister, scribbled in tiny letters, on the inside of the foil.

Don't be afraid
Of buried giants
It's the lightning that's decapitated
To warm matter
Look,
The stars' skin is soft
The plains are naked of it
Walk little man,
Walk:
The same hand caresses and kills
The memory of the knife . . .

Only the two of us remain
In the lion's den,
There I see the ruins
Of cathedrals
Luminous signals,
It's the lighting following us,
Look,

The war is over
The forest has gone silent
Go, little man,
Go
The same hand caresses and kills
The memory of the knife!

A poem by Papa, for my birthday. My fifteenth birthday. The last poem by Daniel Calderón. I couldn't destroy it, little sister, that poem was my life. I read it dozens and dozens of times that evening, with a sick joy, and I learned it by heart, then I rolled it up in a ball and hid it in a crack in the wall of the cell. Invisible. The torturers had stolen our freedom, our integrity, but not our love. A week later, in the middle of the night, the guards carried out a meticulous inspection of the cells, throwing the prisoners out in the corridor. It was there, between two salvos of blows, that I saw Papa's bearded face. He had been tortured, but I knew he had held up. We said nothing to each other, he had just given me a calming sign (he must have known that I was in the neighboring cell) when a hand grabbed me by the hair.

"What's this?"

They had just discovered the little paper hidden in the wall: my treasure.

Daniel Calderón, number 563, was not afraid of dying: he knew why he was there. Not only did he refuse to talk, but by writing a poem he had broken the rules. He was defying authority, seriously. In addition to the usual treatment, beatings and the picana, *they decided to starve him.*

The torturers were not all sadists or confirmed rapists; many were just ordinary brutes who had been given free rein; El Turco would be their puppet. Days went by, then more days. Weakened, "the Poet," as they called him sarcastically, could not hold out much longer. I had known that obsessive hunger in the lion's cage where they had kept me lying down for days. The hardest part was mealtime, when the clicking of the spoons ate away at your stomach and made tears come to your eyes. El Turco and the others made it worse, taunting them through the hole in the door, laughing, moronic and having eaten their fill. Finally the great day came, the one that the whole country was waiting for: June 25, 1978. The guards, the interrogating officers, everyone was talking only about the upcoming match: Menotti's team was going to win that damned final. We heard them braying in the break room, where they had put the television set. Whether it was the end of the forced diet or an offering to the gods of football, that night a bowl of "tumba" was given the Poet. The guards shouted: one goal each at the end of regulation time, Argentina and Holland would play overtime. Taking advantage of the pause, El Turco and his gang broke into Papa's cell: they saw the empty bowl, licked clean, and began to laugh like hyenas. I heard their comments in the corridor, but I didn't understand what made them so mocking.

The television was howling when an enormous clamor greeted the third Argentine goal. The guards were exultant, bellowing with a taurine joy: "Argentina! Argentina!" The roar of victory rose up from the avenue. The River Plata stadium where the final was being played was quite close to the ESMA: the guards in the room with the television set were shouting too loudly to hear it, but the muffled noise that came from the neighboring cell, a compact noise, I was able to clearly identify: it was Papa's head banging against the intervening wall.

The man was fracturing his skull and moaning like a puppy. It was him, little sister.

El Turco and the others came to see me shortly afterward. They had waited until the Poet had finished his revolting stew to show him what they were hiding behind their backs, and what they now exhibited before my livid face: your head, little sister. Your child's head that they brandished like a trophy. The ogres had left your hazel eyes open: the momentary stupefaction that had gone through your mind at the instant they decapitated you could still be read in them.

Die or go mad: Daniel Calderón had chosen to die. Anyway, his head was no longer banging against the wall of my cell. The Poet had died of indigestion with the world, and you in the form of boiled meat that El Turco and the others had made him swallow, mixed with the "tumba."

No, men's cruelty has no limits.

They released me two days later, amid the national happiness, so that I would tell your story. But I won't say anything, little sister, ever. Never to anyone but you. My little poppy.

*

Jana closed the notebook, her eyes staring, chewing her little clots of hatred. No, men's cruelty had no limits.

The stars were tumbling down over the glowing rock, but she could no longer distinguish the colors, the birds soaring off the snowy peaks, the tints of the desert at sunset. She no longer saw anything but that poor girl and her fifteen-year-old brother in the putrid jails of the ESMA, all that love decapitated, which made her weep cold tears. Pale, she closed the accursed notebook where his nightmares lived. Die or go mad! Rubén had survived. Alone.

A blue-gray wave was watering down the sky when the Mapuche raised her head. Rubén was just then walking back to their improvised camp, a few stunted branches in his hands. Jana swallowed the rage that was breaking her heart and stood up as he approached.

"Did you find what you were looking for?" she asked him.

Rubén's face was pale under the moon. He threw his measly branches on the stones.

"No."

"I did," she said.

Jana took off the tight-fitting tank top, let it drop to the ground, and turned to face him. Her scrawny breasts poked out, two little monsters in the starlight. Rubén felt no pity on looking at the Indian's amputated body: her unhappy beauty dazzled him.

Jana took him in her arms first, pressed her chest against him and kissed him. She wasn't afraid of the *winka* who had tried to destroy them. The Mapuches had resisted the Incas, the conquistadors, Argentine army regulars, the *estancieros* and the Indian hunters paid by the number of cut-off ears, the carabineros, the political and financial elites that had bled the country dry: she was a descendant of survivors. Their feet danced a moment on the sand, Jana kissed him, kissed him again.

"Come," she said, detaching herself, "come . . . "

Their clothes disappeared, thrown away, their modesty, the past, the future, whether they would live together or not, the eternal solitude and the words that were never said: they made love, trembling, standing up, holding each other with their eyes as if they might lose each other, entwined so tight it hurt in order to ward off the death that was gripping them, and came together, like demons.

8

Elsa Calderón was one of the hundred and seventy-two children murdered during the Process.

Having no news of her family, Elena had joined the Mothers of the Plaza de Mayo two months before the famous World Cup. Through her knowledge of the enemy, Elena Calderón had quickly become one of the main intellectual leaders of the Association for the Defense of Human Rights. They were the ones who were the military's primary targets. A first roundup had taken place after Astiz's infiltration; he had passed himself off as the brother of a *desaparecido* when twelve persons were kidnapped on coming out of the church of Santa Cruz, among them the first president of the association and two French nuns. End of 1977. To incriminate the Montoneros, the junta had had a false document published, a rather crude photomontage that was disseminated around the world, but the ruse hadn't worked. Voices were raised. The international community got involved. The emotion elicited by the disappearance of the first Mothers threatened to spoil the soccer triumph, so it was decided to use a more subtle method to do away with these madwomen who dared to defy the government. Since their threats had had no effect, the oppressors had thought up an attack by several gangs that would hit them hard, especially Elena Calderón.

The abductions, illegal detentions, and systematic torture were a parallel structure of an effective bureaucratic and hierarchical coercion capable of sowing unprecedented terror among the population; the goal was also to torment the imagination of the living. Of the survivors. Rubén knew that the staging of Elsa's execution and the suicide of the Poet-cannibal could not have been hatched in the minds of the jailers. El Turco and his henchmen were just ignorant, obedient animals. By releasing him, the instigators of this machination hoped to make him their messenger of pain, the surviving witness who would tell his crazy mother how her dear family members had died, sure that the truth would kill her, just as it had killed her husband.

Die or go mad. Rubén had kept quiet, obstinately.

For thirty years, every Thursday, he saw his mother walk around the obelisk in the Plaza de Mayo, unbending in her battle for the truth: there was nothing and nobody who could make her give up, that was the pact. It was *impossible* for her to break this pact.

Nakedness, bodily contact, sounds, smells—it had taken Rubén years to be able to endure situations associated with torture. Beyond the physical trauma, the psychic wounds had taken the longest to heal over: an acute mental suffering then replaced the suffering of the tortures endured, horror rushed into the breaches to the point of making him want to commit suicide as a last act of autonomy. Daniel Calderón had understood that: he had immediately killed himself, fracturing his skull against the wall of his cell.

Not him.

Rubén lit a cigarette, pensively.

Darkness was drawing across the Andean desert. Jana was lying near the fire, wrapped up in the blanket. The flames were giving a reddish hue to her face, calmed after making love, and he couldn't sleep. Images passed through his mind, a confusion of feelings and times in an endless circle. The melancholy his father tried to instill in him had disappeared one night in June 1978, a night of happiness. Words had betrayed him, those of his father's birthday poem, which Rubén had not been able to bring himself to destroy. He had written the *Sad Notebook* years later, in one sitting, as one tears oneself away from a lethal passion, in order to exorcize the core: he had hidden their memory among his little sister's dresses in the apartment across from the intersection where they had been kidnapped, and had never written anything again.

That night, everything was changing.

Rubén put the last log on the campfire's embers and by the light of the flickering fire did something he had thought he would never do again. Jana asleep in his line of sight, he opened Elsa's notebook to the last page and began to write. An hour went by, perhaps two. Abstract time, that cared little for periods, children's ghosts, or death. When it was all finished, Rubén tore out the page and stood up in the moonlight. Jana was still asleep curled up on the sand, her hands balled into fists. He pressed the school notebook in his hands for the last time.

My sweet . . . sweet little sister.

Then he threw it into the fire.

*

The Rock of Seven Colors stretched at the end of the canyon. They woke together, rolled up in the blanket. The logs were just ashes among the blackened stones of the camp. Dawn was growing on the steep ridges. They embraced to ward off the cold that had gripped them, and kissed as a welcome.

"Your butt's frozen," he said, as his hand slipped into her pants.

"And your hand is warm. Brrr!"

She burrowed into him. Rubén was not thinking about what had happened during the night, Jana's face was already radiant, a miracle of youth.

"Sleep well?"

"Yes."

She got up in the pale rays of the sun, her legs bare, and rubbed her nose, which was wet after a night under the stars.

"I've got sand everywhere," she said, shaking out her tank top.

She took off her panties, dusted them off in turn, then exchanged them for another pair taken out of her bag, a triangle of black cotton that she put on without false modesty.

"What?" she asked, sensing that he was watching her.

"Nothing," he said. "You make me laugh."

"Right. Right," she repeated, "don't ever forget that."

He would try. He promised.

The breeze was growing warmer as the sun rose, the mountain range was deploying its stone rainbows. Rubén was picking up the remains of the food that were being attacked by ants when Jana found the sheet of paper folded in two under her bag, which had served as her pillow: a page torn out of the school notebook that had disappeared under the ashes. Jana unfolded it, and her throat slowly closed up:

Seeing nothing in the dew
But the
Dawn split
Like a log.
Nothing remains of the horizon
But the bark,
Cracks,
Images of lice,
Bones . . .
Who kills the dogs
When the leash is too short?
The birds have fled the sky
In the painted landscape
Traces of wings.

Of silence
There remains only the murmur
Implicit,
Cracked clouds
Images of lice,
Bones . . .
Who kills the dogs
When the leash is too short?
Biting words in the mouths of others,
It's like the shadow in your eyes,
I cling to it,
I slip into it on my knees without prayers
To love you inside,
The bottoms of the stars glow there,
Your skin, look, it scintillates as soon as
I touch it
Graze it,
Feed on it,
Still,
It's your heart, more or less,
A sorrow on the straw,
Halfway from nothing at all,
I loiter in you like a path at the
End of the day,
Your hands your fingers your thighs
I love it all,
See,
My wrinkled tears in you
rush down,
Washed-out glaciers,
A disaster at work, it amounts
To the same thing,
And delayed lightning bolts that
Exhaust themselves

In the adored dawn,
Which goes away,
Yet . . .
Trees, surrender your branches,
Raise up the ditches!
To you I sell freedom
To the most thunderous
The use
Of chance
And of time,
What do the crests matter,
Of the path
I won't yield a pebble,
Not a stone
I obey the rivers
The lakes
The vein that takes them to the sea
For you I will pour out my powder
Seller of nothing
On a desert of stones
Or of cutting
Sand,
Become flint again,
Life has its heads,
And in the mirror of the flames
Dancing on the surfaces,
Smooth,
I wait.
If it's not you, Jana . . . The wind.

A poem. The first. For her. Jana held the treasure of the paper between her trembling fingers: no, Daniel Calderón was no longer the only one, his son also had the *duende*. Rubén, who had so often been thrown out of the saddle and, miraculously, gotten back on the horse, Rubén, a loving ghost whom she loved for real. For her as well, everything was changing. Even the ugliness of her ridiculous breasts no longer made her ashamed. Jana had never felt beautiful—she had never felt so beautiful.

"Why are you crying?"

He had come up to her, but Jana couldn't speak. Rubén wiped away the tears that were running down her cheeks, then took her face between his hands.

"I love you," he said. "I love you, little lynx."

Rubén squinted at her a little, to make himself more convincing. Jana finally gave him a smile, a big one, her eyes like diamonds. And the world changed its skin. She, too, had a blue soul.

*

The stony path, the expanse of sand, the bones bleached in the desert, their long shadows stretching back toward the road, the landscape was moving past them in reverse. They were hungry and thirsty, but that no longer seemed important. They reached Uspallata at the hour when the first vehicles were rolling down the main street, passed the closed casino, and ate breakfast on the terrace of the bistro, which had just opened. Scrambled eggs, tea, toast, grilled fat.

"You got your appetite back," she said.

"Thanks to you, big girl."

Their eyes met, amused.

"I'm going to make myself beautiful," Jana said with a defiant air, "you'll see."

Rubén watched her lovely ass in the tight jumpsuit as she walked to the bar, and lit a first cigarette. Sweetness and pleasure—with her ass as a lens, you could see the whole world—which contrasted with the situation. Still no news from Anita, the Grandmothers, or Carlos; on the other hand, the Hyundai would soon be ready. They washed up in the cafe-restaurant's lavatories, bought a newspaper, a little food and water for the road. Eight hundred miles as the eagle flies before arriving in Buenos Aires. They were still gradually returning to reality. It was when they picked up the car at the garage in Uspallata, around noon, that they got the news: Eduardo Campallo had just committed suicide.

He had been found shot in the head that morning, at his home.

9

Three pacts bound the different branches of the military to the Argentine police: the pact of "blood," when subversives had to be eliminated or tortured, the pact of "obedience," which connected the hierarchy from the top to the bottom of the pyramid, and the pact of "corruption," which involved the divvying up of the property stolen from detainees. Alfredo "El Toro" Grunga and León "El Picador" Angoni had gotten rich during the Process, reselling the confiscated merchandise to antique and secondhand stores that didn't ask where it came from. The good old days, those of easy money and the girls that went with it.

His gray hair pulled back, El Picador had prominent cheekbones and wore a thin mustache, fitted three-piece suits that were slightly old-fashioned, and two-tone shoes that looked like those worn by pimps at the beginning of the twentieth century. Taciturn, tormented, a specialist in using the *picana*, El Picador had refined his art to the point that his buddy could have seen it as reverse osmosis, if he'd had the vocabulary. The buddy they'd nicknamed "El Toro." Atavism or congenital mediocrity: his father had already died in the stupidest possible way—he was taking a piss under a tree when it fell on him. Short, stocky, and energetic, El Toro followed his instincts and considered El Picador his best friend. The two men had never done very well in school: the army had offered them something better than a future: a present.

Together with Hector "El Pelado" Parise, they formed a

patota, a trio of rowdy friends. They had kidnapped Reds in the streets or in their homes, blown the heads off countless Jews, eggheads, unionized workers, and darkies, sometimes in full public view, they had extorted confessions using the *picana*, they had quaffed champagne in the glasses of people who were writhing in the ruins of their homes, proposed toasts at their colleagues' birthday parties, supported nonsense and many other half-forgotten things as well that they saw as the memory of a riotous youth.

The end of the dictatorship had marked a turning point in their careers: El Toro and El Picador had been involved in trafficking luxury automobiles with the Soviet embassy, but they had almost been caught red-handed, and had to give up any desire to engage in free enterprise. Not clever enough. Too much the hotheads. They preferred to rely on Hector Parise, their former interrogating officer and the brains of the group, who always knew where the action was.

This operation was to pay off big.

The house that served as their base was comfortable, though a little too isolated for their taste; they'd been there for four days, rotting in that damp jungle where the mosquitoes whined. Finally, Parise and the other men being absent, the two pals could take it easy on the bank of the river. A third man had joined them in the house in the delta, Del Piro, called "the Pilot." The latter, not very talkative, kept his distance from them and affected an aristocratic air.

"Why don't you want to play Truco?" El Toro asked the pilot, who was sulking in a wicker chair. "*Tilingo!*[14] We've got nothing else to do!"

"I just don't feel like it, that's all," the man replied.

Gianni Del Piro didn't feel like playing cards, or dominos, especially with these two guys. He hated dominos, and he didn't

[14] "Don't be so stuck up!"

know how to play Truco. What made it all the crazier were the fucking mosquitoes, voracious monsters capable of biting you through your clothes. A good way to catch dengue—it was endemic in the delta. Gianni Del Piro was ruminating on the bank of the river, in a bad mood. He had planned to meet Linda for an escape to Punta del Este, a resort town in Uruguay, as soon as the operation was over, not to play dominos in a house in the middle of the jungle with two louts who weren't bothered by mosquito bites—a fat one who was outright repugnant with the grease stains on his shirt and his alter ego, thin as a knife blade, the token taciturn one.

Del Piro had had to prolong his mission, and this was unforeseen. Contrary to his dopey wife, Linda was not one of those women that you screw in a motel after eating takeout pizza. The money he was being paid by his former employers was worth a minor misdemeanor, long enough to do a little job that would pay for several adulterous adventures: Gianni Del Piro had lied to everyone, his employer, his wife Anabel, and a few friends who were too curious, but a hitch had forced him to remain in Argentina, and the others had left him hardly any choice. Anabel wouldn't cause any problems, unlike the beautiful Linda. His young mistress had been waiting for him since noon at the hotel in Punta del Este, she was harassing him with messages he couldn't answer, which were getting more and more scathing the longer he remained silent. It would be a euphemism to say that Linda was jealous: possessive, exclusive, anticipating the other person's perversities as if dirty tricks and treachery were ineluctable by nature, putting up with his talk about getting a divorce so long as he swore never to touch his wife again, Linda called several times a day and at the first doubt that formed in her twisted mind, refused to believe in anyone's sincerity, and especially that of Gianni, her Italian male. It is true that the pilot had had some success with women who were impressed with the prestige of his profession. His forced silence was going to drive her crazy.

"Well, are you going to play?" El Toro shouted from the terrace.

"No!"

The pilot was grumbling under the line of pine trees that bordered the watercourse. The mosquitoes were attacking in the twilight, and he was upset by the idea that he might lose Linda—what an ass she had!! A taxi-boat had passed by earlier, too far from the dock to see them, raising a few little sluggish waves along the riverbank. It was the first boat that had gone by for two days. A really remote place.

"*Puta madre*," El Toro yelled, his cards in his hand, "it's no fun playing two-handed Truco!"

"Yeah!"

It was hot on the shady terrace. The fat man turned to his partner and jeered:

"I've got an idea!" He threw the pack of cards on the table. "Come with me!"

El Picador got up without asking what the idea was and followed his friend toward the wooden house. Gianni Del Piro was spraying his clothes with the only mosquito repellent sold in the country when the two men reappeared on the terrace. They had brought the prisoner out of the bedroom, a tranny who couldn't stand up; they were carrying him at arm's length.

Miguel Michellini's eyeliner had run over his eyelids, which blinked when he saw the evening sun through the branches. Del Piro stiffened on his armchair: they had *untied* him.

"Fuck, what are you doing?" he snapped at them, twisting around.

"Ha, ha, ha!"

El Toro was laughing in the transvestite's face. The poor fellow had cried a lot when he'd beaten him. El Picador had not deigned to get involved, leaving the ladyboy to his colleague, who had in fact enjoyed himself—Miguel's wedding gown was still covered with blood.

"Let's go, sweetie," El Toro spluttered, "come play with us."

They lifted up the marionette and dropped him heavily on the chair. Miguel groaned in pain and clutched the edge of the table. His torturers reminded him of those Komodo dragons that devour their prey alive, in a pack, those disgusting beasts whose bites poison the blood of their victims, who are then doomed. The monsters. They had kept his face intact in order to make it up—a transvestite was sort of like a Barbie doll!—and to have fun they'd smeared him with shit. It had dried on the livid little runt's cracked cheeks.

El Toro blew his beer breath on him.

"How about a little game of cards, Madonna?"

Miguel felt tears welling up in his crusted eyes.

"Get fucked, you filthy pig."

"Ho, ho, ho! Did you hear that? Did you hear him, the rebel?"

El Picador, playing his role, limited himself to a faint smile. His buddy stood up, excited.

"Deal the cards, I'll be right back."

Del Piro shook his head and waved his arms wildly to drive away the mosquitoes that were assailing him; he hadn't been present during these "work sessions," but he had heard the little homo's piercing screams. The pilot was expecting the worst, and he was not disappointed. El Toro soon returned to the terrace, a basin in his big hands. It was obviously full of shit.

El Picador, who had dealt the cards as Miguel watched with his haggard eyes, sat back in his chair.

"It's fresh!" El Toro laughed.

He put the disgusting basin on the table, delighted with his trick. Miguel looked away to avoid the stench, while the big guy put on his dishwashing gloves.

"Hold him on the chair!"

El Picador grabbed the poor fellow.

"What the fuck are you doing, for God's sake," Del Piro

growled, spraying himself with mosquito repellent. "You're going to destroy him."

"Don't worry about it! We're going to cook him! Ha, ha, ha!"

Miguel no longer had the strength to resist, hardly enough to spit in their faces. He had told them what he knew, and didn't understand why they were keeping him alive, why they were tormenting him. He closed his eyes while they smeared shit on his face.

The odor of excrement reached as far as the dock.

"Jesus, you guys are really swine!" Del Piro said, not budging from his chair.

El Toro was creating a sculpture *in vivo*, encouraged by the ironic laughter of his acolyte.

The pilot sighed—these guys were making him sick—and headed for the house. They could go fuck themselves with their scatological madness: he would telephone Linda while they were busy, just two minutes, long enough to sweet-talk her—with a little luck and talent, he might be able to calm her erotic fury . . . As night fell, mosquitoes and moths were banging against the kitchen windows. The last thing Gianni Del Piro saw was three men sitting around a card table, a scrawny transvestite, with cards stuck to his face covered with shit, and two men in their forties laughing at him.

"Your turn, Madonna!"

Parise called that same night. The Campallo girl hadn't said that she was pregnant when they tortured the transvestite kidnapped with her as they came out of the tango club. Calderón knew that. Who could have told him except the kid's father? Three months pregnant, according to the information Eduardo Campallo had revealed on the morning he committed suicide. Parise finally had a trail to follow. And the timing helped.

10

The Grandmothers had set up a crisis committee at the association's office. They remained absolutely discreet regarding the goal of their research, reduced their communications to a minimum, and postponed meetings indefinitely for reasons of health, but the headquarters was a beehive of activity. The bits of paper Rubén had brought them were like the Greek fragments of the pre-Socratics, but the Grandmothers had begun by entering the legible names into their database. Drawing on the files of civilian and military hospitals, archives, court records, and reports, they worked in teams to find dozens of connections, often dubious, to verify the leads. Samuel and Gabriella Verón, the parents who had disappeared, did not appear in either the Durán hospital's DNA bank or their files, which suggested that no member of their families had claimed their bodies. Had their loved ones also been swept away by the state machinery? If the DNA of the bones Rubén had dug up corresponded to that of María and Miguel, then they could bring the case before a judge, demand protection for the witnesses, unmask Eduardo Campallo and his wife as *apropriadores*, and expose the people who were trying so hard to hush up this affair.

Campallo's suicide, which they had just learned about, pulled the rug out from under them.

The servants in the house in Belgrano being on vacation, it was Campallo's wife Isabel who had found the body in the early morning. Eduardo was lying on his desk chair, a bullet in his head, the gun still hanging from his hand. Isabel had immediately called 911, but he had put the barrel against his temple and the bullet had blown away his frontal lobes. Her husband had died instantly. He had left no suicide note, but traces of gunpowder, fingerprints, and burns showed that he had pulled the trigger. Since the pistol, a Browning, belonged to him—he had a permit—there was little doubt that he had committed suicide. The elections were approaching, and his death was a hard blow for Francisco Torres, the mayor, who lost both a friend and one of his main financial supports.

For Rubén and the Grandmothers, it was their number one witness who had disappeared. One more.

The detective had a long discussion with the Grandmothers and Carlos as they drove toward the Andes. Since there had still been no response from the pilot's cell phone, the hope of finding Miguel Michellini alive was decreasing. Campallo's death forced them to revise their battle plan, but another character in the drama had just reappeared: Franco Díaz.

The Grandmothers had done research based on the name and the photo of the passport Anita Barragan had sent them. They had a file on the man from Colonia, which Elena had sent to her son's BlackBerry.

Franco Díaz, born August 11, 1941, in Córdoba. Military training in Panama (1961-1964), served at Santa Cruz, Mendoza, then Buenos Aires. Joined the SIDE, the Argentine intelligence service, in 1979. A black hole until 1982 and the Falklands War: a liaison officer in a helicopter unit, Díaz was decorated—his squad had taken possession of the island by capturing the handful of sleeping English troops who were holding the place. At the trial of the generals in 1986, he testified in support of General Bignone, one of those most to blame for the Falklands fiasco, and also suspected of having destroyed the archives concerning the *desaparecidos* before leaving power. Emigrated to Uruguay in the late 1980s.

Retired, Franco Díaz received an army pension and had never again been heard from.

A hero of the Falklands War, a man who was in theory unassailable. An agent close to Bignone, Díaz had been able to keep the ESMA file incriminating Campallo. For what purpose? To sell it to his paperazzo neighbor in order to create an unprecedented scandal? Why would Díaz have decided to torpedo a man associated with his former employers? To take revenge? On whom? On Eduardo Campallo or someone else mentioned in this document? The photo sent to Rubén's BlackBerry dated from the time of the trial, in 1986, but Anita had duplicated the photo in his passport: Díaz hadn't changed much—the same man with an indifferent face, dull eyes under his bald head. Ferreted out in Colonia, the former SIDE agent had gone back to Argentina. Rubén still didn't know whether he was trying to sell or deliver the original document to a third person, but if Díaz took the risk of returning to the scene of the crime, he might lead them straight to the person running the show.

The tankers were followed by semis on the main highway. Jana was concentrating on her driving, the windshield covered with orangish dust blown down from the Andes. They had picked up the Hyundai at the garage in Uspallata and since then had been taking turns at the wheel, stopping hardly at all. The miles rolled by, monotonous; after the stress of the police roadblocks at the provincial borders, the night spent in the desert seemed almost distant. Rubén dozed, his head resting against the side window, exhausted by the hot day, or meditated, his mind full of steaming equations. Jana kept an eye on the rearview mirror, lost in her thoughts. Something had happened during that night: one of the most important events in her life. Why was she so sad? So sad and so happy? The fire that was burning her could drive her mad, she felt it boiling in every pore of her skin, her dirty Indian skin that the *winka* had thrown to the dogs. "Who kills the dogs when the leash is too short?" They would be free. Soon.

The sun was flooding the plains. The Mapuche put her hand out the open window to absorb a bit of coolness, then put it back on Rubén's knee and let it sizzle. He was asleep.

Buenos Aires, 215 miles.

*

Jo Prat had played all night even though he could hardly breathe. These outdoor concerts gave him terrible colds, and even the hieratic calls of the trio of groupies piling up their breasts at the foot of the microphone had left him cold. Drenched with sweat in his tight leather outfit, the asthma attack came over him as he left the stage. Get out of there. Get away from all these people who held his past glory against him.

Prat inhaled two sprays of Ventolin and quietly left the festival through the VIP exit. He had no appetite for sex this evening, and still less for talking to people he didn't know: he took another hit of Ventolin, the third, to ward off the approaching asthma attack. Maybe he was getting old, or he'd given all he had, abused drugs too much, whatever, he dreamed only of getting back to his hotel room, a somewhat antiquated, calm little suite in the upscale neighborhood of Belgrano, where no one would recognize him: he'd take a shower and sleep with the air conditioning turned off until the cold went away.

Living in a hotel was the only luxury that suited him. Calderón and his witness had been hiding out in his flat for several days, but beneath his sovereign airs, the dandy had been shaken by María Victoria's death. The poor little thing. Who would have believed it? Jo was sick about it. Even if the photographer had not told him he was the father (María wanted a baby more than a husband), she was carrying a bit of him in her belly, and she hadn't chosen him at random. Her portrait dominated his loft, and that was after all a proof of gratitude if not of love. Jo had promised the detective a bonus if he discovered the truth regarding the circumstances of her death: Calderón hadn't reported anything, but he had confidence in him—this guy looked as furious as his songs had been back in the day.

Jo Prat sniffled, his head down, his hands in the pockets of his leather pants. He'd gotten past the various barriers, his Sesame badge around his neck. A half-moon escorted him out of Lezama Park. He was thinking about María, about the baby who had died with her, when a pedestrian who was coming toward him stopped.

"Jo Prat?" the stranger asked.

The rocker looked up: a giant with pocked skin was standing in front of him, a bald man about sixty who was going to great lengths to appear friendly. A stranger was always a pain in the ass.

"Sorry," Prat said, "I'm in a hurry."

"The Campallo girl, was she your girlfriend?" the man asked with a fishy smile.

A leaden weight fell on the musician's shoulders. The man who'd come up to him seemed definitely unpleasant.

"If you're a journalist, tell your readers that I have nothing to say." He coughed. "The same if you're a cop."

He tried to start down the lane but the colossus blocked his way.

"You're the one who knocked her up, huh?" the man continued with an aggressive familiarity.

"Are you deaf? I have nothing to say to you, O.K.?"

"Three months along," the man went on. "I checked the dates on her site: you were on tour together when she got pregnant. You're the father of her kid. María Campallo's little pal who informed Calderón."

Parise had seen this face at the photographer's home when he cleaned the apartment, the black-and-white prints she'd hung on a string like trophies. He couldn't make the connection with the moment of the kidnapping, but before he died, Campallo had revealed things about his daughter that had put a bug in his ear . . . The rocker scowled.

"Who are you working for, her father? You're beginning to annoy me with your crap," he growled in a hoarse voice. "Let me by."

His lungs were hurting, and he wasn't wary. The guy with the chalk-white face grabbed his arm, and in a convoluted movement turned it around so that it pressed on his throat. Jo Prat tried to get away but the giant had immobilized him, and he knew how to fight. Prat didn't. The man pushed Prat's forearm against his windpipe so hard that it made tears come to his eyes.

"Let me . . . go!"

Parise dragged the rocker under the trees lining the deserted lane.

"Calderón came to grill you, right?" he growled.

"Leave me . . . alone."

The hold was shutting off his trachea so that he couldn't breathe. He was already suffocating and the bald man seemed to have Herculean strength. Jo tried to wrench himself free, in vain. Parise was blowing his mentholated breath in his face.

"The Campallo girl talked to you about something," he said in a sugary voice. "Something very important, before she disappeared."

"I didn't . . . see her."

"A document," Parise continued without letting up the pressure on his windpipe, "a paper concerning her parents. María Victoria must have talked to you about it. And you talked about it to Calderón."

"No!" Jo spluttered.

Parise glanced furtively toward the park lane, which was still empty. He released the hold that immobilized his prey, balled his fist like an anvil and struck him hard in the stomach. A vicious blow that robbed him of what little breath he still had.

"I don't believe you," belched the former interrogation officer.

Jo Prat held his stomach, a soldier under machine-gun fire, gasping for air that didn't come. With his free hand, the asthmatic grabbed the Ventolin inhaler in his pocket and nervously put it to his mouth. He didn't have time to breathe in life; Parise wrenched the inhaler out of his hands.

"Tell me what you know and I'll give you your medicine back. Are you the one who hired Calderón?"

Jo thought he was going to die. He shook his head, unable to breathe. He was suffocating, for real.

"Yes . . . "

"Where is he?"

"I . . . don't know."

He couldn't resist when the giant searched his pockets and found a little wallet and the key to a hotel, the Majestic in the Belgrano neighborhood. Bizarre. According to the information he had, Prat lived in Buenos Aires, and the papers gave an address in Palermo Hollywood.

"What the fuck are you doing in a hotel? Huh? Why aren't you sleeping at your place?"

Parise waved the precious inhaler in front of the singer's glassy eyes. Jo grabbed his arm; he needed the medicine, urgently. Parise, seeing that he was red in the face and unable to talk, stuck the inhaler between his lips. Jo sucked in a saving gulp that allowed him to escape from the abyss, but Parise immediately took the inhaler out of his trembling hands.

"More," Jo wheezed. "I need . . . more."

His lungs were whistling like a locomotive and he could hardly stand up, a pathetic marionette slipping on a bed of nails. Parise thought hard for a moment under the branches of the trees: Calderón had not returned to his office, the girl that lived with the tranny had disappeared from circulation, and surveillance of the Grandmothers' office had yielded nothing. The detective must have found a hideout for his witness, some place from which he could operate without attracting attention.

"You know where Calderón is," he said.

Jo did not reply, imploring as the man held him up at arm's length.

"Is he staying at your place? Is that why you're in a hotel?"

Gripped by panic, Jo Prat nodded. He reached for the inhaler; he had no strength and soon he would have no air. Parise smiled under the tree that was hiding them. The others were waiting near the gates, in the van.

"Thanks for the information," he said with a smile.

Parise threw the Ventolin into the branches and watched the man suffocate, inexorably, on the carpet of moss.

*

Buenos Aires's towers were emerging dimly through the smog when the Hyundai got caught in traffic on the superhighway. Seven in the morning around the capital. Black smoke spitting out of exhaust pipes, patched-together, backfiring cars, American trucks with shimmering chrome: Rubén and Jana passed through concrete housing developments with washing hanging out over the dirt before reaching Rivadivia, one of the longest avenues in the world—forty thousand numbers.

They arrived at the time when the *cartoneros* were going home.

Raúl Sanz was waiting for them at the Center for Forensic Anthropology. The EAAF[15] had been created in 1984 under the direction of Clyde Snow, an American anthropologist and

[15] EAAF: Equipo Argentino de Antropología Forense

forensic scientist who had offered his knowledge and trained the staff members who were to be his successors. The organization, which was independent, worked in more than forty countries with various institutions, both governmental and nongovernmental. Under Raúl Sanz's guidance, Rubén had learned about ballistics, genetics, archeology, how to exhume and identify bodies, how to locate graves, and how to establish the facts based on the position of the bodies, objects found on the scene of the crime, clothing, fractures . . . Raúl, a man in his forties who was always meticulously well-dressed, kissed Jana's hand before embracing his friend.

"We were wondering if you were going to get here," he said, leading them into his lair.

"We were, too," Jana commented.

Raúl looked questioningly at Rubén, who signaled to him to let it drop. He put down the military sack on the anthropologist's desk.

"A real little Santa Claus," the latter noted when he looked at the contents.

The skulls hadn't suffered too much despite what they'd been through on the trip. Raúl Sanz picked them up like puppies in their basket. DNA results would be available in twenty-four hours, he soon assured them. They exchanged a few words of explanation over black coffee, greeted his full team, and then separated in the Center's lobby. Jana and Rubén had a ten o'clock meeting at the *Abuelas*' office with the Grandmothers and Carlos: that left them time to pass by the apartment to take a shower and feed Ledzep.

"The poor old fellow must be keeping an eye on his food bowl and wondering what we're doing," Jana remarked on the way.

"Losing two or three kilos wouldn't do him any harm," Rubén replied, "or his master, either."

"You're a nasty little puma, not everyone has the luck to have your pelt."

She ran her hands through his hair and saw his tired smile. Jana yawned in spite of herself. She was in a hurry to get back.

Apart from the *kiosco* that was opening up at the corner, the shops on Gurruchaga Street were still closed at that hour. They went around the block twice before parking the car and hurrying into the building's lobby.

The muffled atmosphere in the loft seemed somehow odd, as if they had left a century earlier. They set down the bags in the entry hall. Rubén went to the window with the drawn drapes and saw nothing but vehicles without drivers parked along the sidewalk.

"What is it?"

"Nothing . . . nothing."

Fatigue was playing tricks on him. Or stress. Jana gave him a furtive kiss on the lips, to relax him.

"I'm going to take a shower."

She took her bag from the entry hall, wondered where Ledzep had gone—the old cat must be sleeping in some closet; the blinds were drawn in Jo Prat's bedroom, the heat had withered the roses. Jana put the .38 on the night table, picked out clean clothes. She heard mewing under the bed. She bent down and saw two round eyes glowing.

"What are you doing there, old boy?"

Ledzep's only response was to hiss at her.

Rubén was climbing the glass staircase when Anita called his cell phone. At the sound of her voice, the detective sensed immediately that the news was bad. Jo Prat had just been found dead in Lezama Park: a volunteer at the festival had found his lifeless body and called 911. An asthma crisis, according to the preliminary examination—a Ventolin inhaler lay near him.

"Shit."

"Where are you?" Anita asked with concern.

"At his place," Rubén replied.

The Moroccan lamp gave a soft light in the bedroom: Jana

was getting ready to undress, but something stopped her. She sniffed the air in the room. The objects were familiar, but the atmosphere had suddenly become unbreatheable. The Mapuche drew back: *somebody was in the apartment.* The odor of sweat permeated the walls, and was growing stronger and stronger. She grabbed the loaded revolver lying next to the vase where the dead flowers were turning brown, and sensed a presence at her left.

"If you move or scream, I'll . . . "

Jana fired without aiming: the .38's bullet raised a cloud of plaster dust when it hit the wall but missed its target. She didn't have time to fire again: two harpoons dug into her neck.

"*La concha de tu hermana*!"[16] El Toro whispered, holding his hand to his ear.

Her muscles paralyzed by the shock, Jana collapsed against the night table. El Picador rushed out of the bathroom, sweating in his three-piece suit. Blood was dripping on El Toro's jacket with epaulets; the lobe of his ear had been shot off. The girl lay next to the bed, in convulsions. El Picador set down his attaché case, seized the syringe ready for use, and threw the garrote to the big man.

"Hurry up, damn it!"

Rubén was on the terrace of the loft, talking with Anita, when the detonation resounded on the ground floor.

"What happened?" she cried. "Rubén!"

He turned around and found himself facing two men who leapt through the sliding door, a big bald guy and another whose nose was covered with a bandage. Rubén jumped the latter just as he was pulling the trigger, diverted the shot with a blow of his forearm, and wrapped the man's arm around his neck. Parise aimed his Taser but Calderón pushed Puel back, using him as a shield.

[16] "Your sister's pussy!"

"Get out of my line of fire!" Parise hissed. "Goddammit, get out of the way!"

Puel, who had served in the commandos, felt the bones in his neck cracking: he kicked backward to destabilize Calderón, who sent him flying with him against the screen. The bamboo fencing gave way under their weight; they fell twelve or thirteen feet onto the neighbors' terrace.

Parise trampled flowers and bushes and leaned over the low wall. Puel and Calderón were grappling with each other at the foot of a white plastic table, which had broken their fall. They were hissing with hate as they fought, a ferocious combat that first one, then the other seemed to be winning. A mad, lethal waltz. Parise hesitated to fire. At that distance, he could just as easily hit the wrong target, and as for jumping down to deal with him, he wasn't sure he could get back up. The two men rolled on the tiles, their muscles straining, pummeling each other in a battle that was as short as it was violent. The mask that protected his nose got in his way, but Puel, this time, would not let go of his prey: Rubén was biting the dust on the terrace, his forearm pressed over his windpipe. He struggled to get free, succeeded, and jammed his palm against the base of Puel's broken nose: a flood of blood spurted out under the bandage. Puel felt the flaming arrow shoot up into his brain. In a second, Rubén had turned him over. The detective was breathing heavily to expel the hatred that was restraining his muscles, wedged his hands under the base of the killer's head in order to break his vertebrae, and suddenly froze: there was a child on the terrace.

A youngster in swimming trunks, who was watching them fight, a kid three or four years old as surprised as he was, his eyes of a pure innocence underneath his bobbed hair and curls.

Rubén gripped Puel's head, jaw, and neck in a vise and with a sudden jerk broke the man's cervical vertebrae. The head he was holding in his hands fell down on the chest, which no longer weighed anything.

A stupefying second.

The kid hadn't moved, either.

"Emiliano?" a woman's voice called from inside the apartment. "Emiliano, are you there?"

Perched on the neighboring terrace, Parise had taken out his automatic pistol: the bald man had been about to fire into the pile when he saw the child, that damned rug rat in his Disney swimsuit, who was watching them fight it out to the death.

"Emiliano, where are you, dear?"

White net curtains were blowing through the neighbor's French doors. Parise looked back at Calderón, who, protected by Puel's inert body, was blindly digging through his jacket in search of a weapon.

"Emiliano!"

Parise swore between his teeth. The noise was going to alert the whole neighborhood, the brat's mother was coming, and he couldn't liquidate all the witnesses. The killer retreated, cursing, and rushed down the glass staircase. El Toro was sponging up the blood that was dripping on his soiled coat while his partner was dragging the girl to the front door. They had drugged her and bound her hand and foot with tape. No time for Calderón.

"*Vamos, vamos!*" the team leader barked.

Etcheverry was waiting in the van, double-parked.

Rubén had met the eyes of the bald man who was taking aim at him from the terrace. He found Puel's pistol under his arm and grabbed it to fire, but Parise had disappeared.

The child was still watching, deaf to his mother's calls.

"Emiliano!"

A young woman came through the billowing curtains and let out a cry of amazement when she saw what was going on. Rubén untangled himself from the cadaver without looking at the child and assessed the situation. The neighbors' wall was about twelve feet high, with no handholds that could be used to climb it. The woman rushed toward her child and protected him in her trembling arms.

"Don't hurt us," she implored him, "I beg you . . . "

In his mother's arms, the child began to cry.

Rubén stuck the killer's Beretta in his belt, pushed the garden table against the flaking white wall, put one of the plastic chairs on top of it, and climbed up on the shaky edifice, praying that no one was waiting for him up there. The neighbor watched him, terrified, clutching her child as if he might fly away. Rubén grabbed a bit of smashed fencing and managed to hoist himself up to Prat's terrace. It was deserted, the sliding door wide open. He rushed toward the stairway, his finger curled on the trigger.

The kitchen and living room were empty. He ran to the bedroom, gun in hand, saw the canvas bag on the bed, the roses scattered on the floor. Ledzep shot out of his hiding place and took off toward the hall, his claws slipping on the floor. Rubén pointed the Beretta toward the adjacent bathroom, but it too was empty. He thought he heard tires squealing in the street, raced to the French doors in the living room and onto the little balcony, his heart beating wildly.

Too late: the kidnappers' vehicle had disappeared around the corner of Gurruchaga Street. By the time he reached his car, they would be far away.

It was several seconds before Rubén realized: slowly his face fell—Jana.

11

El Toro was grinding his teeth in the back of the plane's cabin. That little whore had almost blown his brains out: a few inches more to the left and he could have said goodbye to his bonus. In the meantime, the pain in his ear was intense and it was still bleeding despite the handkerchief he was using to stanch the flow. El Picador was teasing him as they sat side by side at the back of the cabin.

"Masturbation makes you deaf anyway!" he guffawed over the noise of the plane's motor.

El Toro shrugged, planning his revenge. In the seat in front of them, Etcheverry was feeling depressed: assigned to drive the van to the airfield, the head of the task force that had staked out the place in Colonia had just lost his best man. Puel, whom he had watched hitting a Slavic giant with chains for hours (the man was a force of nature whose bones refused to break, but Puel had beaten him to death almost without stopping to rest), whom Etcheverry had fished out of the river just a week earlier, while the others were setting fire to the house, Puel was dead. Worse yet, they'd had had to leave him there . . . Etcheverry leaned toward the pilot.

"How long before we get there?"

"Fifteen minutes," Del Piro replied.

They were flying over the delta, an expanse of jungle cut by muddy streams that inspired nothing but disgust in him. Del Piro had had to rush back to Buenos Aires, putting the two brutes in the seaplane and leaving the task of guarding the prisoner to Puel's men, who were accompanying the boss. Parise, who was in charge of the operation, was sitting with his legs jammed up against the instrument panel, wearing a pair of extra-large Ray-Bans. He had just finished a call on his cell phone—the boss was complaining, as usual. Calderón was still at large, one of their men had been left behind, and they had been able to kidnap only the girl. Nobody was paying any attention to her, a simple "package" thrown in the back of the fuselage.

There was little turbulence on this clear, sunny day. Jana came to, feeling like a snake in formaldehyde; her limbs were hobbled, her brain functioned intermittently. There was the sound of a motor—was it an airplane? The Mapuche was lying on the floor, her muscles still aching from the electric shock, her mind hazy. She had been drugged. For sure. Her eyes turned toward the front of the cabin, but she could see nothing more than heads sticking up over the seat backs. Four of them, plus the pilot. Jana thought she recognized the fat man with the swine's face, a red handkerchief pressed against his ear, then felt herself fading as the plane bounced around. Her brain slipped back and sank, in much the same way as one forgets, without realizing it.

A black hole.

*

The house was on the south side of the island, lost in the jungle of the delta. The canal was fairly narrow at that point, and there was hardly any traffic. The taxi boats that roamed the arms of the river could not get through because of the trees that had fallen during storms, and the closest house was miles away. The island was infested with mosquitoes that attacked en masse as soon as the sun went down.

Del Piro had parked the seaplane on the opposite bank, along a dock built where a stretch of water that was broader and less full of branches made it possible to tie up. The plane was bobbing there after its early morning flight. The whole team had assembled on this island in the delta: Parise, the head of the Santa Barbara security police, El Toro and El Picador, his longtime henchmen, the ex-lieutenant Etcheverry, who had been in charge of the task force in Uruguay, Frei, who was the prisoner of his neck brace and moved with all the grace of a turret, and finally Gómez and Pina, who had staked out Calderón's office in vain.

The boss had arrived with them by boat the preceding evening: General Ardiles, wearing a red Lacoste polo shirt and Porsche glasses, escorted by a taciturn gorilla, Durán, and the always stylish Dr. Fillol—Jaime "Pentothal" Fillol, as the pilots had nicknamed him at the time. He was the one who had operated on his friend Ardiles in a Santa Barbara private clinic in 2005, and provided the medical certificates for the old general so that he could avoid going before the tribunal. Fillol owed the general part of his fortune—a clinic with state-of-the-art equipment, ready cash in foreign accounts, a younger wife. He didn't much like thinking about the past, but his name was also on the ESMA form dug up by the Campallo girl. Fillol had attended her mother in childbirth thirty-five years earlier, and pulled her sick brother out of her belly. A strange reunion. The doctor remembered especially the violet-colored head of the baby as it came out of the vagina, the umbilical cord that was strangling it, and what he had done to save it. His profession. The infant's heart had been damaged, suggesting that he wouldn't live long, but he had survived: he was there, before his eyes, thirty-five years later. Miguel Michellini. Yes, a strange reunion.

"What do you think, Doc?"

Fillol gulped on seeing the condition of the broken puppet lying on the table and put away his stethoscope.

"His heart is weak," he said, "but he should be able to hang on a little longer."

Leandro Ardiles was grumbling as he sat on a chair that did not relieve his discomfort. The action had partly failed because the detective was still on the loose.

"O.K.," the general said to the bald man who was to lead the interrogation. "Let's not lose any time."

Jana had awakened in a room with drawn curtains, her thoughts muddy, her ankles and wrists bound with plastic cable ties that were cutting into her skin. She was lying on the iron plate of a table, naked. She didn't know where she was or what had happened to Rubén. Woozy from the chemical vapors, it took her several seconds to realize that she was not alone: a face was across from her, almost unrecognizable under its mask of dried dung, that of Miguel. Or rather what remained of Paula, tied to the neighboring table. The transvestite's white dress had been half torn off and was stained with blood, but he was still breathing. Jana didn't have time to talk to him: a group of men had come into the room to examine Miguel without paying any attention to her.

Jana gulped, her back pressed against the iron plate. There were five of them around the poor fellow, an old man in a Lacoste shirt, his hair dull and his eyes steely, another who must be a doctor was rolling up his stethoscope, followed by a bald giant with pocked skin, a kind of syphilitic pimp, and the fat guy with the pig's face who had Tasered her in the bedroom. They soon turned to her, tied to the table next to Miguel.

El Toro passed in front of the spread-eagled body of the Indian woman and assessed her torso.

"Amazing tits," he said ironically.

The asshole.

"Let's go," Parise urged.

Some people could endure unimaginable physical pain: very few could watch others being tortured without flinching, especially if they were friends or relatives—usually women whose babies were put on their bellies and tortured talked as soon as the kids screamed.

El Picador set up the machine. The *picana*: two copper clamps connected to an electrical transformer that the torturers applied to the most sensitive parts of the body—the anus, the genitals, the gums, nipples, ears, armpits, nasal cavities. The procedure was not new: Lugones, a police chief who was also the son of the great Argentine poet, had already tested the machine in the 1930s. The French instructors returning from the Algerian War had brought it back into fashion.

Miguel was weeping quietly as El Picador put the clamps on his ears. Parise bent over Jana, who was drunk with fear.

"Listen to me, Indian. You are going to tell me everything you know, including your mother's name if you know it, without lying: we're in a hurry, and patience isn't my strong point," he warned her with a grimace that didn't need to be threatening. "That means that the first time you give the wrong answer your homo pal will be transformed into an electrical generating plant. Understood?"

Jana could hardly breathe; she nodded, looking at her friend imploring her.

"Who told Calderón about this? The Campallo daughter?"

"I . . . I don't know."

Parise clicked his tongue to El Picador.

"I don't know!" Jana cried. "I don't know, he was the one who came to find me!"

"Who else knows about it?"

"The . . . the Grandmothers."

"Who else?"

"A cop . . . Anita something. A friend of Calderón's. She's helping him in his investigation. I don't know any more, he hasn't told me anything."

"Who else?"

"Nobody!"

"Who else?"

"Nobody, God damn it! Nobody!"

At a sign from the boss, El Picador switched on the *picana*. Miguel stamped on the iron plate.

"Mama! Ma-ma!"

El Toro smiled—they all ended up calling for their mothers.

"Nobody," Jana repeated, weeping, "nobody . . . stop it, stop it, shit!"

The prisoner writhed even more. Jana closed her eyes but her friend's screams were tearing her apart. Finally they turned off the electricity.

"O.K.," Parise went on. "Now tell me how you found Montañez."

Miguel was moaning like a puppy, she was going to go crazy.

"His name . . . his name was on the internment form," Jana replied, looking away. "The form for the parents, the *desaparecidos*."

Parise turned to General Ardiles, who had a ringside seat. The old man's emaciated face went ashen. He signaled to them to continue the interrogation.

"Did Calderón dig up the skeletons?"

"The skulls . . . "

"To compare the DNA with María Campallo's?"

"Yes."

Jana was panting, she had to have answers.

"Where did this internment form come from?"

"The ESMA."

"I know that," the bald man growled. "I'm asking who gave it to you?"

"The old woman," Jana whispered. "The laundress. She'd kept a copy."

Parise grimaced: the old witch . . . They had, however, searched her shop.

"Calderón," he said, "is he the one who has the original?"

"No, just a copy."

"You're lying, you *India de mierda.*"

"No! No!" Jana begged.

"Who has the original?"

"Díaz!" she recalled. "Franco Díaz!"

Parise turned again to his boss, who responded with a doubtful grimace—clearly the name was unknown to him.

"Who is this Díaz?" the head interrogator went on.

"Ossario's neighbor. In Colonia. He fled after the attack," she said, her eyes full of tears. "He's a former member of the secret services. An Argentine. A retired officer who served in the Falklands War. I don't know him," she added hastily, "I've never seen him."

"And Calderón?"

"He hasn't either, he's looking for him."

General Ardiles wrote Díaz's name in his notebook.

"Calderón was trying to compromise Campallo, but Campallo is dead," Parise continued. "Who are the next targets?"

"I . . . I don't know," she answered, taken aback.

"Don't play games with me, you little whore: the obstetrician, the chaplain, the officer assigned to carry out the extraction, everybody's name is on the internment form!"

Jana stared at him, helpless.

"I don't know . . . "

"You're lying."

"No! No, damn it! You're going to kill us anyway!"

El Toro looked at the weakling on the neighboring table: it was true that he didn't look so good.

"Well?"

"The copy we got was in bad condition," she finally said. "Names were missing, at least half the names! Miguel's mother tore the form into little bits; she . . . she ate the paper, her hair, that was her mania, she was sick, completely crazy. Calderón cut the pieces of the puzzle out of her stomach."

There was a short silence.

"And you think I'm going to believe such bullshit?" Parise said, furious.

He made a sign to El Picador, who flipped the switch. Miguel let out a shrill scream of pain.

"Stop, I'm begging you, stop!"

"You're lying, you dirty little whore!" Parise shouted.

"No!"

"You're lying!"

Miguel was shrieking but Jana no longer heard him. She spat in the giant's face, her saliva landing on his eyelid.

He broke her nose with his fist.

"Take it easy!" Ardiles hissed behind him.

`Jana's head had bounced off the table. The pain burned her face. She felt warm blood running onto her neck, and the tears welling up blinded her. A hellish heat permeated the room, her naked body, her veins. Parise wiped off her saliva with his sleeve and sized up the spread-eagled Indian, her face bloody. He gave the boss a sign to indicate that the session was over.

Doctor Fillol, who had remained silent up to that point, rushed up to the former interrogating officer.

"Do you believe what she said? That my name doesn't appear anywhere?"

Parise ignored the doctor.

"When they dig into Campallo's past, they're likely to trace the matter back to you, General," he said to Ardiles. "We have to go to plan B."

"The monastery?"

"Until we see which way the wind is blowing," the head of security replied.

It took a few seconds for Leandro Ardiles to make up his mind. Since his wife's death two years earlier, the old man had hardly left his guarded residence. What was the point? But the imminence of danger aroused forgotten sensations in him:

courage, duty, abnegation. Should he flee, as Parise advised? They could pounce on him at any time, and at eighty he was too old to run away. Preparations had to be made and his rear secured.

"What about Brother Josef?" he asked.

"First we have to get out of this trap," Parise decided.

The priest had no reason to betray them. Ardiles agreed, his face somber. He had confidence in Parise, who had over time become more than his right-hand man. All right, they would leave as quickly as possible.

"And me?" Fillol asked.

"You'd be better off following us," the head of security replied. "Calderón and the Madwomen have a copy of the document: damaged or not, they might make it public to spread panic. We have to leave, disappear. The sooner the better."

"But . . . my clinic, my appointments . . . "

"Would you prefer house arrest?"

The director of the clinic fell silent. For him as well, things were moving too fast. Parise led the two men out of the room. Jana watched them, trembling all over. Miguel was no longer moving.

"What about them?" El Picador asked, pointing to the prisoners.

The giant hardly looked at them.

"Get rid of them," he said as he shut the door.

El Toro sized up the weeping puppet.

"For a guy who's supposed to have a weak heart, the gigolo's holding up pretty well!"

El Picador set his leather attaché case on the table. Inside were half a dozen *banderillas* and knives of different sizes. He chose the thickest, a steel point several inches long, and stood over the transvestite. Jana couldn't breathe. "No," she moaned. "No . . . "

The poor transvestite was hanging on only by his tears,

soiled with scarlet snot. The *banderilla* went in under his shoulder blade and pierced his heart. Miguel shuddered under the shock; his limbs jerked in a nervous spasm, one last time. The coup de grace.

Jana was trembling with fear on the iron plate. Her broken nose was dripping blood, her vision was clouded, tears ran like razors down her cheeks. Miguel. A foul wind blew on her. El Toro was smiling over her naked body.

"Calderón is fucking you, huh, little whore . . . "

"Your sister too," she hissed in his porcine face.

The fat man sniffed as he unbuckled his belt. He didn't need El Picador for this little *India de mierda*. He unbuttoned his pants and took out his cock, like a relief. It was hard, hot, already enormous.

"What are you doing?" his acolyte asked.

"I'm going to have her first," El Toro replied.

Jana shivered on seeing his monstrous penis. El Toro had sodomized people by the dozens, especially male prisoners—there he went all out. The wags in the barracks had nicknamed him El Toro not so much for his bullish ways as for the size of his cock, a thick, veined log accompanied by testicles that hung like stillborns over his fat, hairy legs. Ten inches long, he'd measured it, of course. With that, there was no need to rape opponents with corncobs, the way Rosas's police did: El Toro had what was needed in his pants. An engine of death. He had ripped apart the little tranny's anus to make him speak, he had perforated his intestines as he was crying for mercy. Adrenaline. He was visibly thriving on it.

El Toro enjoyed the Indian woman's fear as she lay tied to the table. An oily glee lit up his face when he stuck his engine of death between her legs.

"You'll see," he whispered in her ear. "You're going to call for your mother, too."

12

The source of the Paraná River was in Brazil, some 2,500 miles farther north. Carrying everything along with it as it went, it veined the delta before coming out on the Río de la Plata, where it flowed to sea.

A rhizome of water, mud, and jungle, with a surface almost as large as Uruguay, the El Tigre delta had hundreds of canals and as many islands, inhabited and uninhabited; somctimes these were moving islands consisting of the accumulated vegetation carried along by the currents. No vehicles other than motorboats were allowed in the ecological preserve; ports, luxury shops, hotels, residences, or bed-and-breakfasts, activity was concentrated around the city of El Tigre, but all you had to do was navigate a few miles for the houses and cabins to become few and far between. Then nature became luxuriant, wild, omnipresent.

From the back of the boat, Rubén was silently scrutinizing the bank. They passed alongside a thicket of brush, hardly disturbing the birds nesting there. Anita was in front with a detailed map of the region, and Oswaldo was at the helm.

Responding to the commotion she'd heard on the phone, Anita had rushed to Palermo and found Rubén in Jo Prat's apartment, looking haggard. There was a body on the terrace of the neighbors, who were terrified and had called for help, and her childhood friend was in the living room, shattered. He was staring absently at the weapons sitting on the table, and hardly reacted when she arrived. Anita brought him out of his lethargy. His precious witness had been kidnapped in turn, but all was not lost: Gianni Del Piro had made a telephone call the preceding evening. According to the information she had just received, the pilot was currently in the El Tigre delta.

Oswaldo came to pick them up at the marina, where Rubén had asked him to meet them as soon as possible.

An old friend of his father's, Oswaldo lived in a worm-eaten shack in the middle of the jungle: an ERP activist and a great book lover, Oswaldo had taken refuge in the delta after the first roundups in 1976, and had lived there ever since as a hermit, devoting himself to fishing and painting. Oswaldo had retained a phobia for the city and a savage hatred for anyone who wore a uniform. The old man guided the motorboat with a sure hand, his thick beard capturing the sea spray thrown up by the hull. Rubén had explained the situation to him without giving any details, and Oswaldo hadn't asked for any: Daniel Calderón had never seen any of his paintings, Daniel's son was a kind of nephew to him, and he knew the region like the back of his hand.

Del Piro's phone call had been made from a point about twelve air miles from the port of El Tigre. There was no town on the map, just a simple telecommunications relay in the middle of nowhere. The pilot had called from one of the islands scattered along the canals. Rubén felt depressed among the jugs of water and gasoline. He had made a mistake by telling Isabel Campallo about her daughter's pregnancy. She had informed her husband, who, in one way or another, had informed the killers. They had followed the trail back to Jo Prat and discovered the hideout. Jana. The idea that they might harm her revolted him. Die or go mad . . . No, he couldn't go through the same nightmare a second time. And still less at this precise point in his life.

Palm and banana trees grew along the bank. His traveling bag was wedged under the seat where it would stay dry, filled with weapons. Oswaldo was navigating at reduced speed through the zigzagging part of the canal, avoiding the fallen trees and branches on the surface of the water. No one around, only the millions of insects buzzing in the sun.

"This should be the right direction," Anita commented, bent over her map.

Oswaldo grumbled. He didn't like cops, even if they were blond and had big breasts. Pollen and petals were floating in the air as they made their way upstream. An odor of mud emanated from the cloudy water. They passed by the abandoned dock of a colonial house made of wood and adobe, a few stands of pine, and a sprawling willow that held back the alluvium. The last corrugated-iron shacks had disappeared; ahead, there was nothing but miles of dense jungle. Disturbed, an *urutaü*, a local species of owl, fluttered in the branches. Leaving the meandering channels, Oswaldo headed straight ahead and accelerated in the lagoon. The boat was no more than fifteen feet long, but the motor was powerful. Spray flew up from the prow without driving away the birds, who were the kings of the delta. Across from them lay an island like dozens of others. Then there was a quicksilver glint in the sunlight. Rubén looked through his binoculars and felt his heart swell: it was a reflection off a fuselage. A seaplane.

He put his hand on Oswaldo's arm to make him slow down: *they were there.*

Anita was feverish in the front of the boat.

"Do you think they've seen us?"

They had made a loop to pass by at a distance from the island and were now doubling back through the canal on the other side. Rubén didn't answer. He had his loaded gun, his pockets were full of bullets, a billy club, a fighting knife, a pair of pliers, a tear-gas bomb; and a thirty-five-year-old hatred was wringing his stomach. Hugging the shore, Oswaldo brought them upstream, facing the wind. It was growing hotter and hotter as noon approached.

Rubén glanced at his cell phone: he had reception again. The closest police station was not far away, on the Paraná River.

"Call Ledesma," he said. "Have him send a police patrol boat."

"The Old Man?" Anita asked. "O.K., but . . . Shit, what do I tell him?"

"That we've found the people who killed María Campallo and the laundress in Peru Street. Tell him that I take full responsibility, and especially that he should get his ass in gear."

Anita glanced at him from the prow of the boat, met his icy gaze, and typed in the police chief's number on her phone. After a brief discussion, Anita was able to convince Ledesma and hung up, her hair flying in the breeze.

"It's done," she said. "He's going to send a patrol boat. But you're going to be on the hot seat if you're wrong."

Rubén wasn't going to wait the three-quarters of an hour it would take the delta cops to get there. Too late? The island was getting closer as they approached through the wavelets, hardly a hundred yards away. A moorhen was paddling nearby, serene in the current. They passed alongside piles of branches washed up near the bank, a thick vegetation interlaced with vines: Oswaldo was navigating slowly, keeping an eye out for movements in the surroundings.

The seaplane they'd seen earlier through the binoculars was bobbing on the other side of the island. Then they saw a cleared area, logs piled up under the pine trees, and, farther on, in the hollow of a little sheltered creek, the façade of a pink house. Rubén signaled to Oswaldo to land. The hermit turned off the motor. Anita was ready, her service weapon loaded, peering into the shadows under the branches. The boat soon ran up on a pile of pebbles and mud with reeds growing in it; with one leap, they were on land.

"Hide the boat and wait for us here," Rubén whispered. "And be ready to take off in a hurry."

"Don't worry, son."

Oswaldo gave them a reassuring wink and watched them move away through the forest. Anita followed Rubén under the shadow of the pines, more and more anxious. He moved forward, hunched over, noiselessly, and suddenly knelt down behind a thicket. There were two guards on the terrace of the house, a speedboat tied up at the dock, and another sentinel under the pines, about twenty-five yards away. A guy with a neck brace, behind logs of wood, sitting on a deck chair. Rubén had seen him in Colonia.

"Maybe we should wait until the police get here," Anita whispered at his side.

Rubén shook his head. In an hour Jana would be dead. Tortured, raped, her skin burned off with electricity, her love scattered. She might already be dead.

"Wait for me here," he said in a low voice.

Oscar Frei was battling mosquitoes, glued to his chair, an automatic weapon under his armpit. He didn't see the shadow crawling up to the woodpile. The guard sensed a presence behind him, but sunk in his neck brace and his deck chair, he turned around too late: the billy club struck his temple violently. A hand was held over his mouth as he faltered. Frei fell out of the chair, his head full of stars as he was being dragged toward the logs. He tried to stand up, but the sharp point of a knife slipped under his eyelid, slicing the thin skin.

"One move or a word and I'll cut out your eye and your fucking brain too."

Lying on his cottony body, Calderón stared at him with crazy eyes.

"How many of them are there inside the house?" he murmured, very close to the man's face.

The knifepoint was piercing the lower eyelid. On the terrace, Pina and Gómez had seen nothing.

"A dozen," Frei replied, pinned to the ground. "I don't know exactly."

"Are they all armed?"

"No . . . There's a civilian . . . a doctor."

"Is the Indian woman there?"

Frei nodded.

"Where is she? In which room?"

"I don't know . . . I'm on guard . . . I didn't see anything."

Rubén raised his head and quickly assessed the topography of the place. The two guys were killing time on the terrace, which could hardly be seen through the branches. It was an old house of painted wood, built on pilings, with tall paned windows. Frei made the mistake of thinking that Calderón was distracted: he grabbed the detective's wrist, intending to wrestle with him on the needle-covered ground, but the blade immediately sank in. A sudden blow, struck with all the weight of Rubén's body. Frei groaned in Rubén's hand, which was still held tightly over his mouth to muffle the sound. The steel slipped under his eye as if it were butter, pouring out a continuous red flow, before it reached the brain. The man jerked a last time and died.

Rubén was breathing unevenly. He wiped the blade on the dead man's jacket, left the body behind the pile of logs, and crawled back to Anita, his adrenaline pumping full tilt: terrible cries were heard coming from the house.

The blonde was peering through the foliage, watching for him to return.

"Well?"

"There are a dozen of them. You're going to go behind," he told her. "Go around the house through the jungle and be ready. How many cartridge clips do you have?"

"Three," she replied.

"O.K. As soon as you hear the first shots, attack them from behind and shoot into the house."

Anita grimaced.

"Is that it, your plan?"

"They're torturing her," Rubén growled. "Create a diversion, I'll take care of the rest."

"Don't you want to kiss me before I die?" Anita asked.

"You won't die."

"Just in case."

She smiled with all her strength but her hands were trembling. Rubén kissed her on the lips.

"You're not going to die, O.K.?"

"O.K. What if they kill you?"

He raised his eyebrows.

"Then we'll have failed completely."

The blonde with the asymmetrical face blew away her hair. The stress had weakened her muscles; her uniform was soaked with sweat. Rubén looked at his watch.

"You've got five minutes, *querida*."

Anita stifled the fear that was paralyzing her, gave the man she loved one last look, and without another word took off stealthily.

Rubén sneaked up on the house. The guards seemed to be talking on the shady terrace. The pines were too far away from the house for him to be able to hide behind trunks or thickets. Anita would have a better chance behind the house—the jungle probably extended as far as the other bank, where the seaplane was waiting. Three minutes had passed. A new scream came from the left wing of the house, drowning out the buzzing of the insects. Rubén took a firmer grip on the handle of his revolver. At least ten armed men; attacking the house in broad daylight was madness.

Sitting on a garden chair, Gómez was watching the dead branches float by, his submachine gun on his lap. The screams in the bedroom had stopped—the prisoners were having no fun. Pina left to listen to the radio inside. They were signaling to each other through the French doors—yeah, they wanted to get out of this Goddamned mosquito nest. Gómez was settling back on his folding chair when splinters of wood exploded a few inches from his head. An explosion that came from the left. He jumped up, pointed his automatic and retreated toward the house—fuck, they were being fired on! and received the impact right in the chest.

Pina sprayed the yard with bullets as he sounded the alarm. Other shots now crackled, coming from the other side of the house. They were surrounded. Parise was the first to burst into the kitchen, and gave curt orders to his men who rushed out of the bedroom.

"Get a move on, for God's sake!"

El Picador and El Toro posted themselves at the windows and fired a few shots at random while Parise was evacuating the general toward the bathroom. El Toro was swearing between his teeth, crouched down under the window—he hadn't even had time to stick it to the Indian woman. He'd left her there with her pussy bare, his dick still hard. Etcheverry looked out the little window in the vestibule and saw the silhouette of a cop a dozen yards away, hiding behind the oak that bordered the house. The shots she was firing were passing through the windows and the door and whistling into the kitchen. A lethal trajectory. Pina groaned with pain and bent over his thigh, which was spurting scarlet blood. Parise assessed the situation. The cop was going to shoot them like rabbits if they went out the back door. They had to try to make a counterattack on the east side. Etcheverry hunched down and signaled to the bald man who was firing salvos haphazardly, his body braced under the window. The cop stopped firing for an instant. Parise snorted. She was reloading.

"*Vamos!*" he yelled to his men. "*Vamos!*"

El Toro and his buddy burst out the door that gave on the yard. They were about to riddle the great oak with the submachine gun when they saw something that stopped them cold. The policewoman was kneeling on the ground, her hands behind her neck, and Del Piro's Glock was pressed against her blond hair. The pilot had taken her from behind.

Rubén had run toward the west wing of the house as soon as the firing started. He reached the French doors without being fired on, broke the lock with a kick, swept aside the rods and curtains, and pointed his Colt around the room, his brain white-hot. First he saw Miguel's body, a strange *banderilla* stuck in his back, and then Jana, spread-eagled on the table. She was naked, her face smeared with blood, but alive.

"Rubén . . . "

Her nose was broken, her body was sticky, but she was alive. He took out his knife and, keeping his revolver pointed at the door and an eye on the corridor, he cut her bonds with four furious slashes that set her free. The explosions in the adjoining rooms had stopped; Rubén grabbed Jana like a bouquet of fear, and put her on her feet.

"Can you run?"

Her limbs were stiff and numb, and she could hardly stand up.

"Yes . . . Yes."

"Get going, then," he whispered. "Go quickly."

Their hearts were beating as if they were at the muzzle of a gun. A head appeared in the hall, at the corner of the wall next to the torture chamber: Dr. Fillol, obviously disoriented by the gun battle.

"Look out!" a voice behind him shouted.

Fillol immediately put his hand to his mouth, but he no longer had a mouth, half his lower jaw had been torn away by the Colt's bullet, pulverizing his teeth. His finger on the trigger, Rubén pushed Jana toward the broken-in door.

"There's a boat three hundred yards away, on the shore," he told her feverishly. "Hurry, I'll meet you there."

Jana was naked, had no weapon, and a stream of blood was

flowing from her broken nose. Rubén picked up her jumpsuit and T-shirt, which were lying on the floor, and put them in her hands.

"Damn it, Jana, GET OUT OF HERE!"

A shot was fired near them that perforated the wall. The Mapuche met his electric glance one more time, then disappeared through the curtains that a draft was blowing inward. Rubén fired three times into the hall to cover her escape, saw Jana running like a fawn through the pines, and regained hope. A smell of gunpowder hovered in the room. He backed up over the glass fragments and was getting ready to run toward the yard himself when a woman's scream stopped him.

"Rubén! Rubén!"

It was Anita's voice.

"Drop your gun," thundered a voice from the hall. "Drop your gun or I'll snuff her!"

The killers had taken her hostage. The detective swore between his teeth, his hand clutching the Colt .45. One of them was trying to negotiate while the others went around the house. No more cover, no way out: it was a matter of seconds.

"Drop your gun or I'll shoot her!" the voice repeated.

Etcheverry appeared at the corner of the hall, protected by his human shield. Anita raised her arms, terrified, the Glock's barrel against her temple.

"I'll blow off her head!" Etcheverry threatened. He moved forward a few feet, his pistol still pressed against her skull. "Drop your gun, do you hear me, Calderón?"

The killer was a good six inches taller than Anita. The others were hiding behind the wall, close to the bathroom. Rubén gripped his gun—it was too late to escape, he heard footsteps approaching behind him, at least two men who were now blocking any retreat. He leaped toward the hall, met in a fraction of a second the frightened eyes of his childhood friend, and shot her at point-blank range.

Hit hard, Anita fell back against Etcheverry, who still had his finger on the trigger. A fatal second for looking forward. The .45's bullet had passed through the blonde's shoulder, emerged above her scapula, and continued its deadly course: it hit Etcheverry right in the heart. A look of surprise crossed his face; he heaved a last sign as the cop collapsed at his feet and slipped with her down the wall of corridor. Running up behind, Parise fired from the debris of the French doors. Rubén jumped over the bodies on the floor, threw himself against the opposite wall, and emptied his clip on the moving targets. Fillol, reeling near the kitchen and holding the remains of his jaw, was slammed into the sink. Ardiles's bodyguard, hit in the stomach, sprayed the floor with his submachine gun. Splinters of bone flew up in a cloud of dust; hugging the bathroom wall, Pina was dragging his leg—Anita had hit him a little earlier. Rubén fired into the chaos: the last bullet in the .45 fractured the arch of the killer's eyebrows. Adrenaline was burning in Rubén's veins. He stood up, drew his knife, and sensed danger on his right. He looked for the enemy and in an instant located him at ten o'clock and drove the blade home in a single movement. General Ardiles was waiting for him near the bathroom, a Browning in his hand: the knife went into his arm all the way to the bone.

Rubén was pulling out the blade, his eyes shining with hate, when he was hit with fifty thousand volts.

13

The Taser XREP could shoot small paralyzing cartridges up to fifty yards. At close range, it could cause cardiac arrest. Calderón had a strong heart. He was writhing on the floor littered with bodies, his brain fried by the electric shock. Parise sniffed, the weapon in his hand. Del Piro was moving toward him as if he were crossing a minefield.

"Catch the girl," he told the pilot. "Liquidate her and meet us at the seaplane. El Toro, you secure the area. You," he said, turning to his buddy, "take care of Calderón and get all you can out of him. You've got ten minutes. I'll deal with the general."

"O.K., boss!"

The smell of gunpowder was diminishing in the house. The soles of the killers' shoes crackled on the glass shards and cartridge casings lying everywhere. El Picador dragged Calderón's stunned body toward the bedroom while Parise assessed the damage. Six men were down, one on the terrace, four in the hall, another in the kitchen. Dead or dying. Streaks of blood and bits of flesh speckled one corner of the door and the walls, which were perforated by bullets. Etcheverry was no longer moving, collapsed against the wooden interior wall. On the other hand, the policewoman accompanying Calderón was still breathing: she was moaning in the middle of the hall, semiconscious, with a dark hole over her heart. Parise pushed away the weapons on the floor, stepped over the bodies, and reached Ardiles, who was lying in the bathroom doorway, pale as a sheet.

"Will you be all right, General?"

Ardiles had a nasty wound in his forearm, which he was hugging to him as if to protect it.

"No," he said, his eyes bloodshot. "No . . . "

The blade had broken the bone. Parise passed his hand over his sweating face and put away his Taser. Ardiles was losing blood, and his friend the doctor was blowing bubbles near the sink, his jaw lying among the glass fragments.

"I'm going to patch that up," Parise said.

He dug through the medicine cabinet in the bathroom and found bandages and disinfectant. He had to cope with the most pressing things first, then get rid of the bodies, and take off before anyone else got there. Calderón had tracked them to the house in the delta, at least one policewoman knew about it, and perhaps others did as well. They had to throw the bodies in the river, and maybe set the house on fire. The seaplane was on the other side of the river, five minutes' walk away. The old general was grimacing as he cleaned the wound.

"You've got to go back to the plane as soon as possible, sir," Parise told him as he opened up the bandages. "You mustn't stay here."

The cut was clean. The old man was still bleeding and he was showing signs of weakness.

"Are you going to be able to do this?"

"Yes . . . Yes."

"You'll need stitches. We'll take care of that at the monastery, not before, I'm afraid."

"Where is Dr. Fillol?" Ardiles asked.

"Sorry, sir. He was killed in the firefight."

Parise put a bandage on the wound and attached it to the general's arm with adhesive tape. Ardiles gritted his teeth; all he was thinking about was getting out of this house. El Toro returned from his tour of inspection, his clothes covered with thorns and pollen.

"I found an old man hiding in a boat, not far down the bank!" he reported. "He's the one who brought Calderón and the cop here. He told me they were alone," the fat man added, as he caught his breath. "If there were other cops, they'd be here!"

"O.K. What about the guy in the boat?"

"Sleeping with the fishes."

Parise grasped his superior's good elbow to help him get up.

"O.K.," he said. "Go see about your buddy while I take the general to the seaplane. Make Calderón tell us everything he knows and then kill him. We'll meet at the dock in ten minutes. Get going!"

El Toro nodded mechanically, stepped over Etcheverry's body, and disappeared toward the bedroom. Parise supported Ardiles, his red polo shirt soaked with blood.

"Can you walk?"

"Yes," the general said with annoyance.

"In that case, go ahead. I'll meet you there."

He let the general make his way past the dead men, checked his Glock's clip, and turned to the blonde lying on the floor.

Anita was regaining consciousness after the chaos of the firefight. Rubén's bullet had passed through her without hitting any vital organ, but a sharp pain was radiating from her shoulder. The hall where she was lying stank of hemoglobin and gunpowder, and a great chill was invading her numbed body. She tried to get up but the hydrostatic shock had nailed her to the floor. She shuddered when she saw the bald giant coming toward her. An ugly face and a feeling of emptiness that urged her to act. Anita stretched out her right arm, looking for a weapon, but found nothing but blood and dust. Parise briefly sized up the blonde lying at his feet.

"The cops are coming," she whispered to get him to leave.

"They aren't going to save you, old lady," he said, cocking his gun.

Anita had a defensive reflex, but it was in vain: the Glock was pointed at her head.

"Dirty rat," she cursed between her teeth.

Anita had no last thought about Rubén, who was being held prisoner in the next room, or about her cat who was waiting for her, or about the men whom she had loved: Parise shot her in the face.

Anita died in the middle of the hall, her eyes wide open.

*

Cartridge cases lay all over the worm-eaten floor of the torture chamber. The French door was half off its hinges; the curtains were billowing in the wind, letting sunlight filter in.

El Picador had tied Calderón to the table, in the same position as the tranny, the bloody doll lying a few steps away.

"You waking up, Cinderella?" the ignoramus asked.

Rubén was coming to, his stomach next to the iron plate. He was immediately gripped by fear, a child's fear returning to him after its stint in hell. From the ESMA, El Turco, and the others. He didn't know if Jana had managed to escape, if they had killed her, or where Anita was: his muscles ached after the electrical shock, he was tied down and a guy with an emaciated face was digging around in an attaché case on the next table. He saws the *picana* and his throat closed up.

Then El Toro came into the room, his brow beaded with sweat after his run around the house.

"We've got ten minutes!" he announced.

El Picador sorted his utensils, keeping one eye on his victim-to-be—a tough guy, huh? He chose a *banderilla* while his acolyte was tearing off the prisoner's shirt to get him ready. He positioned himself over the naked back, concentrating on the muscles that protruded below the little bones, and chose the point of impact. Rubén pulled on his bonds, a desperate, useless effort: the killer bent over and thrust the *banderilla* into his spinal column. The excruciating pain took his breath away. The sharp point had lodged itself between two vertebrae, literally nailing him to the iron plate. Rubén gasped for air, his brain in a panic, but life seemed to be running away.

"So, you fucking dandy, now you're looking less clever," El Toro gloated.

Rubén smelled his fetid breath like the fumes from a slaughterhouse.

"You're going to tell us everything you know," El Toro said, "and fast. Where did you get the document about Campallo? Huh?"

"Go . . . fuck yourself."

"Ha, ha, ha!"

El Picador put the *picana*'s clamps to the detective's ears. The machine was rudimentary, a portable, manually operated electric generator, but the damage done to the parts attached to it was irremediable. El Toro was jubilant: Calderón was there, pinned down like a butterfly on the plate.

"Let's see what you've got in your belly, my darling . . . "

*

Jana had lit out without thinking of anything but running. She'd seen what they did to Miguel, what El Toro would have done to her if Rubén hadn't gotten her out of there. She ran straight ahead but the world was howling around her. The Mapuche didn't feel the guts under her feet or the blood that was running from her wounded nose, nor the branches that were scratching her: her calluses were thick and fear made her run fast.

She rushed headlong into the jungle, carrying her clothes in her arms. Shots rang out behind her, a brief volley, she didn't know what had happened, if Rubén had escaped as well—

Rubén, Rubén, her heart was beating like a bird against the windowpanes. He had remained behind, in the nightmare house. She was doing battle with the bushes and roots that stuck to her skin, her blood was running down her neck onto her torso, and then there was the fear, the wild thoughts that were coursing through her mind, asphyxiating her. Jana ran straight ahead but her lungs were short of air. She stopped, out of breath, and put on her T-shirt and jumpsuit. The birds had fallen silent, her pulse was beating against her temples. Her whole body was dripping with sweat. She looked all around her, lost. It was dark under the roof of greenery, she didn't know where the canal was, whether she was going in the right direction. Quick, get a hold on herself. A boat along the shore, Rubén had said; that implied that they were on an island. The Mapuche hardly had time to dry the warm blood running over her mouth: she heard the sound of a machete over the buzzing of the insects. Someone was following her. Someone who couldn't be Rubén . . . Jana gritted her teeth and ran to her left.

The vines and branches scratched her skin, the roots made her stumble, but she bounded over the rough terrain and escaped the traps set for her. She stifled a scream as she crossed a wall of brambles, flattened nests of ferns, the calluses of her feet like bloodied soles, tripped again, caught herself on the branches, and then suddenly the landscape changed.

A few giant pines lined the shore, which was flooded with sunlight. Jana filled her aching lungs. The pine needles were softer under her bruised feet, and black birds were zooming along the horizon, but the world was still hostile. She was still bleeding heavily from her nose, and the machete blows were coming closer to the edge of the forest. Reeds and water lilies were growing in inlets along the shore. Jana ran toward the aquatic flowers and reeds swaying gently. The water, earth-colored, was washing up in little waves at the end of the beach.

The Mapuche climbed a small rock, let herself slip into the cool water, and noiselessly hid among the reeds.

Del Piro extricated himself from the jungle, his machete in his hand. Drops of blood marked the trail of the fugitive up to this open area dotted with big pines. No one in sight: but the trail was fresh. Del Piro walked toward the shore, his cheeks covered with scratches. He pushed aside the walkie-talkie to stick the machete in his belt and pulled out his Glock: the Indian woman was there, somewhere.

"Where are you hiding, you little whore?" he murmured into the void.

Del Piro gripped the handle of the pistol in his damp hand, his senses on alert, but heard nothing but the lapping of the wavelets. A few bird cries in the distance disturbed the silence. He scrutinized the surface of the water, looking for a head sticking up, but the canal was smooth, without foam. The pilot went toward the reeds, his finger on the trigger—yes, the fugitive was there, somewhere.

Jana had let herself sink straight down; the muddy water and the lilies would protect her, but she couldn't hold her breath for more than two minutes. The killer's footsteps stopped in front of the mudbed. Duckweed was bobbing on the surface. Del Piro observed the little clump of reeds and the brown water that came up as far as his shoes. The reeds were bending gently in the breeze, the sun was shining in a limpid sky. He bent down, intrigued by the thin colored trickle that, being carried away by the current, was dissolving in the murky water. He smiled. The Indian was there, leaking blood.

The pilot pointed the Glock at the water lilies, bang, bang, when the walkie-talkie on his belt started to crackle.

"Del Piro, damn it, get back here!" Parise yelled. "Fast!"

Jana couldn't see anything; mud and fear were blurring her circuits, and sounds reached her distorted. How long had she been underwater? One minute, two? She no longer had any breath, any autonomy, only a crushing pain in her thorax. They were going to cut her in two. Her lungs in agony, Jana rose to the surface, ready to die.

The sunlight blinded her for a second; she saw the deserted shore, the rocks, but not the man sent to track her down. He had disappeared. The Mapuche remained immobile for a moment, not daring to come out of the reeds. She soon heard a piercing sound: it was the police patrol boat's siren.

*

Jana trembled all along the way. Her feet were lacerated, her arms, her hands, and blood was dripping out of her fractured nose. She made her way along the shore that led back to the house, dripping with mud and stress: where was Rubén? She hadn't seen the seaplane take off earlier, just heard the roaring of the motors when it took off into the sky. The sun was filtering through the branches. She found the boat Rubén had mentioned, hidden under the trunk of a large willow; the leather bag that had belonged to his father had slipped under the seat. She turned toward the woods.

"Rubén?"

No answer. The house was no longer very far away. Her way blocked by thornbushes, she cut toward the jungle, which grew less dense as she approached the house. The voices soon became more distinct: the Mapuche crouched behind the thickets, some forty yards from the house, and observed the scene, the taste of earth in her mouth. The cops had taken over the place, some of them wearing bulletproof vests. Two civilians were fussing with bodies. There were about half a dozen of them, lined up on the ground. Jana shivered under the branches: a kind of odor of terror was floating there. Feverishly, she scanned the row of bodies, a black shadow among the fronds, but none of the men lying there looked like

Rubén. Police officers were exchanging a few words in front of the gray-hulled patrol boat tied up at the dock. One of them, who had been crouching up to that point, stood up and went toward the man who seemed to be his superior. Then Jana saw the two bodies lying on the ground some distance away: a blonde in uniform whose face had been blown away and Rubén, also inert, covered in blood. He was naked to the waist and lying on his stomach, his arms alongside his legs, with two *banderillas* still planted in his back.

Jana retreated under the branches, deaf to the world.

For a time she could never determine, she walked like a robot, haggard, and waited to lose herself in the jungle before she began to scream.

Part Three

KULAN—THE TERRIFYING WOMAN

1

Time had passed, distorted—Mapuche time, which counts seconds as hours and begins the day at dawn. The spirits were floating, but Jana did not recognize them—not yet.

She had waited for the cops to leave before returning to the boat on the shore, hidden beneath the branches of the big willow. Once the police and their adjuncts had left, the island in the delta was left to the chaos of nature. Jana had disappeared. Her nose had doubled in size, but she didn't think about it—she no longer thought. Her brain printed images, actions without goals, moved by an external force, a kind of stubborn will to live that she may have owed to her ancestors. The trip through the meandering canals back to civilization, the boat-taxis she met as she approached El Tigre, the motorboat abandoned near the port, the detour to the rail station, her frightening look, her naked, scratched feet, the streak of bloody snot on her T-shirt, her swollen face ringed with horror that made passersby shy away from her, the suburban train that took her back to Buenos Aires, the *colectivo*: all that remained vague, seen by the eyes of another moribund person.

Jana had arrived at the Retiro wasteland before nightfall, exhausted. The tragedy had reduced her to the condition of a savage. She remained prostrated under the vaults of her workshop. Die or go mad. Now night was falling, and fear gave way to helplessness. The sculpture of iron and concrete in the middle of the workshop, her constructions, her sketches, her rejects—now it all seemed meaningless. Nothing had any value anymore, as if her whole life had never taken place. But she was there, a Mapuche since the beginning of time, and the monsters that she thought she could drive out by her will alone had come back through the door of the Dead. They had never left the Earth: they were rampant, precisely, they were sinking into the freshest wounds, taking delight in evil or coming to terms with it, marked with the human soul trampled by headless gods.

The hours passed, subtracted time that would be taken away later on, when accounts were settled. The torture of the person who witnesses, powerless, the torture of another, the wild thoughts, like those in the notebook that he had had her read in the Andes . . . What meaning to give to that? How could she survive that—should she survive that? Rubén had sacrificed himself for her, in the Christian way she hated.

This evening, it was she who was being tortured, all out.

The wind was blowing on the metal structure of the shed, a vague echo of reality. An evil force was at work in the shadows, a saboteur of dreams as if they had to pay for something, a cruel and obscene monster who had killed her love with the hands of the same executioners who had killed his father and sister thirty-five years earlier . . . No, that made no sense. Jana had not left her community, made it through everything during the crisis and the following years just to wash up there . . . A black anger slowly invaded her. There would be no more kisses at dawn out in the yard, no more little forget-me-not stars in his eyes, his warm hand on her ass, all the caresses to console the world. A premonition, a omen of an imminent end? Jana didn't know why she had run away rather than hand herself over to the police. She had acted under the shock, by instinct, driven back into the jungle by the vision of horror that had swallowed her up better than the vegetation did. Part of her soul had remained with Rubén, in the delta. She'd taken a shower when she got home, but she still felt dirty. The fear she'd felt in the room on the island was unlike anything she'd ever experienced. Jana still smelled the odor of the swine when he'd tried to rape her, the aftershave worn by the bald giant who'd interrogated her, his eyes like those of an eagle in free-fall over her, imprisoned on the table. She recalled the scene. Miguel's death, almost surreal. The old man who witnessed the torture session, the one they called "General." That must be the famous boss, one of the oppressors whose name appeared on the original form. What did that matter now?

Then a name came back to her, a name that the events had pushed into the background: Brother Josef . . . At the end of her interrogation, the general had asked his henchmen what they should do about Brother Josef. The priest Miguel's mother was always talking about, it had to be the same man. They had also talked about a monastery, a plan B, until "the wind turns."

A tropical rainstorm was pecking at the roof of the workshop.

Jana still had a lump in her throat, but she was no longer crying. She had wept too much, her sorrow had dried up. Sadness, impotence, despair—the Mapuches had always fought on to the end. Jana Wenchwn had been a *welfache*, a warrior, since the day the carabineros had broken down the door of her house. She would not kill herself without fighting.

Caupolicán, the Mapuche chief fighting against Spain, had been cruelly tortured in the public square in Cañete: he had been dismembered for hours without making the slightest complaint. Their enemies called them the Auracan, "the rabid ones": Jana had that blood in her veins.

Now she no longer felt anything. Only a boundless hatred.

2

He couldn't sleep. He turned over and over in his bed in the attic, every thought came back to the surface, plunging him into bouts of insomnia that no prayer could end. Hadn't he done his duty? Brother Josef officiated at the Immaculada Concepción de María, the church where Rosa the mystic used to come to spit out her madness and her bitterness, a few blocks from the laundry. Had he done the right thing by informing his superiors? Brother Josef hadn't thought it would go that far. He detested violence, and the sight of blood disgusted him; his world was that of the Holy Scriptures and wise advice given to the tormented souls who came to him seeking absolution. On the other hand, he told himself that he had ignored the consequences of his acts, as if doing his duty would excuse him from having to account for them. But men had come to see him, and they had made him an accomplice to a murder. Since that accursed night in the back room, doubt had gnawed at Brother Josef, to the point that it deprived him of sleep. To whom could he refer the matter, if not to God? Would God even listen to him? And then what did he think, after all, that doing that would settle things, as if by magic?

The street was deserted at that early hour. The priest felt alone with his doubts, more alone than he had ever been. His bare feet jammed into leather sandals, he walked with bowed head down the sidewalk that led to his church, deep in an abyss of reflections. A car with faded paint stopped alongside him.

"Brother Josef?"

An Indian woman was addressing him from a Ford that was in as bad shape as her nose. He stopped, surprised.

"Yes?"

The young brunette got out of the car, swinging open the door in a movement that made him jump back.

"Get behind the wheel," she said in a hoarse voice.

The priest stood there a moment in the middle of the sidewalk, speechless, met the Indian's dark eyes, and shivered when he saw the revolver that she was hiding under her poncho.

"Get behind the wheel and nothing will happen to you," she said. "Go on!"

The man did not react—the sky was pale, the street hopelessly empty. Jana grabbed the collar of his cassock and, planting the barrel of her gun in his back, pushed him toward the seat.

"Move, Goddammit!"

*

The old Retiro train station seemed to have been abandoned, with its disused buildings under a highway interchange and its fallen sculptures lying about pell-mell in the weeds. Brother Josef had tried to reason with the Indian on the way, to tell her that she was taking him for someone else, but she had just guided him to Libertador Avenue, keeping her gun pointed at him. They arrived. With a wan sun as his escort, the man walked in front of her as far as the shed, obediently.

"Our church has no money, if that's what you want," he said, opening the sliding door. "And there's no need to threaten me, I'm not dangerous."

"I am," Jana said behind him. "Move."

It was a weird workshop, cobbled together with whatever

was at hand—a moveable bar, cooking utensils, old car seats. The churchman shuddered when he saw the arsenal leaning against the wall.

"Be reasonable," he stammered. "Put down that revolver and let's talk."

With the barrel of the gun, the Indian signaled to him to back up as far as the stacked pallets that served as a table.

"Kneel and put these on," she said, throwing him a pair of handcuffs. "Cuff yourself to the pallet: both hands. Hurry up!"

Her voice resonated under the corrugated iron roof. In the distance, the noise of traffic on the superhighway could hardly be heard. The priest was scared. No one would hear his calls for help or the sound of a shot. He was alone and at the mercy of this Indian whose eyes were still swollen with tears and who was threatening him with a firearm. He passed the handcuffs through the planks and attached his wrists to the pallet, keeping his eyes on her all the time.

"What do you want?" he whispered. "Huh?"

The position was uncomfortable, his chances of escape nonexistent. Jana stood a yard away and pointed the revolver at his face.

"It's simple, Christian," she said in a neutral voice. "Either you tell me what you know or I'll shoot you down like a dog. Is that clear?"

He nodded.

"Rosa Michellini," she continued in the same tone. "She was one of your parishioners."

It wasn't a question. The priest began to tremble. The Indian's eyes were dark, sad, dangerous.

"Rosa, yes . . . Yes. I . . . I learned that the poor woman died," he said stiffly.

"She was murdered," Jana specified. "Do you know why?"

"No . . . "

She cocked the revolver.

"No!" he cried.

"Answer me!"

"Rosa showed me a document," the kneeling man yelped. "A paper about children stolen during the dictatorship."

So that's what it was.

"A record from the ESMA that concerned her son Miguel?" Jana helped him.

"Yes . . . "

"Who gave it to her?"

"A woman. María Victoria Campallo."

"The old woman showed you the document, and who did you show it to, his father?"

The priest was dripping, drenched with sweat.

"Who did you show it to?"

"To the cardinal," he finally said. "Cardinal . . . von Wernisch."

Jana frowned.

"Who is he?"

"My superior," the brother answered. "When I began my study at the seminary."

She hadn't expected that.

"Why? Was this von Wernisch's name also on the ESMA document?"

"Yes," the young priest replied. "He was the chaplain at the time. The document could compromise him . . . "

Not only the cardinal, but the whole Roman Catholic Church.

Christians.

The Mapuche gripped the handle of the revolver more tightly.

"You warned him of the danger, and von Wernisch rounded up his old accomplices," she went on. "Is that it?"

Brother Josef, still on his knees, paled visibly.

"I don't know anything else," he said. "I swear it."

"Is that right? Where can this von Wernisch be found?"

"In a monastery," he mumbled, "far away from here."

The scene in the delta. The killers. They had mentioned a monastery.

"Are the others hiding out down there?" she began again, her heart pounding. "The general and his men? With the cardinal?"

"I don't know. I swear it!" the priest repeated. "The Los Cipreses monastery, that's where the cardinal resides: that's all I know!"

"Where is it?"

"Near Futalaufchen," he hastened to reply, "a mountain village close to the Chilean border."

The province of Chubut: the old Mapuche territories. Jana's face changed.

"I beg you," the man at her feet squealed. "Let me go. I won't say anything, to anyone, I swear! I swear it before God!"

"You're going to need him, Christian."

She put her gun back in its holster. She couldn't let him go. This traitor would warn the others, the general and the killers accompanying him. Rosa's confidant was trembling, the pallet's prisoner.

"I'm going to leave you there," she announced in an expressionless voice. "Los Cipreses, is that right?"

"What? But . . . "

"The Los Cipreses monastery," she repeated in a threatening tone, "are you sure? Think about it, Christian. Nobody ever comes here. You can shout all you want, no one will hear you."

Her dark eyes were shooting thunderbolts.

"Yes," Brother Josef stammered. "Yes . . . Los Cipreses, near the border. Don't leave me here," he begged, "I won't say anything, I swear!"

"Don't worry, I'm going to leave water for you."

"What? No, wait . . . "

"Save your spit, that's my advice to you. It's a long way."

The sun was climbing into the royal blue sky when Jana left the workshop, her bags on her shoulder. The Ford was waiting in front of the gate. She closed the sliding door, ignoring the priest's supplications. The Mapuche breathed in the air in her sculpture garden. A smell of wild game was floating somewhere between the plains and the tall grass: it was hunting season.

3

Jana hadn't taken much with her: Rubén's weapons, her great-grandmother's dagger with a bone handle, the woolen poncho that had kept her warm ten years earlier on the way to Buenos Aires, the few surviving clothes on her shelves, and herbs from her garden to make poultices. She had thrown the keys into the brush as she left the workshop, threw up what bile remained to her in front of the unhinged aviator where they had kissed, and left the city without regret, her stomach twisted with spasms.

Buenos Aires was no more than an old lady walled up in her memories, counting her last jewels in front of the dreary Atlantic, which no longer looked at her. The Mapuche had been driving for hours, gazing out over the immensity of the pampas. The sun erased contrasts, a shapeless catastrophe that brought her back to the original void. She had eaten practically nothing since leaving the delta, slept not at all, and had the constant sensation that her face was bleeding. Jana drove past great lakes covered with birds, cranes, herons, ducks, and flamingos; everywhere the colors of nature were sparkling, and she saw nothing but dead people.

A furious blast of a car horn made her jump just as she was drifting into the left lane: a cattle truck shaved the Ford, spewing its black smoke on the highway and spreading a slaughterhouse odor in the car, whose windows were all open. Jana stopped at the next service station, stuck out in the middle of nowhere.

Two dusty pumps stood erect in the yard crushed by the heat. There was no employee to fill the tank, just gas vapors that made her dizzy. Jana put her hand on the hood. The Ford's engine was boiling hot—all she needed was for it to give out. The head of an old dog appeared between the pumps. A bit of pink tongue hung from its jaws, a skinny, ageless mongrel whose coat must have been black and fawn-colored. She filled the car's tank, had a look at the shop in the phantom station. The dog observed her from a distance, its long snout in such bad shape that it must no longer smell anything. Jana smiled vaguely—it looked like he had cancer.

She paid for the gas at the counter and went off to the toilet, a dirty hole indicated with letters painted by hand, where she applied a new poultice. Her swollen nose was turning blue in the mirror speckled with filth, but the septum was not deviated. She caught a glimpse of her reflection and shuddered in spite of herself—she had a terrible face.

Four o'clock in the afternoon. Jana took a Coke out of the shop's fridge to help her forget the smell of shit, rejected the plastic-wrapped sandwiches, and located the liquor behind the guy at the counter, who was picking his nose and leafing through a car magazine.

"I'd like a vodka," she said.

The counterman reluctantly looked up from his magazine.

"What kind?" he asked wearily.

"Doesn't matter."

The man turned around, took a bottle off the shelf, stuffed it in a brown paper sack, then picked up the bill on the counter and went back to his magazine. "What about my change?"

"Isn't any. Thirty pesos, can't you read?"

Jana looked at the label. "Piranov. What is that, a brand from Chad?"

"It's the basic vodka," the man retorted. "All the drunks drink it."

What an asshole.

A truck had just stopped in front of the pumps, its chrome glistening in the torrid heat. Jana kept her distance from the elephantine driver who was climbing out of the cab and walked to the Ford. She frowned when she saw the mutt's head looking at her through the side window.

"What are you doing there?"

The flea-bitten dog had jumped through the broken window and was sitting on the passenger seat. He was gazing at her oddly, with his eyes half-closed or pretending to sleep, as if it wasn't really he . . .

"Listen, Brad Pitt, get out of there," she said, opening the door.

The dog perked up an orange ear covered with scabs. His only other reaction was a sigh. Maybe he was deaf, too. She looked at the graying muzzle of the animal, who had clearly made up his mind to get out of this godforsaken place. She shook her head and got behind the wheel.

"Fine, for all I care," she mumbled.

There was still a long way to go before reaching the foothills of the Andes. Jana left the service station without even looking at the patched-up sphinx sitting beside her—the tear running out of his eye must be a year or two old. He smelled of gas, fleas were running all over him, but he suffered them stoically, as if they were old friends.

She named him Diesel.

*

Route 3, which had become Route 22, crossed the country from east to west, angling toward the deserted South. Jana stopped at nightfall, in the middle of the pampas. The Ford's trunk contained violent treasures: a billy club, a grenade, a .22 caliber rifle, three tear-gas bombs, three pairs of handcuffs, an electroshock pistol, and a sniper rifle in its case, along with several boxes of ammo.

It took her almost twenty minutes to assemble the sniper rifle in the dim light of the car, and ten more to align the infrared telescopic sight. It was a model M40A3, based on the old Remington 700. Jana had hunted with her brothers, but she had never fired such a sophisticated weapon. She stuck the six cartridges in the magazine and went out into the moonlight to test the mechanism. The plains were glowing slightly, a smooth, harborless sea that stretched for miles all around. Diesel accompanied her into the grass, his tail wagging, taking advantage of the walk to dissipate his stench of dust and gasoline.

"Do you like that name, Diesel?" Jana asked.

It was the first time they had really talked. The dog did not answer; he was too busy sniffing something or other. The air was sharp, the night violet under the carpet of stars. They walked half a mile or so over the pampas. Finally Jana put the gun she was carrying to her shoulder and examined the virgin landscape around her. Diesel was biting at some fleas, and almost scratched off his ear with his hind paw before finally going off to find a place to relieve himself. The earth was still warm after the hot day. Jana lay down in the grass, put the rifle in firing position, and looked for a target in the dark.

A fencepost a hundred yards away: she aimed and fired, three times. The first two bullets missed, causing Diesel, who was pissing there, to run off; the third decapitated the post.

*

Nothing in her heart but a blue-black storm. A flea-bitten dog and an Indian with a broken nose crying herself empty: that was their team. The Ford was also holding up. Jana crossed San Carlos de Bariloche the next day, her eyes burning after the run against the wind. Her stomach had tolerated the coffee at breakfast and a Coke at noon, but not the sandwich she'd bought in a service station. The foothills of the Andes rose against the blue of the sky, which could do nothing about it. Diesel was still sitting facing the dusty windshield, impassive, looking like an old sea wolf ready to come about. She still hadn't heard his voice. Finally the landscape changed: great, age-old trees dotted the hills preceding the mountain range, their shadows growing longer as the sun went down. Jana crossed green plains toward the mountains perched in the clouds and reached the little town of Futalaufquen late in the day.

After the last Mapuche leaders were defeated, the land had been distributed to greedy *estancieros*, and churches were built to preach the Gospel to the savages who had been spared by diseases. The Los Cipreses monastery had been included within what was now the Los Alerces National Park, a valley lost in the Andes near the Chilean border. According to her map of the region, they were now getting close. The Ford climbed the switchbacks on a stony track, and passed a dump truck stuck on the hill, raising a storm of red dust, before descending toward Los Cipreses.

It was getting dark when she reached the mountain village. A row of houses with closed shutters lined the asphalt-paved road, and there were a few poor-looking farms. Jana slowed down in front of the restaurant, a kind of *pulpería* with a broken sign that seemed to be open, the only sign of life in this ghost town, and then drove on. The monastery was located outside town, a large stone building at the foot of a wooded hill. A waste ground served as a parking lot for visitors. The monastery was dark except for the dim light of a lantern at the entrance. The Mapuche drove slowly around the place and, after a few exploratory detours in the surrounding area, returned to the town.

There was still no one out. She parked on the street.

"Are you hungry?" she asked the dog as she cut the ignition.

Diesel was panting softly on the seat, which was already covered with his hair.

The Los Cipreses restaurant was run by a *mozo perdido*, a young man who had strayed, as mixed-race gauchos were called. His features tanned by the mountain winds contrasted with his youthful eyes, which were somber and timid and must not have seen many female strangers. Jana ordered the only dish on the menu, a cutlet *à la milanese*, while Diesel went through the garbage cans behind the shack.

Half a dozen rickety tables were languishing in the room, on whose walls a few hunting trophies hung askew were gathering dust. The crossbreed was ogling her from behind his tiled counter. Jana didn't utter a word, her mind absorbed by her plans. She had never been in this remote hole, but she knew the region: having been driven out by the carabineros, her family had taken refuge in a friendly community on the other side of the mountains.

"Isn't it good?" the waiter asked, intimidated.

The women with the broken nose had hardly touched her food.

"I'm not very hungry, anyway," she said.

"Can I make something else for you?"

She looked up.

"What?"

The young man shifted from foot to foot, ill at ease.

"It's late," he said. "Do you know where you're sleeping?"

Since the customer gave him a suspicious look, he hastened to add:

"I'm just asking because there's no hotel in the village. You have to go on to Futalaufquen. I live next door, with my family. If you want, we could put you up for the night."

The crossbreed blushed under his young man's mustache.

"No thanks," she said. "Just bring the bill."

Jana paid with Rubén's money and after a disagreeable visit to the toilet, left the little mountain restaurant. The ratty dog was scavenging around the overturned garbage cans; he trotted after her to the Ford, as mangy as his coat, and climbed aboard. He was familiar with the place and began to paw the seat, yapping as if they were coming home to spend an evening by the fire.

"You're completely off the mark, old man," Jana said, starting the car.

The flanks of the mountains stood out against the dark night; she drove as far as the exit from the village, then turned up the dirt road she'd found earlier, which wound toward the wooded hill. She parked the Ford at the end of the track, among the ferns and brambles. The forest became denser when she turned off the headlights. Jana put on her poncho to calm the heat of the night, grabbed the bottle of vodka on the seat and the flashlight. Diesel dug around for a moment in the ditch before following his mistress to the flat, bushy area that looked down on the monastery two hundred yards down the slope, its tiled roof lit by the moon. A good observation post.

As the humidity decreased, so did her fatigue. Jana found shelter under a *pehuen*, a large umbrella tree that had succeeded in slipping in among the pines, and laid out her few things. Moths were beating against the gas lamp, crazy about the heat, and Diesel snapped at them as they looped in and out. She opened the bottle of vodka. The liquor burned her throat, which had been dried out by the trip: she took another drink, but felt hardly any better. The dog had momentarily disappeared, busily nosing around in the thickets. She drank again, but two days of sleeping badly had depleted her reserves. She put out the gas lamp and stretched out on her back.

Chile was on the other side of the Andes, an opaque mass

in the night: her ancestors had lost their lands, but they had kept their magnetic soul. Jana thought about her young sister, her brothers. No, it was impossible to ask their help: they would ask her to return to the community rather than get her revenge, want her to reconstruct herself with them, her people, exiles on their own land. Everything she had tried to do since she'd left would have come to nothing, and she had this dark sun in her heart: Rubén. Jana thought about him, very hard, imagined the luminous spirit floating somewhere in the sky, but in the Milky Way she saw nothing but the diamonds of despair. She closed her eyes, numbed by fatigue and alcohol, a scruffy dog at her side. Slowly, nature took hold of her senses.

Was it the proximity of her people, the Mapuche spirit of her childhood that was calling her back, Ngünechen, the supreme deity of the volcanoes who, from the depths of time, was confronting the dark force of *kai kai*? The specters faced each other in the obscurity; she could almost feel them running over her icy skin. The forces. She felt them boiling up from the earth, spreading through her body, as if the telluric fire that woke the *machi* was still there, crackling . . . Jana suddenly sat up, her eyes wide open.

"Rubén?"

The Mapuche remained motionless under the *pehuen*, short of breath, but there was no answer other than the rustling of the wind in the branches.

*

A pale sun was spreading its mist in the hollow of the valley. Jana had been observing the monastery since dawn, bundled up in her woolen poncho, her eye glued to the gunsight. Six cartridges in the magazine, 7.62 caliber, range 900 yards, with a 10x zoom: she could sweep half the courtyard, invisible among the bushes at the top of the hill.

A monk had made a furtive appearance a little earlier, a young, blond man with thin hair. According to the priest who served as Rosa's confidant, Cardinal von Wernisch, who was very old, had retired there to spend the rest of his life. What about the others? Running about the thickets, Diesel was marking his territory with offhand spurts of urine. The dog finally sat down alongside her, a loyal shadow among the bushes. Jana had still not heard him bark. The temperature was climbing with the sun. Nothing was happening. Diesel soon went to sleep, his muzzle resting on his crossed paws, the ultimate in canine chic. Jana was waiting, sulkily, when her heart suddenly jumped: a fat man in a white shirt had appeared in the courtyard.

Vulgar features, a bovine look: the torturer in the delta, El Toro. He was there, in her line of sight. Part of the world shifted. Jana instinctively put her index finger on the trigger: if she pressed it, she would blow his head off. Images flashed through her mind—this vermin's head exploding, blood spurting onto the walls, bits of brain scattered all around—and then she got hold of herself. At this distance, she couldn't be sure of hitting her target: El Toro could take cover in a few steps. Alerted, the rest of the gang would barricade themselves in the monastery, from which she would never be able to dislodge them. They would send other men to ferret her out, the local police or men under orders to hunt her down. Jana kept her sangfroid: they were there, for the moment that was all that mattered. She had the advantage of surprise. Their vehicle must be inside, in one of the covered courtyards of the monastery where the killers had taken refuge. She could fire into the whole group if they happened to come out—sooner or later, they would emerge to buy cigarettes, liquor, provisions—but a thought shook her: what would she do if they stayed holed up there for a week or two without coming out?

Jana was thinking up suicidal plans for coping with that

possibility. Long after El Toro had disappeared from the sunny courtyard an unexpected event occurred.

A metallic gray Audi parked in the little lot bordering on the woods. A man soon got out of it, wearing a blue blazer of an old-fashioned cut, and walked slowly toward the entrance to the monastery. Jana observed the newcomer in the telescopic lens of her gunsight: a man in his seventies, average height, short brown hair on a half-bald head, rather common features, and two weasel's eyes that she had seen somewhere before. Where? The man was now standing in front of the heavy wooden door, hesitating to ring the bell. Jana finally remembered: the photo sent to Rubén's BlackBerry as they were returning from the Andes. The neighbor in Colonia who had fled. Díaz, the former SIDE agent.

*

Franco Díaz had worked on special operations in and outside the country before joining the intelligence service. Falsifying documents, organizing a giant meeting in order to photograph and identify left-wing militants a few weeks before the coup d'état, infiltrating terrorist groups, liquidating certain targets, planning kidnappings. The dirty war, as it was called. There was no war that wasn't dirty. Díaz obeyed orders. Those who gave them were severe but just. The "Rosario" operation, poorly prepared, had marked the beginning of the end: once the defeat in the Falklands was completed, the military had had to give up power and erase the proofs of what might come back to haunt them. General Bignone had trusted him, Díaz, the shadow agent.

The botanist had fled Colonia, but fate pursued him. A cause-effect relationship, a manifestation of the cancer that was eating away at him? A new bout of illness had befallen him, so violent that he had to hole up in a shabby hotel in La

Plata with his morphine pills. Three days spent in delirium, shot up with drugs, imagining that they were coming to dig up his treasure, or that a storm was devastating his Garden of Eden, that the cops and judges in black robes were condemning him on the spot for damaging the historical memory, daytime visions that sometimes made no sense and from which he emerged haggard, suffering atrocious pain, begging the Voice that guided him to grant him a little of its mercy—for just a little while still. After a bitter, relentless struggle, the Voice had risen up out of the void to extract him from the jaws of the disease. The power of faith in a single God who, better than morphine pills, had put him back on his feet. No, Franco would not die sick and alone in an anonymous hotel room, he wouldn't fail when he was so close to the goal. The cardinal had been his moral guarantee during the Dirty War: Díaz foresaw that the old sage would be able to counsel him one last time, and absolve him as he faced death. Only after that could he go in peace.

Leaving the hotel in La Plata where he had finally made it through the crisis, Díaz soon tracked down von Wernisch via a priest in the provincial diocese. He arrived in the remote village of Los Cipreses after two days of driving on dusty roads, his face sunken with fatigue. The Franciscan monastery to which the cardinal had retired was a vast building of gray stone with a moss-covered tile roof.

Franco parked the Audi and slowly climbed out. The illness was still there, watching for him to make a mistake.

The monastery's door was massive, the bell from an earlier time. The botanist had reached his final objective but now that he was there, something made him hesitate. Retaining his old reflexes, the former agent had not called to announce his arrival. He overcame his apprehensions and rang the bell.

A young monk soon opened the door, looking a little suspicious of the visitor. His austere face changed when Franco introduced himself as an old friend of Cardinal von Wernisch, whom he had come to see about an urgent matter. The monk immediately asked him to wait there, pushed open the ancient oak door that led to the courtyard, and disappeared on the other side of the building, leaving Díaz alone in the entry hall.

A painting was ostentatiously displayed in a gilded frame: a bishop from olden times who looked at him in a benevolent way. Franco took his pills in the shade of the cool vaults; he felt a piercing pain in his stomach. There was not a breath of air in the monastery's internal courtyard; only a few lizards were sunning themselves on the stones. Díaz was sweating under his blazer, his throat dried out by the medicine he was taking and the dust he had swallowed. A fat man then appeared about twenty yards away in the courtyard, a civilian with a puffy face who was coming out of the refectory, holding a plate piled high with food. An empty holster hung under his armpit, and his white shirt was ringed with sweat.

Díaz hid behind the door, his heart pounding. Alert. Red alert. It was not instinct that spoke to him, but the Voice. It warned him of a danger, an imminent danger. He remained crouched there in the shadows. The big man in the courtyard had not seen him; he was entirely focused on his food. Who was this guy, a cop? One of the men who'd been in Colonia? The botanist stepped back slightly. The Voice told him he mustn't stay there. That a plot was being formed against him, a deadly trap. The Voice told him to flee: *immediately.*

Díaz retraced his steps without waiting for the monk to return. The presence of this armed man was necessarily related to his secret. How could they know that he would come here? Von Wernisch was a friend, but they might be using him as bait. The sun dazzled him for a moment as he left the monastery; the car was parked on the waste ground. Franco hurried, seized by an irrational fear, beeped open the Audi's door, and climbed in. Get out of there, fast. He didn't see the silhouette emerge from the nearby bushes; as the car door opened an Indian woman with a furious look jumped into the passenger seat. Her nose was broken, she had mauve bags under her eyes, and she was wearing a poncho that covered a revolver. Díaz immediately tried to defend himself but the Indian stuck the barrel of her gun in his belly. The gun was cocked.

"Start the car or I'll kill you, you filthy son of a bitch . . . "

4

Elena Calderón was still living in the house in San Telmo, in the Avenida Independencia. She and her family had spent their happiest days there. She had kept her door open ever since Elsa and Daniel disappeared thirty-five years earlier, as if they might come back at any time. She would close it, not on the day when their bones were returned to her—this mourning was personal—but on the day when all those responsible were brought to trial and convicted: that was her way of *not mourning*.

The sun's first rays were touching the flowers in the garden. Susana knocked at the varnished wooden door and went in without waiting for a response.

"Duchess? It's me!" she shouted. "Come on, get up!"

The vice president of the Grandmothers headed for the kitchen—unlike her, Elena was a late riser, a habit she owed to her past as a middle-class night owl. Susana took the apricots out of their sack to avoid crushing them, saw the *maté* that was heating on the gas stove, and began to go through the cupboards in search of a suitable pastry dough. Her friend finally appeared at the door to the kitchen, made up and with her hair done, wearing a long embroidered silk dress.

"Hello, Duchess!"

"Hello, my dear . . . "

"Still in frills and furbelows?"

Elena was wearing an extraordinarily elegant dishabille, her shoulders covered with a white angora shawl. Her forehead wrinkled when she heard the cupboard doors slamming as Susana closed them as if there were an animal inside that was going to jump out at her. Elena saw the apricots that had fallen out of the sack, which Susana's tornado had scattered all over the kitchen table.

"How gently you treat things," the mistress of the house observed ironically.

"I can't find the pastry dough," Susana replied. "You must have some, don't you? I've looked everywhere! You'll have to help me, you know I'm a really bad cook, I burn everything!"

Elena Calderón, who never appeared in public without makeup (old age is a disaster, and makeup was her lifesaver), didn't like to speak about personal matters before she'd had her *maté*. She poured herself a cup while her friend bustled about.

"Well?" Susana said.

"Did you look in the fridge?"

"Twice!"

"Look again."

"Aah!" Susana cried, for appearance's sake.

Elena finished the bitter beverage while her friend rolled out the dough in a mold.

"Carlos will be here any minute and you aren't even dressed!" Susana pointed out. The vice president wore a white dress with a cherry motif, simple but very pretty.

"Just be quiet and start cutting up the apricots. I'll be ready in ten minutes."

That was how long it took to cook the fruit.

Elena reappeared punctually, dressed as if she were going to a marriage at the Casa Rosada.

"Is this all right, do I look presentable?"

Straight-line blue dress, white chiffon collar, a white angora shawl big enough to cover a litter of pumas, a touch of mascara on eyelids curved toward the sun like sunflowers: all she needed was a cigarette holder, Susana thought.

"Yes, yes," she assured her. "I'm more worried about the pie!"

Elena glanced at her reflection in the big mirror in the hall—the day before, at the hospital, she must have looked awful . . . The pie was still hot when the journalist honked his horn in front of the gate to the house—Rubén loved apricots.

*

The world was there, with its gasoline lungs, taking him back to the blackest hours of his life. The worst hours. The hours when he had wild thoughts, spurs digging into his sides, fire in his flesh. Rubén knew pain, he had lived with it during his months in detention: die or go mad, the pain that cracked open your body like an oyster, reducing you to a set of bare and unprotected atoms. Rubén had turned to ice. Cold. Nasty. Unbreakable.

He had fallen into a coma after the fusillade in the delta. In his delirium, he remembered his mother at his bedside, the wrinkles of her face and her soft hand caressing his, her eyes closed, as if to wipe out the evil that had inserted itself into his body, as she had done when he was a child to drive away his bad dreams. He'd had one chance in a hundred of surviving: Rubén had fought tooth and nail against his torturers until a second *banderilla* had pierced him. He'd been found attached to the table in the bedroom, bathed in his own blood. Beside him, Miguel was no longer breathing; Rubén was. Thrust into his back under the pressure of the police sirens, the second sharpened point had missed his heart. The emergency team had stopped the hemorrhaging without being able to the bring Rubén out of his coma, but with all the blood he'd lost and the weakness of his pulse when he was taken into the operating room, he could have died ten times over.

His body had stood up to the shock. He had awakened for brief moments, drunk on drugs, entangled in bandages on a hospital bed, the ceiling merging with the plastic tarps that delimited his realm. Chemically-induced hallucinations had cast him back into the pit, struggling amid crocodiles and snakes, two days outside time that left him groggy. Finally, Rubén found his footing in the world—the world and its black lungs.

Sutures, healing, painkillers, blood pressure: Pichot, the surgeon caring for him, had prescribed six days of complete rest before he could think about going home. Rubén remained cold. Anita had been killed by a bullet to the head, the body of his friend Oswaldo had just been found on the bank opposite the island in the delta, but not the body of the Mapuche, who had disappeared in the turmoil.

Rubén lay on the white bed in the hospital room, his eyes circled by dark nightmarish rings. Across from him, Ledesma's face was also grim. The police captain hated hospitals—they smelled like sickness, other people's deaths—and above all he hated the idea of being jeered at when he retired in a few months. The old cop hadn't been able to resist the desire to torpedo Roncero and Luque, Torres's flagship: with Eduardo Campallo's suicide and the men in the delta on the run, their whole house of cards was collapsing. But his investigator, Anita Barragan, had been killed in the operation, and the case had been assigned to the forensic police led by Luque, the very man he suspected of major corruption. A fiasco for which he might have to pay a heavy price.

A large man with a big, pockmarked nose despite his abstinence, Captain Ledesma wore a dark expression mixing anger and grief. He had hardly recognized Anita Barragan's face when her body was brought back to him. Her blond hair was sticky with blood, her head had exploded under the hydrostatic stock: a bullet fired at point-blank range. It looked like a summary execution.

"I don't know how far you're involved in this, Calderón," he concluded in the polluted air of the room, "but I want to tell you right away that the surveillance of Del Piro's cell phone will not appear anywhere in the report, and agent Barragan will be said to have acted on her own initiative, tracking down the Peru Street murderer. There won't be a word about Campallo and his daughter. Luque and Torres will have my hide if they find out that I was carrying on a covert investigation. Moreover, I suggest that you do the same. Captain Roncero will come to question you today, according to what I've been told. Limit yourself to the Michellini case: that's my advice."

"Muñoz falsified the autopsy report on María Campallo," Rubén retorted from his sickbed. "All you have to do is exhume the body."

"After her father's suicide?" Ledesma asked, astonished. "Don't even think about it."

"María was murdered, you know that as well as I do."

"You can explain that to Luque and Roncero, they will probably be curious to hear your version of the story. I'm finished with it."

There was a nauseating silence in the room. Rubén was dying of heat in his hospital gown, flying on an analgesic cloud that did nothing to calm his desire to kill.

"Are you going to let the death of a cop go unpunished?"

"I have no choice," Anita's boss insisted. "Luque has taken over the case, in person, and he's going to make short work of your statements."

The gunpowder and ballistics tests implicated the detective in the killing, and he would be forced to reveal the hidden side of his investigation to Roncero and to Luque and his elite police, who would then never let him go.

"Does Luque scare you that much?" Rubén grunted. "I thought you hated him."

"We often hate what scares us."

"Miguel Michellini's DNA corresponds to María Campallo's, not to their alleged mother's, and . . . "

"Forget Campallo," the policeman interjected. "Harassing a mourning family, and one that is moreover close to the mayor, would blow up in your face, Calderón, you can be sure of that. The report I delivered to Luque is limited to the Michellini case," he said firmly. "You've left a pile of dead bodies behind you, old pal. Whether it was in self-defense or not, you're in no position to attack, you're on the defensive!"

Imprisoned on his hospital bed, his left arm hooked up to tubes, Rubén was almost lost in his pillows. He closed his eyes, suddenly weary. The old cop was drawing back. He was letting go. But he was right on one point: the forensic police had taken over the case and Luque wouldn't do him any favors. Ledesma was shifting his weight from one foot to the other in front of Rubén's chart, simultaneously eager to leave and ill at ease with the idea of leaving the detective alone in his condition.

"Anyway, I'm pleas— . . . sorry about what happened," he said.

Rubén wasn't thinking about the steel point that had been run through him in the bedroom on the island, about his ears burned by the *picana*, or about the electrical furies that were gnawing at his brain, he was thinking about his friend Anita, about his childhood dreams that were dying here on this hospital bed. He thought about her blond smile when she gave him her drawing of a captain sailing over a gray sea speckled with blue . . . Ledesma wanted to say something else, but Rubén bared his teeth, livid.

"Get the hell out of here!"

*

Samuel and Gabriella Verón, the parents who had disappeared, were not Argentines, but Chileans: that was why they weren't entered into any database.

The Grandmothers had finally tracked them down in the archives of Nazareth House, a reception center within the church of Santa Cruz, through which many Chilean refugees passed after Pinochet's coup d'état. Father Mujica, who was close to the poor and the oppressed, had been murdered by the dictatorship's thugs, but the activists had questioned witnesses from the time. Samuel and Gabriella Verón had migrated to Buenos Aires in late 1973, shortly after Perón's death, unaware that the same military junta would take power there. They had gone into hiding after the Triple A roundups, and escaped the death squads until they were finally kidnapped one day in the winter of 1976 along with their baby, a little girl then sixteen months old.[17] Their disappearance had gone unnoticed because, like Father Mujica, their Argentine friends had all been swept up by the state machinery.

What about their family? The Grandmothers had traced them back to Chile, where other associations were fighting the dictatorship's crimes: Samuel Verón had been the student leader of a militant pro-Allende group; in 1971 he married Gabriella Hernandez, whom he'd met at the university in Santiago. After Allende's fall and the general repression that followed, they fled to Buenos Aires. Although Samuel Verón had left everything behind, Gabriella's parents were *estancieros*, the owners of hundreds of acres in the Mendoza region. Killed in a car accident not long after Videla's coup d'état, they had left their land to their sole heir, Gabriella. She hadn't had much time to enjoy it when she and her young husband were kidnapped.

Carlos, for his part, had investigated the public works proj-

[17] Triple A: Argentine Anticommunist Alliance, a right wing group.

ects set up by the junta in order to modernize the city center—to drive out the underprivileged population and construct new buildings for the benefit of private enterprises. De Hoz, the economics minister, had assigned Colonel Ardiles (who was made a general in 1982) to public works. This war on the poor was not new: the junta had reduced by half the salaries of the working classes, done away with free hospital care, and raised the price of cattle 700 percent in order to satisfy the interests of the powerful *Sociedad rural* (an association of large landowners), while whole neighborhoods were deprived of water and electricity. Then forgotten diseases such as summer diarrhea and rabies struck certain areas of Greater Buenos Aires, taking the country back fifty years into the past. Carlos had pursued his investigation: General Ardiles was not unknown, because he was one of the high-ranking officers targeted by the CONADEP at the end of the dictatorship. After spending five years under house arrest, Menem had finally been granted amnesty when the Full Stop law was passed. Human rights groups had repeated their attacks when Kirchner came to power, but the new legal procedures were exploited to create delays, and Ardiles benefited from statutes of limitation and certificates of ill health to escape any punishment. In addition to his army pension, the old general also received stock dividends and attendance fees from various businesses, and obviously did not regret his past. Questioned by a journalist after the dismissal of his case, Ardiles had declared that a war necessarily implied deaths, that it was a matter of "us" or "them"—meaning the Reds.

Susana would have swallowed her false teeth.

Leandro Ardiles now enjoyed activities proper to his age (eighty-four) in the gated community of Santa Barbara that had been built by Vivalia, Campallo's concrete company. Summoned several times to appear as a witness, notably in 2010 for the ESMA trial, Ardiles had never showed up, prevented by medical certificates signed by Professor Fillol, the owner of a private clinic in the same community of Santa Barbara: Fillol, who was one of the victims of the shootout in the delta.

Carlos finished his report with a broad smile that hardly concealed his stubbornness.

"Ardiles," he concluded. "I'm sure he's the colonel who organized the extraction of the Verón couple and the falsification of the birth certificates."

The Grandmothers nodded in silence. A fragrance of apricots was struggling with the sanitized air in the hospital room; Rubén was registering the news, his face pale despite the sunlight coming through the window. Ardiles, an old general: he might be the one responsible for the kidnappings and murders, his name might be one of those eaten away on the internment form. That didn't explain Eduardo Campallo's suicide. Why had Ardiles set up a secret meeting in the Andes, and who was "the man of the *estancia*"? Rubén gritted his teeth as he sat up on the bed.

"What happened to Gabriella Verón's land?"

"That's what we're looking into," the journalist replied. "I've filed requests with the clerk of the commercial court in Mendoza, but that will take time."

"Ardiles can take advantage of that to make himself scarce,"

"If he hasn't already done so," the vice president agreed.

"Don't worry about that, Rubén," his mother told him. "We're not going to let him get away. You can count on us."

"Yes," Susana said. "Rest now."

"Impossible," Rubén replied. "No, impossible."

His voice was hoarse, almost malicious.

"What do you mean?"

"Luque and his gang are going to grill me," he said, his eyes clouded. "If I end up in their hands, I'll never get away."

Rubén was swimming in chemical vapors. He tore off the bandage over his IV, and then pulled the needle out of his vein.

"What are you doing?" Elena asked.

"I've got to find those guys."

"What? But . . . "

Rubén threw off the tubes that tied him to the bed as his mother looked on imploringly. She knew him only too well.

"This is crazy," she said soberly.

"I agree," Susana added. "You'll never make it past the end of the corridor with your blood pressure the way it is."

"I'm feeling better," Rubén lied.

He could see clearly, that was about all. Carlos glanced at his friend's haggard face and understood that it was pointless to insist. He'd had the same look on his face when they told him about the disappearance of Jana, the witness whose body was still being sought. Rubén took the clothes his mother had put in the metallic cabinet.

"You can't leave in that condition," Elena whispered. "You're going to kill yourself."

His eyes were glowing with rage.

"I'm already dead."

*

Jana.

Rubén thought about her constantly.

With the eyes of love, he saw again the room in the delta, her frightened face when they had separated. Three days had passed since the shootout, and she had disappeared. She too had become a ghost. Rubén opened the door of his office in a state of confusion close to dizziness.

Carlos had dropped him off at Peru Street after he had picked up a set of keys at his mother's house. They had left the hospital without anyone noticing, but the news would soon circulate among the staff and get back to Luque.

Rubén walked around the apartment a bit, feeling alien to

himself: the faces on the walls, the couch where she had slept the first night—without her everything seemed lifeless. Useless. Sordid. He leaned on the bar, feeling as if he might faint. The effects of the IV were fading, and the pain in his lungs was increasing, dull, piercing. He took two painkillers from the hospital and put his head under cold water in the sink. A long time. His legs felt cottony but he mustn't stay here—it was the first place Luque's cowboys would look for him. He raised his head, walked into the bedroom at the end of the hall—a few things, weapons, he would take the minimum with him.

Rubén groaned as he slipped aside the chest of drawers on the rug. He lifted the floorboards and remained stunned for a moment: the cache of weapons had been emptied. The grenade, the tear-gas bombs, the handcuffs, the revolver, the ammo, even the sniper rifle and the cash had disappeared. There remained only a set of brass knuckles and the Glock 19, along with its silencer and three cartridge clips.

Rubén's heart was beating faster: Jana. She alone knew where he hid his arsenal. The keys to the office were in her bag, on Oswaldo's boat: they hadn't killed her. She'd escaped. She'd returned to Buenos Aires. Tears of joy welled up, but the mad hope that gripped him quickly dissipated: why hadn't she called the Grandmothers, or tried to find out what had happened to him? Instead of contacting his mother, she had preferred to make off with the weapons in the cache: why, unless it was to make use of them herself? Rubén shuddered beneath his icy armor.

Jana was his sister, his little sister in rage . . . And that was precisely what scared him.

5

Concentrated in the Panama Canal Zone, the United States's military schools had instructed thousands of soldiers who were to train the security forces of future dictatorships: social control over the population, interrogation methods, tortures. By a domino effect, one country after another fell under the yoke of military regimes: Paraguay (1954), Brazil (1964), Bolivia (1971), Chile and Uruguay (1973), and finally Argentina, in 1976. Contrary to his predecessor Jimmy Carter, the Republican president Ronald Reagan did not disapprove of the policy conducted by the Argentine junta: the former actor invited General Viola to Washington; Viola had replaced Videla at the head of the dictatorship, lifted the embargo that blocked loans to financiers and military men, and ceased to support the Mothers of the Plaza de Mayo, who opposed the establishment of "anticommunist" military training bases in their country.

Colonel Ardiles had been promoted to the rank of general by this same Viola, before the disastrous episode in the Falklands. Subsequently, Leandro Ardiles's political and financial supporters had allowed him to slip through the cracks, but the Campallo case put everything in question again—his comfortable retirement in the gated community of Santa Barbara, his independence, and even his freedom. The situation was getting out of control. They had had to flee, his wounded arm still hurt him, and the statue of the commander was beginning to crack under the soldier's veneer.

Leandro Ardiles hated having his fate in the hands of someone else—in this case, those of Parise, the head of Santa Barbara's security police. Even if his name and that of the cardinal seemed not to be on the copy of the internment form the Grandmothers had gotten their hands on, the general's usually temperate character had changed since he knew that he was being tracked. Too many bodies in their wake, not to mention that damned form. Had the original burned in the fire at Ossario's house? He couldn't be sure. Cardinal von Wernisch had guaranteed the monks' silence; the hiding place was secure but, as Ardiles knew, temporary. A military chaplain who urged the armed forces to "bathe in the blood of Jordan" at the height of the repression, then promoted to bishop in 1979, then to cardinal at the turn of the century, von Wernisch thought he would live out his life amid masses celebrated in Latin and papal siestas, when he received a call from Brother Josef, one of his former disciples. The cardinal had immediately sounded the alarm, setting in motion a lethal mechanism.

The two old men were talking in the shaded garden when the young monk who served von Wernisch as a secretary presented himself at the lunch table.

"It's him again, Your Eminence," he said, bending down toward the cardinal's emaciated head. "Franco Díaz, on the telephone. He says it's urgent."

Ardiles met the shining eyes of von Wernisch, then those of Parise at the end of the table. Díaz had come to the monastery the day before and then suddenly vanished. A strange business. Von Wernisch had known Díaz in the past, a pious and patriotic man, a SIDE agent: his appearance here was in no way accidental.

"I'll go with you," the general said, getting up.

"Me too," Parise said.

Díaz's voice was tense and the speaker in the vestibule was of poor quality. He was calling from a cell phone and claimed to have the "original document." Díaz did not explain why he had run away the preceding day; in a few brief words he stated that he wished to deliver the document "immediately" and "to the cardinal in person." The cardinal, urged on by Ardiles, proposed that his interlocutor come to the monastery, but Díaz, who was ill, seemed to be at bay. He suggested a meeting at the Escondida lagoon late that same day, as if the document he spoke of were burning his hands. Taken by surprise, and after a brief consultation with his associates, von Wernisch gave Díaz Parise's secure number to keep in contact, accepting de facto the proposed rendezvous.

"What do you think of that?" the general asked when he had hung up.

"Díaz is a patriot," the cardinal replied. "We can trust him."

His long, bony face bore the weight of years, but his blue eyes retained the lively fire of a theologian eager for a fight: if the former SIDE agent was telling the truth, they had a chance to erase their debts.

The sun was shining on the crests of the mountain range. Sitting at a respectable distance from the barbecue that was smoking up the end of the garden, Gianni Del Piro was moping, blind to the beauty of the Andes. Although the pilot had sweet talked his wife when he returned to this godforsaken hole, he could say goodbye to the hotheaded Linda, who by now must have left Punta del Este, slamming doors and cursing. All this would be paid for in cash—a bonus for the flight, for sure—but losing a mistress who gave him blow jobs *on the rocks* was an incalculable loss. In the meantime, forced to go into exile in this monastery with the general and his bodyguards, the pilot was stuck with these two louts.

El Toro, "on vacation," had put on his favorite outfit, a pair of overalls. Planted with his legs spread in front of the barbecue, he spoke to his acolyte.

"You should taste this!"

"Wait at least until it's cooked!" El Picador retorted.

"Bah!"

El Toro noisily slurped down two big mussels one after the other, spilling sauce all over his undershirt. Since he'd been drinking red wine for some time now, that didn't make much difference. In charge of the cooking, El Picador was impassively watching his friend guzzle. Thirty-five years of experience. El Toro was hungry, you just had to accept him being that way. Virile, even obsessive, with his Sodom and Gomorrah frenzies. That wasn't El Picador's thing. His vice was more scientific, more elegant. After years of experience, he could almost feel the pain in other people's bodies, evaluate it expertly. He sharpened his weapons himself. Calderón had felt pain as soon as he had inserted the first *banderilla*. El Picador had set Calderón in stone, a pain like burning lava slowly spread, a pain that was, so to speak, eternal, and that the addition of the *picana* made absolutely unbearable. Nonetheless, that pile of shit hadn't said anything.

"Wait, goddammit!" he yelled at El Toro. "You can see perfectly well that they're not cooked!"

His starving buddy filched another mussel that was sizzling on the grill, swallowed it in one long, satisfied suck, and wiped his hands on his rather filthy undershirt.

"Mussels are eaten raw!" he decreed.

His crude laugh didn't amuse anyone but himself. The fat man poured a little sauce on the shellfish, making the embers crackle. They'd been doing nothing in this monastery of country bumpkins for three days. It was a haven of peace that the two friends didn't expect to get to—they had almost been caught by the cops in the delta.

"Hey, pour me some wine," El Toro said again.

He handed a glass to the emaciated specter and toasted him for the fifth time. The mussels were almost cooked, and they would soon move on to the meat.

"Finally!" he shouted, sauce glistening on his shaggy chest; the black, thick hair was sticking out of his undershirt.

There was a movement in the monastery's covered courtyard that they didn't notice, absorbed in their meal. Parise crossed the garden, his skull a sickly white under the sun, and stood in front of the embers of the barbecue.

"We're going to take a little ride," he told his men. "From now on, there will be no drinking, understand? And go change your clothes!" he added, looking at El Toro, whose face was shiny with grease. "The general and the cardinal are coming with us. Get going!"

*

They left the Los Cipreses monastery in the middle of the afternoon, jammed into the Land Cruiser with tinted windows. The two henchmen sat in front with Del Piro, Ardiles, and von Wernisch behind them, with the bald giant in the back, where he could stretch his legs. A marked route, handguns; they drove on paved portions flanked with potholes, passing only a few flea-bitten Indians on horseback and a couple of forest industry trucks.

Leandro Ardiles had regained hope after Díaz's telephone call. The former SIDE agent had the original ESMA form; once it was in his hands, it would constitute the best possible protection in the event that somebody decided to sacrifice him. Too many people were involved in this affair. They'd work in the background to find him a pleasant retirement in a country that had no extradition treaty. It was still about an hour to the Escondida lagoon, at the heart of the national park near the Chilean border. An old-man smell spread inside the car; El Toro held his nose and winked at his buddy, gesturing toward the cardinal. Von Wernisch was gripping the door handle, observing the road with glassy eyes. They passed Puerto

Bustillo and its stony *miradors*, and a few poor farms, the last bastions of humanity before the forest. The Escondida lagoon was about a dozen miles away.

Parise was grumbling in the back of the Land Cruiser; he was six foot seven and felt cramped as he scrutinized the map of the ecological preserve. The sun was going down over the pine-covered ridge; the last houses had given way to a dense stand of trees that covered the foothills of the Andes, whose peaks pierced the sky. The road was longer than expected.

"At this rate, we won't get back before nightfall," El Picador remarked.

"Shit, we're going to miss the match!"

"What match?"

"River-Boca!" El Toro snorted.

They had been driving for some time on a dirt track. The Land Rover was accelerating on a hill when Parise cursed in the back: he'd lost reception. All they needed was for Díaz to call just then. The 4x4 was throwing up brown dust in the meanders of the national park. They drove past a limpid lake that could be seen below them. The lagoon. Díaz had to be waiting for them somewhere near the body of water, sick, it seemed. Poor fellow. The 4x4 reached the top of the hill and started down the long slope that crossed the forest. They were gaining speed when suddenly the tires exploded.

El Toro slammed on the brakes with all his weight, skidded sideways, and lost control of the vehicle. Propelled toward the trees, the Land Rover bounced off a trunk and buried itself in the neighboring pine tree, smashing the windshield in the process. In the back, Parise, who was not wearing a seatbelt, went flying, and the others hung onto whatever they could find. Finally, after a last jolt, the car stopped in the ditch.

There were a few seconds of bewilderment, and then the cardinal began to groan, holding his sides. Next to him, Ardiles was grimacing, his arm in a sling.

"What happened?"

El Toro switched off the ignition while his buddy took out his gun.

"Get out of the vehicle!" Parise ordered. "Quick!"

El Picador's face was flecked with glass shards from the windshield. El Toro struggled to open the doors stove in by the accident and was the first to get out. The engine was smoking under the buckled hood; he helped the cardinal extricate himself from the car, still shaky, then freed Ardiles and the head of security. All four tires were flat, the 4x4 tilted into the ditch. Somebody must have spread tacks on the road.

"Díaz set a trap for us," Parise groaned.

He took out his Glock and was warily taking a step toward the road when there was a detonation on his left. Del Piro was thrown against the door of the Land Rover, a large-caliber bullet having hit him in the middle of his chest. He collapsed with a death rattle before the stupefied eyes of the old cardinal.

"Take cover! Take cover!" Parise yelled.

The bullets were ricocheting beneath his feet, and they could be heard hitting the nearby tree trunks: his men pushed von Wernisch and Ardiles toward the pines, abandoning the bloody corpse of the pilot in the middle of the road. The firing was coming from the thickets below them. Parise stumbled on a root and let out a cry, his ankle struck by a bullet. He gritted his teeth to keep from howling, saw the blood and the bits of bone under his sock, and understood that the wound was serious.

"*Vamos, vamos!*" he growled to make them get going.

The giant swore as he hobbled toward the others, who had stopped a little higher up in the woods. They were being targeted from the bushes on the other side of the road. El Toro and El Picador emptied their clips into the bushes.

"Get back up! Get back up under cover, for Christ's sake!"

The two men didn't see that their boss was wounded; they helped the old men climb up the steep terrain, taking them by the arm. Parise covered their retreat, his back against a tree trunk, sweating with pain.

"Goddamned fucking Díaz," he cursed.

A bullet whistled over his head, and another hit the neighboring tree. Precise firing from the bushes down below. Unfavorable terrain. Paris limped after the group that was making its way up the slope, his ankle on fire. Although Ardiles insisted on walking alone, El Picador was supporting the cardinal, who was still complaining about his ribs. A bullet ricocheted under the nose of Ardiles, whose arm was in a sling, and he paled with rage in his Ralph Lauren polo shirt. El Toro pulled him under the branches; bullets were hitting behind them. Short of breath, they cut toward the east, where the terrain was less difficult. The smell of pines had disappeared, or fear had changed their senses. Parise was clumping along, struggling.

"*Vamos, vamos!*"

He fired a few shots haphazardly to cover them. The men advanced, keeping their heads down in the shade of the branches, tripping over roots and clumps of ferns. Von Wernisch was moaning with the effort, he almost had to be carried. Finally the shots behind them became more sporadic, then stopped . . . They went on another hundred yards, and soon heard nothing but their lungs on fire.

"Halt!" shouted Parise, who was bringing up the rear.

It was dark under the big trees. The road below could no longer be seen, only a wall of intertwined vegetation that seemed to grow thicker as the sun went down. Parise was sweating heavily.

"You, help the cardinal lie down somewhere more or less comfortable. El Toro, secure the terrain, we have to stop for a couple of minutes."

"O.K.!"

Ardiles had aged ten years; von Wernisch seemed overwhelmed by what had happened. Exhausted by his trek, Parise sat down to examine his ankle: the bullet had broken the malleolus into several pieces. The stress over, the pain shot up all the way to the knee.

"Did you get hit, boss?" whispered El Picador, seeing the extent of the damage.

"Yeah," Parise said, his head dripping sweat.

His cell phone was still not receiving, and night was falling under the araucarias. No one would come to help them, the place was isolated, and the two old men limited their movements. Parise ruminated: with his ankle in pieces, he wasn't much of an asset. They could leave the old men to their fate—but that would signal to his henchmen that they could do the same thing to him in the event of danger. He had to get back to the road, find a place where the cell phone would have reception.

"Help me get up, I beg you," whispered von Wernisch, whom El Picador had helped lie down. "These infernal roots are breaking my bones!"

Ardiles was mopping his brow, leaning up against a tree.

"So, Parise," he said impatiently, "what is all this crap? Where is Díaz?"

"I don't know, general."

"And you, cardinal? I thought Díaz was supposed to be a patriot!"

"I . . . I don't understand."

Parise tried to get his bearings, assessed the situation. The hidden shooter had at least two weapons, a revolver and a rifle—the more dangerous of the two. He could send his two men to find the shooter, but those two dolts might get themselves shot before they had located the target. El Picador helped the miserable cardinal to his feet; the churchman clung to him as if he were a winning lottery ticket.

"My ribs hurt too much to walk," he yelped, skeletal under his cassock.

"Who's shooting at us?" Ardiles asked again. "Díaz?"

"In any case, it's not the cops."

"Your job was to protect me!"

"My job is to get you out of here," Parise growled, the pain making him ill-tempered. "O.K.?"

The old man shut up.

It grew damper as night fell. El Toro soon returned from his inspection, out of breath.

"I didn't see any movement," he said. His suit was covered with dirt. "I don't understand what the plan is, boss!"

"I don't either," his pal added.

The giant got up, his jaws tight to hold in check the pain in his ankle.

"We have to get back to the road," he said. "The shooter is moving; we'll go around him."

"The Land Cruiser is out of commission, boss."

"Not to mention that I left the keys in it," El Picador added.

"And your credit card number, did you think of that?"

El Toro laughed at his joke, then changed his mind when he saw his companions' gloomy faces. The sun had gone down on the other side of the hills, and night was now falling in waves. Parise asked the question he was fearing.

"Where do you think the road is?"

"That way."

"There."

"There."

"I'd say there . . . "

They'd pointed in three different directions. Only Ardiles shared his opinion: five o'clock.

Parise ordered El Toro to carry von Wernisch as far as he could. The compass had been left in the glove compartment of the Land Rover, they had no flashlight, they could hardly see, and they had only a lighter that burned El Toro's fingers. Somehow, the little group got into marching order. The insects were coming out as it grew dark. They struggled five hundred yards uphill and then turned toward the right, down the slope of the hill. Parise was hoping to find the road sooner or later, but after a time that seemed to him too long, the slope stopped descending. Worse, it began to rise again.

"What the fuck is going on?" El Toro grumbled. He was sick of carrying the old man. "I thought we were going to find the road!"

Parise was limping along at the rear of the group; they could hardly see each other in the darkness. The trees were tall and dense, almost covering the sky and the stars, if there were any. They fell silent, waiting. An opaque silence enveloped the forest. It would soon be completely dark.

General Ardiles was the first to understand. They were lost.

6

A smell of humus permeated the earth. They had felt their way several hundred yards over uneven ground before giving up the hope of finding the road. The vegetation was too thick, and forced them to make detours; they no longer knew where they were, whether north was in front of them or behind them. No one knew anything about the stars, and besides, they couldn't see them, and they were in danger of becoming even more lost if they continued to walk on blindly. Hector Parise was hobbling along, bent over and pale as a sheet in the shadows. Von Wernisch, bent over El Toro's shoulder, was complaining about his hip and his ribs, which had probably been fractured in the accident; Ardiles was also showing signs of weakness, as if the prospect of danger had reawakened the pain in his wounded arm.

They stopped among the tree trunks and ferns. It was totally black.

"We're going to wait until it gets light," Parise decided. "There's no point in going on."

In fact, they could hardly see their hands before their faces. The others acquiesced, exhausted, but worried about spending a night in the middle of the forest. El Toro's lighter ran out of fuel just as the group was settling down between the roots of a centuries-old tree whose top seemed to belong to another world. They had asked each other the same questions over and over without finding an answer, and were demoralized, while von Wernisch moaned and called on all his saints, his old bones killing him. They felt a need to come together, an ancient gregarious instinct.

After the damp, the cold gripped them. They were not equipped for it. And all the strange noises around them that made them jump. They stopped talking. Ardiles was squinting into the dark, a wild animal without prey, walled up in a furious foreboding silence. At first, El Toro had boasted loudly that he was going to "kill that fag Díaz," but he too had lowered his voice. He was dying of thirst after their forced march, and the forest was beginning to scare him. You couldn't see anything, the moon had never come out again, and the stars had disappeared.

Time went on and on, interminably. No one spoke anymore. The dark took them all in its coils, oppressive, an almost physical mass that seemed to crush them more every minute. A feeling that El Toro didn't know inexorably invaded him: claustrophobia. A foretaste of panic, which had to be kept at a distance. He could no longer distinguish the others at the foot of the tree where they had made their improvised camp. There remained only the odor of the shriveled-up old men, stinking of fear and death.

"Maybe we should make a fire," El Picador murmured alongside him. "I've got some matches."

"To make it easier to locate us! That's a great idea!"

"We can't see a damned thing in this fucking forest, boss!"

"Another reason to stay hidden until dawn," Parise growled.

The pain was making him nasty. The silence surrounding the forest became even more suffocating, punctuated by the creaking of the branches overhead. Branches or something else. As if they were being watched.

"What if there are animals?" El Toro asked with concern.

"What are you afraid of, jaguars?" his buddy teased him.

"Are there any?"

"In your ass!" the other mocked him.

"Shut up and open your eyes," the bald man grumbled in a hostile tone. "We're going on guard duty while the others rest."

But in the darkness, with this mass around them, minutes had become hours. Time went on. The old men no longer complained, shivering with cold. The wind was shaking the tops of the trees, but it was barely audible, as if the forest stifled everything. It was only eleven o'clock by El Toro's digital watch, a knockoff with a leather band that irritated his fat-ringed wrist. He cursed the dark and the hunger that were tormenting him, slumped in a bed of scratchy ferns, thought about that night's soccer match to drive away his bad thoughts. A snapping sound quite close to them made him jump. It wasn't a bird. Too heavy.

He shook his companion.

"You hear that?"

"Huh?"

"That noise," he whispered.

"Nah . . . a squirrel, shit . . . "

El Picador didn't like to be scared—not like that. Once someone had told him a story about guys whose car had broken down at night. One of them had set out for the closest village to get gas, and had never come back. His friends, who had stayed in the car, had been awakened by a dull, repetitive knocking against the door: the head of their companion, who had gone to get gas.

"And that?" El Toro jumped.

"What's going on?" Parise whispered on their right.

The fat man could have sworn he saw a form move through the trees. Very nearby.

"I saw something go by," he whispered.

"What?"

"I don't know, damn it!"

El Picador peered into the darkness, his hand gripping his

automatic pistol and his senses on full alert. They heard a series of slight cracks behind them, like furtive footsteps, at eight o'clock. They turned around, aimed their guns into the dark, and waited, their hearts pounding . . . Not a single sound more.

Parise had stood up without putting weight on his wounded ankle, his eyes dilated.

"There's someone there," El Toro whispered. "I saw a figure . . . "

"It's pitch-black, stupid!"

"Exactly!"

The old men stood up in turn, waiting to see what would happen.

"What's going on?" the old general asked.

Then El Picador saw it on his right, for a fraction of a second: a shadow striped with white slipping at high speed among the trees. Vertical stripes. A fucking ghost. He fired three shots one after the other into the bark of a nearby tree.

"There's something there," he shouted. "There!"

"Where?" the bald man growled.

All he could smell was gunpowder and the fear of the others clinging to each other.

"At ten o'clock!"

They had lost their bearings, and the shadowy figure had disappeared.

"What?" Parise said angrily. "What did you see?"

"An animal," El Picador retorted. "An animal with white stripes . . . they were phosphorescent!"

"Yeah!" El Toro confirmed.

They couldn't see anything but the trembling darkness.

"You're crazy!" Ardiles grumbled. "You've become completely sick!"

Time remained in suspense: then he also saw it, on his right, a ghost or animal whose shadow was turning around them at high speed.

"There! It's there! On the right!"

The shots crackled in the saturated air of the forest, unveiling for a brief instant their dumbfounded faces, but if there was a figure, it had disappeared.

"It's the devil," von Wernisch burst out. "It's the devil who has led us here!"

The general felt around blindly, caught hold of Parise's jacket, and did not let go.

"Give me a gun!" he ordered. "Give me a gun!"

The giant wrenched himself free. They had only three pistols and the clips were still under the Land Cruiser's seat. Then the head of security thought he sensed someone behind him. He hesitated to fire for fear of wounding one of his own people, but it was certain: something was roaming around them. *Something* that didn't seem human.

"What is it?" El Toro roared.

"We mustn't stay here!" the cardinal repeated. "There are evil spirits in these woods, I feel them. I feel their presence around me. They're on the prowl. Don't you feel them?"

The devil was moving through the forest, all around them. A terrible threat that would soon strike. Even General Ardiles was trembling alongside him. The old fear of the dark had taken him by the throat. There was a breath of panic when the phantom's head appeared behind a tree trunk: a white stripe, hardly perceptible in the obscurity, ten feet away from him.

"Give me that!" Ardiles hissed, grabbing for Parise's pistol, but the bald man brutally shoved him away: the two old men were losing it. Thrown to the ground, Ardiles howled with pain when he fell on his wounded arm. A bullet grazed Parise's skull and ricocheted off the araucaria's trunk. A bullet fired by a revolver at very close range. No, they weren't ghosts or phantoms, but instead several hunters lying in ambush. Parise crouched down and opened fire, at the risk of making himself a target.

"Get out of here!" he shouted, aiming his automatic weapon. "Goddammit, get out of here!"

He pulled the trigger. The clicking of the firing pin stunned him. He tried again, in vain: the Glock was empty.

"*Mierda!*"

A bullet split the shadows on their right. El Picador started to squeal, waving his arms around him.

"Damn, I've been hit! Aah! Goddamned fucking piece of shit!"

"Where is it?" El Toro yelped in panic. "Where is it, goddammit! I can't see anything!"

"*La concha de tu abuela!*"[18] El Picador swore. "My fucking leg is broken, I'm sure of it!"

The bullet had broken his tibia. He was leaning against the trunk without knowing how he could stand up. Parise cursed in the dark: they were going to be shot down like rabbits if they stayed there. He no longer had a weapon and the killer was observing them at this very moment.

"Every man for himself!" he growled, helping the general to his feet.

The boss took off. Panicked, El Toro and El Picador fired three times to cover their escape, abandoning von Wernisch to his fate. Supporting his wounded friend, El Toro made his way between the brambles. Parise had gone in the opposite direction with Ardiles, leaving the cardinal under the tree—they were out to save their skins. The giant banged his head on branches, recovered, gritting his teeth to keep from howling.

"Wait for me!" the general cried. "Parise! For the love of God, wait for me!"

"Hurry up, shit!"

The forest was haunted, you couldn't see anything. El Toro and El Picador groped their way, thinking only of getting out

[18] "Your grandmother's pussy."

of the trap. They heard the cardinal's calls for help behind them, frightening cries that froze their bones. They continued on through the thickets, needles in their blood.

"It hurts!" El Picador swore a few yards away. "It hurts, damn it!"

"Shut up for fuck's sake; they'll hear us and know where we are!"

Somehow they moved on, groping, wandering through this tangle of vines and brambles that led nowhere. El Toro went first, his hands bloody from pushing through the thorns; he tried to step over the roots, the bushes, and bounced around like a mad pinball. His mind occupied with fleeing the hell into which he had been led, he walked headfirst into a tree trunk.

"Fuck!" he swore in a low voice.

Furious, he swept away with his hand the bits of bark encrusted on his forehead and caught his breath, peering into the dark all the while. He didn't know how many bullets he had left in his pistol; his pockets were empty, and fear was dripping down his face. Then he realized that he was alone.

"Picador!" he shouted. "Where are you?"

No answer. He swallowed, out of breath: he'd lost his buddy. He'd been right behind him just a moment ago—at least he thought he was. A whiff of fear gripped his heart. Should he go back? To do what? To be skinned alive by those damned striped phantoms?

"Where are you, for God's sake? Pic! Hey! Pic!"

The darkness muffled his calls. Still no response. Only a resounding emptiness. All he could hear was the rustling of the wind in the treetops and the creaking of the branches below, the forest sounds that made his skin crawl. El Toro thought he sensed something on his left, and fired two bullets into the forest. Sweat was running into his blind man's eyes; he opened them wider, in vain. His intestines were in turmoil.

"Hey! Where are you?"

El Toro drew back, aiming his gun at an invisible target, stumbled on roots, and caught himself by grabbing the vines. "*Hijo de puta, hijo de puta,*" he cursed, his pulse racing, gripped by an unfamiliar fear. The shots could come from any place, hit him any time, the forest was a fucking giant hood around his head. Then he heard footsteps in the leaves, footsteps that were coming closer. He fired his last two bullets, which disappeared into the night.

"*Hijo de puta! Hijo de puta!*"

He pulled the trigger several more times before hearing the firing pin clicking at the end of his arm. His eyes went wide; frightened, he tried to move backward: he was being watched. Somewhere. Between the branches. There was something there, he could feel it, there, in the heart of darkness. Suddenly his hair stood on end: the shadow was rushing toward him like a tiger. Too late to retreat. He screamed, ready to strike with the butt of his pistol. A red point appeared on his chest: El Toro was about to strike the unearthly beast when an electric charge atomized his nervous system.

He staggered in the damp air of the forest, and collapsed heavily onto the roots, his muscles paralyzed. A few seconds passed, outside time.

"*La concha . . .* "

The beam of a flashlight dazzled his bovine eyes. El Toro made a desperate effort to get up, but in vain: the rifle butt fractured his jaw.

*

It had rained during the night, transforming the clearing into a mire. The first thing El Toro saw when he opened his eyes was a woman's vagina that was pissing on him. A stream of lukewarm urine was dripping from a tuft of black hair, the kind of pussy he liked best, crouched a few inches from his face.

El Toro tried to move but his limbs were bound and his head riddled with countless wood splinters. Images came back to him, in disorder: the mad flight through the forest, the panic that had made each of them take off in a different direction, the total darkness, the disappearance of El Picador—he'd been right behind him!— the beast that had attacked him . . . He turned his head aside: the piss was running over his split lips, and the open wounds were burning.

"That's to keep you from getting septicemia," Jana said as she finished emptying her bladder.

The blow with the rifle butt had demolished his mouth and part of his upper jaw. El Toro spit out the two incisors that had ended up at the back of his mouth, and almost suffocated as he rolled on the mud. He blinked his eyes. The Indian was buttoning up her jumpsuit—she looked pretty scary with her broken nose and her eyes still ringed in black. He started back: it was the girl from the delta, what the fuck was she doing there?

"Don't worry, I'll be back," she said, disappearing among the branches.

Her daubed face and her sepulchral voice made him shiver. El Toro sniffed down clots of blood, lying on the ground, still unable to stand up. As for speaking, the slightest movement of his jaw brought tears to his eyes. He was completely naked, thrown like a sack of dirty laundry in the middle of a clearing, his mouth in shreds. Above him, immense trees swayed in the wind; their tops could be seen in the early morning light.

How long had he been there? His hands were tied behind his back, and his feet had also been hobbled with handcuffs that cut cruelly into his skin. The fat man twisted around and saw El Picador lying a few steps away, also naked, next to an old man whose bones stuck out of his emaciated body—the cardinal and his sad face. Bound hand and foot, the prisoners could hardly raise their heads. Von Wernisch seemed to be praying, his eyes half-closed, curled up as if to hide his withered penis. El Picador was in a similar position, dazed and livid. His leg was broken, an open fracture exposing the tibia which, to judge by the dull glow in his eyes, seemed to be causing him to suffer atrociously.

A flea-ridden dog was observing them from the thickets, impassive, his paws crossed under his gray muzzle. El Toro's head was spinning terribly; he made a painful effort to sit up, grumbling into his blood-soaked beard. The little whore had broken his jaw. It took him several seconds to fully recover his wits. A damp cold was seeping into his bones. He still had some reserves. Where were the others? Parise, General Ardiles? The clank of a chain on his right made him jump: a man with a bald head was crouching at the edge of the clearing, a guy in his seventies chained to a tree by his neck, like a dog. Was it Díaz? El Toro met his crazy eyes, and the inexplicable fear he'd felt in the forest gripped the pit of his stomach. Another sound caught his attention. He turned toward the araucaria: the Indian woman was digging a hole, a little farther on, under the branches.

A grave.

Jana was toiling away, completely absorbed by her work, in order not to think.

Among the Mapuches, there are no prison sentences, only reparations.

7

The old docks in the port of Buenos Aires had been replaced by the Waterfront, an ultramodern complex designed by famous foreign architects. Relatively small boats still tied up alongside the brick warehouses, but the other buildings had been bought and converted into luxury lofts, with Jacuzzis and views of the artificial port.

Rubén knew that he couldn't get far in his condition: coughing made him weep, his pain surged up in furious spikes, and his brain transmitted only sordid images. Joggers with streamlined glasses were trotting down the promenade. He followed the sycamore-lined lane that led to the Costanera Sur dike, walking slowly, his mind sluggish under the effect of the painkillers. It was 2 P.M., a few English tourists in their checkered shorts were sitting idly on the terraces of the restaurants, mellowed by the local Malbec wine. He stopped near the frigate Sarmiento, the old training ship that had been made into a museum: Isabel Campallo was drinking a Perrier on the terrace of the bar where they were to meet.

Rubén had called her at home before leaving his office, and he had left her the choice. Either she agreed to see him in a public place, alone, or he would tell Rodolfo what he knew regarding the theft of children, with DNA tests to back up what he said. Looking distractedly at the tarped sailboats bobbing in the port, and incognito behind her large sunglasses, the widow was brooding on her misfortunes in the fog produced by the antianxiety medicine she was taking. Not until the detective sat down at her table did she notice his presence. Her bun carelessly made, looking a hundred years old in a black dress, her right arm in a sling, the sign of a recent fall.

"My daughter and my husband are dead, Calderón," she said as a greeting. "What more do you want? Don't you think I've suffered enough?"

Women pushing strollers were gossiping as they walked past the terrace. Rubén ordered an espresso from the waitress, lit a cigarette while she moved away, and then turned to the *apropriadora*.

"First, thanks for agreeing to this meeting," he said, changing the subject. "As I explained, everything you say to me will remain between us. I will not speak about it at the trial, to the cops, or to anyone. I am going to tell you what I know and I ask you to do the same."

María's mother did not flinch; she was on the defensive. Ever since Calderón's first appearance at their house things had gone from bad to worse: she had lost her daughter under tragic circumstances, then her husband. She now had only a son who was virtually catatonic since the revelations at the cemetery, and her beautiful eyes to weep with.

"I found the bodies of María's parents," Rubén continued without animosity. "Samuel and Gabriella Verón, a young Chilean-Argentine couple who were murdered in September 1976. The Center for Forensic Anthropology has confirmed that their DNA matches that of María Victoria and Miguel Michellini. Your children's birth certificates are forged, as you know."

Isabel Campallo shook her head.

"No."

Rubén's espresso arrived.

"Listen, Mrs. Campallo. For the moment, the press doesn't know about this, nor do the judges, but the Grandmothers have a file of charges against you, and whether you are in mourning or not, you're still subject to punishment as an *apropriadora*. You could get seven years in prison. It's up to you whether you want to stain your name and that of your husband."

There was a silence along the promenade where couples were entwining to the clacking of halyards. Isabel Campallo hunched a little more over her bandaged arm.

"Well?"

"One day Eduardo spoke to me about children," she finally said. "Two young children. He told me they had been abandoned in front of a hospital, that we could adopt them. I believed him."

"Sure, Rodolfo was found under a cabbage leaf and María in a flower . . . Summer '76, you know what was going on then, don't you?" he snapped at her.

"Yes, the military was in power. But the dictatorship didn't prevent people from abandoning their children."

"Before they were liquidated. *Desaparecidos* whose children were stolen from them."

"When two babies are put in the arms of a sterile woman, she is ready to believe anything at all," Isabel Campallo retorted. "And then, however it happened, these children didn't have parents," she said in her defense. "We gave them the opportunity to have the best possible education. That's what we did. Always."

Rubén blew his cigarette smoke in the widow's face.

"You claim that you knew nothing about the conditions under which your children were adopted, or about the people who allowed it?"

"No. I believed Eduardo's version. Perhaps because I wanted to believe," she conceded. "I lived with it."

"But you never told your children they had been adopted."

"No."

"Why?"

"It was convenient."

"And cowardly: you must have suspected that they had been taken away from their parents."

"No, I wanted to love them, that's all. You aren't capable of understanding that, Calderón?"

Silent tears were running down the *apropriadora*'s cheeks.

"Love them while hiding the truth about their origins," Rubén said. "A fine little neurosis you've got going there."

"That doesn't make us monsters," Isabel said, gaining control of herself. "My husband and I have always loved Rodolfo and María Victoria as though they were our own children."

"I'd hardly expect you to detest them because they came from murdered parents," he replied angrily.

Piqued, Isabel rebelled.

"Your memory is short or selective, Mr. Calderón. At that time the country was threatened with anarchy. There were murders every day, in the open street: police officers, judges, soldiers, CEOs—the terrorists were killing everybody! Montoneros, communists, or followers of Che Guevara, it didn't make much difference: they all wanted to change the world without asking whether the world wanted to pay the price—in blood! Why do you think Argentines welcomed the military putsch? Mistakes may have been made, but those who were secretly interned were interned for good reasons: it was them or us!"

Rubén could have put his cigarette out on her face; he threw it away instead.

"You have strong arguments for someone who doesn't ask questions," he observed cynically. "Why didn't you say anything to me when I came to tell you about your daughter's disappearance? We might still have had a chance to save her. Did you think of that, or had your ideology consumed your heart?"

A disquieting veil passed over the detective's waxen face.

"Rodolfo was present," she said, embarrassed. "I . . . I couldn't talk about the subject in front of him."

"Maintaining your lie was more important than saving your daughter's life, huh? You disgust me," he said between his teeth.

Isabel held back her tears. People were strolling past the terrace, deaf to the drama that was being played out there.

"Do you know why your husband committed suicide?" Rubén asked.

The widow shrugged her thin shoulders.

"Out of sorrow . . . Obviously."

"He didn't leave anything behind him?"

"No."

"Don't force me to break your other arm," he said in an icy tone. "If your husband had killed himself out of love for his daughter, he would have left a note to explain. So?"

"It's at the notary's," she said.

"What's at the notary's?"

"Eduardo left a letter, dated the morning he died."

"What does this letter say?"

"That he was leaving his fortune to Rodolfo," Isabel replied. "I retain only the house, plus the property from my family."

Rubén grimaced.

"Your husband disinherited you?"

"No. Eduardo knew that I didn't need money. My family is very rich, that's not it." Isabel sighed under the black corset of her dress. "It was rather a last act of love for our son," she explained. "My husband suspected that Rodolfo would someday find out the truth about the adoption. I think he wanted to prove to him that despite our silence, we loved them, him and his sister, as our own children. That we wanted to protect them."

This piety did nothing to sway Calderón.

"No," Rubén rasped. "No, something else happened. Something that pushed your husband to kill himself."

The bubbles in Isabel's Perrier were beginning to evaporate in the warm air of the terrace. She looked up, surprised.

"What could have led Eduardo to commit suicide?"

"The truth," he said. "The truth about the death of his daughter."

Isabel was pale on the other side of the table, and soon became transparent.

"Explain yourself," she said.

"Your husband seemed alarmed the other day when I told him about the circumstances of María's murder. Think what you want of me, Mrs. Campallo, but I wouldn't have come to disturb your mourning if I hadn't been sure that she was killed. I believe your husband understood that too, at that moment: and that it was a shock for him."

Isabel's forehead furrowed.

"Between the burial and his suicide, who did your husband see, aside from his family? The forensic police? Luque?"

"No . . . No."

"The mayor? Torres was his friend, wasn't he? He's the one who set up the elite police force: your husband might have asked him for an explanation regarding the falsified autopsy report and the murder that was being concealed from him. They must have seen each other, or talked on the telephone."

"Yes," she said. "Yes, Eduardo went to see him on the morning of the day when . . . "

Isabel didn't finish her sentence.

"The day he committed suicide," Rubén went on. "Think about it. Your husband met his friend Francisco Torres, then dictated his last wishes at the notary's office before putting a bullet in his head. Why did he do that, in your opinion?"

Isabel Campallo stared at him, disconcerted.

"Because Eduardo had understood that his friends were

hiding the truth from him," Rubén said, driving the point home. "That they were themselves involved in the murder."

"No." She shook her head, incredulous. "No, Francisco is an old friend. He would never have done such a thing. He has nothing to do with the dictatorship. He was barely twenty years old at the time. It's impossible."

"Torres could have given in to the pressure. Lots of people are involved, an old general and others, perhaps people close to him."

"No," Isabel repeated. "I tell you that Francisco is a family friend: he knows María Victoria, Rodolfo . . . I refuse to believe you."

"Nonetheless, your husband committed suicide after they talked."

"I'm telling you that's impossible. Francisco is an honorable man."

"Precisely, he might have admitted to Eduardo that he was implicated in the affair, how the murder was hushed up by Luque and his clique."

"Why in the world would Francisco do such a thing?" she countered.

"Maybe in order to protect someone. Someone whose name is on the internment form proving the adoption of your children."

"That was more than thirty years ago. Francisco hadn't even done his military service: how can you suggest that there was a relation with your old oppressors?"

Rubén lit a cigarette, which didn't make him feel any better. Then the answer came to him like a lightning bolt—why hadn't he seen this connection earlier? Isabel Campallo was right about Torres. It wasn't himself or one of his friends that the mayor of Buenos Aires was trying to protect: it was his father. Ignacio Torres, the man who had gotten rich in the wine trade before launching his son's political career. Gabriella Verón had owned land in the Mendoza region . . . Ignacio Torres was the man of the *estancia.*

*

His head was throbbing, accompanied by the jolting of the apparatus. Too many events all at once—the hospital, Campallo, Torres's betrayal—and he could hardly stand up. A sequence of blows that he received right in the face, like a boxer on the ropes. Jana. Rubén had turned the equation around in his head hundreds of times, and had found only one answer to her silence: if she had taken the weapons from his cache without notifying the Grandmothers, it was because she thought he was dead. There was no other explanation. Rubén trembled when he thought of what she might do. He had no way of contacting her, the Ford was no longer in Peru Street, where Miguel had left it: Jana had left the city without contacting anyone, with his weapons. Did she have a lead, a lead he didn't have? The fear of losing her was still with him. What did she think, that she was going to liquidate them, all by herself? Had she gone mad?

Rubén was slumped in the rear seat of a light plane, suffering from the turbulence and his pain, using his bruised flesh as a cushion. A tubby walrus was at the controls of the Cessna, Valdés, the head pilot at the El Tigre airfield. The detective had found him in his tumbledown shack, playing endless games of solitaire on his computer, as if nothing had changed since the preceding week. Valdés hadn't heard from Del Piro but he'd bared his big, nicotine-stained teeth when he saw the stack of bills Rubén laid on the counter.

"We're almost there!" he finally brayed from the cockpit.

Sweat was running down Rubén's face.

Mendoza, ten in the evening. He needed a bed, a hotel where he could rest. The detective walked slowly across the tarmac, his left arm glued to his side as if he'd broken his shoulder. Rubén was gritting his teeth, he was tough: the Glock was in his bag, and he shot with his right hand.

*

The Torres family belonged to the oligarchy of landowners who had divided up the country among themselves two centuries earlier. Ignacio had grown up in the fertile valleys of the Uco, the pride of Argentina. He loved his region, which was magnificent, the wine that was made there, the power he had inherited, and the money that sustained it.

The province of Mendoza produced the best wine in the country for a domestic market that was at the time very strong. Wine was the popular drink par excellence, but Ignacio was a visionary. Argentina, which had prospered by supplying a devastated Europe after the war, exported its raw materials: wine would be the new El Dorado. As early as the 1970s, Ignacio Torres had understood the predominance of capital over labor. With the liberalization of markets, financial speculation soon became more profitable than local agropastoral or industrial production, especially if the profits were invested abroad. However, a fairly strong society had to be created before entering these markets.

Ignacio had taken advantage of the ups and down of the dictatorship to increase the scope of his holdings, tripling the extent of the family lands in order to build the wine estate of his dreams, which he called Solente.

The main vineyards in the region were concentrated around Luján; Solente was farther south, off the beaten path. Torres had brought in the best winemakers from Europe and America to improve the syrahs and cabernets that had, up to that point, been consumed only by common, unsophisticated drinkers, and to build the his winery's reputation. Afterward, he had counted on an intense advertising campaign and prospected on export markets and influential milieus, especially *Mondovino*, the specialized magazine that established the ratings, judiciously: the Argentine wine industry's sales exploded in the 1990s, in particular those of Solente, whose bottles now cost six times more than they used to. What did it matter if the majority of his compatriots no longer drank wine because they could not afford such luxuries? Exports more than compensated for the decline of the domestic market.

Solente. The geographical location of the winery was ideal, with its hundreds of acres of vines lining the Andean foothills, and although the family chapel was reminiscent of Pinochet-style architecture, the building that received the public and merchants was ultramodern. A vast exposition hall with sculptures and contemporary works of art, gardens with exotic plants; an air-conditioned gift shop selling bottles of wine and other merchandise with images of the vineyard; a restaurant and lounge with a terrace offering views of the fabulous mountain range and its snowy peaks: more than a wine estate, Solente had become a brand. And Ignacio Torres had amassed enough money to launch his eldest son on a political career.

He'd made it to the Casa Rosada: at seventy-three years of age, that represented the culmination of a lifetime's work. His son Francisco had the stature of a president, the capacity for work, the charisma, and for his part, he had solid support in financial and industrial circles. The mark he would put on the country would be irreversible: the Torres mark.

To be sure, Ignacio had a few problems, but he had no intention of changing his methods. As he did every year in this season, the master of the vineyard had come to supervise the harvest. The few clouds attacking the Andes dissipated over the extinct volcano Tupungato, the guardian of the valley of his childhood. Yes, he could be proud of his work. The bunches of grapes gorged with sun extended as far as the eye could see, to produce a wine that promised to be exceptionally good that year. Ignacio tasted a grape, spat out the skin, and judged for himself—perfect acidity. Protected by a broad-brimmed hat, the old man was ambling down the row deep in thought when a voice hailed him:

"Mr. Torres?"

Interrupted in his reflections, Ignacio showed a certain surprise. He had a brief moment of hesitation. Romero had dropped him off at the top of the north parcel so that he could inspect the vines before the harvest, and the quad had stopped down below. He couldn't see Romero and a man was coming up the dirt path: a big, brown-haired man dressed in black, who was walking with the slow and cadenced pace of a legionnaire.

"What do you want?" Torres called.

"I have to talk to you," the man replied as he approached.

After sleeping poorly for ten hours in a hotel near the airfield, Rubén had rented a car and driven to Solente, stuffing himself with painkillers.

Still ten yards before reaching the boss.

"If you're a journalist, you must have been told at the reception desk that I receive visitors only by appointment," Ignacio said, irritated. "You can see for yourself that I'm busy."

"Yes," Rubén said in a weary voice. "I called at noon. I was told that you were at the vineyards to supervise the harvest. I'm not a journalist."

The detective stopped at the bottom of the row, dripping with cold sweat after his forced march over the hills. Ignacio Torres had a broad, flat body in accord with his cowboy getup. His lively eyes soured.

"Who are you?"

"Rubén Calderón," he said. "I work for the Grandmothers."

It was impossible to discern the landowner's reaction behind his Ray-Bans.

"What do you want?" he asked curtly.

Rubén was dying of heat in the sun and he had no time to lose.

"The truth about the theft of land from the Verón family,"

he said point-blank. "September '76, you remember? Colonel Ardiles brought you Gabriella, the sole heiress to these lands, a young woman accompanied by her husband. They had been extracted from the secret jails at the ESMA."

Ignacio sensed the danger: he glanced toward the bottom of the parcel, saw the quad halfway up, but still not that dolt Romero.

Romero was resting between the vines, a bullet in his chest after a duel that hadn't lasted long.

"Nobody will come to save you, Torres," Rubén said, reading his mind. "Certainly not one of your men disguised as *piqueteros*. You're the one who sent them to track down Montañez, aren't you? With whose help, Luque's?"

Torres quickly scanned the plantations: the winery was too far away for them to be seen.

"I have nothing to say to you," he replied, with his customary authority. "You had better go back where you came from before I call security."

He took a cell phone out of his checkered shirt. Rubén grabbed Torres's wrist and, using his right hand, twisted it until the phone fell to the ground. Torres swore at the brute, who was impassive despite the sweat running down his forehead, and held his wrist as if he might fall. Rubén took the Glock out of his jacket, the silencer still screwed onto the barrel, and pointed it at the old man's belly.

"What do you want," Torres grumbled. "Money?"

Rubén shook his head slowly.

"Vulgar to the very end, huh? Tell me instead how much Gabriella Verón's land was worth at the time. Did you buy it for a song, or did she and her husband cede it to you in exchange for the lives of their children?"

The old boss's jaws remained inflexible.

"I have nothing to say to you," he repeated. "Take it up with my lawyers."

"Why didn't you have them fill out the sales contract while they were being tortured at the ESMA?" he asked in a sugary voice. "That would have been simpler, wouldn't it?"

"I'm a businessman, not a soldier. You've got the wrong person."

"Let's say instead that you preferred to manage the affair with Ardiles, who brought you Samuel and Gabriella Verón to sign the sales contract before they were liquidated. Who else did you pay off, high-ranking military officers? Was the couple kidnapped for the purpose of stealing Gabriella's land or did you learn of their existence while they were at the ESMA? Huh? Who told you about them, Ardiles? In any case, the sales documents and the signature were extorted from them by force, from defenseless people, people who were tortured before their children were stolen," the detective said heatedly.

Torres put on a face of false pity.

"You'll never be able to prove that," he grumbled.

"We'll see about that at your trial."

"There won't be any trial," the landowner boldly assured him. "You don't know what you're getting into, Calderón."

"I do, actually. You financed your son's political career by profiting from lands stolen from the *desaparecidos*. The ESMA form María Campallo got her hands on threatened to taint you, so you made an unholy alliance with your old accomplices to protect the property you acquired in such a criminal way. You're the one who had María Campallo kidnapped and killed, who gave the order for the dirty work to be done, relying on the networks of your old friends, first of all Ardiles. Luque and his elite cops were ordered to cover up the affair, at the price of sacrificing one of your main supporters, Eduardo Campallo, whose daughter you had killed. Your son's friend. It's terrific, that morality you're always talking about."

"You're crazy."

"Crazy enough to put a bullet in your belly and let you lie here dying for hours." He cocked his pistol and changed his tone. "Tell me where Ardiles is hiding. Tell me right now or I swear I'll leave you here like a piece of shit in the sun."

Torres got scared: Calderón was staring at him with the eyes of a rattlesnake, his finger curled around the trigger. He was going to shoot.

"In a monastery," he said. "A monastery in the south . . . "

"Where in the south?"

"Los Cipreses," Torres said, his mouth dry. "In the lake region."

Ruben gripped the handle of the gun, seized by nausea.

"Who's hiding him?"

"A former chaplain . . . von Wernisch."

"Is his name also on the ESMA form?"

"Yes."

A warm breeze was coming up over the hills.

"We're going to check that right now."

Rubén crouched to pick up Torres's cell phone on the ground and held it out to him.

"Call the monastery's number and turn on the speaker," he ordered. "You must have it in your contact list."

Torres had lost his haughtiness. He took the phone.

"What do I say?"

"Ask for news of Ardiles. Just that. You try any funny business and you're dead."

The old man nodded under his Stetson and obeyed, the Glock aimed at him.

A monk answered the phone. Torres introduced himself, asked about the health of his military friend, and received a mixed response: Mr. Ardiles had gone away with the cardinal on an urgent errand. They would be back before nightfall, that's all he knew.

Rubén signaled to Torres to hang up. He wasn't lying: they

were there. Rubén hesitated. The lake region was more than 250 miles away, several hours' drive over a highway in poor condition. By the time Rubén got there, Ignacio Torres would have been able to warn Ardiles and his men. He turned toward the patriarch. He couldn't be left free to move around. He also couldn't be thrown in prison: Ledesma would lose his nerve. Ruben's eyes, already somber, grew even darker.

"You like land, huh, Torres? Well then, eat it!"

Ignacio paled behind his Ray-Bans.

"What?"

"Eat it!" Rubén ordered.

"But . . . "

The Glock's barrel raked across Torres's face: Torres bit the dust, his hat rolling against the vines. Blood ran into his hands speckled with brown spots, dripping from his split lip.

"Eat it!" Rubén yelled, pushing him with his foot. "Eat that goddamned earth or I'll kill you!"

A deadly spark crossed the detective's retina. Ignacio, lying among the vines, picked up a clump of soil in a shaking hand. This guy was out of his mind.

"Eat it, I tell you!"

He carried the clump to his mouth and reluctantly put it on his tongue.

"More!"

Trembling, Torres obeyed and raised his head, his mouth already full, but Calderón was still aiming at his belly.

"More!" he hissed, the hammer cocked. "Go on!"

Torres chewed, with difficulty. Rubén was about to burn up under the heat of the sun. It would be hours before they started getting worried about the absence of the boss, who had gone to inspect the vines. Torres was feeling sorry for himself among the grapes, his chin covered with brown earth and blood, close to vomiting. Rubén lowered the silencer and fired two shots that pulverized Torres's kneecaps.

8

Ituzaingó 67: the Grandmothers were feverish as they opened the gate to Franco Díaz's garden.

They had received Jana's letter at the association's offices, a few laconic words, barely credible, without further explanations. It had been sent two days earlier from Futalaufquen, a small town in Chubut province. Elena and Susana hadn't hesitated long. Carlos had met them with the required equipment at the Buquebus of Puerto Madero, where they had taken the first boat to Colonia del Sacramento, on the other side of the estuary. The crossing, in their state of excitement, had seemed to last a century. Finally they arrived. Ituzaingó 67: a blazing sun was flooding the botanist's garden. Leaving the gate open, the trio went down the charming walk where bees were busily at work. The immaculate flowers of the *palos barrochos*, the hollyhocks along the wall, the violets running along the flowerbeds, azaleas, orchids—Díaz had created a little paradise around his *posada*.

"I'd like a nice cold beer," Carlos remarked as he put down his equipment in front of the *ceibo*.

"Dig first, then we'll see," Susana kidded him.

"Besides, you already drank two on the way over!" Rubén's mother added.

Sheltered by a straw hat, the journalist grumbled about them being pains in the neck, then set about the task without complaining. The *ceibo* the letter mentioned dominated the back of the garden, next to Ossario's house—the blackened walls of his terrace and the collapsed roof could be seen over the hedge. Carlos dug around the base of the tree, taking great precautions. Elena was sweating heavily under the white scarf that protected her from the heat—that never happened to her.

"Are you all right, Duchess?" Susana whispered.

"Yes."

Elena opened her eyes wide as if she had to hold reality in them lest it escape.

"An agent never destroys his archives." According to Jana's letter, the former SIDE official had buried the original document at the foot of a young *ceibo*, the Argentine national tree. The guardian of the temple, Díaz, was supposed to have fled, leaving the document where it was: among the roots of the totemic tree. The Grandmothers waited impatiently behind Carlos, who was no longer young, notwithstanding his propensity for drinking alcohol at unsuitable times.

"Well?" Susana encouraged him.

"I've got it," the bearded man finally said.

The two friends peered over the shoulder of the journalist, who was clearing away the last soil attached to the roots: a small cylinder was caught in the rhizomes. He pulled it out and then went to take refuge in the shade. Elena, who had the best eyes, adjusted her glasses and the magnifying glass they'd brought for the purpose. Then she unscrewed the lid. Inside the cylinder was a roll of film, just as Jana had said.

"What is it?" whispered the vice president, who couldn't see anything. "The ESMA form?"

Elena unrolled the film, still incredulous.

"Well?" Susana persisted. "What's going on? Elena? What's going on?"

"It looks like . . . a microfilm," her friend murmured.

The names and dates were illegible at this scale, but they were miniaturized cards: some of them carried the infamous symbol of the ESMA, others did not. Elena Calderón continued to unroll the film, inspected it several times with the magnifying glass, and suddenly the Earth seemed to move. It was not only Samuel and Gabriella Verón's internment form: there were dozens, hundreds of others.

"Susana," Elena whispered, shocked. "It's the microfilm . . . "

"What? Do you mean *the* microfilm?"

Elena nodded under the scarf that protected her from the sun.

"Yes," she said, convinced. "Yes, this is it. The microfilm of the *desaparecidos*. This is it, Susana. It exists. They're here."

Susana and Carlos held their breath. The military men had destroyed the reports on clandestine operations in the late 1970s, General Bignone had done away with other documents in 1982, and the federal police had burned everything else a few days before Alfonsin was elected, but there were rumors that all the documents connected with the *desaparecidos* had been duplicated on a microfilm that was concealed in a safe in Panama or Miami, or more likely had been destroyed . . . Now, there it was before their eyes.

The reception of prisoners, the processing and recycling of information, periodic reports on the advancement of the "work," names and matriculation numbers, actions authorized by the hierarchy, tours of guard duty, nocturnal thefts ordered by authorities further up the chain of command—Díaz had preserved on microfilm the internment forms of all the Argentine *desaparecidos* in a secret state document that had been entrusted to him, the patriot. The Grandmothers' eyes misted over. Their whole life was there.

Not only the truth about what had happened to their children and husbands: the truth about the disappearance of thirty thousand persons abducted by the dictatorship, what had been done with their remains, the part of Argentine history that had been stolen.

Susana pressed her sad Duchess's hand. The fate of Daniel

and Elsa had to be on one of these miniaturized documents, but Elena Calderón was not afraid to confront it. Rubén believed that the truth would kill his mother, just as it had killed his father. He was wrong: Elena was fighting because a country without the truth was a country without memory. The fate of her husband and their daughter was only one part of the tragedy that bound together the Argentine people, victims and tormentors, passive participants and complicitous. Justice was there, between their trembling hands.

The Grandmothers could die in peace.

"Our search is over," Elena whispered, her throat tight.

The old women shed a few tears as they thought about their compatriots, all those unfortunate people who, like them, could soon begin their work of mourning over all the unfathomable voids that the microfilm's revelations would fill, over the sick hearts that could finally be reconstructed. They wept in the garden, no longer knowing whether they were crying with joy or with relief as Carlos took them in his arms. He too was having a hard time controlling his emotions: "The truth is like oil in water: it always ends up rising to the surface," as activists said.

The midday sun was blazing. Elena called Rubén, impatient to tell him the incredible news, but he didn't answer his cell phone.

The old woman's face grew dark.

"What is it?" Susana asked.

Elena tried again, several times, in vain: there was no answer.

9

Franco Díaz thought Argentines weren't ready to wash their dirty linen at home: that wouldn't happen for years, when his generation had passed on. It would be a long time before the *ceibo* tree in his garden grew and, as it flourished, one day spat out the truth. By that time, he would be gone, killed by cancer, and the last actors of that time would be dead, too.

Díaz didn't know that his neighbor, who had lost the suit he'd filed the preceding year, was spying on him day and night to prove that he was in fact polluting his garden. He also didn't know that Ossario was paranoid enough to have installed an infrared video camera at the window of his living room that covered his neighbor's whole Garden of Eden. And he didn't know that when Ossario was viewing one of the cassettes he had seen him bury something at the foot of the a young *ceibo*—Franco had even made the sign of the Cross over it before covering it with earth, looking all around him as if he were afraid someone might see him. The following night, Ossario had sneaked into Franco's garden, dug around in the still loose dirt, and found a cylinder that he had taken home with him. What he'd discovered that night went beyond anything he could have imagined. Díaz didn't know that Ossario, obsessed with the mystery, had feverishly copied dozens of pages of microfilm, put the cylinder back in its place just as dawn was breaking, and begun to work his way through the internment forms on *desaparecidos*, looking for witnesses. It was the scoop of his life. The name of Eduardo Campallo, the businessman who was constantly in the news at the time of his disgrace, was on one of the ESMA forms, as an *apropriador*: imagining his revenge as a springboard, the former paparazzo had contacted his daughter, María Victoria, and by that very act signed their death warrants. No, Franco Díaz didn't know the hidden agenda, but that didn't matter anymore: after spending five hours bound hand and foot in the trunk of the Audi, suffocating on the gag, without morphine to relieve his pain, the old SIDE agent had told her everything he knew.

Jana had listened to his revelations without showing the slightest emotion, and then offered him a deal. Paralyzed by the violence that emanated from her irises, already feeling the cold knife in his sick flesh, Díaz had obeyed all her orders.

The forest where she had dragged him was compact. Chained to the trunk of a large araucaria, the SIDE agent had watched her silently daub her face with black. The Mapuche had left before dawn, carrying her backpack, her rifle, and her other weapons, still without saying a word. The night had been long, cold, and anxiety-producing. What if she had abandoned him there? What if she never came back? Díaz had thought he heard gunshots far away in the forest, then it was silent again. He had finally dozed off, frozen with cold and fear.

The Indian woman had reappeared shortly before dawn, leading her prisoners. There were three of them, tied up; the thinnest was staggering, his tibia obviously broken, and he was being supported by an old, emaciated man in a cassock. The third man was unconscious, wrapped in a blanket that the Indian was dragging through the trees. Franco recognized his friend von Wernisch despite his pitiful appearance: the cardinal, manifestly shaken by what had happened to him, tried to communicate with him, but Franco Díaz didn't dare reply. He was forbidden to talk, to move, or to make signs to anyone: the Indian had been clear about that. First, she grouped the prisoners in the middle of the clearing, tied their feet, and then gagged the wounded man and the wretched cardinal. Then, terrible under her painted mask, she used a dagger to shred their clothes.

Kept at a distance, Díaz was given favored treatment: fresh water, his ankles unbound if not his wrists, and he was allowed his precious doses of morphine, which the Indian gave him in small amounts. On seeing the captives, the botanist shivered: the big guy he'd seen two days earlier in the courtyard of the monastery emerged, his face bashed up and covered with piss and blood. A few paces away, the Indian continued to dig her hole, silently, methodically.

"What . . . What are you doing?" Díaz dared to say.

But, concentrated on her task, she seemed not to hear him.

The Mapuches had assimilated horses better than the *winka*, who had brought them to the continent. Their horses were faster and had more endurance, and the rest was settled with lances. Since treaties bound only those who believed in them, native surprise attacks and raids were common along the frontier. The warriors brought mounts and captives back to camp, where each victory over the *winka*, the invaders, was celebrated. White women were treated according to the chief's appetites, and the men were literally thrown to the dogs. Reduced to sleeping outdoors, half-naked and starving, the Christians soon looked as wretched as the dogs. Beaten, humiliated, gnawing on the remains that had escaped the greedy jaws of the canines, shivering with cold and despair, the captives' lives depended on chance. The Mapuches killed them before eating their hearts; the head was then carefully stripped of its flesh and contents and transformed into a *ralilonko*, a trophy cup from which they drank *chicha*, a corn liquor. The leg bones were emptied out, cut, and used as flutes to make the souls of the sacrificed sing. Among the Mapuche, during wartime everything was daubed in black, from the symbolic weapon of the *gentoqui*, the master of the battle-axe, to the warriors, the *conas*, who painted their faces with charcoal before going into battle. Jana had found suitable pigments, which she had mixed with water to obtain a dark-colored paste. In using the pigments of her childhood, she rediscovered her artist's soul, her Mapuche soul. That did not console her.

An hour passed, punctuated by the rasping of the shovel and the first bird calls. Diesel roused himself from his torpor, stretching his stiff limbs after a nap in the ferns. The sun was coming up over a forest redolent of moss, and the prisoners didn't move from their mire. The gags made breathing difficult for them, and they suffered from cramps, cold, and despair. El Picador glanced painfully at his friend: a viscous liquid was oozing from his tibia fractured by a large-caliber bullet, every movement cost him great pain, and Parise had abandoned them to their fate. At his side, immured in his torment, the old cardinal had stopped moaning: he was watching with glassy eyes the movements of the devil flitting among the tree branches. El Toro, by far the most rebellious despite the condition of his jaw, was still grumbling, his wrists bloody from his efforts to free himself. A dense rage that left him powerless. They were no more than three stiff bodies thrown in the mud of a remote forest, naked and drenched to the bone, with that fucking dog that kept coming to sniff their asses.

"Get out of here!" he muttered into the mess in which his lost teeth were soaking.

El Toro wanted to kill every living being, and the girl was still digging. She hadn't gagged him, as she had the others, and she had urinated on him to clean his wound. What was she saving him for?

Diesel limped over to his mistress, who no longer saw him. Sweat was running off her face, making rivulets in the remains of the black pigment. The hole was deep and her hands hurt, but Jana was no longer of this world. A cosmogony of disaster.

In the drama of the dead, she had become Kulan, "the terrifying woman."

Jana dropped the shovel, tears in her eyes.

Diesel, who was lapping the water that had collected in the mire, perked up his ears and instinctively ran away when she approached. Alerted by the mutt's brief yapping, El Toro snorted. The Indian's silhouette was coming out of the thicket, her face blackened, fearsome under her madwoman's mask. The prisoners twisted about in an effort to escape, but tied up as they were, they wouldn't go far. Jana caught El Picador by his good foot and dragged him into the trees. Díaz hid behind his trunk, pursued by the prisoner's muffled groans. She attached a rope to the ankle of El Picador's broken leg and threw it over a branch of the big araucaria.

Yes, Jana was crazy: crazy with pain.

El Picador screamed through his gag when she winched his leg up to the branch.

*

Diesel had disappeared. A gentle rain was falling at dawn and a breath of horror floated over the clearing.

Hanging by his ankle from the araucaria, El Picador had stopped moaning. Jana no longer had the strength to haul his whole body up, despite her leverage system; half his torso was touching the ground, his whole weight pulling on the suspended leg with its fractured tibia. The Christian was no longer moving, his eyes rolled back and his gag loose, as if the fear of being dismembered had frozen him in this improbable posture.

Jana was waiting in the shade of the branches: Mapuche time, which counts seconds as hours and starts the day at dawn. The winching and El Picador's muffled cries had terrified the captives. They had tried to get away, but naked and hobbled, they had succeeded only in paddling about in the morass. Von Wernisch wouldn't last much longer; a stunted skeleton shivering with cold, an artillery shell from another war forgotten in the mire, the old cardinal had faded away. El Toro was still mumbling; he was probably used to muck and insults. Jana was meditating in the shelter of the trees, her eyes closed, immobile, a cruel and magical statue. The spirit of Kulan was still prowling around her, but she was no longer alone with her double: Shoort, Xalpen, Shenu, Pahuil, her grandmother's spirit ghosts were returning to her after a long journey, all her old dream companions, cousins in blood and matter, all the old witnesses of the aboriginal time that accompanied her in her agony. She saw again Rubén's face in the bedroom when she had left him—memories with blinded eyes.

Jana opened hers, but that didn't help. Diesel had left, his tail between his legs, and had not come back. The animal had probably understood what was going to happen. A melancholy drizzle was falling. Jana got up, a metallic taste in her mouth, and walked toward the center of the clearing where the prisoners were floundering. Von Wernisch's crumpled face was whey-colored; he was praying silently, turning his back on El Toro, a greasy mass crawling in the mud out of which he had been born. The killer must be looking for a stone, something with a sharp edge. Jana grabbed the cardinal under his arms and pulled him backward toward the dry ground. "Uuh! uuh!" the old man yelped through the gag as she dragged his stiff body, but he no longer had the strength to resist. El Toro stopped creeping, on the alert. Von Wernisch implored the Indian, pitiful tears in his eyes, and panicked when he saw the pile of earth next to the hole. He struggled, kicking weakly, and vigorously shook his head: Jana pushed the howling package into the grave.

The priest's body disappeared from the surface of the Earth. El Toro, on his knees, gulped. Chained to the tree trunk,

Franco Díaz observed the scene with terror: the Mapuche had lied to him. The agreement they'd made was a fool's bargain; she wasn't going to spare him, as she had promised, in exchange for his obedience: the savage was going to massacre them one by one. Jana did not listen to von Wernisch's muffled cries and supplications at the bottom of the grave: she took up the Selk'nam knife and went toward El Toro.

The man tore madly at his bonds and threw back his head, uttering what had to be taken for threats. She crouched down next to him; he was grimacing with his smashed jaw.

"El Toro, huh?"

Jana turned toward the edge of the clearing and the araucaria where El Picador was hanging

"See your little pal?" she said in a voice that was too calm. "I'll make a deal with you. If you rape him to death, the way you did Miguel, I'll spare you; otherwise I'll bury you alive with the old man."

A veil of stupefaction passed over the prisoner's eyes. Jana did not depart from her falsely tranquil tone.

"You have a choice, El Toro: it's you or him."

He could hear von Wernisch moaning in the pit, very nearby. El Picador was no longer moving, his twisted foot attached to the branch. A grimace of hatred made the torturer's bloody mouth even uglier.

"*India de mierda!*" he muttered.

Jana stood up. The fat man was squirming at her feet, mad with rage. Of course. He raped boys but he wasn't like Miguel, no, not El Toro. Jana was a Mapuche, one of the people whom the Spaniards hunted with dogs trained to devour them, people who were paid by the number of ears they cut off. She would begin with the worst: the pig.

She jumped on him and made him roll in the mud. He fought back, shoving her desperately with his shoulders, but she straddled him, her eyes blazing. Jana grabbed El Toro's scalp as he lay on the ground, and took a firm grip on the handle of the knife. A tear of cruelty rolled down her Indian's cheek.

"This is for Paula," she said as she cut off the first ear. "And this is for Rubén."

10

Diesel was waiting in the trees, impassive in his dog's way. A timid sun pierced the clouds after the first rain of the morning. The animal was sitting on the bank of a stream that flowed there, examining the limited horizon as though a hypothetical vessel of flesh and bone might emerge from it. A familiar odor diverted him from his hungry reverie: suddenly cheering up, Diesel abandoned his observation post and trotted toward his mistress, who was approaching him.

Jana had left the clearing and was walking like an automaton toward the stream, which she had found the day before. The sight of the animal didn't affect her one way or the other. Diesel licked her hands to welcome her, wagging his tail, without seeing the collar of ears that was dripping blood on her stunted breasts. Jana was no longer herself. Neither a sculptress nor a Mapuche ghost or Selk'nam risen from beyond the tomb to avenge her people: she remained crouched at the edge of the stream, her cracked paint on her face, her eyes empty. The T-shirt under her jacket was sticky with blood, and El Toro's cries still echoed in her head, but she wasn't done yet. The two others were still out there: Parise and Ardiles. Only afterward could she go back to her own. Rubén . . .

Diesel yapped, as if trying to bring her back to the right side of the world, a mouse's squeal that was lost in the lapping of the stream. Jana washed her hands and the knife in the water, which briefly took on a rosy tint. The air was blowing over the carpet of moss as she stood up. The fugitives had gone north.

According to her detailed map of the park, there was only one trail that could be taken across the forest: the one that led to the former mission. They must have waited for daylight so that they could get their bearings. They had one, maybe two hours' head start. The Mapuche put on her backpack, shouldered the rifle, and started off between the trees.

Diesel followed her through the ferns, wagging his tail.

*

The birds were singing again among the damp branches. Mist still lay on the ground after the terror of the night; his ankle hurt, but Parise could walk. They seemed to have lost the killer who was following them, but apart from that the situation was not promising: he was out of ammunition, he had nothing but a pocket knife and his jacket, which was too thin to protect him against the cold, and the pain was making him nasty. Fifty-nine years old. The former interrogating officer was no longer young, but he'd manage, as he always did. Ardiles had chosen him for that—even crippled, this guy remained a force of nature.

The two men had fled in the darkness, plunging straight ahead, deaf to the cries they heard behind them. They had made their way through the anarchic vegetation; one hour had seemed like a hundred, until they finally stopped somewhere right in the middle of the forest, exhausted. It was too dark to go on. In any case, they were lost, and they both needed a rest to regain their strength. They had taken turns keeping watch, slept a few hours with fear in the pit of their stomachs, until dawn finally came. Parise's pale face had hollowed as if it had been sucked inward, the bullet stuck in his ankle hurt him, but the daylight appearing between the foliage had perked him up a bit. The giant had chosen a heavy branch that would serve as both a cane and a club. Soaked, their bellies empty, they had set out again, keeping an eye out for shadows in the undergrowth.

The light guided them through the thorny brush. The forest grew less dense as they moved higher; the two men followed the ferns that led under the foliage and after an hour's forced march, they found a marked trail. It rose gently uphill toward the ridge.

"What do you think, Parise?" Ardiles asked, out of breath.

"This trail has to go somewhere. A road, or a pass . . . With a little luck, we'll get some reception."

They decided to continue north. It would be very surprising if they didn't find civilization. As for the mysterious killer who was tracking them, they preferred not to mention him—it was a miracle they'd survived that night. The drizzle accompanied them through the forest. At 6,500 feet, their blood was short of oxygen, and the slope was getting steeper. The general struggled on, but the wound in his arm had started acting up again—that brute Parise had knocked him down when he'd demanded a weapon—but this was not the time for making acerbic remarks or settling accounts. They kept going, in silence. Sweat and rain ran down their faces. The ground was slippery, the pines fewer.

"We're coming to the summit," the head of security announced, looking even paler.

They came first to a low stone wall amid the ferns, and then rockslides; a little higher up, they found more walls, the remains of an ancient building that had been overtaken by vegetation.

A former mission.

The fugitives approached it slowly, wary of unpleasant surprises. Bushes and weeds had covered the crumbling walls, but the outline of the monastery could still be discerned; given the state of the ruins, it must date from the Conquest of the Wilderness.

"Let's stop," Parise panted.

The wind was stronger on the heights, and the sky was finally clear, despite the gathering clouds. He sat down on a low wall to rest his wounded ankle while the general explored the ruins. Ardiles's shoes slipped on the rocks; he caught himself by grabbing with his good hand the scrawny bushes thriving there, swore under his breath, and soon reached the back of the building. The mission was located on a rocky outcropping that overlooked the wooded valley. The foothills of the Andes, whose summits had never seemed so near, stretched out under the vaporous clouds. The old soldier frowned. A lake glimmered in the distance, inaccessible; a ravine about thirty feet deep blocked the way. Below, a mass of tangled brambles and bushes spread out like a sea of thorns and rock. They'd come all this way to end up stuck in a dead end.

*

Jana walked for more than an hour before finding their tracks. The giant was wounded—she'd hit him in the ankle the day before, along the road—and the footprints in the mud were of unequal depth. The old man who was with him was not in much better shape. A bird of prey soared over her in the pale sky; she climbed through the forest, her throat dry despite the full supply of water in her pack. Diesel was still sniffing around alongside her, more concerned with the dragonflies than with their own odor of carrion: Jana could almost smell it despite her crushed cartilage, an odor of death, intoxicating. She followed the tracks on the damp soil. Old hunting reflexes. Things would have been different with her brothers, but what did that matter now? El Picador's and El Toro's ears were coagulating on her breast, and she no longer thought about them. No longer thought at all. The revolver was loaded, she still had five bullets, and six more in the rifle. Jana, who up to that time had walked at a steady pace, slowed down. The sun had climbed higher, now it could be seen through the sparse treetops, and the fugitives were no longer very far ahead. What would they do once they were backed up against the old mission? Would they retrace their steps, or would they try to go around the obstacle by going along the precipice? The Mapuche hadn't reconnoitered that far, guessing that seized by panic they would flee in the direction opposite the gunfire. She moved forward, full of apprehension, and reached the first ruins.

Shadowing his mistress faithfully, Diesel stopped whipping the ferns with his tail. He saw her crouch amid the vegetation, lifted his head toward the high ground, and, his nose to the wind, suddenly started to bark. A hoarse bark that echoed through the valley.

"Fuck," Jana grumbled. "Fine time to open his mouth."

She kicked the mongrel away and kept her eyes glued to the mission for a long time: no one. But they were there. Diesel kept his distance, ashamed, his tail between his legs to beg her pardon.

"Get out of here, damn it!"

Putting actions to her words, she drove the animal away; he took off without protest. A few feverish seconds passed. She soon found an observation post at the edge of the woods, put down her rifle, lay down among the ferns, and sought a target through the telescopic sight. Two hundred yards of open ground between her and the ruins of the mission. Jana hesitated. The tracks led here, but she didn't see any others. She crept forward between the low crumbling walls, the Remington pressed against her shoulder, on her guard. It had started to rain again, a few large drops that bounced off the leaves of the succulents. The soles of her Doc Martens crackled on the little stones; she advanced little by little, in the shelter of the walls, sweeping the site as she approached the main building. Diesel had disappeared; his stupid barking had betrayed her presence, but no one was making any sign of life. They couldn't have gone very far: the old general must be exhausted, and the bald man burning with fever with his ankle in fragments. Jana moved forward again, very cautiously, without realizing that her advance was being watched.

Parise had been trying to make a bandage with part of his shirt when the dog's barking made him sit straight up. Someone was coming: it had to be the killer, the one who had set a trap for them on the road. But this time it was broad daylight and they were the ones who had the advantage of surprise. Parise limped back up and took cover behind a hole in the wall through which he could observe the enemy without being seen. Ardiles, who had been wandering along the edge of the ravine, had rejoined him, anxious.

"Did you hear that?" he whispered.

"Yes."

The two men crouched down, watching the movements at the edge of the forest. Parise's heart jumped when he recognized the girl who had escaped from the delta. The whore had tracked them to the dead end and was trying to flank them on the right. She was no longer very far away, about sixty yards, a furtive silhouette among the plants and rockslides.

"Get up, general."

"To do what?" murmured the old soldier as Parise was helping him to rise. "Be careful of my arm, for God's sake!"

Fatigue and fear made him stagger. Leandro Ardiles hardly had time to regain his balance.

"Sorry, general, but I have no choice."

The giant pulled him toward the slope.

"What are you doing? Parise! Parise, stop! Aah!"

Ardiles tried to grab the collar of Parise's coat but lost a shoe and slipped on the pebbles.

"Parise! What . . . "

The bald man gritted his teeth as he awkwardly put his weight on his broken ankle and pushed the old man toward the ruins down below, where the Indian was hiding.

Jana heard his cry. She waited a few seconds, her hand gripping the handle of the revolver. Then she heard his calls for help. She put down her things, released the safety, and climbed up under cover. The moans were coming from the summit. She moved slowly closer, keeping an eye on the shadows under the rain, her weapon in her hand, and found Ardiles lying among the thornbushes, against a wall that had checked his fall. He was moaning and holding his wounded arm, pale as a sheet. Jana pointed the revolver at him, felt the icy wind hit her, too late: she turned around and found herself face to face with Parise, who leaped out of the ruins. She pulled the trigger just as he brought his club down on her wrist. The bullet dug several inches into the earth and the gun flew out of her hand. Jana stepped aside to avoid Parise's charge but the giant grabbed her by the hair and threw her brutally to the ground. She fell facedown and the killer immediately jumped on her. Rolling over on her back, she fought with the energy of desperation. She shouted as she kicked haphazardly, hoping to break what remained of his ankle, but Parise was too quick, too heavy: he pinned her to the ground, 250 pounds of hatred weighing on her rib cage.

"Dirty little whore!" he hissed into her hot face.

He used his knees to immobilize her, but the Indian was still fighting like a wildcat: she scratched his eyes, ripped the skin off his eyelids, short of breath, her muscles without oxygen. Jana resisted the killer's pressure with all her strength but she was caught in the trap. Parise got up on his knees, brandished his enormous fist, and brought it crashing down on her broken nose. A stream of blood spurted out. The killer was breathing heavily, lying on his prey, expelling the adrenaline that was flowing through his veins. Held down by his weight, the Mapuche no longer moved. His fist was still balled as he looked at the girl with the painted face stretched out under him: he hadn't missed her. Parise looked around him nervously, long enough to adapt to the situation, which was finally turning to his advantage. The girl seemed to be alone, with her nose pissing blood.

Ardiles was moaning two paces away, stuck between the wall and the thornbushes.

"Help me . . . Parise, for the love of God, help me!"

Jana saw stars in the sad sky, and the brute over her who was crushing her. Tears clouded her eyes. She had her knife in its scabbard, all the way down there, stuck in her Doc Martens. She bent her legs while he was holding her, his knees pressed on her torso. Her hand felt the damp soil, desperately sought a handhold, and gripped the handle of the knife at her fingertips. She pulled out the blade and with her last strength, planted it between the giant's ribs.

Hector Parise froze for a second, electrified by the sting. His grimace of surprise changed to anger when he realized the treachery. Jana had failed to pierce the liver, or to hit any vital organ: the blade had slipped between the giant's ribs without sinking in deeply. He seized the hand that was still holding the handle, twisted it to make her let go, and furiously threw her ancestor's knife away.

"You wanted to do me in, huh?" he belched, beside himself with rage. "You wanted to do me in!"

She moved her head, incapable of freeing herself. His knuckles white, Parise stared at his prey. An icy breeze was blowing over the mission heights. Jana tried to protect her face with a last defensive movement, but it was useless: he massacred her with blows of his fist.

11

Rubén had abandoned Torres amid the sun-drenched vines and left the Solente vineyards that afternoon. An undulating road through the desert ran alongside the mountain range. 250 miles. Rubén gritted his teeth until dusk; with each rise in the road his stomach tightened more and more the butcher's hooks sunk into his guts. He came out on the crests, his body feeling as if it were soaking in formaldehyde inside the car. He was thinking feverishly about Jana, the emptiness of her absence, and the men holed up in that remote monastery. The sun was going down behind the snowy peaks when he reached the first foothills of the mountain range.

The Los Alerces National Park extends over more than 700,000 acres. Ancient forests cover the hills, bordering rivers and clear lakes. Rubén followed the paved road that ran through the preserve, drove past closed campgrounds, a few small farms without tractors where a hog sometimes snorted, potato fields, isolated cattle, a schoolhouse . . . As a result of the painkillers' side-effects, hyperthermia, and a convalescence that resembled suicide, he arrived at the Los Cipreses monastery in a state of confusion close to intoxication.

Night had fallen over the mountain village. Rubén finished off the bottle of water lying on the seat of the car, checked to see that the Glock was loaded, and walked slowly up to the bells hanging at the entrance to the building. The medications and the dust had ended up drying out his throat, and the water he drank by the quart didn't help; his body was begging him to lie down, to close his eyes, or to change his skin.

"Yes?"

The monk who opened the door was almost as wan as he was. The guy they'd talked to on the phone, to judge by his faint voice. Rubén apologized for disturbing him at such a late hour, introduced himself as a friend of Mr. Torres, and asked to see the cardinal. The young man with tattered sandals frowned at him with annoyance.

"It's just that . . . they haven't come back," he said. "Neither His Eminence nor his friends. We are still waiting for them."

"It's 11:30 P.M.," Ruben noted.

"Yes, I know. I'll admit that we're worried."

It was difficult to tell whether he was lying or not; he could hardly be seen by the pale light of the lantern. Rubén pulled the monk outside, and with his right hand slammed him against the wooden door.

"Listen, Friar Tuck," he said angrily, "I'm tired and I don't have time to lose with your nonsense. Is Ardiles there, with the others?"

The monk's Adam's apple bounced up and down under the detective's burning eyes.

"As God is my witness," he said, "someone called the monastery this afternoon and asked to speak to the cardinal. They left shortly afterward for the meeting."

"What meeting?"

"I don't know, the cardinal didn't tell me. Not very far away, I think: they were supposed to be back before nightfall."

"Who called the monastery?"

"Somebody named Díaz."

The botanist who had fled Colonia, the ex-agent of the SIDE.

"The cardinal left with Ardiles and his men?" Rubén growled.

"Uh . . . yes."

"What kind of vehicle?"

"A 4x4."

"What kind?"

"A black Land Rover," the monk replied, his eyes rolling with fear, "with tinted windows."

Díaz. He must be trying to sell the original document. That didn't explain where they had gone, or why they were so late. The monk obviously didn't know anything more.

"Did an Indian woman come here in the past few days?" Rubén asked. "A tall brunette around thirty, a Mapuche?"

"No." He shook his shaved head. "No."

Rubén scowled at the friar's pale face. They were getting away from him, once again. He went back to the car while the monk locked his door, and left the parking lot. It was a dark night. He parked a little way down the road, on the edge of a forest. He waited for more than an hour in the shadows of the car, watching for movements at the entrance to the monastery, but no vehicle showed up. The wind outside was rustling the trees, full of water. Exhausted by fatigue and the effects of the drugs, Rubén reclined the seat and plunged headfirst into a sleep without memory.

Jana's ghost didn't visit him that night, but he had the same evil foreboding when he woke up. He had slept like a stone for six or seven hours and his cold body was now like one long moan. The sun was coming up over the ridge and the monastery's empty parking lot. Rubén wasn't hungry but he wouldn't last long in this condition.

A cat who'd lost an ear was guarding the overturned garbage can at a restaurant with drawn curtains; it was still closed at this hour. Rubén drove on to the neighboring farm, looking for an open bar, when he spotted a jalopy with faded paint. The backyard of a farm. He stopped short: an old Ford was sitting in the puddles, its passenger-side window missing.

It was Jana's car, he would have recognized it anywhere. His heart beat faster. Rubén got out and walked toward the building, miserable under the drizzle that had started to fall. In the shelter of a lean-to covered with corrugated metal, someone was working on the axles of a 4x4: a Land Cruiser. Rubén looked feverishly around him, his hand on the butt of his gun, but detected no movement behind the flaking window frames. The farm seemed to be deserted, except for the guy under the lean-to that served as a garage.

"Hey!"

A teenager slipped out from under the car and sized up the stranger approaching him. He was a half-breed about twenty years old, and he was wary of *winkas*.

"I'm looking for the woman who drives the Ford," Rubén said, pointing to the old banger behind him. "Is she here?"

"No."

"Where did it come from then, this pile of junk?"

"It belongs to my father," the young man stammered.

"Registered in Buenos Aires," Rubén commented. "Are you playing games with me?"

"No . . . "

Felipe blushed all the way to his ears.

"Listen," Rubén said more gently, "I'm a friend of the woman the Ford belongs to. Tell me where she is!"

"I don't know. I wait tables in the restaurant, that's all."

"Sure. And this 4x4?" he said, pointing to the Land Cruiser, that was shot through with bullet holes. "Are you going to tell me that it fell out of the sky, right here in your lousy courtyard?

The *winka*'s eyes went right through him.

"My father and my brother went to town. They're the ones who brought it back, I . . . "

"I don't give a damn about the 4x4," Rubén interrupted. "All I care about is the guys who were in it. Them and the woman who was driving the Ford. This concerns a murder. Tell me what you know before you get yourself in a world of trouble."

Felipe hesitated, but ended up admitting that the two vehicles had been abandoned the day before in the forest. The 4x4 was damaged; he'd had to pull it out of the ditch with his father and his brother, who had gone to get parts, but the Ford was in running condition. They'd brought the cars back to the farm to repair them.

"Who told you that these vehicles had been abandoned?" Rubén asked.

"The Mapuche. Jana . . . "

Rubén stuck some hundred-peso bills in the adolescent's pocket. "Show me where."

Stones on the road were ricocheting off the bottom of the car. Felipe remained silent in the front seat of the car. He'd seen the butt of the pistol that was poking out of the stranger's jacket, his face dripping with sweat despite the open window, and the pain in his eyes. They drove through the forest, at top speed in third gear on a road that had become slippery. The young man was worried, looking with a melancholy eye at the rain on the hills. He wondered if this guy was lying to him, if they would be accused of theft, and what murder he was talking about. They climbed a switchback and entered a long curve through the forest. Felipe signaled to Rubén to slow down: it was nearby.

A remote place among lakes and hills, in the midst of araucarias and impenetrable thickets. The next farm was miles away. Rubén looked at the tracks along the edge of the road. It had rained, but a tree was leaning over near the ditch. A pine tree, with paint marks on its trunk. He bent over and saw fragments of a windshield in the grass, bits of plastic, cartridge casings. There were at least a dozen casings, of several calibers, scattered around the area of the accident. Rubén stood up, his blood tingling. The half-breed kept his distance, worried about the idea of earning so much money so easily.

"Jana's the one who told you to pick up the 4x4? And her Ford too, you're sure?"

Felipe nodded. The preceding evening. Rubén cautiously turned toward the forest. The vegetation was dense under the branches, the sky a chemical white beyond the hills.

"Is there a path through the forest?" he asked.

"Yes. A little higher up, in the village. But it goes nowhere. There's nothing around here, only the ruins of a monastery, one or two hours' hike from here."

Due north, that was the direction. Rubén went up the trail on foot, following the half-breed's instructions. The painkillers were making him feverish, the pain radiating from his left side, from an inflamed point just over his heart. He moaned as he walked along the path, almost invisible under the trees. Roots and brambles slowed his advance, and rain was falling in large, scattered drops filtered by the branches, increasing the smell of humus. He found another cartridge casing on the ground; it came from a rifle. 7.62 caliber. The same as his Remington. Jana. She had hunted them in the forest. Rubén followed the path that climbed slowly through the forest, his lungs hurting, hearing nothing but his pulse pounding in his temples like a call for help. He stopped a moment to drink a little water, threw away the empty bottle, and walked on, the pockets of his coat heavy with cartridge clips, listening for noises in the forest. The rain had soaked him without cooling him off. Jana was out there somewhere in that ocean of greenery, hunting or hunted. He stopped again, lost, exhausted by this race like a fall into the void. The mud was sticking to his shoes when croaking sounds led him to a nearby clearing.

A sullen wind was sweeping over the little mire. A man was

hanging underneath a tree, a naked and grotesque puppet, with his twisted head resting on the ground and his stinking foot still attached to the branch. The fractured tibia had poked through the flesh; the skin was a purplish-black, as if gangrene were already attacking it. Rubén had to chase away the crows to see that it was the torturer from the delta. The crows had been eating away his eyes and he no longer had ears: a clean wound that hadn't been made by the birds.

Rubén vomited at the foot of the tree. He stood up but the sky was spinning. He saw the shovel abandoned near the pile of turned earth a few paces away. A grave, freshly dug. Nausea gave way to dry heaves. He found a few full bottles of water in the ferns, a gas lamp, plastic wrappings: the remains of a campsite. Of a massacre. Rubén was splashing through the puddles when a sort of squealing on his left pulled him out of his torpor: Díaz was hiding behind a tree trunk, chained up, his eyes half mad.

"Help me," he yelped hesitantly. "Help me, please!"

The botanist had dreamed of dying amid his flowers, not of starving to death in this hole, shitting his pants with fear, and begging. He was crying like a puppy, unable to control his trembling. Did he recognize the detective? Rubén came up to the tree to which he had been chained, his heart sinking. Jana: it was no longer vengeance but suicide.

"Where is she?" he asked. "Where is the Indian woman?"

"He, he, he . . . "

Yes, Franco Díaz had gone mad. Rubén pulled on the chain around Díaz's neck.

"Where did she go! Goddammit, tell me!"

"There . . . " He pointed toward the woods, his fingernails full of dirt. "There . . . I beg you, unchain me."

Farther north. He had to believe him, there was no other choice. Rubén turned toward the trees in the drizzle and without saying a word left the captive to his fate. The botanist's pleas quickly faded away behind him; he called out Jana's name in the forest, several times, but his legs could hardly carry him. He was breathing with his belly, his mind vague in a crystalline body. He no longer knew if he was getting lost, losing her, losing everything. The Glock in his jacket weighed a ton, the clips in his pocket seemed to be pulling him down.

"Jana! Jana!"

Tears of impotence welled up in his eyes as he called, in vain. He had lost his bearings and was walking without knowing where he was going. The lion's cage, the orphans' little steps, Elsa, Daniel . . . History was stammering. Rubén was losing hope in the middle of the forest when a dog appeared through the brush. A mongrel with a dirty coat that yapped strangely as it trotted toward him.

"Where did you come from?"

It was hard to tell whether his tail was wagging or he was starving to death. He sniffed the stranger, held up his graying muzzle as a sign of something or other, pawed the ground, and turned round him like a carousel. To whom could such a fleabag belong except Jana? The animal seemed to be waiting for him. Rubén followed him through the woods. The sun was coming through intermittently, he was boiling with fever, but this scruffy dog was somehow familiar and clearly knew where he was going. The pine trees became less dense. The dog turned around and looked at the man coming along behind him, as if to urge him to hurry, but Rubén was already on the verge of breaking down. A gunshot suddenly cracked in the damp air. It came from farther up the slope, three hundred yards perhaps. The old mission. Rubén hurried forward, his heart in his mouth. Every yard cost him a life, but this dog, the pale sky, and the rain no longer existed: two figures were lying higher up among the ruins.

A woman with black hair and a bald giant towering over her who was pummeling her face with his fists. The sutures on

Rubén's back were cracking open, and he could feel the blood running down under his clothes, or else he too was going crazy. A bad dream.

"You wanted to do me in, huh? You wanted to do me in!"

Parise was breathing so hard to expel his hate that he didn't hear the footsteps approaching behind him: when he turned around, he saw two gray blades speckled with blue staring at him, and the black mouth of a Glock.

Rubén immediately pulled the trigger. His head thrown backward, the giant spun briefly around before falling to the ground. A cloud of gunpowder evaporated. Hit at point-blank range, Parise's head had exploded. The dog yapped, frightened. Sensing a presence, Rubén pointed his pistol to the right and saw the old man trembling against the wall. Ardiles. He was holding his bandaged arm against his body, crouched among the thornbushes and moss-covered stones, without a weapon. Jana was not moving, crushed by the weight of Parise's body. Rubén knelt down and moaned as he pulled the brute's 250 pounds off her.

"Jana . . . "

Bits of gelatinous flesh had landed on her. She was inert; Rubén could see nothing but her dreadful face under the cracked paint, and didn't know what to do: her nose, lips, eyes, all the blood that was flowing out of her. He found the necklace of cut-off ears on her breast and shuddered with horror.

"Jana," he murmured. "Jana . . . "

The arches of her eyebrows had been shattered by Parise's blows, her broken nose had been reduced to a pulp, her mouth split. No bullet holes or wounds, only the poison of barbarism in her veins. Rubén tore the bloody necklace off her neck and threw it away.

"It's over," he said, holding her. "It's over."

The drizzle was falling on the ruins. Her hair was sticky with blood. He rocked her, imploring her to live.

No, Jana was a brave woman, she couldn't die, not now, not after all they'd been through. He shuddered when he felt her pulse against his heart. She sighed and opened her eyes, subdued.

"Rubén . . . "

Her voice rose up out of the depths of time. Had he become a ghost, like her? The Mapuche remained incredulous for a moment, staring at Rubén, her eyes full of pink tears, and then she saw Diesel at her side, sniffing the killer's body. Everything became clear and real again: the ruins of the old mission, the pale light of morning, the drizzle. Stupefying seconds. Rubén.

"I thought . . . they'd killed you," she murmured.

"No."

Jana hugged him with all her strength and the hate that had been twisting her stomach into knots for days seemed to disintegrate. Rubén had brought her back from the dead. He said comforting words to her, words of love, as they embraced each other, to give her time to realize her terrible mistake. The gentle rain cooled their faces; Jana's had been only a mask of pain; bloody tears were running down her cheeks, but she no longer felt them. Rubén tried to help her up but he was the one who staggered. She saw his pallor, the arm he could hardly move, the pieces of his blue soul that clung to life.

"Will you be O.K.?" she asked.

"Yes."

There was water at the campsite, and the descent through the woods would take them to the clearing where Díaz was waiting for them, chained to his tree. The Grandmothers needed the testimonies of the ex-agent of the SIDE, the general, and the others. They would all be put on trial, right down to the last one. Diesel was mounting a needless guard over Ardiles, who was watching them from the thornbushes, his eyes glassy. Jana put Rubén's arm over her shoulder to help him walk. He would walk. They would never leave each other again—never.

Their enemies called them the Auracans, the rabid ones. The Mapuche kicked the old man on the ground.

"Get up, you dirty son of a bitch."

Acknowledgments

An *abrazo* to the Magnificent Seven, my faithful companions in adventure, constant from Niceto to La Mascara; to Sergio Nahuel, the all-purpose photographer; to Daniela, Leslie, and Karla, the little Mapuche fairy picked up on the road of the *machi*; to Miguel and Barbara, *flores* and nightime ramblings in Buenos Aires; to Nicolas and Emilie Schmerkin for the forename, the contact, and your humane parents; to the delicious Rodolfo De Souza and Marilù Marini of the book theater; an *abrazo* to Sophie Thonon, a pugnacious lawyer, and to Rosa the subtle *Abuela*; to Danielle Mitterand's France Libertés Foundation; to the Argentine Collective for Memory, Alicia in Paris and the others; to you, the girls; to Fabien the anthropologist and to the help provided by Quai-Branly; to Florent for the information about aviation; to my readers Clem and Stef of the Collectif des Habits Noirs; an *abrazo* to you, Aurel, for the words that were needed; to Susana's placid patience during the preparatory courses ("*Las putas al poder!*"); to Florence Malgloire for the first apartment in San Telmo; to Eugenio for the Breton *asado* in the delta; to Jose and his Mapuche brothers detained in Chile (*Pewkawal!*)—but that's another story . . .

About the Author

Caryl Férey's first novel to be published in English, *Zulu* (Europa Editions, 2010), was the winner of the Nouvel Obs Crime Fiction and Quais du Polar Readers Prizes. In 2008, it was awarded the French Grand Prix for Best Crime Novel. *Utu* (Europa Editions, 2011) won the Sang d'Encre, Michael Lebrun, and SNCF Crime Fiction Prizes. *Mapuche* is his third novel to be published by Europa Editions. He lives in France.

www.europaeditions.com

EUROPA EDITIONS BACKLIST
(alphabetical by author)

Fiction

Carmine Abate
Between Two Seas • 978-1-933372-40-2 • Territories: World
The Homecoming Party • 978-1-933372-83-9 • Territories: World

Milena Agus
From the Land of the Moon • 978-1-60945-001-4 • Ebook • Territories: World (excl. ANZ)

Salwa Al Neimi
The Proof of the Honey • 978-1-933372-68-6 • Ebook • Territories: World (excl UK)

Simonetta Agnello Hornby
The Nun • 978-1-60945-062-5 • Territories: World

Daniel Arsand
Lovers • 978-1-60945-071-7 • Ebook • Territories: World

Jenn Ashworth
A Kind of Intimacy • 978-1-933372-86-0 • Territories: US & Can

Beryl Bainbridge
The Girl in the Polka Dot Dress • 978-1-60945-056-4 • Ebook • Territories: US

Muriel Barbery
The Elegance of the Hedgehog • 978-1-933372-60-0 • Ebook • Territories: World (excl. UK & EU)
Gourmet Rhapsody • 978-1-933372-95-2 • Ebook • Territories: World (excl. UK & EU)

Stefano Benni
Margherita Dolce Vita • 978-1-933372-20-4 • Territories: World
Timeskipper • 978-1-933372-44-0 • Territories: World

Romano Bilenchi
The Chill • 978-1-933372-90-7 • Territories: World

Kazimierz Brandys
Rondo • 978-1-60945-004-5 • Territories: World

Alina Bronsky
Broken Glass Park • 978-1-933372-96-9 • Ebook • Territories: World
The Hottest Dishes of the Tartar Cuisine • 978-1-60945-006-9 • Ebook • Territories: World

Jesse Browner
Everything Happens Today • 978-1-60945-051-9 • Ebook • Territories: World (excl. UK & EU)

Francisco Coloane
Tierra del Fuego • 978-1-933372-63-1 • Ebook • Territories: World

Rebecca Connell
The Art of Losing • 978-1-933372-78-5 • Territories: US

Laurence Cossé
A Novel Bookstore • 978-1-933372-82-2 • Ebook • Territories: World
An Accident in August • 978-1-60945-049-6 • Territories: World (excl. UK)

Diego De Silva
I Hadn't Understood • 978-1-60945-065-6 • Territories: World

Shashi Deshpande
The Dark Holds No Terrors • 978-1-933372-67-9 • Territories: US

Steve Erickson
Zeroville • 978-1-933372-39-6 • Territories: US & Can
These Dreams of You • 978-1-60945-063-2 • Territories: US & Can

Elena Ferrante
The Days of Abandonment • 978-1-933372-00-6 • Ebook • Territories: World
Troubling Love • 978-1-933372-16-7 • Territories: World
The Lost Daughter • 978-1-933372-42-6 • Territories: World

Linda Ferri
Cecilia • 978-1-933372-87-7 • Territories: World

Damon Galgut
In a Strange Room • 978-1-60945-011-3 • Ebook • Territories: USA

Santiago Gamboa
Necropolis • 978-1-60945-073-1 • Ebook • Territories: World

Jane Gardam
Old Filth • 978-1-933372-13-6 • Ebook • Territories: US
The Queen of the Tambourine • 978-1-933372-36-5 • Ebook • Territories: US
The People on Privilege Hill • 978-1-933372-56-3 • Ebook •

Territories: US
The Man in the Wooden Hat • 978-1-933372-89-1 • Ebook • Territories: US
God on the Rocks • 978-1-933372-76-1 • Ebook • Territories: US
Crusoe's Daughter • 978-1-60945-069-4 • Ebook • Territories: US

Anna Gavalda
French Leave • 978-1-60945-005-2 • Ebook • Territories: US & Can

Seth Greenland
The Angry Buddhist • 978-1-60945-068-7 • Ebook • Territories: World

Katharina Hacker
The Have-Nots • 978-1-933372-41-9 • Territories: World (excl. India)

Patrick Hamilton
Hangover Square • 978-1-933372-06-8 • Territories: US & Can

James Hamilton-Paterson
Cooking with Fernet Branca • 978-1-933372-01-3 • Territories: US
Amazing Disgrace • 978-1-933372-19-8 • Territories: US
Rancid Pansies • 978-1-933372-62-4 • Territories: USA

Alfred Hayes
The Girl on the Via Flaminia • 978-1-933372-24-2 • Ebook • Territories: World

www.europaeditions.com

Jean-Claude Izzo
The Lost Sailors • 978-1-933372-35-8 • Territories: World
A Sun for the Dying • 978-1-933372-59-4 • Territories: World

Gail Jones
Sorry • 978-1-933372-55-6 • Territories: US & Can

Ioanna Karystiani
The Jasmine Isle • 978-1-933372-10-5 • Territories: World
Swell • 978-1-933372-98-3 • Territories: World

Peter Kocan
Fresh Fields • 978-1-933372-29-7 • Territories: US, EU & Can
The Treatment and the Cure • 978-1-933372-45-7 • Territories: US, EU & Can

Helmut Krausser
Eros • 978-1-933372-58-7 • Territories: World

Amara Lakhous
Clash of Civilizations Over an Elevator in Piazza Vittorio • 978-1-933372-61-7 • Ebook • Territories: World
Divorce Islamic Style • 978-1-60945-066-3 • Ebook • Territories: World

Lia Levi
The Jewish Husband • 978-1-933372-93-8 • Territories: World

Valerio Massimo Manfredi
The Ides of March • 978-1-933372-99-0 • Territories: US

Leïla Marouane
The Sexual Life of an Islamist in Paris • 978-1-933372-85-3 • Territories: World

Lorenzo Mediano
The Frost on His Shoulders • 978-1-60945-072-4 • Ebook • Territories: World

Sélim Nassib
I Loved You for Your Voice • 978-1-933372-07-5 • Territories: World
The Palestinian Lover • 978-1-933372-23-5 • Territories: World

Amélie Nothomb
Tokyo Fiancée • 978-1-933372-64-8 • Territories: US & Can
Hygiene and the Assassin • 978-1-933372-77-8 • Ebook • Territories: US & Can

Valeria Parrella
For Grace Received • 978-1-933372-94-5 • Territories: World

Alessandro Piperno
The Worst Intentions • 978-1-933372-33-4 • Territories: World
Persecution • 978-1-60945-074-8 • Ebook • Territories: World

Lorcan Roche
The Companion • 978-1-933372-84-6 • Territories: World

Boualem Sansal
The German Mujahid • 978-1-933372-92-1 • Ebook • Territories: US & Can

Eric-Emmanuel Schmitt
The Most Beautiful Book in the World • 978-1-933372-74-7 • Ebook • Territories: World
The Woman with the Bouquet • 978-1-933372-81-5 • Ebook • Territories: US & Can

Angelika Schrobsdorff
You Are Not Like Other Mothers • 978-1-60945-075-5 • Ebook • Territories: World

Audrey Schulman
Three Weeks in December • 978-1-60945-064-9 • Ebook • Territories: US & Can

James Scudamore
Heliopolis • 978-1-933372-73-0 • Ebook • Territories: US

Luis Sepúlveda
The Shadow of What We Were • 978-1-60945-002-1 • Ebook • Territories: World

Paolo Sorrentino
Everybody's Right • 978-1-60945-052-6 • Ebook • Territories: US & Can

Domenico Starnone
First Execution • 978-1-933372-66-2 • Territories: World

Henry Sutton
Get Me out of Here • 978-1-60945-007-6 • Ebook • Territories: US & Can

Chad Taylor
Departure Lounge • 978-1-933372-09-9 • Territories: US, EU & Can

Roma Tearne
Mosquito • 978-1-933372-57-0 • Territories: US & Can
Bone China • 978-1-933372-75-4 • Territories: US

André Carl van der Merwe
Moffie • 978-1-60945-050-2 • Ebook • Territories: World (excl. S. Africa)

Fay Weldon
Chalcot Crescent • 978-1-933372-79-2 • Territories: US

Anne Wiazemsky
My Berlin Child • 978-1-60945-003-8 • Territories: US & Can

Jonathan Yardley
Second Reading • 978-1-60945-008-3 • Ebook • Territories: US & Can

Edwin M. Yoder Jr.
Lions at Lamb House • 978-1-933372-34-1 • Territories: World

Michele Zackheim
Broken Colors • 978-1-933372-37-2 • Territories: World

www.europaeditions.com

Alice Zeniter
Take This Man • 978-1-60945-053-3 • Territories: World

Tonga Books

Ian Holding
Of Beasts and Beings • 978-1-60945-054-0 • Ebook • Territories: US & Can

Sara Levine
Treasure Island!!! • 978-0-14043-768-3 • Ebook • Territories: World

Alexander Maksik
You Deserve Nothing • 978-1-60945-048-9 • Ebook • Territories: US, Can & EU (excl. UK)

Thad Ziolkowski
Wichita • 978-1-60945-070-0 • Ebook • Territories: World

Crime/Noir

Massimo Carlotto
The Goodbye Kiss • 978-1-933372-05-1 • Ebook • Territories: World
Death's Dark Abyss • 978-1-933372-18-1 • Ebook • Territories: World
The Fugitive • 978-1-933372-25-9 • Ebook • Territories: World
Bandit Love • 978-1-933372-80-8 • Ebook • Territories: World
Poisonville • 978-1-933372-91-4 • Ebook • Territories: World

Giancarlo De Cataldo
The Father and the Foreigner • 978-1-933372-72-3 • Territories: World

Caryl Férey
Zulu • 978-1-933372-88-4 • Ebook • Territories: World (excl. UK & EU)
Utu • 978-1-60945-055-7 • Ebook • Territories: World (excl. UK & EU)

Alicia Giménez-Bartlett
Dog Day • 978-1-933372-14-3 • Territories: US & Can
Prime Time Suspect • 978-1-933372-31-0 • Territories: US & Can
Death Rites • 978-1-933372-54-9 • Territories: US & Can

Jean-Claude Izzo
Total Chaos • 978-1-933372-04-4 • Territories: US & Can
Chourmo • 978-1-933372-17-4 • Territories: US & Can
Solea • 978-1-933372-30-3 • Territories: US & Can

Matthew F. Jones
Boot Tracks • 978-1-933372-11-2 • Territories: US & Can

Gene Kerrigan
The Midnight Choir • 978-1-933372-26-6 • Territories: US & Can
Little Criminals • 978-1-933372-43-3 • Territories: US & Can

Carlo Lucarelli
Carte Blanche • 978-1-933372-15-0 • Territories: World
The Damned Season • 978-1-933372-27-3 • Territories: World
Via delle Oche • 978-1-933372-53-2 • Territories: World

Edna Mazya
Love Burns • 978-1-933372-08-2 • Territories: World (excl. ANZ)

Yishai Sarid
Limassol • 978-1-60945-000-7 • Ebook • Territories: World (excl. UK, AUS & India)

Joel Stone
The Jerusalem File • 978-1-933372-65-5 • Ebook • Territories: World

Benjamin Tammuz
Minotaur • 978-1-933372-02-0 • Ebook • Territories: World

Non-fiction

Alberto Angela
A Day in the Life of Ancient Rome • 978-1-933372-71-6 • Territories: World • History

Helmut Dubiel
Deep In the Brain: Living with Parkinson's Disease • 978-1-933372-70-9 • Ebook • Territories: World • Medicine/Memoir

James Hamilton-Paterson
Seven-Tenths: The Sea and Its Thresholds • 978-1-933372-69-3 • Territories: USA • Nature/Essays

Daniele Mastrogiacomo
Days of Fear • 978-1-933372-97-6 • Ebook • Territories: World • Current affairs/Memoir/Afghanistan/Journalism

Valery Panyushkin
Twelve Who Don't Agree • 978-1-60945-010-6 • Ebook • Territories: World • Current affairs/Memoir/Russia/Journalism

Christa Wolf
One Day a Year: 1960-2000 • 978-1-933372-22-8 • Territories: World • Memoir/History/20th Century

Children's Illustrated Fiction

Altan
Here Comes Timpa • 978-1-933372-28-0 • Territories: World (excl. Italy)
Timpa Goes to the Sea • 978-1-933372-32-7 • Territories: World (excl. Italy)
Fairy Tale Timpa • 978-1-933372-38-9 • Territories: World (excl. Italy)

Wolf Erlbruch
The Big Question • 978-1-933372-03-7 • Territories: US & Can
The Miracle of the Bears • 978-1-933372-21-1 • Territories: US & Can
(with **Gioconda Belli**) *The Butterfly Workshop* • 978-1-933372-12-9 • Territories: US & Can